BLUE
MOUNTAIN
ROSE

BLUE MOUNTAIN ROSE

A Novel in Five Acts

JULIE HAMMONDS

Soulstice PUBLISHING
books with *soul* • Flagstaff, AZ

Soulstice Publishing
PO Box 791
Flagstaff, AZ 86002

This is a work of fiction. All of the characters, organizations, and events portrayed in this novel are either products of the author's imagination or are used fictitiously.

First published in the United States by Soulstice Publishing
www.soulsticepublishing.com

Blue Mountain Rose: A Novel in Five Acts

ISBN: 978-1-7349899-8-4 (hardcover) 978-1-7349899-5-3 (ebook)
LCCN: 2024920702

Cover design: Lindy Martin
Cover images: Shutterstock.com
Author photo: Matt Anderson
Frontispiece: based on a sketched reconstruction of Shakespeare's Globe Theatre by Joseph Q. Adams; Science History Images/Alamy Stock Photo
Editorial services: Merlina McGovern and Milli Ondras
Interior design: Erin Stanford
Text font: Adobe Garamond Pro
Printed in Canada by Friesens

First Edition: 2025
29 28 27 26 25 1 2 3 4 5

For my parents,
Jim Hammonds and Catherine Bell

What I have done is yours.
~William Shakespeare

The Blue Mountain Rose Theatre Company presents

The Tragedy of HAMLET Prince of Denmark

DIRECTED BY RICHARD KEANE

DRAMATIS PERSONAE

Ted Harrington as
Claudius, King of Denmark

Isabelle Rivette as
Gertrude, Queen of Denmark, and mother to Hamlet

Peter Dunmore as
Hamlet, son to the late King Hamlet, and nephew to the present king

LaShia Shay as
Horatio, friend to Hamlet

Margaret Graham as
Polonius, Lord Chamberlain

Bryce Benedict as
Laertes, son to Polonius

Fawn Tucker as
Ophelia, daughter to Polonius

Aaron Jensen as
Rosencrantz, courtier

Carissa Karvelas as
Guildenstern, courtier

The Ghost of Hamlet's Father

Ambassadors, Clowns, Courtiers, Gentlemen, Ladies, Lords, Messengers, Officers, Players, Sailors, Servants, Soldiers, and other Attendants

DIRECTOR'S NOTE

Some of you have seen or read this grand play many times; for others, the 2009 Blue Mountain Rose production of *Hamlet* will be your first experience of the most brilliant play ever written in the English language.

It is not necessary to understand the details of the plot to appreciate what you're about to see. But for those new to the storyline, in brief: When death claims King Hamlet of Denmark, his son, also named Hamlet, comes home for the funeral. Soon after, Hamlet's widowed mother marries his uncle, his father's brother, who is now king. Amid these confusing events, Hamlet sees his father's ghost. Claiming he was murdered by his brother, this ghost urges Hamlet to seek revenge.

Hamlet is the most written-about and most frequently performed of all Shakespeare's plays. It carries a fearsome reputation, but there is no reason to fear it. Certainly, this grand play explores powerful themes such as familial bonds, loyalty, betrayal, and revenge. But if you've ever trusted a friend, considered taking justice into your own hands, or lost someone you cared about, then you've shared the emotions Hamlet feels so deeply and expresses with such power.

Hamlet is the most questioning of all Shakespeare's characters. From first line to last, he ponders aloud what he can or should do. You might see him as a noble person faced with a terrible choice, or as an emotional weakling who can't do the right thing, or as something else entirely. People have been trying to understand Hamlet's character for more than four hundred years. Like them, you will find much to contemplate in these next few hours.

This play's greatness is evident in every expressive line, yet *Hamlet* is sparsely written in important places. Much is left open to the viewer's interpretation. But every character in the story has their story, their motivations and challenges.

Whether this is your first or tenth encounter with the tragedy of the Prince of Denmark, you are co-creators with us. Bring your heart, mind, and imagination to the task as we embark on this journey together.

–Richard Keane

PROLOGUE

April 2009

Kate uses the master key to open the wrought iron gate, then clangs it shut behind her and slides the deadbolt home. A copper coin embossed with the masks of Tragedy and Comedy swings from her key ring. She rubs it for luck as she returns the key to her pocket; superstitious, perhaps.

She walks through the open yard where the groundlings stand on summer evenings, sometimes raucous and other times rapt. Climbing the stairs into the lowest audience gallery, she drops a cushion onto the front bench and settles in. Only now does she look up. The familiar sight of this open-air Elizabethan stage always lifts her spirits.

The Blue Mountain Rose Theatre wears its winter robes. Removable rolling doors seal the inner stage in the offseason, and waterproof drapes protect the elaborately carved balcony railings from snow. Supported by two gaudily painted posts, a built-in roof called "the heavens" shields the outer stage. Beneath that holy protection, how many times has doomed love sighed away its brief hour?

The stage is Rome and Verona, palaces and London streets, alehouses and battlefields. Eleven years of joy and drama flash across her mind. Prince Hal, carousing shirtless with Falstaff and his merry ruffians; Rosalind and Celia, innocents at play in the Forest of Arden; Mark Antony, holding the restless crowd spellbound with the power of words.

In half an hour, a crew will knock at the backstage door, and their work of preparing the theatre for *Hamlet* will begin. Tech rehearsal starts in a week, and on this day in late April there is much to do. Kate's clipboard holds the list of tasks needed to ready the Rose for her sixty-third season. Though the crew know their jobs, Kate is their hub, the center of a wheel that must turn smoothly from now to October. She must be ready to answer questions, give directions, and guide the work when the crew finds new wear and damage from this winter's snow and rain.

She will be ready; Kate is always ready. But here in these stolen moments before the day's rush, she doesn't have to think about any of it. She can simply sit in this enchanted space and breathe.

ACT 1 *January* 2009

ACT 1
SCENE 1

PETER

Peter rolled over in bed and looked out through enormous windows at the ocean. Every morning, his first task was to gauge the water's mood. A storm two days back had sent it lashing and slashing like a hungry cat whose claws stung his skin during his daily swim. That cat was now a kitten, fur sparkling in the sun.

Throwing on a pair of sweats and a faded T-shirt, Peter padded down the staircase in bare feet, his hand brushing the cool, chrome railing. This borrowed house was all curving white walls and the sheen of metal. In his mind, Peter called it Denmark, from *Hamlet*:

> HAMLET: Denmark's a prison.
>
> ROSENCRANTZ: Then is the world one.
>
> HAMLET: A goodly one, in which there are many confines, wards, and dungeons, Denmark being one o' th' worst.

Some of Peter's London friends had made light of his predicament, calling unruly fans the price of sudden fame, even saying he should enjoy their attention while it lasted. Rory had said, "If you need a place to lie low, the keys are yours. Why d'you think I bought it?"

A week later, Peter had swung the front door wide and looked across the living room at plate glass windows framing the face of his new best friend, the South Pacific. Not a prison and comfortable enough; even in his loneliest hours, Peter was grateful. Mostly.

He knew living in these particular confines by choice meant a world of difference between his Denmark and a real prison. But hadn't Hamlet also chosen to go to Elsinore Castle? Did having the choice improve his mood?

Continuing down the stairs, Peter ran the lines in his head:

> ROSENCRANTZ: We think not so, my lord.
>
> HAMLET: Why, then, 'tis none to you, for there is nothing either good or bad but thinking makes it so. To me, it is a prison.

Better stop thinking then, Peter told himself as he walked into the palatial kitchen.

The fridge was nearly bare, but there were eggs and the last of a regal block of whitestone cheese. Peter scrambled the eggs and cut a banana, apple, and kiwis for the day's fruit salad. *A trip to town is in order*, he thought, jotting a grocery list. But every such trip meant the risk of being recognized. As usual, he would ring up Rory's friend Huatare and ask him to pick up groceries. Maybe Huatare could stay for dinner. Peter tried to remember the last time he'd had company, and it didn't take long: Huatare, groceries, two weeks before.

Since moving to New Zealand in July, Peter had hosted a few guests to relieve the loneliness of self-imposed exile. In October, Rory and his girlfriend, Sienna, had come for a visit, their dinner parties filling the house with lively chat. But now Sienna was on a movie set, Rory was rehearsing a Broadway show, and Peter was alone.

He drank his coffee and ate the salty eggs while sitting beneath the porch umbrella. The early sun of a January morning on the coast of New Zealand warmed his feet. He checked his phone for the London weather, as he did every morning, and laughed, as he did every morning. Four degrees Celsius and raining, of course. Must be twenty-four here already and still climbing. *Do I miss London in January?* His laugh turned into a sigh. A quick shake of the head released the clouded mood. *Best not go there.*

Rinsing the dishes, he looked out at the ocean where long, lazy swells rolled in, rippled by a slight breeze. Small breakers would greet him once he made his way down the path from the cliff to the beach;

bursts of white energy, then a shush as the water slid up the pebbles to kiss his toes. It would feel delicious to step into the ocean's domain, stopping a moment to savor and then striding out confidently, the water ruffling the hair on his legs, sliding against the muscles of his chest and back, teasing him until he embraced it with arms strengthened by months of daily swims in all weather.

I'll swim out to the headland twice today, he decided, rummaging in the linen closet for a towel. He quickly packed the beach bag: water and juice, sunglasses, Rory's orange swim cap that protected his head but made him look like an ocean-going fruit. For company between swims, he added Huatare's book on Māori theater.

It wasn't until he'd walked out across the yard, through the seaside gate, along the cliff path to the stairs, and all the way down to the cove that he remembered his swim trunks—hanging to dry in the upstairs bath. Swimming in sweatpants was an unappealing option. *Oh well, there's nobody here to see me; nobody within five miles. Bare it is, then. Again.*

Setting his things on the picnic table, Peter stripped off the T-shirt and sweats, slathered sunscreen on his nose and shoulders, and snapped the orange cap into place. *I'm going to scare a few seals today*, he thought, grinning.

Up on the cliff, unseen, the photographer clicked her shutter.

After Huatare left that evening, Peter sat at the dining table with a second glass of Pinot Noir, musing again on his own personal Denmark. Rory's house held the world at bay, sheltering him from the zealous fans who'd dogged him in London. Denmark offered plentiful solitude. *Not always welcome, that.* In escaping to Rory's, he'd accidentally chosen a monk's life.

His thoughts returned to Hamlet and Rosencrantz. Hamlet, moody son of a dead king; Rosencrantz, unfaithful friend and would-be accessory to Hamlet's murder. *The people in Shakespeare's mind. No wonder the man couldn't sleep.*

When Hamlet called Denmark a prison, Rosencrantz could neither empathize with his friend nor let the claim go. "We think not so, my lord," he countered, igniting nearly twenty lines of wordplay that left Hamlet suspecting his schoolmate had been called to Elsinore to spy on him. *So then, false friend; game on.*

Opening his laptop, he pulled up *Hamlet* from the Folger Shakespeare Library in America and searched for "prison." In the first reference, the Ghost of Hamlet's Father calls Purgatory his "prison house." Peter scanned the rest of the Ghost's speech and shivered. Quickly searching on, he found what he was seeking. *There, in act 2.*

"On your feet now." He heard the voice of every director who ever sat in comfort behind the magisterial table. *Up, then.* Carrying his laptop and wineglass into the living room, Peter let his eyes absorb Hamlet's words. He set the glass down on its chrome coaster on the coffee table, then the laptop beside it.

> ROSENCRANTZ: We think not so, my lord.

Peter drew a deep breath, released it slowly, drew another. Rocking forward and back on his feet to ground himself, he flexed his knees, then went still. "'Why, then, 'tis none to you, for there is nothing either good or bad but thinking makes it so,'" he said aloud in a playful tone. He paused a moment, his eyes taking in the high-ceilinged room with its spare furnishings, its graceful proportions. *How do I dare be unhappy here?* And yet, as Hamlet says, "'To me, it is a prison.'"

> ROSENCRANTZ: Why, then, your ambition makes it one.
> 'Tis too narrow for your mind.

That's rich. Provoked by Rosencrantz's willful misunderstanding, Peter walked to the pavers in front of the fireplace and turned, calling out Hamlet's words: "'O God, I could be bounded in a nutshell and count myself a king of infinite space, were it not that I have bad dreams.'"

> GUILDENSTERN: Which dreams, indeed, are ambition,
> for the very substance of the ambitious is merely
> the shadow of a dream.

You're missing the point, Guil, just like Rosencrantz. Between the two of you, I don't have even half a friend. "'A dream itself is but a shadow,'" he argued to the quiet room.

ROSENCRANTZ: Truly, and I hold ambition of so airy and light a quality that it is but a shadow's shadow.

I just told him this castle feels like a prison, and he's waxing poetic about shadows. He thinks I have the ambition to be king? Musing on memories of his movie premiere in America—photographers shouting his name, fans chanting lines from *Thirst* when he stepped out of the limousine—Peter thought, *I've had a taste of royal life; I didn't like it. Well then, let's put kings in their place, as Shakespeare did—in plays his company performed before royalty, no less.*

"'Then are our beggars bodies, and our monarchs and outstretched heroes the beggars' shadows,'" he argued rationally with the invisible Rosencrantz. Ambition as the shadow of a king that is a shadow of a beggar, ephemeral.

The next lines rolled through his mind, but now a magnet was pulling him forward to one of Hamlet's great monologues. He didn't need the laptop for this one; he had it by heart.

"'I have of late, but wherefore I know not, lost all my mirth,'" he began. *You nailed that one, Shakespeare my friend. How'd you know?*

As Shakespeare's words began to echo through his chest, Peter recalled the feeling of standing onstage at London's Olivier Theatre. Known among actors as "the great barn" for its unforgiving acoustics, it rose before his mind's eye as Rory's living room faded from his awareness. Reaching to the last row of an imagined audience with his trained voice, he continued, "'This goodly frame, the Earth, seems to me a sterile promontory.'"

The air filled his lungs, vibrating his ribs.

"'This most excellent canopy, the air, look you, this brave o'erhanging firmament, this majestical roof, fretted with golden fire—why, it appeareth nothing to me but a foul and pestilent congregation of vapors.'"

Lost in the scene, Peter scanned the ghostly faces of the audience. He was looking for the one he wanted to see, the face that had always been there, in every audience since the beginning. *When I was in what, sixth form? And we performed* Ariadne's Thread *at school.*

So quickly did grief snatch him up in her talons that he didn't have time to protect himself. *She's not here, I can't find her; she's not here and never will be here again, the face I want most to see, the one person I need more than anyone else so I can ask her "Why?" and hear an answer.*

Released, Peter dropped to his knees on the thick rug, head in his hands, trying to breathe. Then he shouted the question that kept him pinned here in this elegant space, locked away from the world, paparazzi and crazy fans be damned.

"Why, Mum?" Then a whisper: "Why?" And now he was in tears, the solitude of his Denmark a comfort, for where else could he rage, where else could he grieve his mother in peace but here?

"You're having me on." It was the only thing he could think to say when his agent, Martin Pierce, called unexpectedly three days later, rousing Peter from sleep.

"Fabulous feature on the front page of the *Evening Standard*, above the fold, with the headline arranged to preserve the eyes of delicate viewers but not much else left to the imagination," Martin reported. "What's with the orange cap?"

A wave of cold fury washed through Peter's body. *They've found me. Here.*

"Just something Rory left behind. What's the headline?"

"Not that anyone will be reading it because they'll be checking out your abs, and might I say, impressive, but it's 'Vampire lord living alone in paradise.' You've been working out?"

"It passes the time," Peter groused. "Do they say where I am?"

"I'm afraid they do: 'A gated mansion owned by Rory MacNair, his costar in the recent hit *Thirst*.' Sorry, but it won't be long before the address is on the fan chat boards."

"Then I'm stuffed." As the wave of fury ebbed, his chest felt hollow.

"I'm afraid that's the sum of it."

"I can't let them come here. I can't let that happen to Rory's house. Denmark has been good to me."

"I thought you were in New Zealand?"

"Never mind. I just need to figure this out. Again."

Martin sighed the sigh of the long-suffering. "I'll get you another movie," he urged Peter. "Send you to farthest Uzbekistan where there's nobody but crew for a hundred miles. You'll have all the privacy a person could want."

"Not another movie, Martin, thanks; not yet."

"So you're off again? How many friends do you have with gated mansions?"

"Enough," Peter said, though he couldn't think of any at this particular moment.

"And where will you go now?"

"I don't know. I thought I'd have more time here."

"Call me when you get there, wherever 'there' is."

Without saying yes, Peter rang off. He sat in Rory's bed for a long moment, hands tangled in the sheets, looking out through the great glass windows at the ocean.

"One last swim, and it's goodbye," he whispered.

ACT 1
SCENE 2

KATE

Kate Morales walked into the conference room and set her briefcase on the scarred oak table that Richard called "The Table Round." Technically, it was oval, with inserts to extend the seating down the room to hold twenty, but Richard had granted himself a lifelong Poetic License. Many years back, before Kate's time, someone had wood-burned a Celtic dragon into the central leaf. Around it, in florid calligraphy: *veritas, sapientia, venustas*. Truth, wisdom, beauty.

Richard was Irish, but he loved the Arthurian legends. He'd recently wondered aloud to Kate, "How is it nobody's made a truly great play from them?" When she suggested the musical *Camelot*, he'd scoffed.

"A few catchy songs adrift in an ocean of tears," he'd said. Difficult to argue with; but then, when was Richard ever easy to argue with?

The table was in its smallest configuration. For today's early season production meeting, Kate added two inserts and pulled folding chairs from the storage closet. Like nearly every room in this office building that was the worn-down home of the Blue Mountain Rose Theatre Company, the conference room did triple duty, providing storage and extra rehearsal space as well.

Ten chairs: one for Aurelia Rotch, the company's dramaturge and speech coach; one each for season directors Paul Rubineau, who had flown in from LA, and Linda Sutera, who lived in town; one each for the company's music director, costume designer, properties designer, and scenic designer; one for Serena Scott, the company's marketing manager; and the final two for Richard and Kate. Under Richard's leadership, this team knew how to build productions an audience would remember.

Hamlet and *A Midsummer Night's Dream* would form the 2009 season's Shakespearean core, with Martin McDonagh's recent black comedy *The Lieutenant of Inishmore* as the high-season modern production and Sarah Ruhl's *Eurydice* as the smaller autumn show. Kate was especially looking forward to Ruhl's play. After seeing it off-Broadway, Richard had enticed the playwright to come to Arizona for an artist's residency while her play was being staged.

Kate was turning on the wall-mounted video screen when she heard Richard singing in the hallway. "'Camelot! Camelot! In far-off France I heard your call,'" he proclaimed in a lively tenor. "'Camelot! Camelot! And here am I to give my all.'" Then the man himself swept into the room, and as usual, his presence transformed the workaday space into a stage.

"Guenevere, how do you on this congenial morning in Camelot?" he broke off mid-song to ask. "Is that your brand-new dress? It's grand."

Looking up at her boss, Kate took in his purple silk tie with the yellow fleur-de-lis that perfectly matched his pale yellow shirt, and the tweed sport coat with its subtler hues of cinnamon, burgundy, and dandelion.

Richard James Aloysius Keane: raconteur and *bon vivant*, recent recipient of the National Medal of Arts for his contributions to the American theater, executive director of the Blue Mountain Rose, and Kate's longtime boss. A wave of carefully styled silver hair framed his classically handsome face, with its high cheekbones and strong jawline. Smile lines accented the corners of his bright blue eyes.

"Thank you for the compliment, Lance," Kate replied pertly. Richard knew she loved designing clothes. She'd sewn her dress from two other dresses and a suede jacket found at the secondhand store. "And may I say, you're looking particularly handsome today."

"You may," he allowed with a regal tilt of the head.

Kate rolled her eyes at him and smiled. "An exciting day, working with the whole team for the first time this season."

"The world-building begins," Richard agreed. "*Hamlet*'s to be set in a European country, early in World War II. I asked the designers to think about France during the occupation; muted colors, vaguely militarized touches. With *Midsummer*, Paul and I want a magical woodland abounding with fairy spirits. He has free rein, so we'll see what they've come up with."

The video link to Stratford-upon-Avon was ready, so Kate asked Richard, "Do you want to say hello to Art?"

"O Art, Ancient Muse, Fiery One, much-feared Apollo," Richard invoked, arms raised, eyes seeking the heavens, "To you I say, hello."

Used to his theatrics, Kate shook her head. "Arthur Ryerson? In Stratford." Richard's dear friend Art worked for the Royal Shakespeare Company in Britain but assisted Richard with play selection and other matters of artistic direction at the Rose. He would arrive in mid-June to direct *The Lieutenant of Inishmore*. "Let's see if he's set up."

"Yes, let's." Richard settled into his chair. As soon as Kate confirmed his friend was online, the two were sending greetings across the wide Atlantic, stealing the opportunity for what Richard called "a chinwag." Kate waved toward the camera, smiling when she saw that Art, too, had opted for a purple tie, though his was the color of ripe grapes.

"Kate, how lovely to see you," Art said. "I was just telling Richard the other day that we need to entice you up onto the stage this season."

"I am the one, and possibly the only, thing you'll never see on our stage," Kate replied. The entrance of two of their designers saved her from once again explaining the stage fright that kept her work behind the scenes.

"Our meeting gathers," Richard told his friend. "Katherine will mute you until we begin, and I warn you, she'll do it again if you stray out of bounds!"

"Since when have I ever—" Art protested. As Kate tapped the mute button, cutting off the rest of his speech, Richard's genial laugh seemed to say, "When has he ever not?"

All afternoon, an ebullient Richard popped in and out of Kate's office to praise the set design and costume ideas he'd seen at the meeting, as well as the snippets of music he'd heard. After eleven years at the Rose (with the last five as company manager), Kate was used to the aftermath of Richard's creative storms. She'd come to define her role as "managing Richard" as well as the company, and it was far too late to train her boss out of the habit anyway. She'd become deft at maintaining a part of her concentration undisturbed by his disruptions.

She was just looking at a report of season ticket sales when Richard came back in and sat down heavily in the chair she kept for guests. It wasn't like him to pause for long on such an exciting day.

"It's going all to pot," he announced sadly. "We're skint."

"You've been talking with Merle?" she guessed. Merle Blanchard was currently the treasurer of the board of directors; before that, he'd been the company's accountant. Richard had nicknamed him "Merlin." With a wave of his magic wand, Merlin made money appear, especially when Kate needed to write a contract for a popular actor.

"Merlin holds the strings of our proverbial purse, so when he calls, I must answer," Richard said. "I should have fled instead. He gave me the most unwelcome news."

"What is it this time?" Kate teased. She thought back to September, when the Lehman Brothers collapse set off discussions between Merle and the company's management team about the company's finances. It was hard to understand how the fate of big investment banks back East could possibly affect the Blue Mountain Rose, but a December announcement that the country was officially in a recession (and had been for the past twelve months) emphasized Merle's point.

It had been only the latest cloud in a broiling storm of financial news. A year ago, they'd opted to be prudent with their 2008 productions, scaling back the earliest, grandest designs. Thanks to Merle's cautious guidance, they'd avoided drawing on the company's capital reserves that season. Their productions had been leaner than usual, but their actors remained top-notch. Perhaps welcoming the distraction from real-world problems, audiences had remained solid and enthusiastic.

"He thinks 2009 will be worse than 2008," Richard said. "He envisions the country going to hell this year."

Kate recalled recent headlines about banking failures and consolidations. It was difficult to understand what was happening or why, and she'd tried to put it out of her mind, telling herself that events in the New York banks couldn't hurt their safe theatrical nest in far-off Flagstaff, Arizona.

Richard had apparently been doing the same. "At first, I thought the Goose was winding me up," he said, using Merlin's other nickname, The Goose That Laid the Golden Egg.

"But then he asked me, 'Have you seen house prices lately? People won't come to our shows if they can't put gas in the tank and food on the table. They're walking away from their mortgages.' The Goose warned me to prepare for the worst. He thinks ticket sales will shrink by 30 percent or more over 2008."

"Let's go to the break room. I'll make you a cuppa, and we'll talk," Kate suggested.

Richard shook his head. "We sailed through this past season by adjusting our sheets to the prevailing winds, but we may capsize next time. To stay afloat might require drawing on the endowment. With the stock market at full ebb, we'd be robbing from the future to do it, but Merlin thinks it may come to that."

"Merle is right to warn us, but it's on us to think it through," Kate reminded her boss. "I was just going to look at the season ticket numbers. Shall we?" She gave Richard an encouraging smile, but the data they found erased it. Season subscribers were their most loyal fans, drawn from Arizona's many arts patrons and from people near and far who built a pilgrimage to the Blue Mountain Rose into their annual calendar. Some subscribers who had been coming to Flagstaff since they were children now brought grandchildren to see a play here. Kate had access to decades of information about their buying habits. The numbers were grim.

"Down 21 percent from this time last year and 24 percent from the average of the ten years leading up to 2008," she said, reading the graph. "We know they're delaying their purchases, and maybe worse. It's early yet, but it looks like Merlin might have a point."

"'*Et tu*, Brute?'"

"I am not stabbing you in the back, Caesar," she protested. "I'm telling you what's real so we can deal with it."

"I know, my loyal Mark Antony, as you always do. Maybe Merlin is right. I must meet with the board. We have to scale back again, and this year it may mean cutting salaries, not simply trimming production budgets. Perhaps we even drop one of the shows."

"We can look. I'll run the numbers for those scenarios."

"It's all well and good, running numbers, looking at projections, trimming what we can, but I'll tell you what Merlin said that stole the wind from my sails."

"He said more?"

"Indeed. 'This is it for me,' our magician told me. 'I can't take the stress.' He spends his days guiding clients on how best to soften their fall from the cliff this market has created. He told me, 'I can't do it much longer. I'll serve out my term on the board, but I'm retiring from Blanchard and Blanchard after tax season.' Turning the firm over to his son. I wish I had the luxury."

"Of turning the company over to your son?" Kate asked gently, knowing she was treading on personal ground. Richard had dated a number of accomplished women over the years but never married.

"Of retiring," Richard answered.

Shocked, Kate said, "Not you!"

"Why not me?" Richard raised his eyebrows. "Merlin thinks I should follow his example. Ride off into the gilded Tucson sunset and leave the problem of the Rose—that's what he called our beloved stage, 'the problem'—to others to solve."

"You won't have to retire," Kate said. "In a day or two, I'll have projections you can look at with the board. We'll figure it out."

She saw his shoulders rise, then fall as he released a steadying breath. When he met her gaze, his blue eyes were troubled by storms.

"We shall try."

ACT 1
SCENE 3

Richard

A week passed—momentous in its way, at least from Richard's perspective. The US government's $700 billion Emergency Economic Stabilization Act of the previous October had failed to slow the country's economic free fall, and as stock markets roiled at home and abroad, the Rose's endowment shrank with every closing bell.

The temper of the times required daily calls with Merlin and Kate as Richard prepared for an emergency meeting of the Rose's governing body. The board of directors would make the tough decisions, but they relied on his advice.

To assess their situation, he and Kate projected a 20 percent drop in ticket sales and assumed that donations other than grants would drop by half as compared to 2008. Then they analyzed two scenarios in which full productions would be cut: a season without *Inishmore* or a season without the smaller *Eurydice*. For a Shakespearean theater company to cut *Hamlet* or *A Midsummer Night's Dream* would have signaled imminent doom to the media and audiences, so they didn't even whisper those alternatives aloud.

At week's end, the board accepted the worst-case projection and reviewed the scenarios. Neither looked wiser, financially, than retaining all four plays with smaller budgets. The board directed Richard to reduce production costs by 10 percent, with specific cuts left to each director. They would fill the remaining gap from interest on the endowment capital (if any) and, if the year lived down to Merlin's dour predictions, the capital itself as a last resort.

They asked Richard to identify at least one full-time staff member whose working hours and salary could be reduced to part-time. "Absolutely not," he'd answered, offering instead to lower his own salary temporarily by 10 percent.

In "the most unkindest cut of all," as Richard termed it, the board had passed a resolution tabling plans they'd been working on since 2005 to upgrade the Blue Mountain Rose. It was Richard's long-held dream to offer a more comfortable and expansive festival venue, upgrading the facilities for theatergoers and actors alike. He'd also sketched plans to improve the grounds around the theatre to provide a stage for a green show (a pre-performance entertainment tradition at other venerable Shakespeare festivals such as those in Oregon and Utah). The millions of dollars required for a "bigger and better Blue Mountain Rose" had seemed within reach of their fundraising efforts as recently as early 2007, but the financial news since then had frozen shut the checkbooks of major donors.

With those decisions made, Richard could turn his attention toward more pleasant challenges. On this frosty Tuesday morning, they would start in-person auditions for the acting company.

In the coming month, they needed to find at least forty-three actors to cover the parts across all four productions. A handful of seasoned performers already lived in Flagstaff. These actors held renewable contracts that practically guaranteed employment, following the local audition that was always held in mid-January.

Richard might also hire a few actors without previous contracts based on this local audition. Among these were theater majors at Flagstaff's Northern Arizona University. They would stay in town over the summer to work as crew or perform a spear-carrier role in the Shakespeare plays.

As usual, though, most of this year's company would come from the wider world. Veterans of regional theater companies throughout North America dreamed of getting into the Rose, and stage actors from New York and other big cities who coveted a classical performance credit knew none was more golden than this one.

Such actors would have their agents send a bio and headshot to Emilia Valdez, a freelance casting director. She had worked with Richard long enough to earn not only his trust, but a nickname. Richard called her Artemis, for the Greek goddess of the hunt.

Because he trusted her taste implicitly, Richard didn't look at the many hundreds of contacts they received each year. *I leave the talent-hunting to Artemis the talent-hunter.* Emilia gave the green light to actors she thought Richard would want to see during closed auditions in New York and Los Angeles at the end of January.

The company also drew talent from Britain, thanks to its ties with Art at the Royal Shakespeare Company, the revered RSC. "Ryerson's Recruits" were recent RSC actors willing to forgo time in Stratford-upon-Avon to spend a season at the Rose. They auditioned for Art if he hadn't seen them perform recently.

Following auditions, Emilia would work with the season's directors on their selections and backup choices. Once the directors made their choices, Emilia contacted agents with the good news. She did that for all the directors but Richard, who preferred to call his actors himself when he was directing a production. The thrill of telling someone they'd made this year's company had never lost its shimmer in his thirty-eight years at the Rose.

The start of audition season was usually a high point of Richard's year. Today, embroiled as he was in the month's financial news, the winter clouds matched his mood as he entered the large rehearsal hall.

The room's tan-colored walls contrasted with bright red floor tape that marked off a space the same size and shape as the Rose stage. Green floor tape indicated the location of permanent stage features such as doorways, pillars, and balcony posts. Any actor with imagination could read these cues and visualize the performance space.

Emilia and Kate were already seated at the production table, leafing through Emilia's binder of headshots. Giving his colleagues a wan smile, Richard settled himself between them. Elbows on the table and chin resting in his hands, he was a captain at the helm of his ship, ready to guide her out of the harbor. *Focus on this,* he told himself, *and only this: our stage and its players-to-be.*

The first actor was Fawn Tucker, a young actor Richard already knew and liked, a renewable contract player he was considering for Ophelia, Hamlet's love interest.

"'Once more, unto the breach,'" he said.

Some actors entered the hall diffidently, eyes darting as they read the space for the first time. Others strode in confidently and launched into their prepared speech without a cue.

Many of the monologues were from Shakespeare, but actors could use any speech they'd performed in the past, no matter the source. There were Pucks and Mirandas, Walter Youngers and Violet Westons, and now and then an audacious Ophelia or Hamlet, though never the "To be or not to be" speech. The consequences of blowing that in front of Richard Keane were the stuff of theatrical legend.

After each actor left, Richard gave Emilia and Kate a short assessment. "Needs coaching, but might do for Borachio," he said after a young man delivered a solid "O, that this too, too sullied flesh would melt." When Richard said something like, "Strong voice, possibly the right energy for Gertrude," he smiled as Emilia wrote it down. Having worked with many of the local actors in past years, he wanted everyone to succeed in their bid to join this year's company.

Just before lunch, Emilia turned a page in her binder and slid it over to Richard. "He's from New Zealand, but he's agented by Martin Pierce at Buchwald," she said. "Living here in Flagstaff temporarily, who knows why. So I told Marty we'd see him here instead of making him go to LA."

Richard's first impression was of hair: a tousled mop contrasting with a neatly trimmed mustache and beard. *And suddenly, it's 1968 again*, he thought. *We're not doing* Hair *this season, Peter Dunmore.*

The actor clicked open the door and began speaking as he passed across the green tape that marked the stage right rear entrance without looking at the floor. Speaking early was usually an amateur error. But there was nothing amateur about the stage whisper that filled the space.

"'To be or not to be,'" he began, "'that is the question.'" Richard raised an eyebrow at Emilia, who grimaced to indicate she hadn't remembered to warn the actor away from Hamlet's forbidden speech. Returning his attention to Dunmore, now standing center stage, Richard saw Kate glance at him, no doubt shocked that someone dared to bring this speech to audition at the Blue Mountain Rose. He squinted and jutted his chin in the actor's direction. *Bold in his choice, and he's gone all in, wearing black and carrying a dagger. Let's see what he can do.*

"'Whether 'tis nobler, in the mind to suffer the slings and arrows of outrageous fortune,'" Dunmore continued, his voice gathering force even as his distraught face seemed to dismiss this possible course of action. "'Or to take arms against a sea of troubles and, by opposing, end them.'"

His voice crossed over from whisper to low growl as he touched the dagger to his bare forearm, tenderly proposing, "'To die, to sleep—no more—and by a sleep to say we end the heartache and the thousand natural shocks that flesh is heir to—'tis a consummation devoutly to be wished.'"

Richard registered the surprise on the actor's face as he puzzled through the consequences if he "shuffled off this mortal coil" only to be plagued by dreams after death. Dunmore looked around the room, a confused soul seeking solace, making brief eye contact with Emilia, then Richard, then Kate. The young actor—*New Zealand, Artemis said?*—was demonstrating familiarity with the use of direct address. Actors who spoke straight to the audience were common in Shakespeare's time, and the Rose proudly carried this tradition forward. But as Peter continued the speech, Richard stopped thinking about performance technique and allowed himself to be drawn in.

This was not an actor, but the Prince of Denmark, his heart in turmoil as he protested that everything from "the whips and scorns of time" to "the pangs of despised love" should be considered rational grounds for suicide. Then he was overcome by "the dread of something after death, that undiscovered country from whose bourn no traveler returns."

As Hamlet decided to "bear those ills we have," Richard remembered to breathe again. It had been a long time since anyone surprised him this much. *Today, of all days.* A wave of gratitude swept his heart.

Dunmore knelt and set the dagger down. Slowly rising to his feet, he admitted, "'Thus conscience does make cowards of us all'" with a rueful half-smile. Suddenly, as if startled by a sound just offstage, he turned and whispered, "'Soft you now, the fair Ophelia.'" He held the position for a moment.

Richard leaned back and set his hands behind his head, waiting for the actor to collect himself. Then he called out, "Thank you." Dunmore shook out his shoulders, showing no hint of nerves as his eyes met Richard's. He nodded in quick acknowledgment and turned for the door.

Richard turned to Kate, who mouthed a silent, "Wow." Once the door clicked shut, he gave Emilia the single note for her list:

"Our Hamlet."

ACT 1

SCENE 4

KATE, RICHARD, PETER

After auditions, Kate drove into town to pick up her daughter. Tuesdays, Beth had chorus after school with her friend Lauren. Afterward, she would do homework in the community hall until she saw Kate's car pull up out front, promptly at five fifteen.

Tuesday was chorus, Wednesday piano, Thursday dance class. Beth was a busy girl with the ambition and diligence to become an actress, but she was only ten. "Next month I'm eleven," she'd reminded her mother approximately eighty-seven times, as if Kate could forget. It would be years before Beth could drive herself to lessons, and truth be told, Kate was glad. She loved working at the Rose, but time with her daughter was the most precious coin in Kate's purse.

On the drive home, Beth asked about auditions. "You remember Fawn Tucker, from *All's Well That Ends Well* last year," Kate began. Beth did, having a prodigious memory for faces.

"And Fawn was in *The Comedy of Errors* in 2007," Beth reminded her mother. "I like her. She has pretty hair."

"She wore it up in a fancy braid today," Kate replied. "We also saw a few other actors from *Comedy*, including that tall guy who played Dromio."

"Aaron Jensen," Beth filled in. "He came here from the Oregon Shakespeare Festival."

"From Ashland, you're right." Unable to keep her thoughts from the actor who'd made Richard so happy, she added, "And we saw a new actor, new to the Rose anyway, who actually did the 'To be or not to be' speech from *Hamlet*. For Richard, can you believe it?"

"Did he remember his lines?" Beth was a diligent memorizer who usually had no trouble remembering hers.

"Better than that. He was marvelous. He looked a bit scruffy, but he had that charisma people will come from far away to see. Richard was thrilled. He thinks he may have found our Hamlet."

As he drove home, Richard mused on the many actors he'd seen perform the Prince of Denmark. Fresh out of drama school in 1963, he'd watched Peter O'Toole at the Old Vic, the year it first became Britain's National Theatre; a pivotal performance. He recalled the American Richard Chamberlain turning Birmingham on its head in 1969. Derek Jacobi had played it at the Rose in 1977, on tour from London with the Prospect Theatre Company. That was Richard's first *Hamlet* as director and the third of seven performed at the Rose since 1947, by Richard's count; each one different, all quite fine.

This unknown New Zealander could be set to join a bright constellation of stars. Is it possible he might shine brightest of all?

Since he'd sat in Kate's office and blurted out a wish to retire, Richard had been pondering it. As he pulled into his driveway, his thoughts turned to his winter home in Tucson, a cherished haven. He could live there full time and perhaps summer in Britain, take on directing jobs as he wished, and set down the burden of running a repertory company. *Keep my hand in the game while stepping away from the fiscal tribulations of this demanding job.* The idea was growing on him, though so far, he hadn't shared it with anyone but Kate; not even Art knew he was seriously contemplating such a drastic move.

This may be the last Hamlet *I direct, but I'll go out on a high note if I can see Peter Dunmore on his way to becoming the next great Prince of Denmark on our stage.*

Peter drove straight back to his motel room on Route 66 after auditions and ducked inside. He didn't think he'd been recognized at the Rose, but the rest of the world posed a problem, too. Fortunately, he'd collected enough food in a single raid on a grocery store on his way into town to eat indoors for a week at least.

It could be a month before he heard back. Peter understood the audition season and knew he'd face competition from the finest actors in America and perhaps Britain as well before it was over. He hoped going first had given him an edge. And he couldn't help finding encouragement in Richard's demeanor when his audacious audition speech ended. The man had seemed to forget himself for a moment. Peter wondered when an actor had last surprised the legendary Richard Keane.

He was aware of a metallic taste in the back of his throat, the aftereffect of nerves. It had been three years since *Macbeth* at the Young Vic; three years since he'd found a mark and filled his lungs, preparing to launch a Shakespearean speech to the last row of the balcony like a comet pulling a fiery tail through the velvet sky.

Oh, how he missed it. Hearing the rush as the audience breathed with him, seeing their rapt faces, feeling the reaction when he singled one person out from the crowd and spoke directly to them in a sweet moment of intimacy, direct and personal as a kiss. Today, there'd been just three in the chairs: two assistants and the Great Man himself.

Richard Keane.

Already well-known as a director in London when he'd crossed the Pond to join an up-and-coming Shakespeare company in Arizona, he'd blazed a path for other British and Irish actors to follow. The fact that Hollywood was just a day's drive away had given this festival international allure. But the Rose was also that rare thing, an Elizabethan stage with a yard for groundlings and three tiers of audience galleries. Built as a faithful echo of the Globe Theatre from Shakespeare's day, she was widely known as "an actor's house," with an enthusiastic audience that demanded one's finest work. At the Rose, an actor could perform the best-known plays in the English language under someone who held a sterling reputation as a director worth crossing an ocean to serve.

The man was a legend. In casting about for a place to land after he'd been found in New Zealand, Peter had only really considered this one option, driven toward Richard by the questions that awakened him in the night, inexorably drawn to the Rose by his actor's soul.

ACT 1
SCENE 5

RICHARD, PETER

"We want you for Hamlet," Richard told Peter on the phone a month later. "Your audition was brilliant."

Between mid-January auditions and the day Richard could finally call his chosen actor and deliver the news, Richard and the other directors had worked with Emilia to solve the daunting logic problem that was repertory theater.

They had four shows to produce, with overlapping casts. In mid-May, *Hamlet* would open first and run solo for two weeks. Then *Midsummer* would open. Not only would *Hamlet* and *Midsummer* proceed in rep, meaning they would run concurrently until *Hamlet* closed at the end of July, but *Midsummer* would then overlap *The Lieutenant of Inishmore*, and *Lieutenant* would overlap *Eurydice* in September at the end of the production season.

Many actors would perform six or seven parts, in a mix of roles that matched their skills and experience working in a repertory company like this one. Before auditions, Kate and the season's directors had drawn up a master planning sheet that showed the preferred combinations while avoiding rehearsal and performance conflicts.

Richard would never ask any actor playing Hamlet to take a significant role in a show running concurrently, like *Midsummer*, but he might invite them to play a smaller part in that play and something more significant in a later production. Richard had decided to offer Peter the additional roles of Lysander in *Midsummer* and either Padraic in *The Lieutenant of Inishmore* or Orpheus in *Eurydice*.

All in all, this was the sweetest offer he could make in these belt-tightening times. He was nonplussed when Peter thanked him, cordially but coolly, then said, "I'll need to talk with my agent."

Although he preferred to hear unqualified excitement coming across the line, Richard aimed for a note of unruffled charm as he replied, "Of course; take whatever time you need."

"Would you be open to the idea of a shorter season for me—perhaps only *Hamlet*?" Peter asked.

Richard countered, "We'd prefer not to, but I'm open to the discussion. May I ask why you might prefer a briefer tenure at the Rose?"

Peter explained, "I, erm, have other offers I've kept on the table, waiting to see if *Hamlet* would come through."

"Ah, I see." Richard maintained his even tone. "Then I'll look forward to hearing from you."

As he rang off, Richard ran through the options in his mind. *Eager to get on to other things so soon? Or perhaps simply daunted by the challenge of repertory.* That latter possibility being the least objectionable, Richard chose to believe it while he awaited further developments.

As the phone went silent in his hands, Peter looked around at the four familiar walls of the motel room where he'd spent the past month waiting for this very call.

"Eejit," he chided himself aloud. "What's your problem, then?"

The month had not been wasted. He'd started learning Hamlet's lines, here in the room or while hiking and running the tangled forest trail system just uphill from his motel, the only two places where he spent much time.

"Why learn eight hundred lines if you don't mean to take the role?"

The feat of memorization required to perform Shakespeare's plays in repertory was prodigious. The Rose's actors might commit five times as many lines to memory as most modern stage actors. But Peter had always enjoyed this part of an actor's job. Hamlet's words now rolled through his mind at odd hours, even when he was watching American movies on the motel television. *Memorizing lines is not my problem. What is it, then?*

In his research, Peter had stumbled across an apt quote from none other than Richard himself, in a *Newsweek* magazine article headlined "Shakespeare is alive and thriving in America."

"No ordinary roles, these," Richard had opined. "Shakespeare's characters are ancient souls, well-known to our audiences already and thus capable of creating the deeply empathetic feelings only familiarity makes possible."

The anything-but-ordinary role of Hamlet was the universally acknowledged test of an English-speaking actor's skill. *Better actors than I have run from it.*

Peter thought back to *Macbeth.* Learning a major part was challenging, but performing it was a thrill; sheer joy, speaking that text night after night as each new audience fell captive to the spell of Shakespeare's words. *Fear of playing Hamlet isn't my problem, either.*

He kept returning to the surprise in Richard's voice when he'd asked for time to think. He'd only seen Richard the one time, but the man's charismatic presence loomed large in Peter's mind. You wouldn't want to get on the wrong side of such a man.

You also wouldn't want to let him down. *Maybe that, then; I'm scared of Richard. Scared of letting him down?*

Maybe that.

ACT 1
SCENE 6

KATE

When Richard took Peter's call the next morning, Kate was sitting in his office. She watched her boss's face light up as he listened. "Hamlet and Lysander" he whispered to her, his hand over the receiver. Sharing his relief, she gave an encouraging thumbs-up as Richard said into the handset, "We appreciate your coming to the Rose, and as director of *Hamlet,* I very much look forward to working with you. I'm sure Paul Rubineau will feel the same for *Midsummer.*"

When she called Peter the next day to discuss his contract, Kate was surprised to learn he had stayed in town after his audition.

"I'm between jobs, and this is a fantastic place to pass the winter," Peter told her. Looking out her office window at the snow that silvered the pine trees, Kate smiled.

The company provided a housing stipend or free lodging to actors from out of town. Stipends were offered when rehearsals started on April 1, but Kate could be generous with the free lodging even before rehearsal season began. "In that case, I have a deal to offer, if you're interested," she told him.

Kate described the Arden Court as "part motor inn, part cabin chic, and all quirk." Owned by the Blue Mountain Rose since the 1970s, it had housed such luminaries as Michael York and Judi Dench. A stay in the "Forest of Arden" was part of the company's mystique, especially for British actors. Its grounds included a renovated motor inn, as well as two dozen cabins for those who wanted a true taste of the American West.

The Arden was open to the public all year, but few tourists wanted to stay in a cabin during the cold months. If he was willing to accept their rustic charm, Peter would pretty much have the cabins to himself for the next six weeks, until other cast and crew members began to move in.

"I'll take the Arden, and thank you," he told her.

"Our pleasure."

Kate was in a hurry as she entered the code to the Arden's back gate and drove past the cabins and down the hill to the motor inn parking lot. After this meeting, she wanted to get back to the office for a check-in with Richard. He'd said again on Tuesday that he was considering retiring and even mentioned making his winter home in Tucson his permanent residence. The thought still shocked her, but it had also sparked her to think of making a major change of her own. *What if?* she wondered. *What if 2010 is the year I step up to replace him?*

It wasn't the first time she'd thought about directing the company. Kate had worked at the Rose since earning her master's degree in theatre management and producing from Columbia; 2009 would be her twelfth season. She knew the Rose from *A* to *Z*, from managing a large acting troupe that performed in repertory to writing grant applications. It would be a natural progression for someone with her experience to step up to the leadership role.

Kate had assumed she would direct a company somewhere, at some point in her career, but as long as Beth was in school, Flagstaff would be their home. Until Beth left for college, the Rose was Kate's only option. And she'd never imagined Richard would retire so young.

Part of her thought it was a star too high to reach for; nobody could replace Richard, and who was she to dream of it? Another part of her—the part that had trained in New York and once considered making a career there, before fate sent her home to Arizona—believed she had the skills to carry the company forward should Richard truly decide to step down.

Sure, she lacked the international connections Richard had built over the decades, but if she stepped into Richard's chair, Art Ryerson in Stratford and casting director Emilia Valdez would ensure the company continued to attract the best talent from both sides of the Atlantic.

Lofty dreams aside, she was here at the Arden to get Peter Dunmore into his cabin. He was the only actor checking in early. The hotel manager had already sent a cleaning crew. All Kate had to do was guide their Hamlet to his new Elsinore, hand him a welcome packet, and be on her way. Then, after talking with Richard, she needed to pick up Beth from school, fix dinner, listen to the song Beth was rehearsing for chorus, and get the two of them into bed at a reasonable hour.

She was accustomed to the sheer number of things to be coordinated, the seeming impossibility of finishing it all by ten o'clock, but it still startled her sometimes to look at how many plates she could spin in the air at once. Add to this, the top position at the Rose?

Kate was just getting out of her car as a small sedan pulled up beside her and parked. The man who stepped out was taller than she'd remembered. As he unfolded his six-foot-two-inch self from the rented Honda, the smile he sent her way seemed warm but diffident.

"Katherine?" he asked. "You must be. I remember you from my audition."

She reached out her hand. "Please call me Kate. We're excited to have you with us this year, Peter."

They were standing in the parking lot of the motor inn, two small, L-shaped buildings separated by a covered breezeway that made a convenient shelter for picnics when it rained. Each building had two stories. He looked up and asked, "Will I be sleeping on the balcony?"

She couldn't help but smile at hearing his accent again; it was pleasant on the ears. "No, we're settling you in one of the cabins up the hill. We think you'll like the space and cooking facilities. And when you go home to New Zealand, you'll have a story to tell about what it's like to live in what we call the Forest of Arden."

He didn't answer, just turned to open the trunk. "You don't have to unload here," Kate interrupted hastily. "There's a service road around the side, through that gate, that will take you to the cabin parking lot. It's much closer. I'll meet you."

She handed Peter a map of the Arden and showed him which cabin was his. "At the gate, punch in the code 1623," she said, pointing. "Then continue up to parking spot eleven. There's a paved trail to your cabin from there. Do you have much to carry? I can help."

"No, go on, it's just two bags."

"See you there, then." Kate turned to walk up through the breezeway to the cabin. She didn't see the look of appreciation on Peter's face as he took in her swinging curtain of straight, dark hair and the long, embroidered coat she wore with innate grace.

Peter's cabin was a single, an A-frame for one person. It had a kitchen, dining area, and living room up front, a bedroom and bath behind that, and an upstairs loft just large enough for a desk and chair. A covered deck encircled the lower floor. The next-nearest cabin was a good thirty yards away, through the native forest of stately ponderosa pines.

Kate walked through the furnished space, turning on lights. Thanks to the trees, these cabins could be dark despite Flagstaff's famously bright skies, and she wanted Peter's first impression to be a cheerful one.

Then he was in the front room, setting his suitcases down with a thump and admiring the southwestern decor. He declared the pullout couch "brilliant," the dining table set with flowers for his arrival "fantastic." Any impression she had of his being reserved faded away.

His enthusiasm encouraged Kate to look around the space with fresh eyes. For one person spending about five months here, she thought it might be just right. Simple, yet sufficient.

"Welcome to the Forest of Arden," she said.

"'Ay, now am I in Arden, the more fool I. When I was at home I was in a better place, but travelers must be content,'" he said in a lilting tone. "'If this uncouth forest yield anything savage, I will either be food for it or bring it for food to thee,'" he continued, dropping into a playful bow.

"'For my sake, be comfortable,'" she replied from the same speech. An appreciative smile brightened his green eyes.

"Your given name is Katherine?" he asked suddenly.

"Yes, it is. Richard probably called me that, when he talked with you. He's the only person who uses it. He's formal with names."

"Maybe that's why I thought of *Henry V* when I saw you," he mused. She raised her eyebrows. "When I saw your coat, I had an idea that Katherine of France had worn it onstage at the Rose."

Kate laughed. "You think I robbed the costume shop for it? I'm flattered—I think. But no; I made it for myself. It's lined, you see?" She unbuttoned the coat and held it open so he could see the fleece inside. "For winter."

"You made that? It's brilliant."

Continuing the short tour, he admired the fully stocked kitchen, and as she led him up the curving iron stairs to the office loft, he approved of that, too. *He wants to appreciate everything*, Kate thought. It was easy to like someone who approached a new living situation with such a positive mindset.

They went back downstairs and up the short hallway, past the bathroom, which he pronounced "choice," opening the large hallway closet to admire its wide shelves, and on to the bedroom. Together, they looked at the quilted, queen-sized bed that dominated the space.

Suddenly feeling shy, Kate asked, "Is it at all like where you live in New Zealand?"

Peter smiled, but she saw him bite his lip. "There's a thick forest near where I live, but my house proper is by the ocean, so you get mist and fog. It's not like here, where every day is bright."

She noticed he hadn't quite answered, but let it go. "I do hope you'll be very comfortable here."

"I'm sure I will be, and I'm grateful you let me move in early."

"That was Richard's doing. He's rather keen on your Hamlet." Her compliment was answered by another wry smile from Peter. "I'll leave you to settle in, but if there's anything you need, just let the site manager know, and we'll take care of it."

Turning to go, she realized she'd forgotten to give him the key and welcome packet. She turned back and found him looking at her with such guileless appreciation that it stole her breath.

She returned his gaze for a moment, absorbing the sight of his red-gold hair and neat beard, his bright green eyes. Beneath the scruff was an undeniably handsome man. Then she reached out her hand, from which the key dangled. His fingers brushed her palm as he took it. She didn't breathe again until she was walking down the porch steps and back into her life, where the list of things to do awaited her, suddenly far less urgent than it had seemed just half an hour before.

ACT 1
SCENE 7

RICHARD, PETER

After a long weekend at his Tucson house, Richard returned to his office late Tuesday morning. The moment he walked inside, decades of memories embraced him.

Pictures from notable performances occupied almost every inch of wall space not claimed by bookshelves that held the finest collection of Shakespeareana in Arizona. On a shelf behind his desk, the Regional Theatre Tony Award stood alongside the National Medal of Arts in its velvet-lined box. Other accolades were scattered throughout the room.

The thought of taking his personal mementos down from the walls and walking away for good gave him a pang. The Rose had been his world since the day he arrived in America at twenty-nine to assist the company's illustrious founder.

Adam Condell had overseen construction of the original outdoor stage in 1947, on a hill just north of Flagstaff. Condell, who grew up in Flagstaff and earned his degree from the Arizona State Teacher's College, taught drama with Angus Bowmer at the Oregon Shakespeare Festival. Inspired by Bowmer's vision, Condell designed the stage for his beloved hometown with the help of John Ashby Conway, designer of Ashland's first and second stages.

The location proved ideal. Flagstaff's position on Route 66 pulled in motor tourists from as far away as Chicago and Los Angeles. Nearby was State Route 180, the road to the Grand Canyon.

As tourists began including the Rose in their Arizona itineraries, the performances, delivered with verve by well-trained actors, hooked them. Word spread, return ticket sales were strong, and Condell's idea, that the West could support another summer-long Shakespeare festival in addition to the brilliant original in Ashland, had proved right.

When Richard arrived in Flagstaff in 1971 as a guest director, bringing his *The Taming of the Shrew* cast from London's West End, a second and grander version of the Rose stage had just been constructed.

"The setting of the wooden O makes one feel embraced by a wise forest whose ancient trees have gathered round to witness high art," a writer from the *Los Angeles Times* had gushed when it was built.

Richard had seen Shakespeare performed outdoors, of course, notably at Regent's Park and Brownsea Island, but never in a theatre purpose-built for the task and of such classic Elizabethan design. He had blocked *Taming* for performance on an indoor proscenium stage. Making it work on the Rose's thrust stage, where his actors were nearly surrounded by attentive and sometimes raucous groundlings standing in a seatless space called the yard, changed his life.

"It's like theater-in-the-round almost, innit?" he'd asked Condell, who laughed and told the young director, "Yes, and the more you embrace the possibilities of that and let the actors play *with* the audience rather than simply *to* them, the better it gets."

Upon returning to London, Richard stayed just long enough to pack his bags. He'd received a calling as clear as a religious conversion. He wanted to continue directing Shakespeare's plays, but only on the Rose stage—the stage still in use today.

Oh, to be twenty-nine years old again and just starting out, Richard thought as he looked around his office. A tentative knock interrupted his reverie. *Speaking of which.*

"Come," he said, and in walked his Hamlet.

He'd invited Peter to a meeting the day the actor signed his contract. A role of this stature merited the focused attention of director and actor long before formal rehearsals began. And because Peter was unknown to him, Richard took great interest in introducing himself personally.

Now, with a genial demeanor, Richard showed Peter to the table where, every year, he hosted scene work with small groups of actors. In his mind's eye, the chairs were filled by everyone from John Gielgud and Lynn Redgrave to Kenneth Branagh and Emma Thompson. Peter Dunmore was taking his place among these ghostly eminences.

"Tea?" Richard offered, and Peter agreed. They made small talk as Richard heated the kettle and asked his preference between English Breakfast and Darjeeling. When Peter hesitated, Richard suggested the Darjeeling as a robust support when there was mental work to be done.

As Peter accepted the cup and buried his nose in the steam, they were interrupted by another knock. This time it was the company dramaturge. Richard made introductions as he prepared Aurelia's herbal tea, and soon the three were seated with scripts in hand.

"Very well then; let's begin at the heart of the matter," Richard said. "Who is Hamlet to you?"

It was a test, but Peter had always been a diligent student of Shakespeare. He cleared his throat, then answered, "He's a young man who's led a sheltered, pampered life as the Prince of Denmark. And now grief is driving him mad."

"Ah, good. How will you play that sheltered early life and that new experience of grief?"

"Well, I hope."

Richard smiled. "No doubt. You haven't played Hamlet before, is that right?"

Peter thought about the biography he'd concocted, which mapped his London stage career onto the more limited opportunities available to a player in New Zealand and Australia.

"That's right," he replied, "but I have played Benedick and Macbeth, as well as smaller roles."

"How did Mackers go for you?" Aurelia asked.

Relieved to have a break from Richard's searching gaze, Peter thought back to his performance. To play in front of a big, adoring crowd was a powerful rush. The reviews had gushed with praise, the seats stayed full, and the actress playing Lady Macbeth had proved a notable partner onstage and (for a time) in bed. But how much of this could he share with Aurelia and Richard?

"Erm, we were a tight company, and I enjoyed playing Macbeth. Shakespeare gives him so much to do, with an astounding economy of writing."

"Not so with Hamlet; no economy here." Richard laid gentle fingers on his script. "And what's your approach to delivering this grand text?"

"No matter the play, I think Shakespeare's lines are conversational. Whether the words are prose or poetry, it's meant to be real people saying meaningful things to each other. Driving themselves and each other to thought, emotion, action. Bringing the audience along for the ride."

"So you think our audience is capable of following the action?" Aurelia asked.

"Oh yes! Elizabethan audiences would have recognized the beauty in these speeches, the way they recognized the beauty of words spoken in church. But they also would've understood them."

When Richard nodded, Peter turned to look his director in the eye. "Especially here at the Rose, where you've made such a tradition of the actor/audience connection, audiences can understand Shakespeare. But to get there, the actor has to grasp what the character is saying and why. I need to understand Hamlet's words, through the lens of his limited experience of the world and his fresh and powerful experience of grief, and then play them so the audience can empathize with his choices."

It was a passionate speech and one Richard agreed with wholeheartedly.

"Bravo," he said. He considered them well launched into a discussion of the play that would shape all the work to come. They would spend the rest of the morning talking about Hamlet's objectives and tactics, looking for interesting answers to an actor's all-important questions, "What does this character want now, and what is he prepared to do to get it?"

After today, Aurelia would be available whenever Peter needed to delve into what specific words meant or referred to. Her deep knowledge of Shakespeare's England and her understanding of the world Richard wanted to create in this production made her advice golden.

"Think of her as you would of me, and call on her anytime," Richard told Peter as they said goodbye as the meeting ended. "I'm here as well, when you're ready to discuss intentions and choices. We'll meet regularly once rehearsals begin, and we shall work the soliloquies with especial care."

"I look forward to it," Peter said.

"As do I."

When Art Ryerson answered Richard's ring, it was just after dinnertime in Stratford-upon-Avon. Richard pictured his friend relaxing in the leather easy chair in his historic cottage, crystal whiskey glass sparkling in the lamplight. Richard wished he could pop across the Pond, pour himself a stiff drink, and sit down to talk things over with Arthur, but these were not those times.

"I wanted you to know, for the first time I'm thinking of hanging it up," Richard said in a Galway brogue barely dimmed by decades among Americans. "It's all so much in the best of times, and now with the banking crisis, the times are anything but. My contract comes up for renewal again next year. I'm thinking of giving notice this fall so the board can prepare for transition. The Rose needs a captain who can steer her through dangerous financial waters, and I'm afraid I'm not up to the task anymore." He drew a long breath. "I'm tired, Arthur."

The shocked silence went on for so long Richard started to wonder if he'd lost the connection. Then he heard Art swallow a sip of whiskey.

"This banking mess is quite troubling here as well," Art said. "We're seeing all manner of turmoil and upheaval. At the RSC, our big donors are tightening their purses, and season tickets are down."

"Here, too, which is why we've cut production budgets. It's more than that, though. I have to tell you, the Rose herself is showing her age."

"Lost a bit of sparkle, has she? The dear old girl." Art tried to lighten his friend's mood. "Get the actors together to give her a new coat of paint, like you did when Branagh brought his *Much Ado* cast in '93, and she'll be good as new."

Richard chuckled. "Remember when I handed Kenneth a tin of gold paint and invited him to figure out where it should be applied? Branagh looked round and round before he saw that the only gold in our wooden palace is on the ball atop the flagpole!"

"As I remember, he had a few creative ideas about where you could put it to use, starting with gilding your own precious self," Art said, laughing with Richard.

"Those were good days." Richard's laugh turned to a sigh.

"These hard times will pass."

"Will they? I met with the buildings and grounds manager last week. He's done his usual flagpole-to-basement preseason checkup. Did you know, the Rose will see her fortieth season next year? She's showing her age more brazenly every year. Dry boards are splitting, joints are parting, the electrical system has developed gremlins, and the ancient plumbing puts the dressing rooms at risk of a flood during every monsoon."

"That bad, is it?"

"Aye. She needs significant help: not a paint job, but an overhaul from stem to stern. And with the endowment under siege, I don't see whence cometh our help."

"What say your money people?" Art asked, knowing the answer already.

"They tell me now's the time to tighten the belt, not rebuild a theatre."

"Is that what she needs, rebuilding?" Art asked, shocked again.

Richard recalled the long list. "The board's resolution tabling the upgrades we'd dreamed of was a blow. Forget the upgrades and she still needs new electrics and pipes and work around the foundation. The audience would appreciate more bathroom stalls, thank you very much, and the actors want more dressing room space."

"When have they ever not wanted that," Art pointed out.

This time, Richard didn't laugh. "I'll tell you the truth of it, Arthur, and be done. It's not just me who should retire. I've half a mind to suggest that the board consider closing her down after next season, as well."

"My word." Art took another sip of whiskey. "You can't do that, you simply can't. There's been a theatre on that site for more than sixty years, man. Don't shut her doors now. You'll find a way."

"But that's the crux of it. I don't have the energy or the ideas anymore. To direct, yes; I still have the spirit for that. My undiscovered Kiwi prodigy will be the next Peter O'Toole if he proves up the way I think he will. But the rest of it, bah. It might be the wiser course to close her down gracefully rather than let her fall to bits."

"About your New Zealand nobody," Art mused. "What if you cancel that contract and invite someone famous to play it instead? David Tennant was superb in the role last year at the RSC. He started out looking as sober as an undertaker and then believably lost his mind. Wit has never disguised itself so artfully in witlessness. He might take it on if you asked him."

"Tennant is one to watch," Richard sighed noncommittally.

"Your regular players are among the finest actors there are, but do yourself a favor and bring in a big name this year. Get a Hollywood hotshot who wants to prove he has the talent for a live stage. Better yet, find a leading lady to play it. Garner national press and jack your ticket prices through the roof, bank crisis be damned. Make a pile of gold that will have your money people eating their words."

Richard thought back to the morning's meeting with Peter and

Aurelia. After their thoughtful discussion, he felt more confident than ever in the actor he'd chosen. "We don't need to cast some callow Hollywood youth who needs to be cued from line to line. I like this lad enough to place my wager on him. Perhaps he'll show us all something new."

"Find someone to take the rest of it on, then," Art counseled. "Grant yourself a new job title; director emeritus would do nicely. Direct there on contract and let someone else figure out how to give the Rose another forty years of life like the grand old dame she deserves to become."

"I want her to live on; I do. And the thought of keeping my hand in beyond next year does appeal. My name would still attract donors. But who would want to take over as executive director? They'd have to navigate the company through this present storm and find a way to renovate the Rose. Meanwhile, I'd be hovering like Banquo's ghost, fingers itching to reclaim the helm if they did manage to steer us into calmer waters. It's a thankless job I'd be handing over. Who would want to do it? Would—"

"Not me," Art said, cutting off the thought his friend had barely begun to voice. "You know I'd never leave Stratford. Besides, I thought you liked me better than that."

Richard chuckled. "You're right. It will have to be someone with the gumption to battle the storm and right the ship, but someone I simply don't like."

"Let the search for a hated new captain begin," Art said.

ACT 1
SCENE 8

Peter, Kate

A month passed; a month in which Peter cocooned in his tiny cabin at the Arden and devoted himself to the study of *Hamlet*. He read everything he could, devouring essays that analyzed the play and the character. Sometimes he called Aurelia, asking questions and learning more about Shakespeare's Elsinore. Twice he emailed Richard, receiving lengthy replies each time.

It was a larger task of memorization than he'd ever done, one that wouldn't be finished until he and the other actors set the play up on its feet and began playing with the relationships between their characters. But learning lines alone was not enough to occupy his whole mind. The work that absorbed him was puzzling out the conundrums of character and circumstance. Saying Hamlet's words was one thing; finding ways to play his emotions, his soul, was another.

His father died, and his mother married his father's brother. Typical family dysfunction, right? The "antic disposition" Hamlet puts on, a virtuoso performance at the knife's edge of madness, and the trouble he causes for himself and those around him are legendary acting challenges.

The day Peter worked on the very long second scene in act 2 in which Hamlet says, "I could be bounded in a nutshell and count myself a king of infinite space," he laughed out loud and looked around at his small cabin with appreciative eyes. It was indeed a nutshell. Everything had its place, with no room for abandon or increase. He'd bought a winter jacket and a few long-sleeved shirts, and the closet was full. He could eat here, sleep here, study his part here, bounded within this cozy nutshell, and what more did he need? Through every window he saw the upright, red-gold trunks of pine trees, an endless series of repeating lines. When he sat on the porch to read, the wintry silence was profound. He was a king of infinite space indeed.

He'd set a few photos of his mother on the bedroom windowsill atop her favorite scarf and, beside them, a treasured bottle of her perfume. He talked with her often, saying how much he missed her or sharing something from his day, maybe something new he'd found to play with in *Hamlet*. He asked her questions and sometimes, if his heart was quiet, he heard her voice in his mind, encouraging him to puzzle it out for himself.

Grief remained a durable dye that turned even bright days indigo. He'd avoided talking about grief with Richard, but it only made the days following their first meeting lonelier. After all, who better to talk with about the loss of a parent than the director of a play infused with themes of grief and madness? But Peter had resisted the temptation to unburden his conflicted soul.

Now and then, a powerful wave of sadness washed through him. He might be reading lines, or washing dishes, or staring out at the forest; he never knew what might trigger it. A pang of sorrow would slice through his body, sending his heart thudding. He'd learned to stop what he was doing and let the flood come. No use fighting it. Tears would flow, and just as he'd experienced in the grandeur of his oceanside Denmark, here in the bounded privacy of his cabin nutshell, there was no reason not to cry, or scream, if that's what the fit demanded. His mother had been gone a year, but his pain in losing her remained fresh and raw.

Richard's right-hand woman, Kate of the soulful brown eyes and impressive skills as a seamstress, had called after his first week at the Arden to ask how he was getting on. Remembering to put on his New Zealand accent, he'd said everything was shaping up well.

"Are you getting out much, maybe going for hikes?" Kate had asked. "I know it's winter and snow can get in the way, but the Rose is the highest-elevation professional stage in the country. It's no joke. Everyone needs to adjust to it, to perform at their best."

Remembering the aerobic exercise suggestions tucked into the welcome packet, he explained he'd been out for runs on nearby trail systems between Flagstaff's brief and pleasant snowstorms. "I was shocked I could only run five minutes before I was gasping for breath the first time I went out. Then I saw a group off in the distance, running like a herd of"—he reached for a swift herd animal native to New Zealand, but nothing sprang to mind; he hadn't been there long enough—"gazelles? And I thought, 'Come on, man, you can do five minutes more.'" At Kate's giggle, his mouth curved up in an answering grin.

"When I started running here at Buffalo Park, which is flat and easy, it was alternating between running two minutes and walking a minute for twenty minutes, and I was done for the day," she told him. "It gets easier."

"But 'easier' doesn't mean 'easy,' I'm guessing," he said, matching her tone.

"No, it's never that!"

In that momentary pause, he'd thought, *I should invite her out.* But everything about it daunted him: a date, after a year of celibacy; the idea of being in a public place, where anyone might recognize him; the fact that they would be working together for the next few months. A date gone wrong, with Richard Keane's beautiful right-hand woman, would have consequences.

Before he could sort it all out in his mind, she'd broken the silence to ask, "Do you cross-country ski?"

"Erm, no, I don't actually." *Am I about to reveal my ignorance of New Zealand geography?* "There's not a lot of that, right where I come from."

"Oh, right," she said. "Well, if you ever want to try it, we have a good facility out north of Flagstaff. It's higher elevation than town, and there's usually snow. You can rent skis and take lessons there. I'd be happy to show you around if you like."

Hearing that, the *No* in his mind easily became, "Yes, I'd like that very much."

He found her an easy companion, kind and encouraging on his first day out, lending a hand when crossed skis sent him tumbling. He laughed at himself as he brushed snow from his beard. She patiently showed him the motion that would carry him most easily uphill.

Apparently, his large sunglasses and woolen hat, along with the beard, were sufficient disguise out here on the ski trails. He hadn't been recognized at the Rose or the grocery store, either. He was starting to think he might be able to stay unrecognized even once performances started.

Just one vampire-free season, that's all I ask had become his mantra. One season as Peter Dunmore, succeeding or failing on the Rose's fabled stage by talent alone. Then he would go back to the real world, reclaiming the McKenzie name and all that came with it.

With Kate, he felt safe in his disguise. And so the next Monday, they went out again before Kate went to work at noon. Mondays were dark onstage here, as at other theatres. Years ago, Kate had negotiated a late start to her workweek that gave her a precious, free weekday morning. For Peter, it was just two hours of rough exercise and companionship in his otherwise solitary life, but he appreciated the latter perhaps even more than the former. Kate knew her Shakespeare, for one thing, sharing his delight in the poetry and pathos of *Hamlet.*

The third week, Kate offered to run lines with him as they drank cocoa on the ski lodge deck. She didn't have the play by heart, of course, but she found his cues with ease and spoke them with grace. He asked whether she sometimes acted in the shows.

"No," she'd told him. "Stage fright."

"I'm sorry. I know it can be debilitating. Laurence Olivier said his throat closed up. Is that what happened to you?"

Kate thought back to the *Much Ado* she'd stage-managed in grad school. Friends in the company lured her onstage during one rehearsal to play Beatrice in a scene with Benedick. Their Benedick, Wyatt Randall, had star power—most of the women in class had a crush on him, including Kate. It could have been lust or fear that tied her tongue that day, but either way, she'd flubbed and stumbled through a scene she knew by heart, scared to look at her friends, knowing they were embarrassed on her behalf. She'd never tried again.

"It didn't go well. I remember my heart racing, and then when I tried to get a word out, my mouth was so dry I coughed." She rolled her eyes. "I was performing a scene I knew, with a guy I knew, in front of my classmates who were friends of mine, and I still couldn't do it. Lord knows how I'd survive the eyes of a paying audience."

She laughed, but he was still looking at her with calm concern, so she added, "I've made a life in theater, but to stand up there and bring the audience all the way into the story, to feel their response, is something I will always wish I could do."

He asked with genuine curiosity, "What is it you do, that you love as much as I love to act?"

"Fabric art." Her face brightened. "Designing, buying, building, sewing, decorating, all of it. I love making costumes. Sometimes I even wear them myself, and then I feel . . ."

"Beautiful and powerful and true," he filled in.

"Exactly."

"As I feel onstage." They smiled into each other's eyes before looking away.

"Have you played Hamlet before?" Kate asked as they sat drinking hot chocolate after their fourth Monday ski.

Peter bit back a humorous retort about not all British actors being cast in the role before they were thirty. *She doesn't know I'm British*, he reminded himself. *And it's an honest question.* "No, I never have. I was offered it once, but I chose Horatio instead. I didn't feel ready for the big role."

"Why not? Or if it's too personal, forget I asked." Kate blushed.

"Nah, it's all good," Peter reassured her, using one of Huatare's favorite phrases to make himself sound Kiwi. "I just didn't feel old enough, or maybe 'mature' would be the word. I might only have one chance at it. I wanted to do the thing right."

"There are a lot of different questions to decide, I know: Is he mad or pretending or maybe both, and if he starts out pretending but does go mad, when does that happen—that sort of thing?"

"Yeah, definitely that, but I studied the lines in school, and even then, I had an idea of a direction to take on it. The thing was, back then I couldn't figure out why he does the things he does. How he behaves toward the Ghost of Hamlet's Father, as an example."

"What about it?"

"He questions the Ghost and goes back into the castle, yeah? And then walks around talking to himself and other people, for four acts." Peter gazed up into the trees. "Why doesn't he ask the Ghost more questions, at least?"

Kate sat back and looked at him. "Maybe there are no questions worth asking when your ghost comes back to haunt you. Maybe the chance to see that face one more time would quiet every question."

"I suppose you're right," Peter mused. "Seeing a ghost will throw you off your game, I guess. He was probably freaked out. But he puts it behind him so quickly."

"To me, the confusing thing is what he doesn't do. He doesn't run crying, away from the Ghost or into his arms. He doesn't go back to the battlements every night on the off chance of meeting him again."

"He moves right along to the task at hand," Peter agreed. "The actor might choose to show some other action with the Ghost, but not based on the words Hamlet says."

"And this play was written by a man who had lost a son. Recently, too, if the biographers are right in their guesses." Kate shook her head.

"William Shakespeare must've known what it was like to grieve. The Elizabethans had more firsthand experience of death than we do, but people back then still had feelings."

Peter nodded. "*Hamlet* is far from being what I'd think of as an accurate psychological portrait of grief."

"Unless in Ophelia's madness. She tells King Claudius, 'I cannot choose but weep to think they would lay him i' th' cold ground.' He gets that right," Kate said. "Maybe we don't need a scene in which Hamlet . . . ?"

With a sharp intake of breath, she looked down. Peter could see she was moved and working to control it.

He gave her a moment, then asked softly, "A scene in which Hamlet?"

"What if he sees the Ghost and just bursts into tears? Because that's what I'd do if I saw my dad. I'm sorry; I didn't mean for this to turn dark. Sometimes it catches me off guard."

Peter looked at her with wide eyes. "When did you lose him?"

"Three years ago. A long time."

"Time doesn't matter, I've found."

"Oh. You too?"

Moved by the vulnerability she'd shown, hungry to talk about his mother with someone after so many months alone with her ghost, he said, "My mum. A year back."

"Oh." They sat together in the silence of shared grief. After a long moment, he noticed that her chest was rising and falling in time with his; they'd synchronized their breathing.

It happens sometimes onstage when you're absolutely in tune with a scene partner, Peter thought, *but I've never noticed it happening with another person in normal life.* He looked at Kate, who returned his gaze. *I wonder what it means.*

ACT 1

SCENE 9

PETER, KATE, RICHARD

After more than a month alone at the Arden, Peter was happy when the *Hamlet* cast began to move in as April neared. It was a risk, but soon there would be rewards; line partners, scene partners, even picnic partners as the weather warmed.

Kate told him most of the younger and newer actors would probably prefer the motor inn over the cabins, and that proved true. They chose among rooms named after famed Shakespearean actors and directors who had worked at the Rose: national and international luminaries such as Jean Smart, Simon Russell Beale, Kate Winslet, and Sam Mendes; beloved regional players such as Mark Murphey, Robynn Rodriguez, Brian Vaughn, and Marco Barricelli.

The older actors and those who'd brought partners tended to prefer the cabins, but they generally chose the larger two-bedroom units, just uphill from the motor court. Even once everyone was in place, Peter still had no neighbors near his nutshell. It made life easy; he could choose to interact, or not, and as it was still early days, he chose not to, cultivating something of a loner's reputation to protect his lonely heart.

But he couldn't avoid their eyes when the full cast met for the first time.

Kate came to the meeting with a job to do: presenting the personnel policies on harassment and inclusion. She stood in a quiet corner of the big conference room, watching as people entered. Richard, by the door, greeted each actor with a hearty handshake, then gestured toward the table where coffee and teas were set out alongside two gorgeous platters of fruits and cheeses; the king, inviting his guests to the banquet.

Kate could sort the actors who had worked with Richard before from those meeting him for the first time. The old hands walked in with a smile as bright as Richard's; the rookies trembled, but his genuine warmth soon reassured them.

Kate felt he was at his best on days like this. Not that she was entirely happy as she watched him greeting this season's Laertes. Richard had rebuffed her the day she asked to be considered for his job. She had prepared her case carefully, even practicing it with Beth, who made a stern Richard until she broke into giggles. In her speech, Kate listed her advanced degree in theatre management, her many different stage-related jobs throughout college and grad school, and the prodigious variety of experiences she'd gained since coming to the Rose as an intern.

"Not that I could replace you, Richard," she'd told him. "Nobody could. And I don't want you to go. But if you're moving on, I hope you'll consider endorsing my name to the board as a potential successor. You'll never find anyone more committed to Flagstaff and the Rose than I am."

"I know it, Katherine," he'd said. "Your talents are many, your skills even more numerous, and your claim to this throne is a righteous one. Yet I hesitate." He gave her an earnest look. "It's not your youth, and heaven knows it is not your sex. Talented young women lead their own companies here and in Europe, but not enough of them. We would do this company proud if we could add your name to that banner. And still, I will say no; at least for now."

She tried to keep her expression neutral as he continued, "To be honest, you don't know what you're asking for. It is not a bright, new coin I can press into your hand and say, 'Spend wisely.' It's more like a millstone I'd be setting around your neck; you of all people. I would not wish it on you, Katherine, truly."

She'd pressed her case once more and been pushed back again. Since then, she'd puzzled over it but could not settle on an explanation that fit his words. "You of all people," he'd said. What did that mean? Why wouldn't Richard even consider her for his "throne"? Maybe he already had someone else in mind, someone like Arthur, with decades of experience and thousands of connections in the British theatrical world. Or maybe she hadn't projected enough confidence. She didn't want to believe her youth and sex weighed against her, but the possibility planted a seed of disappointment in Richard, an unpleasant emotion she fought to ignore.

The nearer they'd come to the all-hands meeting, the more nervous Peter felt. Someone in the cast might recognize him from his movie or remember him from London. Peter could imagine in detail the scene in which his cover was blown and he had to either face the consequences or turn and run once more, straight to the airport for the next plane out.

He'd fought the better angels of his nature throughout one Monday ski. Finally, reluctantly, he asked Kate about the cast list, not wanting to lean on their friendship but curious beyond the limits of his self-control. She'd been coy. Richard never shared the list publicly ahead of the first meeting, she'd told him. The secret created a bit of theatricality Keane immensely enjoyed.

But it's a matter of life and death, Peter thought, recognizing immediately that it wasn't. "Then never mind," he'd told Kate.

Looking into the mirror that Friday morning, he had a crazy thought of shaving off the beard, cutting his hair short, dyeing it black, and strutting in prepared to be instantly recognized. "Hey, you're that guy," someone would say, and they'd be off to the races. "You're the guy in that movie." Or worse: "You're that guy from the photo." Though they'd never know him from the photo—*not with my clothes on anyway*, he amended morosely. *No, I am most definitely* NOT *that guy.*

Instead, he used trimmers to shape his mustache while still mostly hiding his upper lip, then carved his beard closer to his jawline, cleaning up his neck where he'd let the mountain monk thing go on too long. He hung a gold hoop in one ear and added gold cufflinks to his red button-down shirt. Ripped blue jeans and boots completed the look.

He'd turned himself into a pirate, estranged from the clean-cut image of his stage work and his darkly seductive look from the movie. If they didn't recognize him the moment he swaggered in, he could hide in plain sight. *That's the hope, anyway.*

Lifting one eyebrow, he gave himself an over-the-top pirate scowl in the mirror, then laughed at himself. One thing was sure: He appeared much different today than he had in *Thirst*. For that movie, they'd dressed him in black and used colored contact lenses to give him a dark-hearted glare. He could never frighten anyone today. *Good.* He wanted to draw attention to this new character, "Peter Dunmore," a beach bum from New Zealand with a flair for the dramatic who happened to know his Shakespeare. Looking in the mirror one last time, he told himself, *Prepare to flirt and flirt hard, Kiwi pirate.*

Kate knew most of the actors already, and some came to greet her once they'd met Richard and poured themselves a steadying cup of coffee. If they hadn't already connected casually at the Arden or acted together in previous seasons, she introduced them to each other by both real name and character. It was fun to watch their faces light up as they met scene partners. Her highlight so far this morning had been introducing Ted Harrington's Claudius to Margaret Graham's Polonius.

She noticed Peter the moment he walked in. She'd grown used to his scruffy beard, puffy jacket, and knitted ski cap; she hadn't seen his hair in a month. Today, he looked positively dashing, with his beard trimmed and a red shirt that accented broad shoulders. He shook Richard's hand and returned his greeting, then turned away; *to the drinks table*, she thought, but no. He scanned the room, looking from one actor's face to the next. Then his eyes found hers and stopped. He sent her a smile. Returning it, she was startled to feel her heart jump. *No*, she commanded herself. *Not for a player. Not ever again.*

"You look quite the Hamlet," she said as he walked over. "'Th' expectancy and rose of the fair state, the glass of fashion and the mold of form, th' observed of all observers' indeed.'" She gestured around the conference room at the people who were looking their way, curious to assess their leading actor for the first time.

He scanned the room again quickly before declaiming to Kate in a plummy British accent that would have made Sir Ian McKellen proud, "'O, what a rogue and peasant slave am I!'"

"'A dull and muddy-mettled rascal' you are indeed,'" she teased.

"That I am," he agreed, switching to the broader New Zealand vowels. "And yet I just shook the hand that shook the hand of Olivier. The great Richard Keane."

"Richard the Great, he likes to be called."

"Richard the Great it is then." He seemed nervous, and she wanted to ask why. He'd already met Richard, she knew, so it couldn't be that. *First day at school*, she thought. To ease his jitters, she introduced him to LaShia Shay, the female actor playing Horatio, and stepped aside to let Hamlet meet his one true friend in Elsinore.

Richard was perhaps the only person in the room for whom nerves were not an issue. How many first cast meetings had he enjoyed here in this very room, seated in King Arthur's throne (in reality, a humble oak chair with his last name carved into the back)? *Too many to count*, he thought.

There was one person he especially looked forward to welcoming. She came in last, as befitting a queen; after Claudius, after young Hamlet himself with his long hair and earring. (*A hippie Hamlet; an audacious choice*, he'd thought.)

When their Gertrude, no less a personage than Isabelle Rivette, swept into the room, he could hear the chattering actors grow quiet as all eyes turned her way.

"Isabelle," he said, stepping forward. "*Bienvenue*."

"Richard Coeur de Lion," she said, her English softened by a whisper of her native tongue. Isabelle was the most highly decorated French actress of the past twenty years.

He kissed her cheeks, then held her hand for a long moment. "We're honored by your presence. Welcome to the Blue Mountain Rose production of *Hamlet*." Then, knowing everyone was listening, he turned to address the room. "Welcome to you all. Please be seated, and let us begin."

At the end of the long day, Peter was glad to return to his nutshell. Opening the front door, he said, "Hi, Mum," to the quiet room. He no longer felt sheepish about such things. She was here as much as she was anywhere, and he wanted to talk with her.

"First cast meeting today," he continued. "Remember Isabelle Rivette, from the touring cast of *Phèdre*? She's to play Gertrude! I'm chuffed to work with her."

He set his papers on the dining table and walked the few steps to the kitchen to warm some soup for dinner.

"Once she came through the door, nobody looked at me again. I can be anonymous as a church mouse and just play my part. 'O day and night,' what a relief that is."

Peter opened a fresh loaf of bread and dropped two slices into the toaster.

"We went round the table and introduced ourselves. Nobody recognized me. My Kiwi accent is spot on, thanks to hanging out with Huatare." He smiled, thinking of his friend.

"We introduced our characters and talked about trust. Who does our character trust, and why? Who do they distrust, and why? Hamlet, of course, trusts nobody but Horatio. Horatio is my Huatare."

Peter carried dinner to the table and sat down, then popped back up to pull a bottle of dark ale from its cool cupboard as a treat. "The woman playing Horatio is called LaShia Shay. She's played the Rose before. She came up through the New Orleans Shakespeare Festival at Tulane and the Alabama Shakespeare Festival. Seems a good sort." Peter took a long, appreciative drink from his bottle, then raised it as if making a toast.

"You always loved first meeting, Mum. When you played Medea, you brought me to the National. I sat by the wall and watched everyone greet everyone else. So much excitement in the room, so much tension. You were the star of the show, just like Madame Rivette today."

He paused, remembering his mom's tailored gray suit, her warm, gold hair curled and pinned up to accent her high cheekbones and graceful neck. "The beauty of the world, the paragon of animals" indeed—and now a quintessence of dust.

Grief came knocking, but he blinked away tears as they formed. To distract himself, he said, "Speaking of trust, we have the first fight rehearsal in a week. You know how I love a good sword fight. The choreographer wants to use rapier and dagger. I hope I can trust the guy playing Laertes not to stab me through the heart." He laughed briefly before his face turned somber.

"I was glad not to be recognized, but it made me lonely, too. It's one thing to hang out here, reading Shakespeare. He's good company, and so are you. It's quite another thing to stand in a room of strangers and realize nobody knows my real name, much less who I am, what I'm like, what I wish for or fear or—want."

He recalled the electric flash he'd felt when he caught Kate's eye through the crowd.

"Amend that. Kate Morales was there. I think maybe she knows. Not who I am in the world, but something of who I am at heart. Whether she knows what I desire, how could she? I've kept it close. I have to."

The soup cooled as he stared off through the window into the darkening forest.

"I talked with Richard Keane again today, Mum. *The* Richard Keane. Well." There was so much more to say, but the words caught in his throat.

"That's it for now, I guess. Time to eat." He tried to imagine his mother's kiss on his forehead, her wise green eyes, darker than his own, and for a moment he almost could.

ACT 1
SCENE 10

Richard

Richard invited Kate to sit in on the April board finance committee meeting, something he'd never done before. He felt bad about dampening her ambition to succeed him. Being at the table as the board made difficult decisions about the company's finances might change her mind about angling for his throne.

It was a gray Friday morning in Flagstaff, and a cold wind played with Richard's coat as he walked up the hill toward the office. He paused a moment, looking across the field of dry grasses at his theatre. The Rose in her grove of attending pines looked as durable as the mountain range behind her. *If only she were,* he thought.

After the board president called the meeting to order, Merle gave his report. He covered their financial status before describing the global economic conditions that made their situation feel so unstable. "Last month, the Dow Jones hit its lowest level so far, having dropped 54 percent from its peak of 14,164 in October 2007. They're starting to compare this crisis to the Great Depression. I hate to say this, but the only change I see coming is for the worse. I am profoundly pessimistic about the economic outlook for at least the next year."

"And these international economic problems affect us how?" nudged Eric Oliver, the development director.

"They affect us like a monsoon affects a tall pine tree in a meadow," Richard answered gloomily. "We know the rain and wind will blow our branches to hell and back. What we don't know is whether a bolt of lightning might strike us dead where we stand."

"As Richard says, this is an economic storm, unprecedented in its global scope, unlike anything most of us now living have ever seen," Merle continued. "At last week's meeting of the G20, tens of thousands of protestors marched in London, demanding substantive change in global financial institutions. Unemployment is up, foreclosures are up, people feel unsteady on their feet. That affects us in ways we're already seeing and ways we can't yet foresee. Kate?"

Kate cleared her throat. "Season ticket sales are sharply down," she said, bringing up a slide on their big screen. "So are advance sales for *Hamlet* and *Midsummer*. We haven't started selling regular tickets to *Inishmore* or *Eurydice* yet, but we expect to see the same types of numbers. Grant income remains steady because it's from grants we won last year thanks to Eric, but how that will go this year for the 2010 season is anyone's guess." She looked at Eric, who shrugged. "But here's the toughest news. Corporate donations are down by nearly 40 percent over last year, and private donations aren't even that good."

Eric chimed in. "I've been working the phones harder than ever, and everyone is singing the same tune. 'I have to tighten the belt this year. Maybe we can do something next year. I'm sure you understand.' I do, but we still need money to run the company in 2009."

"If we accept these numbers as reality, we have difficult decisions to make," Richard followed. "We may dig quite deeply into the endowment, cut production budgets further, or even consider a reduction in staff through layoffs." The silence in the room was profound. "I have no desire to do any of these. However, we must be aware of our options in order to choose wisely. Let's take them one by one."

As he returned to the big conference room later that morning for the fourth day of rehearsal, Richard did his best to drag his eyes away from the dark clouds of financial catastrophe looming on the horizon so he could attend to brighter, closer possibilities: the script, the cast, the work.

The conference room quieted as he entered. "Well met, everyone," he greeted the room, trying for a note of cheer. A chorus of "hellos" and "well mets" washed over him in reply.

Richard and the cast were spending their first week together in a table read of the full script, act by act. The actors were in good voice, he felt, and they'd all studied diligently since being hired into this year's company. Most were nearly "off book," meaning they'd memorized their parts, but at table read, everyone kept a script open. It allowed them to listen deeply to each other, instead of worrying about their next line. When the group paused to consider some question, discussions were lively but focused. Richard could see friendships forming amid moments of laughter and insight around the table.

"Your characters are real human beings," he'd told them Tuesday at their first rehearsal. "They must be so in your mind first, so they can be so in your audience's eyes and heart. As we prepare to present this play, we have an opportunity to become wiser people, more empathetic people. We will be strengthened in our knowledge of the human condition. We must be open to that growth, or else the contract between the Rose and our audience will be broken. They come to our stage expecting to be invited into a brave new world and shown something true and enduring about their own. *Hamlet* can deliver on that promise—because of each of you."

Each day, Richard kept one ear especially tuned to the voice of his Hamlet. Peter Dunmore had a rich, emotive vocal instrument, well-supported by a strong diaphragm. He was quiet and attentive at the table, but he always had something insightful to say when the opportunity presented itself. He displayed a ready wit and was at ease with the other actors.

With Richard himself, Peter was more reserved. In Richard's estimation, he might not have the acting pedigree of some in the room, such as Isabelle Rivette, but his training in New Zealand had been solid, and his gifts were undeniable. *This is only day four; his youthful awe will wear off as the weeks pass and we continue to work together*, Richard thought.

With everyone settled in, scripts at the ready, Richard felt their eyes on him. "Acting in a Shakespeare play is no small feat," he began. "It requires a healthy body, capable of enduring nearly three hours of performance, sometimes twice a day. It requires a keen mind to know the lines and what they mean, a translation across more than four hundred years. It requires an inner fire the audience can see burning as the character comes to life inside you. And it requires great heart and true capacity for empathy, whether you're playing a hero or villain or, as we would be wise to consider all of Shakespeare's characters, somewhere in between."

Richard looked around and saw that everyone was watching him. "But I soliloquize," he said, releasing them with a smile, "and that is Hamlet's job." His eyes circled the room, stopping on Peter, who acknowledged his look with a nod.

"Speaking of which: Peter, it is time for us to begin considering the soliloquies together. Tahoma?" Richard turned to stage manager Tahoma Begay, sitting to his left. "Please schedule Peter and me for weekly rehearsals to focus on Hamlet's speeches. Say, Tuesday mornings?" He saw Peter nod again as Tahoma wrote the note.

"Very well then; let's begin. I believe we've reached act 4, scene 1. Tahoma?"

"A room in the castle," Tahoma read the stage directions. "Enter King, Queen, Rosencrantz, and Guildenstern."

Richard's eyes turned to the broad-shouldered actor playing Claudius.

"Where is your son?" Ted said.

In the late afternoon, snow began to fall. Richard sat at his desk and reviewed the budget for *Hamlet* once more. He and the other directors had to reduce costs by 15 percent to 20 percent below their original budgets. They'd already found 10 percent. To do more was like squeezing blood from a stone, but they had pledged to try. Art, Linda, and Paul had also offered not to take salaries for directing their shows. Saddened but touched, Richard had promised to consider it if they showed it to him as part of the overall budget cut.

Picking up the phone, he called Serena and Eric into his office. Once they were seated, he said without preamble, "I have something to tell you in confidence." He waited for their nods of assent.

"I am considering giving formal notice to the board this summer that when my contract is up next year, I will not be seeking a renewal." He watched the emotions ripple across their faces.

Serena was first to speak. "Is it the financial news? It can't be that bad, can it?"

"It can be, and it is," he said heavily. "But here is what I'm pondering. If I am to present my successor with an opportunity rather than an insurmountable problem, could we begin now to plan a funding campaign? Perhaps weave it through the summer and culminate with a gala fundraiser in the fall, at a thousand dollars a plate? If three hundred people buy in, that's money enough to make some difference."

Eric said, "I agree with the idea of a campaign, but to find that many people willing to eat a big-ticket banquet dinner in these economic times won't be easy."

"In the meantime, who knows what the markets are doing," Serena chimed in. "Things could turn around, right?"

"It's theoretically possible." Eric's tone was skeptical.

"No matter what the markets do, we can benefit the Rose by doing what we do best: putting on a show," Richard said. "At this banquet, what if we perform a variety show: musical numbers, scenes, skits? That should fill the seats. We have enough singers and dancers in the company for a stellar cabaret. I announce I'll be stepping down next year, and we call it my retirement party."

"I see where you're going with this, Richard," Serena said. "But if the headlines are still bleak, it'll be hard to spin the idea of your leaving as anything other than a sign of bad times at the Blue Mountain Rose. To many people, you ARE the Rose."

Eric added, "I like the idea of an event, though. How about if we do a cabaret on a smaller scale? Sooner rather than later. If it's not a big production, we could probably pull something together as quickly as next month."

"Both summer shows will be deep in rehearsals in May," Serena said. "Would the actors really want to devote time to this?"

"They would if I told them to," Richard answered sharply. "If I said the life of the company was at stake."

Eric disagreed. "I'm with Serena. The moment you say that, everyone assumes we're on the brink of failure, and if there's one thing I've learned in twenty years of fundraising, it's that nobody wants to back failure."

"How about this, Eric," Serena asked. "We put out a quick spring fundraising letter that also promotes a cabaret evening just before *Hamlet* opens."

"That could work. We keep expenses down, invite actors to donate their time."

"I like it," Richard mused.

"With the proceeds, I assume you'd return some funds to production budgets?" Eric asked.

Richard shook his head. "It won't go towards productions. The Rose herself needs the money." Asking them again to keep what they learned in confidence, he reviewed the report from the buildings and grounds manager, sparing no detail of the work needed.

When he was done, Eric whistled. "No wonder you're thinking of retirement."

"I don't want to leave her in ill repair," Richard said, "but perhaps there is no way to prevent the inevitable. For the first time in my life, I simply can't see a way forward. Maybe my replacement can."

ACT 1
SCENE 11

KATE

On the way home from school that night, Beth said, "Mom, I have something to ask you."

The ten options that flashed through Kate's mind ranged from "Can I get a tattoo" to "Can I sleep over at Lauren's house tomorrow night," and the answers "Not in a million years" and "That would be fine" were ready on her lips when Beth silenced her with the question, "I want you to tell me who my dad is. Please? I want to know."

Feeling her throat drop to her stomach, Kate glanced at her daughter, sitting composed and prim in the passenger seat, an expectant look on her face. *You have no idea what you're asking*, Kate thought.

She took a deep breath. "Honey, you've kind of surprised me," she said, forcing herself to project a calm she didn't feel. "Where is this coming from?"

"I'm going to middle school next year. Of all my friends, I'm the only one who has just a mom."

Kate thought of the work and love that went into being "just a mom" and cringed. But she knew Beth didn't mean it that way.

Into the silence, Beth said, "My friends know he's not around, my dad. But in middle school, there will be lots of new kids. I want an answer for when they say, 'Just your mom? Where's your dad?'"

"Can't you tell your curious new friends your dad isn't part of the picture and let them get used to the idea the way your old friends have?" Kate asked, reasonably, she thought.

"I can, but why do I have to? I don't want to," Beth argued. "If I know who he is, I can explain. And that's not the only reason. I want to know what he looks like. Can't you just tell me? I want to know."

The conversation was playing on auto-repeat in Kate's mind the next afternoon. Having dropped Beth off at Lauren's for a Saturday-morning play date, she sat in her office looking at depressing numbers on her computer screen. Richard had emailed the staff, letting them know a spring cabaret fundraiser was in the works, but Kate was brainstorming more options, places to economize, ways to ask past season-ticket buyers to subscribe again without sounding desperate; anything she could suggest that might help.

It was dispiriting work, and she was glad of the interruption when Devon Whelan tapped on her door.

"First fight rehearsal today?" she asked their fight choreographer.

"Come see," Devon answered with a grin.

"Wish I could," she said.

Turning back to the screen, Kate tried to attend to the stories her numbers were telling her, but after twenty fruitless minutes, she had to admit it was no use. Releasing herself from the keyboard, she stood and stretched. A quick visit to rehearsal would give her something more pleasant to ponder than her daughter's unhappiness last night when she'd said, "I'm sorry, but no. Honey, please don't ask me to do that."

In the large rehearsal hall, Richard and Tahoma welcomed her to the production table. Settling herself next to Richard, she saw Devon standing at the edge of a long, blue gym mat on which Peter Dunmore and Bryce Benedict, their Laertes, were at work. The three men were building the first part of the fight scene in act 5. With Devon's guidance and suggestions, the actors would use Shakespeare's text to build a framework for the duel that finally brings *Hamlet* to its poetic end.

As Kate watched, the actors nodded to each other, then lifted their rapiers to their foreheads in a formal gesture. They started in, with Laertes advancing. "Forward, two, thrust," Devon said, "and Hamlet back, back, parry, riposte."

Richard always started fight choreography early in the rehearsal period. He'd once told Kate that if it's left for later, the choreographer's original vision often has to be sacrificed. It's cut back as either too dangerous or too complicated for the actors to learn at that point in the process.

"We'll start early and do the thing right," Richard had said. "The actor playing Hamlet kills three people onstage. The more confident that actor feels in the fight scenes, the less they have to worry about. And an actor unbound by worry can devote full energy to performance."

The bottom line, though, was that like just about anyone who was once a kid, Richard loved a good sword fight. Devon always gave him what he wanted: planned mayhem that looked more complicated than it was. "Grab audiences by the throat and don't let go" was the fight choreographer's creed.

Watching Peter and Bryce build their fencing match stole Kate's thoughts from her spreadsheets. She had seen Peter ski over some tiny, invisible obstacle and tumble, laughing, into the snow. *Give him a rapier and he moves like an athlete*, she thought, amending it to, *They both do*. Bryce was in many ways Peter's opposite: shorter and stockier, clean-shaven and with neatly barbered hair. Of the two, it was Peter she watched most. At one point, he thrust the rapier at Bryce and held a deep lunge, looking to see whether Devon approved.

"Could you do it every performance, let's say four shows in a row, and not pull a hamstring at the Sunday matinee?" Devon asked, smiling.

"How does it look?"

"Like Hamlet is putting it all out there, knowing Laertes has mad skills but thinking maybe there's value in wanting it more than your opponent."

"That's what I was going for. I can do it."

As the choreography went on, Kate saw that Peter listened carefully to Devon and Bryce, attention absorbed in his task, but at one point he looked over to the production table. He flashed them a happy smile that made her grin widely in return. Then her mind spun back to Beth. For someone who was not yet a teen, her daughter's skills at the silent treatment were prodigious. The smile faded from her face.

"Come in," Devon told his fighters. As they met in the center of the mat, he nodded to each. "Good stuff, guys. We made a solid start on the polite part of the fight, using rapiers and daggers as Shakespeare wrote it, all very formal to start, very gentlemanly. There's a lot to work with here in terms of civility and respect, even forgiveness. How far you want to play those qualities is up to you and Richard. As we move deeper into the scene, things get chaotic. They're going to hurt each other. We'll keep working toward that next week." Peter and Bryce thanked him, then shook hands.

Devon stepped back as Tahoma stood and called out, "That's a wrap for the day. Don't forget to get your workouts in. At this high elevation, long fight scenes and speeches can take it out of you if you let them."

As Devon walked to the table to discuss the choreography Richard and Tahoma had seen so far, Kate looked over to where the duelists were collecting their scripts and chatting. Finding no excuses for delay, she stood up and headed for the door, trying to force her thoughts back to the waiting spreadsheets. It was no use. The need for groceries turned her mind ahead toward what she anticipated would be a quiet dinner with Beth. What could she say to her disappointed daughter to ease the sting of hearing a mother's firm no?

Then Kate felt a tap on her shoulder and turned to find Peter smiling down at her. "Can I walk you out?" he asked.

"Sure. I just need to stop by my office."

He loitered by the door, watching her close down her computer and stuff her briefcase. His wavy hair was in disarray, and there was bright color in his cheeks.

"You look like you had a good time with Devon and Bryce," she said.

"Fighting is fun; I don't deny it. Half of us choose Shakespeare just to handle a sword now and then. It's nearly as fun as skiing. And speaking of which—"

Kate estimated that her day was about to get worse: Now that Peter had a full calendar of rehearsals and calls, their ski Mondays were done. *Too good to last*, she thought.

"About skiing—"

"You have a lot to do," Kate interrupted.

"Yeah, nah, it's not that. I've been hearing about this Museum of Northern Arizona. Devon's mum is a docent. He says it's an amazing place to learn about the Navajo and the other Indigenous people here. I'm curious about similarities with the Māori. There might be overlaps, right? Would you like to go explore it with me?"

And just that simply, the carousel that was Kate's whirling life of work and motherhood spun to a momentary stop. The words *Not a player, not ever again*, whispered through her mind like warning bells from someplace far, far distant from where she stood. To quiet them, she said, "Yes, I'd like that. Let's do it."

They wandered the gracious, stone-walled museum, marveling at wonders. Peter was the same at the museum as he'd been when exploring his cabin at the Arden: appreciative. His praises began with the reconstructed skeleton of a small dinosaur in the entrance hall. They continued as he and Kate wandered through the room explaining northern Arizona's geology and into the great hall featuring stories of the Navajo, Hopi, Zuni, and other Native American cultures, all still very much alive and thriving.

It was easy to share his enthusiasm as he pointed out motifs in a grand Navajo rug that reminded him of Māori designs. They examined a piece of Pueblo pottery over a thousand years old, declaring its hand-painted geometric designs more beautiful than anything ever made by machine. Peter was curious about everything, and Kate found that her mood brightened in his company. They had the hall pretty much to themselves and spent the better part of an hour exploring its displays.

"Here's something special you haven't seen yet." Kate called him over to the reconstruction of a Hopi kiva, a ceremonial room with a storytelling mural celebrating the blessings of rain. They sat on a low bench along one wall, looking up, trying to imagine what it was like for Hopi people to take part in the intimate kiva ceremonies. Kate told Peter about the time she went to the Hopi reservation for a social dance and a friendly family invited her to sit on the roof of their home.

"Such kind generosity," she recalled, telling him how the family's teenage daughter had explained certain aspects of the dance for her benefit. Peter absorbed her story, smiling. Kate was surprised when he didn't match it with one of his own. He didn't seem to be the kind of guy who always needed the final word; she liked that.

They wandered outdoors, to a central courtyard alive with birdsong. The day was warm for early April, and they sat down on a stone bench, admiring the bark of a venerable juniper tree nearby. Peter told her about his friend Huatare, who had taken him on a weekend adventure to see *Tāne Mahuta*, the largest known living kauri tree.

"Huatare stood there, staring upward. He closed his eyes, and I did the same. Later, he told me he was breathing with the tree, taking in the oxygen it gave so freely, expressing his gratitude. I always think of that harmony now, when I see a fantastic tree like this one."

They sat side by side, looking up at the juniper. Kate closed her eyes and took a peaceful breath, inhaling the tree's faint scent. Opening her eyes, she had a quick impression that Peter was looking at her, but when she turned her head, he was looking away.

Noticing an urge to take his hand, Kate stood up. *Friends*, she told herself sternly. *Colleagues. That's enough*. Plainly, her heart disagreed. To distract its attention, she said, "There are two more rooms you can't miss; my favorite rooms in the whole museum."

Kate loved the museum's trove of paintings. She had spent many happy hours learning about the artists from her dad, a painter. When they walked into the first room, Peter exclaimed in delight and began wandering from one northern Arizona landscape to the next. Kate let him go, making her own path through the room. One or two of her favorites were hanging, including Joella Jean Mahoney's powerful *Summer Sky*, with its fractured, geometric cloudscapes. She greeted the painting like an old friend.

After a few minutes, Kate noticed that Peter had quieted. She walked over to stand beside him and gaze at the enormous painting that had captured his eye. It was an Ed Mell oil painting of the Grand Canyon, with Mell's trademark incandescent sunset. The things Mell did with line and color; Kate remembered her dad's delight in this same painting.

"I've never seen anything so beautiful," Peter murmured. "We have to go there."

Kate's heart registered the "we" as her thoughts spun. "I . . ." she began, wanting to say something, anything, before realizing she didn't know how the sentence would end.

Peter only heightened her dilemma by setting a hand on her back, just between the shoulder blades, where she stored all of life's tensions. She felt them drain away under his touch. The internal battle between her misgivings and her feelings was intense, but brief. Finally, she looked up. There was an invitation in Peter's eyes. The desire to protect herself fell away as her heart declared its answer. Turning into his embrace, she reached up to meet his questioning kiss.

ACT 2 *April* 2009

ACT 2

SCENE 1

PETER

Richard had fixed Peter in his unerring gaze and was not letting go. "Let us begin with the first soliloquy," he declared.

Settling in at the table on Richard's veranda, Peter stole a moment to appreciate the view. Pictures he'd seen of Mount Fuji came to mind as he looked at the San Francisco Peaks, sparkling in the morning sun after an overnight dusting of snow. Faced with such grandeur, it was hard to turn his attention to words on a page—even words as resonant as Hamlet's.

But he'd come here to work with his director on the famously daunting soliloquies. After a sip of tea and a quick look at the script in front of him, he said quietly, "'O, that this too, too sullied flesh would melt, thaw, and resolve itself into a dew, or that the Everlasting had not fixed His canon 'gainst self-slaughter!'"

He glanced at Richard, taking in the older man's blue eyes and sharp nose before looking away. *Get your mind in the game,* he told himself sternly.

"How does my accent sound?" Peter asked. "It's quite different to Isabelle's, who's meant to be my mum. Do you want me to tone it back a bit? Or even," he said, switching over hopefully to his own Oxbridge accent, "D'you want me to go Brit?"

Richard laughed. "Heavens, no. I like our polyglot. Claudius is solidly American, Gertrude softly French, Polonius brings us the mist-covered moors of Margaret's native Yorkshire. You might make the New Zealand drawl a touch crisper, but stay natural, so nothing sounds forced and the meaning comes through clearly. Yes?"

"All good," Peter acquiesced. *I had to try, anyway.*

At Richard's cue, he continued through the thirty-one lines of text, demonstrating he understood the words but not acting them strongly.

When he finished, Richard nodded approvingly. "Tell me something. What is Hamlet doing in this speech? Besides thinking aloud, I mean."

Peter considered for a moment. "Winning the audience to his side, to his view of things."

"How?"

"By enlisting their empathy. He wishes he could kill himself and says his heart is breaking—ironically because he cannot speak. Those are intensely self-reflective, personal statements. He grows up quite a lot in the space of these lines."

"Why would he need to enlist our empathy, do you think?"

Peter took another sip of tea, pondering his answer. "He's going to need us on his side if he's to kill the king as he's been urged to. We're the mob, I suppose. But no, hold on. I don't think of him as political. He's no Mark Antony, inciting a crowd to riot and revenge. This is a very personal fight to him. Maybe he just doesn't want to feel alone in it."

"Go on. What else?"

Fathers and sons. "He's taking his father's side right off against his mother."

"Aha? How so?"

"He compares his father to Hyperion, the Titan who's the son of earth and sky, and Hercules, famous warrior and son of Zeus. Gertrude doesn't recognize the superman Hamlet describes. I have a guess no man is that great in the eyes of his wife."

Richard chuckled. "I suspect you're right. We'll see whether Isabelle plays it that way."

Setting down his cup, Peter continued, "Hamlet paints his father as an earthly god, and I guess that's how we all see our parents or would like to." He looked toward the mountains, trying to stay calm. *I can't speak her name; not here, not to Richard.* "Describing his father as a perfect man justifies his outrage at his mother's crime of marrying again."

"And why is he so outraged? As the usurping Claudius points out, everyone loses a father at some point."

"There has to be something he wants that was once within reach but is now beyond his grasp. There's the throne, though Hamlet doesn't mention any royal ambitions until act 5. There's a Peter Pan possibility—"

"To be a boy who never has to grow up—"

"Exactly, though I don't buy that either. He's obsessed with his mother and what he thinks of as her infidelity, as if she'd cheated when his father was alive. He almost seems jealous."

"So you go with the buried Oedipal desire to kill his father and marry his mother?"

"Exactly as he thinks his uncle has done. It works for this speech, yeah?"

"Do you think so?"

"I'd like to play that jealousy where it suits the text. Sometimes here, he sounds like a disdained husband. He doesn't sound like a son when he says, 'O, most wicked speed, to post with such dexterity to incestuous sheets.' Who's he to think of her sheets, incestuous or no?"

"How do you play that?"

Peter paused to collect himself. "Maybe he's out of his head, but then there's a moment when he comes back into himself and realizes what he's saying."

"Show me," Richard encouraged.

Peter stood up. Quietly, he said, "'Within a month, ere yet the salt of most unrighteous tears had left the flushing of her gallèd eyes, she married.'" He lit Hamlet's next words on fire and threw them toward the silent pines with muscular force: "'O, most wicked speed, to post with such dexterity to incestuous sheets.'" He shook his head slightly and drew a breath. On the exhale, more quietly, almost mournfully: "'It is not, nor it cannot come to good.'"

After a moment, Richard said, "I see it."

"Perhaps it can be part of the arc toward madness," Peter suggested, reclaiming his chair.

"Shakespeare writes this speech in verse," Richard pointed out. "He never writes mad characters in verse."

"This is his first private speech," Peter answered. "He still hears himself. He still senses the boundary of sanity, but perhaps he's flirting with that edge. Later on, when Hamlet sees the Ghost again, in his mother's chamber, he switches to prose. Maybe that's where he will lose his grip on things?"

"So, your Hamlet shall go mad?"

"Yes. And then sane again, before the end." Peter's answer was clear.

"I look forward to seeing you play that. What drives him there? The thought of his mother's sheets?"

Peter bit back a laugh at hearing Richard say such a thing.

"Erm, no," he smiled to take the sting out of what he meant to say. "I don't think his mother's sex life, questionable as it may be, is truly his concern. I think it's grief that does it."

"Grief."

"Oh yes. Grief can drive a man mad." *Just look at me.*

"It can indeed." Richard looked at Peter speculatively. "Not to pry, but you've had some experience in this realm?"

Peter swallowed, determined not to give his mother away. "I have, yes. In Hamlet, I see a young man who's the focus of everyone's attention in any room he's in. He's the prince, heir to a kingdom. They watch to see if he'll stand by while his ascent to the throne is delayed. As his behavior slides sideways, they watch him even more closely to see whether they can rely on him, on the chance he does become king."

"All eyes on him," Richard said. "If you want it, we can place courtiers in any scene we choose, even without lines."

"Yeah? Maybe as they watch him, they can write things down or take photos, if it's right for the world-building."

Richard made a note on his pad.

"It's being watched that nudges him out past the bounds of sane behavior," Peter added, thinking of the fans and photographers who had dogged his steps in London. "He has no private place to grieve his father."

"I feel for him. He's been dealt a tough hand. He's just trying to work it out."

Peter looked at Richard, surprised. He felt a strong urge to share the particular tough hand he was trying to work out. Instead, he said, "So when he's alone, he talks out loud. Does that seem mad?"

"Depends how you play it."

"I'm asking myself, who's he talking to in this speech? The audience is out there, but who is it he sees? We've said it's not a mob he's trying to persuade to his side."

"Not a mob. Who then?"

"A mirror? Seems too cold. He's not looking at himself. He's feeling, and what he's feeling is someone else's pain."

Richard sat still, head tilted to one side. *He's letting me find something I can play*, Peter thought. *I see why actors have lined up to work with him for more than forty years.*

"Oh. Of course." The answer seemed obvious now. "In all that crowd, he's searching for the one face he most wants to see—his father's. He's saying, 'I feel your pain, Dad.' He hopes that with the power of his empathy, he'll be able to connect, just one more time, with the person he holds most dear."

ACT 2
SCENE 2

Kate, Peter

Kate invited Peter over for dinner to celebrate his first soliloquy session with Richard. She'd pulled off a hearty bean soup paired with fresh bread from the bakery, with apple crisp for dessert. She and Beth would get another dinner from the leftovers before she had to cook again.

Introducing Peter to Beth felt like a big step. Kate typically didn't take it unless she felt things might go somewhere, so it hadn't happened more than two or three times in the past eleven years. She always made sure to describe the person to Beth and ask her daughter's permission to allow that stranger into their home. Kate felt that just as she had the authority to vet Beth's friends when they first came over, Beth should have the authority to vet hers.

Describing Peter, she'd said, "Remember that new actor Richard wanted for Hamlet?" When Beth did, Kate added, "I've taken him skiing at the Nordic Center, and we've run lines. He has a fun accent and lots of stories about life in New Zealand."

Still upset with her mother for saying she couldn't meet her dad, Beth crossed her arms, but skepticism is a tough act for an eleven-year-old with a loving heart.

Kate recognized that her daughter was holding back. She continued, "He used to go swimming in the ocean every day, can you imagine?"

Beth, who adored marine mammals as only a child born and raised in landlocked Arizona could, asked, "Did he see dolphins?"

"I don't know!" Kate felt pleased. She knew her daughter was trying to exile her to emotional Siberia, and she knew why. Any sign the freeze was warming made her glad. "Let's ask him."

"I wonder if they have dolphins there," Beth mused.

Peter made himself popular by arriving with gifts: a bottle of New Zealand Pinot Noir for Kate and a bracelet kit for Beth. It sparkled with glass beads in the colors Kate had said she favored, blue and green. To the kit, Peter had added a small enamel charm of a flying kea, a New Zealand parrot. He'd removed it from his own fleece jacket to give to her, but he didn't tell her that.

Kate didn't kiss him at the door, although she wished to. The wish gave her something to ponder as she and Beth gave him a quick house tour. He was Peter being Peter, praising the colorful decor, the comfortable furniture, and the picture windows looking out into the forest. Beth grinned widely as his New Zealand accent landed in her ears for the first time. *A good start*, Kate thought.

Following Kate and Beth into the kitchen, Peter said, "This is quite a house. You're on a bit of land, I take it? The driveway seemed a hundred meters long."

Kate wanted to explain, but where to start? "It was my folks' house. They thought they'd have a big family when they bought it, but it turned out to be just my sister and me. We grew up here. After Dad died, my mom didn't want it anymore. I bought it from her, so now Beth sleeps in the bedroom I had when I was a girl."

Peter gave her an understanding look. "Are there things of your dad's here?"

Kate smiled as she looked around the kitchen and dining area. "In every room—starting with that." She pointed to a small oil painting of an aspen grove in autumn gold. "He taught business at Northern Arizona University, but he loved to paint. Honey, would you take

Peter back to the family room and show him your granddad's paintings?"

"Come on, Peter," Beth said. As they left the kitchen, Kate heard Beth ask, "Did you really used to go swimming every day in the ocean?" sounding so grown up that it gave Kate's heart a pang.

At dinner, they talked about the ocean and its creatures. Beth even asked to be excused to go get a drawing she'd made in school of an orca whale. To an appreciative audience, she read aloud the accompanying paragraph about whale biology.

Peter seemed willing to talk whales all night, but eventually Kate turned the conversation toward favorite childhood books and movies instead. She and Peter had both read the trilogy called *The Lord of the Rings*, and Beth knew of the movies filmed in New Zealand.

"Were you in them?" Beth asked brightly.

Peter squirmed, thinking *Peter Dunmore of New Zealand would have been.* He found it very tough to lie to Kate and Beth. "I was up in Australia most of the time those were filmed," he said; still a lie, but one with fewer details to remember than if he went the other direction and Beth asked which scenes he'd been in.

"I like your accent," Beth declared. "Can you do other ones?"

Kate chimed in supportively, "I wonder if we can tell the difference between a New Zealand accent and an Australian one."

Peter looked from one to the other. "There's not much difference between how Aussies talk and how us Kiwis do it," he said, making the letter *I* in "difference" sound like "ee." "If you can get someone to say 'fish and chips,' you'll hear that the Kiwis soften the vowels more than Aussies do." He pronounced the words for them several times, hoping he was getting it right. Finally, Beth exclaimed, "I hear it!"

"It is really hard to tell which is which," Kate said. "Nice job, Beth!"

"Can you do another one?" Beth asked. "Can you sound Irish, like Richard?"

In a merry tone, Peter answered, "Can I sound like Richard? You be the judge. I declare the Rose the finest outdoor Elizabethan theatre in the Colonies, 'either for tragedy, comedy, history, pastoral, pastoral-comical, historical-pastoral, tragical-historical, tragical-comical-historical-pastoral, scene individable, or poem unlimited,' and I dare any man alive to say otherwise."

He had them both laughing now. "You sound just like Richard!" Kate praised him. Peter raised his eyebrows at her.

"Now British," Beth commanded, a bright look in her eye.

"Ah, the Brits, but which ones?" Peter said, sounding like a London native. "From Yorkshire to Cornwall to London town, 'An Englishman's way of speaking absolutely classifies him. The moment he talks he makes some other Englishman despise him.'"

Kate laughed, recognizing lines from a song in *My Fair Lady*, her favorite musical. Peter continued in his natural voice, "In some ways, this so-called Received Pronunciation accent is the most difficult to pull off. We've all heard it in movies or on the news, so every audience is aware of its nuances. As actors, we need confidence to bring it out."

"Here's a tough one," Kate said. "How's your American accent?"

"Americans can always tell when foreigners try to imitate your accent." He pitched his voice low and gave it a rough edge, emphasizing every consonant. To Kate's ear, he sounded solidly Midwestern. "As actors, we're trained that in American English, every letter is sounded out, but your Rs are monsters. It's bloody hard—I mean very difficult—to get it just right, and you catch us out on every mistake."

Beth had grown wide-eyed, and for a moment she didn't speak. Then she said teasingly, "Say this in American, Peter. Say, 'If they're going to treat us like monsters, then monsters we shall become.'"

Kate saw Peter swallow, but he was his own happy self again so quickly she thought she'd imagined the shadow that crossed his face.

"Honey, what does that even mean?" she asked her daughter.

"Peter knows," Beth said, sounding more confident.

"Peter knows what?"

"He knows who he is."

Confused, Kate looked at Peter. He'd raised his eyebrows again. "I think you have me confused with someone else," he said, his relaxed New Zealand accent back in place.

"Who? Who does Beth have you confused with? I'm lost," Kate said. Peter gave Beth a long look but stayed silent.

"You're him, aren't you?" Beth asked, sounding a little less sure of herself. "Aren't you Onyxx the Vampire? From that movie *Thirst*?"

To Kate, it seemed that Peter froze in his chair. Then he laughed and said, "Oh, that guy, eh? What's his name—I forget. I'm flattered, Beth. He's quite a handsome lad. But no, I'm just plain Peter Dunmore from New Zealand."

"How do you know that movie, Beth?" Kate asked, mothering instincts on overdrive. Now it was Beth's turn to squirm. Kate watched the emotions play across her daughter's face, whose every expression was known to her. She saw Beth consider, and wisely discard, the idea of trying to lie.

"Um, Lauren and I saw it. We went to see *WALL-E*, but we snuck into the other theater." Then, in a rush: "I'm sorry, Mom."

"I think *Thirst* was PG-13, wasn't it?" Kate said.

"I guess, yeah."

"And was it too old for you?"

"Yeah, but everybody at school was talking about it, so we wanted to see it."

Kate heard Peter clear his throat. She kept her eyes fixed on her daughter. "Not 'Yeah, but.' I think that movie was too old for you, and I think you think so, too. One more apology, and this time not because you're sorry you got caught."

Beth blushed. "I'm sorry we snuck in to see a movie without asking. I didn't like it. I was sorry we did it, but then I was too embarrassed to tell you."

Kate, aware that Peter was witnessing a parenting lesson when all she'd wanted was for him to enjoy a home-cooked meal and meet Beth, chose to let it go.

"Apology accepted. Please don't do that again without asking, OK?"

Beth nodded.

"Now who wants dessert?"

As they sat in the family room with bowls of apple crisp and vanilla ice cream, Peter gamely returned the conversation to ocean creatures, trying to get Beth back on his side.

"Another great New Zealand movie I bet you'd like is *Whale Rider*. Maybe you've already seen it, eh?" Beth shrugged, keeping her mouth tightly shut.

"It's about a girl, around your age, who wants to become a whale rider, a leader of her people. But her grandfather says she can't because the chief is always a boy."

Beth couldn't help herself. "That's not fair."

"No, no way," Peter agreed. "But the girl, Pai, is very brave and holds onto her dream. I think you might really like it if you see it."

"I will if she'll let me." Beth indicated her mom with her elbow.

"It sounds like I wouldn't have a problem with that one." Kate's voice sounded tired.

Soon after, Peter rose to go. Kate walked him out. The moment she shut the front door and they were alone in the darkness, she began to apologize. "I don't know what got into Beth."

"No, we're fine," Peter said soothingly. "She just got an idea in her head."

"She turned eleven in February, and suddenly everything's much harder than it was a year ago. Most of the time, she's still my sweet little girl, but when she's upset, she wants the world to know. Sometimes it makes my head spin."

"You're doing a great job with her. The love between you is plain as day."

"I hope so." Kate willed herself to accept his comfort.

At the car, Peter turned and placed a hand on her waist, his eyes asking a question. Sheltered by the darkness and hidden from the house by his car, Kate stepped forward into his embrace. Leaning her body against his, she gave him the sweetest of kisses. It was like taking a tiny sip of nectar. She couldn't help herself; it had been a long time, and she was starved for touch. Forget taking a sip. She wanted to down the bottle.

They lingered, kissing and letting their hands make tentative explorations, rewarding each other with sighs of pleasure, making out like teenagers until, finally, she pulled herself away.

"I need to get back inside," she whispered, breathless.

He grinned, lifting his arms in a stretch that became a groan. Kate felt the same way.

"Thank you for dinner," he said. "And, um, this."

"Yes, this. This was…mmmm."

Peter was still smiling as he drove down the long, dark driveway, but once he turned onto the gravel road that would take him toward town, he remembered.

I've gone unrecognized for so long, I thought I could pull it off forever. Guess I was fooling myself. An eleven-year-old just proved me wrong.

ACT 2
SCENE 3

RICHARD, KATE

Watching his actors assemble for rehearsal the next day, Richard felt unquiet. The *Hamlet* cast was coming together well, collaborating with the skill of long experience. But something was off.

Blame it on *Hamlet*. The play was a mountain no less formidable than the 12,000-foot San Francisco Peaks. Some of his players scaled its heights with ease. Their Hamlet was one of those. The Dunmore lad seemed to have an intuitive sense of his character's motivation in each scene, the all-important *Why*, as in "Why does he say that? Why does he do what he does or, in Hamlet's case, not do it?"

With one or two of the other actors, character motivation was proving harder to find. Surprisingly, Isabelle was one of these. Performing in her second language was not the source of the French actor's troubles, in Richard's opinion. She hadn't yet found a way to empathize with the Queen of Denmark's choice, made before the play began, to marry her husband's brother so quickly after that king's death.

In Richard's estimation, the audience would allow and even be charmed by a French accent. They would not appreciate an actor who failed to convey her character's motivations.

To help their Gertrude find herself, Richard had directed Tahoma to set aside the first forty-five minutes of rehearsal on this bright Wednesday morning for more table work before moving back to the rehearsal hall. Their theme would hardly be cheerful: Richard thought it necessary for the cast to talk about grief. To avoid turning the work session into group therapy, he had invited Kate to be their moderator.

Richard valued Kate's people skills highly. But as the main characters assembled at the Table Round, he sensed she was ill at ease. He saw her give Peter a long look, but when their Hamlet felt her gaze and turned to make eye contact, she looked away quickly and began talking with Margaret. One of Ryerson's recruits from the Royal Shakespeare Company, Margaret had been cast across gender to play their Polonius.

What's the story with Kate and Peter, Richard wondered. Then he pushed the thought away. Liaisons between permanent staff and seasonal company members were infrequent. Such relationships could lead to problems, and, for that reason, Richard considered them unfortunate, but such connections were not forbidden. *Kate's private life is her own. Best to let it remain so.*

Kate set the ground rules with a natural poise, stepping easily into the moderator's role. She enjoyed helping groups solve problems.

It was difficult not to look at Peter. She could tell he was trying to connect, but she quickly took a seat at the head of the long table, where she faced only Richard at the far end.

"We're going to talk about something your characters wrestle with," she began, "and that's grief. It's a powerful theme in this play and something Richard wants us to work with." Richard nodded but didn't interject.

"We all experience grief," Kate continued. "It comes with any loss, whether of a person or a pet, a job or a relationship; even the loss of a dream or an idea of something that might happen, that doesn't." With this last note, she couldn't help looking at Peter before moving on.

"We don't need to talk about our own griefs here this morning—"

"Oh, thank goodness," interrupted LaShia with an exaggerated wipe of her hand across her brow, making everyone laugh.

"Although I will say that the Blue Mountain Rose strives to provide a safe environment where people can do the work they need to do—whatever that might be," Kate countered.

"Our practice this morning is to help you find the grief your character is experiencing," she went on. "Ask yourself: What did my character want, that it now appears they won't get? What or who did they love that's now gone? It can be something they lost even before the play begins, like Hamlet losing his father."

"Are we going to act it out?" asked Bryce.

"Eventually, sort of. Was that equivocal enough?" Kate replied, to another general laugh. "We'll go around the table and invite you to speak from your character's point of view about what you're grieving. Be specific. Then you'll take this to the rehearsal hall, where Richard will have you work on your feet."

This was Richard's cue. "It's an exercise we call 'embodying grief,' to help you find specific ways to express that feeling in movement. We'll work with questions like, 'Where does my character hold grief in the body?' You'll walk in character, mourning. If you have lines that express grief, how does your character hold their sorrow in or let it out through physical action when speaking? If they do not have lines, can they express it silently? We'll give you time and structure to consider those ideas. Then we will break into smaller groups for a wrap-up discussion."

"As I said at the start, this is a safe space for you to consider and express your character's grief," Kate said. "It's going to get noisy in the rehearsal hall, and that's OK. I'll say right now, the expression of grief may mean anything from whispers and tears to pounding your chest and screaming your heart out."

"But if you decide that your character needs to rip your costume, we'll need to warn the costume department," Richard said. Everyone laughed again.

"Let's get to work," Kate concluded.

After the table work and the "embodying grief" exercise in the rehearsal hall, Richard grouped the actors with scene partners in twos and threes to run lines together. He would go from group to group, listening and asking questions, guiding their final explorations.

He had grouped Peter with Isabelle and Ted, bringing Hamlet's core family group together. In addition to playing Claudius, brother-killing newly crowned King of Denmark, Ted would also be playing the Ghost of Hamlet's Father.

Ted went first. Decades had passed since he'd played football while studying acting at Fresno State, but he still carried himself with an athlete's bearing. Like Isabelle and Margaret, he'd made his life in theater, building a career on Shakespeare festival stages from San Diego to Stratford, Ontario.

"'O, my offense is rank, it smells to heaven,'" he said, somberly introducing the first line of Claudius's most famous soliloquy. Then, in his regular speaking voice, he added, "It's interesting to reconsider Claudius's words about guilt, mercy, and repentance in light of our discussion of grief."

"Say more about that," Richard encouraged him.

"He asks if he can be forgiven for murder when he still has the bounty he acquired as a result. This speech is usually played as an exploration of guilt. But if he's grieving, too, maybe he's mourning the innocence he gave up when he committed the crime."

Isabelle asked, "What do you mean with 'the innocence'?"

Ted knitted up his brows. "We don't know what the court was like before Claudius killed his brother. But let's imagine Claudius has a crush on Gertrude. He never says it. He feels he would make a good king, but he never says that, either. He bottles it all up inside, until one momentous day. Now he knows the man in the mirror can kill. He can never unlearn it. Innocence lost; that's what I mean. Looking at Claudius this way, I feel for the guy. We're all capable of things we'd rather not consider possible."

"Would you like to try it on your feet?" Richard asked.

"I'll think on it some more. Let's give Peter his turn."

"Very well," Richard said. "Peter? Ready?"

Peter looked at Ted. "I found some things for 'Hold, hold.' Cue me in?" When Ted nodded, Peter stood, drawing a deep breath. Then he looked down at the floor, and it was as if his whole being, body and soul, were being pulled downward by a force stronger than gravity.

"'Adieu, adieu, adieu. Remember me.'" Ted's sonorous voice gave Peter his cue.

Peter started softly and let the volume build. His body began to straighten as if the earth itself were filling him with energy in a wave that began at his knees and ended at the crown of his head.

"'Hold, hold, my heart, and you, my sinews, grow not instant old, but bear me stiffly up. Remember thee? Ay, thou poor ghost, whiles memory holds a seat in this distracted globe.'"

Now standing tall, he fixed Ted in a gaze that combined awe and heart-rending sorrow.

"'Remember thee? Yea, from the table of my memory I'll wipe away all trivial, fond records, all saws of books, all forms, all pressures past, that youth and observation copied there.'"

He brought his hands together and swept one palm across the other. Hamlet's voice had thickened with nostalgia for the innocent youth he'd been just ten minutes earlier. That youth was gone now. Hamlet the man began to speak his mind with force.

"'And thy commandment all alone shall live within the book and volume of my brain, unmixed with baser matter.'"

At this, Peter paused, holding his firm stance a moment before shifting his feet and rolling his shoulders to release the tension.

"Well played," Richard said. As Peter sat down, everyone looked toward Isabelle. The French actress sat straight-backed, a pensive expression on her aging, beautiful face. After a moment, she mused, "I have nothing so rich as this to play. Until her final, formidable scene with her son, Gertrude has only lines that are single sentences. In all the first three acts I think, she must be in grief about her dead husband, but will she ever say so? No. It is difficult for me to like her."

"Perhaps the goal is not so much to like her as to find enough ground in common to understand her," Richard suggested.

"Common ground? I do not see it. The memory of my husband, Jean-Philippe, to me is sacred."

Ted nodded in sympathy. "You think she's mourning her husband, but there's nothing to work with."

"With grief? No. All she does is talk about her son. 'Did he receive you well? Did you assay him to any pastime? And for your part, Ophelia, I do wish that your good beauties be the happy cause of Hamlet's wildness.'" She shrugged.

"Is there something of grief to play in that?" Richard asked.

Isabelle considered the question, lips pursed. "She has much to grieve in Hamlet. Through a mother's eyes, his behavior is very strange. He might lose everything if he continues. Love, advancement; things that matter to her, very much." Isabelle smiled at Peter. "Our boys are our greatest joys and our greatest worries. We want them to succeed in the world yet remain by our side. But Queen Gertrude's son, he holds himself apart from her. He will not sit beside her when the Players perform; he chooses Ophelia. And when he does come to her, he says such terrible, shocking things."

"And kills good Polonius," Ted added.

"Oh yes, he talks to a ghost she cannot see, and murders a man in her bedchamber," Isabelle agreed. The three men listened, letting her find it.

"She has good cause to grieve her lost boy. That, I can play."

As the session ended, Richard drew everyone into a circle.

"Quality work," he told his actors. "Today you faced one of life's heaviest subjects. As Katherine said this morning, we all have grief in life, and working with grief in character can bring up grief in reality. I know I've had cause to reflect this morning. Anyone else?"

There were nods and murmured assents. Then Margaret said, "Richard, if I may?"

"Please."

"It's important for us to take care of ourselves with some extra kindness now." Margaret ruffled her fingers through her short, gray hair. "Grief work is big stuff. And we've invited it to express itself in our bodies, so my suggestion is to start there. Go for a walk or a run, or just go over to that lake—"

"Frances Short Pond?" Fawn offered.

"That's the one. When I need to get grounded, I go outside. A walk around the pond is just the thing for me. What about you?" she asked, looking around the circle.

There was silence for a moment. Margaret rode it out.

"I'm going for a run at Buffalo Park," Bryce said.

"Can I join you?" LaShia asked. "I need to get my heart rate up." Plans were quickly made for a quarter of those present to carpool to the park and do a loop or two on its wide trails over the lunch break.

"Peter?" Bryce asked.

"Think I'll walk 'round the pond, if Margaret will have me."

"Hamlet and Polonius, out for a walk," Margaret said, smiling. "We can discuss the shapes of clouds."

After a quiet moment, Tahoma stood. "That's lunch. Afternoon call is at two."

"Thank you Lunch," the actors replied.

ACT 2

SCENE 4

KATE, PETER

"Margaret and I are off to the pond for a walk. Want to join us?" Peter had knocked on the half-open door of Kate's office to make the invitation.

Kate flashed him a look. "Not this afternoon. I have to finish this before I get Beth from piano."

Rebuffed, Peter stepped back. "All good. See you 'round, then."

Kate stopped him. "It would be good to talk soon. Just not here."

Peter swallowed. "You know, don't you."

From down the hall, Bryce called out, "Sure you won't join us, Peter?"

"Yeah, nah, have a good run," Peter called back; then more quietly: "Kate?"

"Let's eat lunch outside when you get back from the pond," Kate offered reluctantly.

They agreed to meet in forty-five minutes in the grandly named Calliope's Grove, a circle of benches beneath the pines where a devoted cadre of volunteers gave educational talks before performances.

As Kate collected her meal from the staff fridge, she thought once more about what to say to Peter. She hated to do it but felt compelled. If nothing else, this was a chance to prove to herself that she had the fortitude to be a leader—even if it meant cutting off a promising personal relationship.

Peter was sitting on a bench in the grove, his shoulders hunched in his jacket. Walking toward him, Kate remembered the day they met at the Arden. *Was it only two months ago?* She recalled the pleasure of sitting down after their Monday skis, drinking hot chocolate and talking about *Hamlet*. Peter, with his way of noticing the good in everything, his clumsiness on the ski track and his self-deprecating laughter, his vulnerability when he told her about his mom. He'd become a friend, and more than that. She'd introduced him to Beth. But she had a job to do.

As she sat down, Kate could see the morning's work with grief still in Peter's eyes and the set of his shoulders. Remembering her dad, Kate found a softness in her heart that let her meet his gaze with kindness.

"How are you?" she asked. *That wasn't how I planned to start out, but I guess it's as good a place as any.*

He smiled, but without his usual warmth. "All good." He looked away, then back at her. "Just worried about what you're about to say."

To work, then, Kate thought. Leaning forward, she said, "You're not who you say you are."

"No," he replied after a moment in which all the air seemed to leave his body. "It's true, I'm not. Beth?"

"She's great with faces and voices. We looked at pictures from *Thirst* on the Internet. She showed me Onyxx the Vampire. He looked so different from you. I told myself it wasn't the Peter Dunmore I knew. But then I rented your movie. Oh, Peter."

"I know."

"I'm still upset with her for seeing it. It's too old for her."

"Indeed it is."

"I wanted to prove she had the wrong person. You can't imagine how much I wanted it to be someone else."

"I wanted that, too, believe me."

"But there you were. Your hair was a different color, and your eyes. Contact lenses?"

"Black ones."

"And you had an American accent, but I recognized your voice, and . . . you. You're Onyxx the Vampire."

"Yeah," Peter groaned. "God help me, I'm Onyxx the Vampire."

Watching Kate straighten her back at his admission, Peter let his eyes linger on her dark hair and brown eyes, fringed in long lashes. *I care about you*, he wanted to say. *Can't we just drop this and go back to those kisses?* He wished he could brush the serious look from her face with gentle fingers. But they were a long way from that softness now.

"I'm sorry I didn't tell you before. I wasn't telling anyone; haven't told anyone for months, and it's become a habit."

"What are you doing here, Peter McKenzie?" Kate asked, using his real name for the first time. "Slumming?"

He snorted. "Hardly! This isn't a stage for slackers."

My cover's blown anyway, so I may as well enjoy what I can from it. Dropping the New Zealand accent, Peter began speaking in the familiar tones of his London home. It was a relief not to strain after the right pronunciation for a change.

"I wanted to see if I could still be here." He gestured toward the Rose's brown-painted timbers. "To see if I could still have a career in Shakespeare. After everything. Fans breaking into my flat. Photographers chasing me. I missed this so much, you have no idea."

The shift from casual New Zealand to the precise tones of a BBC announcer startled Kate, and she looked at Peter with fresh eyes. He was no longer an actor from Wellington chasing his first big break in American theater. She and Beth had read that after his performance as Macbeth at the Young Vic, he'd been acclaimed the next great interpreter of Shakespeare on the stage. Michael Billington, the esteemed theater critic at *The Guardian*, had described him as "a cross between Sir John Gielgud and the young Ken Branagh."

"No, I do have an idea," she said, trying to stay firm, though her heart went out to him. "I understand wanting to act—really, I do. But here's why I have to be angry with you, Peter. You gave us a false résumé to get in here."

"But I am an actor," he protested. "I've acted in Shakespeare onstage, in all the plays I said, in those roles."

"I know. Just to make sure, I searched your name on the Internet."

"Oh," he said, then, "Ohhhh. You've seen the pictures."

Kate blushed and looked down at her hands for a moment, remembering that silly orange swim cap and; well.

Peter knitted his brows. "Never mind. I'm not here on a lark. By reputation, this is the finest Elizabethan stage in America, a country that does right by the outdoor performance of Shakespeare. I had to see if there was still a place for me in this world I love."

"But to do that, you snuck into our company," Kate reminded him. "And if you're going to stay, then I'm sorry, but you'll have to tell Richard."

He's the last person I'll be saying my name to, Peter thought. Shaking his head, he said, "I can't do that." He could see he'd shocked her.

"But you have to."

"No, I don't. And I absolutely can't."

"Why not?"

He took his time before answering. *Because if I tell him who I am, he'll know who I am* was both truth and nonsense. How to explain himself without explaining himself? *If I blame it on the vampires, she'll have some of the truth, at least.*

Peter's voice was filled with emotion. "The moment it's known I'm here, this place will be overrun. I'm not being egotistical when I say the fans will flood this place on the heels of the reporters and paparazzi so quickly, you won't know what happened. I'll not have a moment's peace, to rehearse, to work, to eat, to sleep. The Arden—"

He shook his head, thinking of his precious nutshell. "Behind every tree will be a fan with an autograph book or a photographer with a long lens. I won't be able to brush my teeth without sharing the flavor of toothpaste with the world. Kate, please. Don't ask me to do this."

All the light had gone out of his eyes. Kate searched for something to do or say that would rekindle it. More than anything, she wanted to set her hand on his. But she couldn't step across the space between them with a touch.

"It must have been difficult for you when all this first happened," she said. "I can only imagine."

He took a slow breath. "I'd been living a normal life: booking work as I could, going out with friends, never recognized unless I was onstage. After *Thirst* came out, my anonymity was gone. Overnight, life as I'd known it evaporated."

"You didn't know how this would go when you made the movie?"

His grimace told the story. "I thought an American movie would gain me the kind of money a British stage actor only dreams about. My friend Rory had done one. He said the celebrity side of it wasn't bad. I could handle it and then it would die down. But *Thirst* went far bigger than any of us thought. It was everywhere. And the fans." He paused to collect himself.

"People dressed cap-à-pie in black started following me around London. On the street, or in one memorable encounter, on the Tube, before I stopped taking it. Touching my clothes, my hands, my neck." He gave her a sad smile. "Remember how, in the movie, vampires like to taste human skin?"

Kate had grown wide-eyed. "Yes."

Peter looked up at the pines, their boughs whispering in a light breeze. "They would come to my flat after dark and sit in a circle on the steps, chanting 'Onyxx, change me, Onyxx, take me.' Everywhere

I went, to the market or the theatre or the—" He stopped, swallowing hard. "The hospital. Vampires everywhere."

"The hospital? Oh, Peter. Your mom?"

He glanced at her fiercely, eyes bright with unshed tears. "She took ill when the movie was in post. We were on a press tour ahead of the premiere. I stopped doing events to spend time with her. That drove the media mad. Any reporter who respected our privacy was replaced by one who would get the story no matter what it cost us. Two made it past hospital security. They took pictures of my mum and me." Tears streaked his cheeks now. He brushed them away brusquely.

Kate couldn't help herself. She reached across the table to take his hand. He gripped her fingers tightly for a moment.

"As soon as I could, I ran."

"All the way to New Zealand."

"Rory had a house there, where I could have privacy. It was a good place. Until it wasn't."

"And now you're here."

"I really want to stay, Kate. But I can't possibly tell Richard Keane who I am."

Kate let go of his hand and sat back, considering his words. If she backed down, would it mean she wasn't ready to lead the Blue Mountain Rose when Richard retired? But what kind of leader did she want to be? She needed time to think.

"How about this?" she asked, meeting his troubled green eyes with what she hoped was rational reassurance. "Let's take a day to think about it. I'm asking you to do something really hard. I didn't know how hard, or why. I understand it better now. But you're asking me to hide something that matters. I owe Richard my loyalty, and loyalty means honesty. So let's each try to think about it from the other person's point of view. Will you do that?"

Peter nodded. "I'm an actor. Thinking about the world from another person's perspective is my job."

ACT 2

SCENE 5

Peter

On Saturday, the *Hamlet* actors living at the Arden hosted a picnic to welcome the incoming cast members of *A Midsummer Night's Dream.*

Some actors would perform in both plays, of course: Bryce was getting ready to dazzle as Theseus and Oberon, and LaShia would play Hermia to Peter's Lysander. But eight new actors who would only appear in *Midsummer* had arrived in the past few days to join the repertory company, and on Friday, they'd held their first cast meeting with Richard. Full rehearsals for *Midsummer* would start with table reading the following Tuesday.

The picnic potluck had been LaShia's idea. She asked everyone to bring food to share, whether that was chips and salsa (Ted) or a baking dish filled with Chicken Creole (LaShia herself, who hailed from New Orleans). Bryce arrived with enough beer to quench everyone's thirst. It was a time to relax and get to know one another in the casual setting of the picnic tables clustered in the covered space between the motor inn's two wings.

On this mid-April day, the sun was shining and spring was in the air. Peter had baked his Aunt Dianne's cheese scones that morning and now brought his bounty to the sharing table. Walking up to the patio, he looked around nervously, seeking out new faces that might bring trouble.

"Hey, let me introduce you to someone," Bryce said behind him, clapping him on the back. He turned to find his friend standing next to a tall, blond woman whose wide-set blue eyes gleamed like chips of glacial ice beneath arched blond brows.

Peter felt his breath catch in his throat. It didn't take more than a few seconds for Freja Lund to see through the beard.

"Peter?!" she exclaimed, stretching out her hand. She turned her head so he could kiss her cheek, which he did politely but with great reluctance.

"You know each other?" Bryce asked. Before Peter could intervene, Freja said, "We did *Macbeth* together at the Young Vic! What was it—three years ago?"

"Yeah, 2006," he agreed reluctantly.

Bryce narrowed his eyes. "The Young Vic in Britain? I thought you'd never been north of the equator until now!"

"Erm, yeah." It flashed through Peter's mind to pull Freja aside and explain his situation before she destroyed everything he'd been hoping to protect. She might remember the tabloids; she might take pity on him. On the other hand, this was Freja, his Lady Macbeth and sometime bed partner. When they weren't onstage, he'd never been able to predict what she would do.

"Hey Freja, let's sit and catch up," he said quickly.

"What's this accent, Peter?" Freja asked. "Is your Hamlet an Australian?"

"It's New Zealand." Peter's pride was stung. "Let's get some food, and I'll explain everything."

"Hang on, I want to hear this!" Bryce was grinning. "You've been holding out on us, bro."

Freja gushed about *Macbeth* as they loaded their plates. Peter could feel eyes on him, listening to his terse replies as she played "Where are they now?" with the entire cast list from their 2006 production. He desperately wanted time to think, but he hadn't come up with anything by the time she sat down beside Bryce and across from LaShia at one of the picnic tables, leaving him to slowly settle into the hot seat waiting for him.

"They acted together in *Macbeth* in London," Bryce was explaining to LaShia.

"I thought your career was in New Zealand and Australia?" LaShia asked Peter.

"Double, double, toil and trouble, fire burn and cauldron bubble," Peter thought. *Nothing for it but to come clean.*

"That's quite a beard," Freja said flirtatiously. "I preferred you with smooth cheeks."

LaShia laughed. "We tried to get him to shave last week, but he got the costume designer to say he could keep it. They said Hamlet needs someplace to hide."

"In his beard? I don't think so, though he may have breakfast hiding in there." Freja reached across the table as if to flick food from his furred cheek. Peter saw Bryce's eyes grow even brighter as he watched her gesture. He was obviously enjoying Peter's predicament.

Leaning back, Peter broke contact with Freja as he reached for a beer. He drained half the bottle in one long, meditative gulp before setting it down next to his plate.

"I guess I have something to tell you," he said, looking at Bryce.

Once he began, it was an unexpected relief to admit to the details of his identity. Bryce and LaShia didn't seem surprised that he'd acted on some of London's great stages, which made him proud. Neither one had seen *Thirst*.

Maybe it isn't as popular here as I thought? He entertained a moment of hope.

LaShia disabused him of that idea. "No, I've heard of it. Everybody has. I'm not a big fan of the books, so I didn't feel like I had to see the movie."

Around them, Peter saw other actors tuning in to their conversation. He pitched his voice low, but that only energized the force field of curiosity. He didn't know whether it was the word "London" or the fact that he'd let go of the New Zealand accent halfway through his story. People were definitely catching the drift of his conversation. He saw Isabelle lean toward Ted and ask, "What did he say?"

Finally, he gave up. Standing, he declared loudly, "'To be or not to be.'" He smiled as light laughter circled the tables. "That is not the question. It's to tell, or not to tell. And I've decided to tell. But what I have to say needs to be kept a cast secret."

Fawn made a pouty face at him. Ted said, "What's the big secret?"

"Where do I begin? I'm not really from New Zealand, and that's just for starters."

He set it all before them: his stage career in Britain, his decision to make an American movie, the resulting celebrity, his decision to run when the fans made his life miserable. He kept to himself the part about his mother; they didn't need to know that bit. Finally, there came the question he'd been dreading.

"Have you acted in American theater before? Should we know you?" Ted asked.

"No, this is my first time onstage in the States," Peter answered.

"What's your real name, then?"

Swallowing, he looked over at Freja. "Before I tell you that, I need to ask you the favor I mentioned."

"What is it?" Bryce cued him supportively.

"Please don't tell anyone, and I mean anyone, that I'm here."

"But why not? I don't understand," asked Fawn.

"If I'm going to stay here, I need to be able to keep hiding from my fans," Peter replied. "The movie I made was called *Thirst*."

"You're Onyxx!" Fawn squealed. "But you don't look anything like him!"

"That's on purpose, because yes: The part I played was called Onyxx the Vampire."

There was a hubbub of talk as those who had seen the movie filled in those who hadn't, but everyone had at least heard of last year's blockbuster, and, quickly, Peter had all eyes on him again, assessing, admiring, wanting. *Five minutes ago, I was one of the troupe; now I'm odd man out.* He felt itchy inside his own skin. He raised a hand.

"I need—nobody can know Onyxx is in Flagstaff, right? Not just for me, but for you."

"This could bring in big crowds to see our show," Fawn said, doubt in her voice. Looking at Freja, she amended, "Our shows."

Peter heard a murmur of support. *I need to squash this right now, but what can I say?* he thought desperately. "I've already talked to Kate Morales about what would happen if the vampires came to town. I've been through this before, and I'm telling you, the place would be unrecognizable. It wouldn't be the Rose anymore."

"Does Richard know?" Isabelle asked.

"No," Peter admitted, "and he can't."

"But our director has to be told," Ted said.

Peter closed his eyes briefly. *What reason can I give that will satisfy them?* Then he flashed on Kate's calm face, her hand in his, and took a deep, steadying breath. *Tell as much of the truth as I can.*

"Here's why I'm asking you to keep my secret," he said, squaring his shoulders. "I came here for the same reason you did. I love Shakespeare. I want to play Hamlet with you. I can't do that if vampires are chanting 'Onyxx, change me, Onyxx, take me' from the third row."

Fawn laughed, recognizing the reference from the movie, but nobody else did, and her face grew serious.

"If you broadcast my presence, I'm done for," Peter said. "My life, the thing I love most to do, will be finished. And I'll have to leave. Because I won't do that to you." He paused and looked at Bryce.

"Although if I did leave, that would be great for you, because you're my understudy."

"No, man. Under those conditions?" Bryce laughed. "I don't want it."

"I'm asking you—I'm begging you. No photos, no calls home about this, not even a hint," Peter urged them. "Let me do this one play, and I'll owe you my life."

"I've got you. We've got you," Bryce said, looking around. "Right, guys?" When the support they voiced didn't live up to his expectations, he stood up next to Peter.

"Right? Guys. Our brother has asked us for help. Are we going to let him down?"

"No," the group answered, some hesitantly, the rest with more conviction.

"I said, 'Are we going to let him down?'" Bryce shouted.

"NO!"

Peter knew it was the best he was going to get. He prayed it would be enough.

ACT 2

SCENE 6

PETER

Just one vampire-free season; that's all I asked. This was Peter's dejected thought as he sat on the porch of his nutshell cabin, trying to study lines on Sunday afternoon. The script waited, open on his lap, but the words blurred as he thought about his predicament.

Beth had found him out, and now Freja had exposed him to the acting company. Beth might tell her friends this delicious secret, and they might tell their parents, and then word would spread through town. The actors had promised not to expose him, but how long could that promise hold?

So I have to go, is that it? I have to hide again? Sipping his Earl Grey as it sent tendrils of steam into the cool spring air, he remembered the Grand Saloon at the Theatre Royal Drury Lane, where he and his mother had taken afternoon tea on special occasions.

What shall I do, Mum?

Looking down at his script, Peter sighed, remembering the past week of rehearsals. As they worked through the scenes together, the actors were seeking meaningful moments, trying out different ideas for Richard's feedback. Meanwhile, Tahoma recorded where each actor decided to work during each scene, including entrances and exits. His blocking notes would help the actors remember their movements a week or two later when they returned to that text.

The work called on everything in Peter: mind and heart, body and spirit. *How many opportunities do we get to do what we love to the very best of our ability?*

Peter was a professional, and he felt his duty to the Rose keenly. Not just that—he was making friends with the other actors, especially with (as he thought of them) Hamlet's family, Ted and Isabelle, and with Hamlet's friend, LaShia, and his rival, Bryce. He owed it to them and to his profession not to mess up the production.

If I leave now, with four weeks to go, they can polish Bryce, Peter told himself. *He has six seasons at Utah to draw from, so he knows what he's about. He would pull it off.* If he squinted, he could almost see them opening *Hamlet* without him. *It's a proficient company. They'd be fine, and so would—*

"Kate," he said out loud. Her name conjured to mind her long-lashed brown eyes and the kindness in them as she'd tried to help him do the right thing by the Rose.

She'd urged him, "You can tell Richard and ask him to keep your confidence." *If only it were that simple.* He couldn't explain his reasons to Kate; only his mother would understand. For Peter, the Blue Mountain Rose was a place of both allure and danger. Telling Richard would place everything at risk.

She's been kind to me, and I've left her in a rotten position, he admitted to himself. He was asking her to keep an important secret from her boss. Peter knew she loved her job. Who was he to expect she might place his needs above those of Richard and the company?

Better for her if I go. He didn't like to contemplate it, but it seemed true. If he left, there would be no reason for her to keep his secret. She could tell Richard—tell the world if she liked—he'd been here. It wouldn't matter to him anymore.

Maybe I can go back to Denmark, he thought, remembering his New Zealand hideaway with its spare, bright rooms, the bedroom with its enormous bed and wall of windows, so different from this tiny cabin. He looked around at the bars of sunlight slanting down through the pines and drew in a breath of sweet-smelling mountain air. He'd begun to fall in love with this place; no doubt about that. Best to leave before the condition became permanent.

I'll hate saying goodbye to Kate. He sighed again, taking another sip of the tea before it cooled. He valued her friendship and, if he was being honest, their brief exploration into the intriguing realm of Something More. He had liked her calm demeanor when she'd led the group through its discussion of grief. In their discussions of *Hamlet*, she'd possessed a quick mind. And when he'd kissed her in the darkness, she had responded with every inch of her body.

He'd wanted to find out whether they might have something real. But she would understand why he had to go, and, in time, she would forget him. He would do the same. *I would*, he told himself. *It's always been short affairs for me anyway. Why should this be any different?*

Forcing himself to look down at his script, Peter tried to let the decision settle in.

> HAMLET: Why, what an ass am I! This is most brave,
> That I, the son of a dear father murdered,
> Prompted to my revenge by heaven and hell,
> Must, like a whore, unpack my heart with words…

Laughing at himself, he drew a deep breath and looked away from the script as he began to speak. The words felt rich in his throat as he gave each one its weight and meaning, the force of his trained voice rolling out through the trees for only the wind to answer.

"'Now I am alone,'" Peter said, looking past Richard and up toward the mountains. It was Tuesday, and that meant soliloquy work.

Peter had long since stopped thinking of Richard Keane as a famous director, Tony Award–winner, recipient of the National Medal of Arts, et cetera, blah, blah, blah. The nerves in his stomach on their first day of private rehearsal now made him laugh. Today he dreaded their practice for another reason. He needed to tell Richard his plan, ideally without telling the truth about why he had to go.

He'd imagined walking in and saying, "Richard, I have something to tell you," in the spirit of ripping the plaster off the wound. But when he arrived, Richard was plating breakfast for them. He'd already set the table out back. His first words to Peter were, "Be a good lad and take that tray out to the patio, would you? I'm just pulling the quiche out of the oven." The smell of Swiss cheese set Peter's stomach growling, and that was that.

Over the first two weeks of rehearsal, he'd come to appreciate Richard's vast knowledge of Shakespeare's work, as well as his way with actors. Richard wasn't dictatorial. He listened acutely and asked insightful questions. His notes were brief but thoughtful, placing as much emphasis on what was working as on what might need further attention.

Peter had anticipated that the secrets of his heart—and his respect for Richard's standing in the theatrical world—would help him maintain a formal distance from his director. He hadn't expected to like the man, but the plain truth of it was that he did. And now, sitting over slices of quiche, mouth crammed with French bread he'd slathered with Fortnum & Mason marmalade, Peter found it impossible to say what he'd planned to say.

Today's work would consider Hamlet's third soliloquy from the end of act 2. Hamlet's decision to act crazy is throwing everyone into confusion, possibly including himself. Instead of killing the uncle who has usurped his father's throne, he's having doubts.

About the Ghost of his Father, who urged him to revenge, Hamlet says toward the end of this speech: "The spirit that I have seen may be a devil, and the devil hath power t' assume a pleasing shape; yea, and perhaps, out of my weakness and my melancholy, as he is very potent with such spirits, abuses me to damn me."

Peter sympathized with that weakness and melancholy. He'd looked forward to working on this speech with Richard, that was the truth. He didn't want to give up the opportunity.

One more rehearsal with the old man before I make my exit, thought Peter. *What the hell. At least I'll have this memory.*

"'O, what a rogue and peasant slave am I!'" he confessed to Richard, launching the morning's work.

As they had at the cabin, the words rolled through him, seemingly from the stones buried deep in the earth below his feet, up through his body, into his lungs, and out to the very tips of his fingers. He started the speech quietly, letting each line surprise him, letting his Hamlet discover the conundrum. Hamlet has just seen an actor break down in tears when enacting a scene. "What would he do, had he the motive and the cue for passion that I have?" Hamlet asks, imagining the actor would "drown the stage with tears." Comparing his own behavior, he notes that he's said nothing on behalf of his murdered father. "Am I a coward?" he wonders.

The words built momentum as Peter embodied the desperation of a man trying to force himself into action. Then, when Hamlet says, "Why, what an ass am I," he let the energy of anger fade into embarrassment.

Hamlet's brave enough in private, it seems, Peter thought. *But anyone can play the hero in the sanctuary of solitude. What about when it comes time to say what you need to say?*

On he went through the speech's nearly sixty lines, finding the beats where different emotions might crest and fade as new emotions built. He was so absorbed in the task that when he reached the final line, it took him a moment to look around and notice his audience.

What a thrill, he thought. *Could there be anything more delicious than playing Hamlet? Richard was an actor once, in Ireland, before he went to London and then came to the Rose to direct. Maybe he'll understand. Why I came, if not why I have to go.*

Richard sat, hands steepled, elbows on the table, chin barely grazing his fingers. Peter was pinned under his gaze. Richard's eyes weren't steel-blue; there was nothing hard about them. They held the blue of a calm ocean beneath a summer sky. Peter couldn't help himself. He smiled and bowed, and Richard gave an appreciative chuckle.

"That was very fine," he said. "Your teachers would be proud to see your work. Sit, and let's talk through a few questions."

"Richard, before I go, there's something I need to tell you," Peter said hesitantly as their session drew to a close. He hadn't been sure until this moment that he would say anything at all, and now what he did say startled them both.

"I'm not actually a Kiwi," he began. "What I mean is, my acting career has not been spent in Australia and New Zealand."

"No?" Richard sat back, giving Peter an appraising look.

In for a penny.

"I changed my bio because I didn't want anyone to know who I was. I, erm—did an American movie last year—quite popular, in fact, one called *Thirst*. Have you heard of it?"

Richard pursed his lips. "I don't follow American popular cinema."

"After it came out, I was a celebrity to a degree nobody expected. In Britain—erm, I'm British, by the way," he said, dropping his New Zealand accent mid-sentence, "polls briefly showed I was more widely known than anyone outside the royal family." He made a scoffing sound, watching Richard's face for a reaction, but Richard just narrowed his eyes as he registered the change in Peter's speech.

"Sounds fantastic, perhaps," Peter continued. "The reality was not. Fans and photographers, everywhere I went. Suddenly, I had no peace nor privacy. I moved to a friend's house in New Zealand to get away. It was quite a nice hideout, really. Until the paparazzi found me." He let himself stop talking and drew a deep breath.

Richard raised an eyebrow. "And have you performed onstage—that much at least is true?"

"Oh yes." Peter was surprised by the question. He'd hoped it was obvious.

"Where?"

"The National Theatre and Shakespeare's Globe, the Young Vic, the Chichester Festival Theatre. I've played Macbeth and Benedick. For my bio, I mapped my actual performances onto companies in Australia and New Zealand and hoped they wouldn't be checked."

"I knew you'd performed on a grand stage somewhere!" Richard responded with vigor. "There's no hesitation in you. When you get on your feet to deliver a speech, it comes through with force and, dare I say, trained brilliance."

Peter blushed. "I'm honored you think so."

"Royal Academy of Dramatic Art, if I don't miss my mark." It wasn't a question.

Peter nodded. "I hope you can understand. I didn't disclose myself when I arrived because—" He stopped, biting back the truth. "I detest being famous the way I am now. I've played Macbeth; I would hate to be known just for *Thirst*."

"Then why tell me?" Richard asked in a reasonable tone of voice.

"Ah. You know Kate's daughter, Beth?"

"Of course. Delightful girl. Precocious."

"Indeed. She'd seen the movie. When they had me to dinner, she found me out. Kate didn't believe her at first, but then she watched the movie, too. And one of the actors in the *Midsummer* cast has recognized me."

"Fame can't be all bad, can it?" Richard asked. "Having fans could be a benefit, I should think."

"For the Rose, you mean."

"Aye, and for you. Having fans who admire your movie work so much they'll sit through a three-hour stage production might have a salutary effect on the ego. I remember when Kenneth Branagh brought the company from *Much Ado About Nothing* here in 1993. The American movie actors Keanu Reeves, Denzel Washington, and Robert Sean Leonard were in that production. They did a sold-out six-week run here. Sir Kenneth told me later that he was as proud of their work on this stage as of the movie they'd made, and that won him a London Film Critics' Circle Award for direction."

"I know. Branagh came and talked to my Shakespeare in Performance class at RADA. He told us about the Rose. Called it a 'jewel box' if I'm remembering right."

Richard said in a persuasive tone, "Wait until a full house is leaning forward as you enter, ready to absorb your first words as Hamlet. It's a rush like no other. Your fans will eat it up."

"That's what I'm afraid of." Peter thought of the female vampire who'd grabbed his hand and licked his wrist before he pulled away. The paparazzi had caught that moment, too. The caption read, "Tastes like chicken?" He blinked rapidly, trying to push the memory away.

"Things are different now to what they were when Branagh and Thompson were here, or Jacobi, or the rest. Fans are different, or perhaps it's just my fans; I don't know. They'll overwhelm this precious place, Richard. I'm not talking about people who stand at the stage door for autographs. I could live with that; I have lived with that."

"It can't be all that different now, can it?" Richard asked in a doubtful tone.

"You have to understand, in this movie *Thirst*, I played a vampire. Fans of that character dress as vampires, act as vampires. They would follow me at all hours, surround my house at night, take outrageous liberties. I had to stop going out in public. They like to sniff my wrist because the blood is close to the skin there. They try to lick my neck."

Richard snorted. Peter knew it sounded funny. Living through it had been anything but.

"A crew of them broke into my flat, not for mementos but to sleep in the bed of their vampire leader. That was a—difficult night. For weeks afterward, I would wake up with my heart pounding in my chest, convinced I'd heard them at the bedroom door. It's no way to live, and I won't. I fled London to escape them. I'd rather leave the Rose than go through that again."

Now he'd shocked Richard, he could tell.

"If I'm going to stay, I can't be—myself. I can't do that here. I'm telling you who I am because—" He almost said *because Kate said you deserved to know*, but he held back. No need to tell Richard that Kate had been his first confidant. "Because as my director, you deserve to know who I am. But I'm asking you not to tell anyone else. If I stay, it has to be as Peter Dunmore, a bloke from New Zealand with a zeal to play Hamlet. If you need to tell the world who I am, then I'm sorry, but I'll have to go."

"You've put me in quite a position. I'm not sure I agree these are the only two options."

"It's not an ultimatum. I'm just telling you my situation."

"Parsing the difference would take a poet's skill—or a lawyer's."

"I'm sorry. But can you at least promise you won't make my identity known without giving me a chance to respond first?" Desperation filled his voice. "Not to fall back on Hamlet, but I'll say to you as Hamlet says to Horatio and Marcellus, the night he sees the Ghost: 'Never make known what you have seen tonight.'"

Richard narrowed his eyes, but Peter stayed firm.

"'Nay, but swear 't.'"

Richard gave him a reluctant half-smile. "'O day and night, but this is wondrous strange.'"

"'Upon my sword?'" Peter asked, putting out his hand. Richard took it.

"I swear not to share the news without your consent."

ACT 2
SCENE 7

Richard, Kate

The more Richard thought about the celebrity actor who'd come to Flagstaff to play Hamlet, the more delighted he felt.

The lad had talent in spades, and talent alone would have brought people to see his splendid *Hamlet*, Richard felt sure. Word of mouth, bolstered by advertising, would gradually have built the audience. He'd hoped for sold-out performances in the final weeks of the ten-week run.

But this unexpected celebrity opened a new vista before Richard's dreaming eyes. Fond of the Rose, loath to leave it in disrepair or to tell the board it might be time to close it down, he asked himself, *What if this changes everything?*

What if Peter's fans filled the seats from opening night? What if they had to add performances to meet demand? What if these fans also bought tickets to see him as Lysander in *Midsummer*, plumping up the numbers for that show as well?

It could change their whole season. Suddenly, the Rose would be this summer's must-visit stage. Ticket sales would not just revive to prerecession levels, but soar. Far from needing to tap the endowment, they would add to it, while also tackling the stage's maintenance needs for the long term. Then Richard could spend 2010 preparing for retirement by training a new executive director to lead a fresh and vibrant Blue Mountain Rose—or not retire at all.

These thoughts brought lightness to Richard's step as he popped into Kate's office that Tuesday afternoon and shut the door. She turned from the computer and greeted him with a smile that grew bigger once she saw his own.

"Good news?" she asked.

"'Well, well, we know,'" he quoted enigmatically.

"We know what, Richard?"

"'We could an if we would.'"

Belatedly recognizing lines from *Hamlet*, Kate raised an eyebrow and waited.

"It turns out our unknown Hamlet is not so unknown after all."

"No," she said, surprised. *He told Richard!* "He's rather well-known."

"Rather well-known! He's the most famous actor to grace our stage since Sir Patrick Stewart played Prospero in 1998."

"Infamous, you mean."

"Six of one. He tells me his fans are vampires."

"He means it literally."

"Be that as it may. Battalions of vampires. If vampires carry purses, we'll fill this house every night."

"He said you can use his name?"

"No," Richard admitted. "That he did not. Spoke against it most adamantly; told me not to tell a soul. We have work to do there."

"We?"

"Think of it, Katherine: every seat filled, night after day after night. Our coffers full, our stage restored to former glory, our star ascendant once more. I tell you, it's enough to make a man feel young again."

"Oh, Richard. He's not going to want to let you use his name. It has—difficult—consequences for him if you do."

"You mean *when* we do. He's going to let us. We shall persuade him. We've had experience with fame here. We will teach him how to dance with these black-caped fans instead of fighting them. He simply needs to learn the steps, is all."

Kate considered her words. "You're hoping he'll let us use his name to help the Rose."

"I am."

"Are you saying you wouldn't retire then?"

Richard smiled with genuine joy.

"Richard, Peter has no reason to place our needs above his own. He simply wants to act. Surely we understand that here. If we take away his anonymity, he thinks he won't be able to play Hamlet. He thinks he would have to quit the company."

"And I think him wrong." Excitement swelled in Richard's voice. "He was born to play Hamlet, and he shall play him here. You'll tell him, won't you."

"Tell him he was born to play Hamlet? It seems a bit…I'm not sure that will hold him here if he's this nervous about his fans."

"Tell him the Rose needs him. Tell him of our financial trials this past year and more. Knowing what's at risk will surely change his mind. We can protect him from these fans, I know we can. Won't you tell him that?"

Kate sighed. "I'll try."

The next evening, they walked out to Kate's favorite meadow, one she and Beth often explored because it was so close to their house.

Beth was walking between Kate and Peter. When Kate had asked her that morning, "Do you want to hike with me tonight after piano?" Beth had been noncommittal, but when she'd added, "And Peter?" Beth had squealed, "Onyxx!"

"You can't call him that, Beth; it's a secret," Kate had reminded her.

Now in Peter's company, Beth was doing her best to be good, but her antic energy made Kate laugh. For her part, Kate felt a bit shy as they walked down through the pines toward the meadow. There was so much to say, yet it didn't seem right to launch straight into the subject most on her mind. She brought up *Hamlet* instead.

In what Kate still thought of as his "London accent," Peter talked about scene work and fight rehearsals. Beth asked what they were fighting with. Picking up a branch fallen from a ponderosa and a short, stout twig, he demonstrated how a rapier and dagger allowed the actors to move the action from polite to deadly in an instant.

"Not literally, though," Kate reminded her daughter. Walking on, Peter shared his opinion that Isabelle Rivette's Gertrude was shaping into a performance to admire. Kate explained to Beth that Isabelle was a famous French actress.

Their small talk helped Kate feel more at ease. It was still hard to see how the funny, humble Peter she knew could perform so convincingly as lord of the vampires, but that was the actor's art. She wouldn't treat him any differently just because she'd seen him in a movie. She wanted him to know he could be himself around them.

Once in the meadow, they had new things to talk about; namely, the beauty of the San Francisco Peaks in dusk's softening light. Beth explained that the Peaks were actually a volcano like Mount St. Helens in Washington, which Kate had taken her to see. "San Francisco Mountain exploded too, only a really long time ago," she told him. "The Peaks we see are just the shoulders of the old volcano."

Peter asked about the bright green patches on its shoulders, and Kate explained these were aspens coming into leaf.

"They turn yellow in the fall," Beth told him.

"People drive up from Phoenix to walk in the aspen groves," Kate added. "It's like walking in a Klimt painting, all golden orbs catching the sunlight."

There was a tank in the meadow, a depression lined with a wide dirt wall, where rainwater would collect. "For wildlife," Kate explained. While Beth walked along the wall to look for elk tracks in the soft earth, Kate and Peter sat down on rocks nearby to watch and see if anything would come.

"There's something Richard wants me to tell you," Kate began tentatively. "It's about the Blue Mountain Rose."

Peter listened as she explained the company's financial struggles of the past year and how they were facing a deficit and big infrastructure repairs that meant continued difficulty.

Keeping his eyes fixed on the Peaks, which were holding the day's last light as if unwilling to let it fade, he said, "Why did Richard the Great ask you to tell me this? I imagine I can guess."

"I imagine so. He thinks if we can tell the world you're our *Hamlet*, the Rose can make money this season instead of lose it. And he thinks we can protect you from—your celebrity—because famous actors have worked here before. We would insulate you from the audience. He's not asking you to endure what you lived through in London."

"He isn't." Peter looked at Beth, who was balancing on a rock at the far end of the tank. "But you are." He smiled a little to soften the words, and she nodded.

"I'm asking you to consider it. Can you really keep running from these fans? Is that how you want to live? Maybe he's right. Maybe we can help you turn and face them."

Peter looked down at his hands with a troubled expression. "You have no idea what you're asking me."

"I know. You've told me, but I can't really understand it. Maybe only another actor can. That's why I'm just saying, please think it over."

"I asked him to keep this a secret. Will he still do it if I don't agree to go public, do you think?"

"I think he's a man of his word. He also cares about the Rose and lives to serve her needs. If he can see a way to help her, he will."

Beth had completed her circle of the tank and returned to show them the heart-shaped rock she'd found. As they leaned closer to admire it, she said, "Peter! You have to come eat with us so I can show you more. I keep finding these everywhere I go."

"She really does," Kate affirmed. "It's one of her superhero powers."

"I can't miss the chance to see a superhero's rock collection," Peter told Beth.

Finally looking Kate in the eye, he added, "I'll think it over, but I'll tell you now: I'm not doing that for Richard." As they began the walk back to their cars in the rosy light of dusk, he took her hand.

ACT 2

SCENE 8

KATE

Richard emailed Peter first thing Friday morning, inviting him to a lunch meeting. He copied Tahoma so the stage manager would know what he was up to with their Hamlet. Then he popped his head around Kate's door to invite her as well.

"I already talked with him," Kate told her boss. "He said he would think about it."

"That's what we're going to help him do. We're going to help him reach the right conclusion."

Kate wasn't sure they could do any such thing, but she admired Richard's optimism. It was comforting to see him acting more like his familiar, can-do self. And anyway, she looked forward to seeing Peter again.

Their post-walk dinner had been simple: leftover pasta salad, steamed broccoli, and snickerdoodle cookies for dessert. He was helpful in the kitchen and generous with praise for the meal. After dinner, Beth showed off her collection of heart-shaped rocks. The two of them went online to explore the area's geology, studying how her red, white, and purple stones had achieved their unusual shapes.

Watching them, Kate had thought again about Beth's desire to find out who her father was. Beth enjoyed Peter's attention, and not because he was a movie star. Having another adult in the house made a difference Kate could feel in her daughter's demeanor. She only wondered whether Peter would remain in their lives after this season or even this week, if Richard continued to pressure him.

When she'd walked Peter out to his car after dinner, she found the answer to something else she'd wondered. Her desire for him was matched by his for her. It was a thrilling, humbling truth, proved in a whitewater rush of kisses that seemed to make it both impossible to breathe, and unnecessary. If she could have gone to his cabin at the Arden that night, she would have. She was ready to share his bed, and he clearly wanted the same. This kind and positive man wanted her. The knowledge filled her body with desire.

"Beth," she finally said, reluctantly pulling herself away.

"I know," he'd replied, catching his breath. "We can't stay out here all night, and I don't fancy trying anything in this little sedan. We can't go to the Arden and leave her alone here. Does she ever do sleepovers with friends?"

Kate had laughed at the plaintive note in his voice. "Yes, she does. I think that can be arranged."

"Good. Because Kate?"

"Hmmm?" She snuggled into his arms for a goodbye hug.

"I want to do a sleepover, too."

Now in Richard's office, she recalled that goofy proposition and blushed. Just then, Peter tapped on the door and entered. When he saw her, his smile became a sunbeam.

Richard invited Peter to a seat. "Kate tells me the two of you have talked about your celebrity and the enormous benefit that would accrue to the Blue Mountain Rose if we could announce that a movie actor of your celebrity were here to perform in *Hamlet*."

"Yes," Peter began, but Richard raised a hand.

"Before you make a decision, I have an offer." He looked toward Kate, then back to Peter.

"We recognize that publicizing your presence has consequences you are keen to avoid. So we will provide secure housing and hire a team to safeguard you from, shall we say, your more bloodthirsty fans," Richard offered regally. "The Rose has seen celebrity. We know what we're about in this regard."

As Peter opened his mouth, Richard raised his hand again.

"If you agree to stay under these conditions, we offer to extend your contract for let's say two more seasons. We can do that right now. We will add 20 percent to the contracted amount for this season and in each following season."

"Richard," Kate interrupted. "How can we afford that? Not that you're not worth it, Peter," she said, turning to him with a smile she tried to keep professional. "But as you both know, finances this year aren't looking great."

"Peter's fans will more than make up for it. We had calculated a worst-case scenario of 60 percent of seats filled. Now I think we can count on 85 percent. They will come in droves to see this young man onstage. Or so I am given to believe."

Peter saw his opening. "You make a good offer, and it's one I appreciate."

Smiling, Richard leaned forward in his chair.

"But I have to say no."

The smile dropped from Richard's face as he tilted his head to one side. Kate could see his disappointment, but he quickly collected himself.

"May I ask why?"

"As I said at your house, my fans aren't like the people who interrupt your restaurant meal to ask for autographs."

"The likes of Sir Patrick Stewart himself have trod our boards. His star-trekking fans comported themselves well. We will take measures. I'm proposing that we protect you, leaving you free to do your work upon our renowned stage."

Peter snorted. "I'm afraid that every time I appear onstage, these fans will chant the name 'Onyxx' just to get me to look at them. They won't respect our work, Richard. You want their money, you want them to fill the seats, but as I warned the cast last week, this is what we'll get."

"You told the cast?" Richard and Kate asked in unison. Peter glanced at Kate, then looked away.

"I had to. One of the new *Midsummer* actors, erm, recognized me. They all promised to keep it a secret."

"Be that as it may," Richard said. "If these fans of yours misbehave in our theatre, we'll bounce the first who do, set a public example. The rest will see it's not allowed."

Peter appeared to be struggling with himself as he shook his head. "Just one vampire-free season, that's all I wanted. I'm here to be an actor, but what you're asking will make it impossible for me to do that."

"I don't think so."

"I'm telling you, it will. You're saying it won't. And I say you're living in a dream world." Peter's voice was rising. *Please don't,* Kate thought. She tried to catch his eye, but he wouldn't meet her gaze.

"I know you think I'm going to save the Rose for you. But I'm not your—you don't even know me. Don't put that on my shoulders." He stood up and pushed back his chair.

"Don't do this, I'm begging you," he said, pausing at the door. "I don't need your money, Richard. Don't try to use my fame."

Afterward, Kate patiently endured ten minutes of Richard's inspired venting before escaping to her office and shutting the door. He'd been eloquent, pure Richard James Aloysius Keane, but she wasn't the person he needed to persuade.

Winding down, he'd said, "You see what you'd have to deal with in my job. I'm still a young lad of sixty-seven, but these types of personnel issues will be the death of me."

That, combined with the sight of Peter giving vent to his temper for the first time in her presence, left Kate feeling low. She tapped his number into her desk phone, but it went to voicemail. Checking Tahoma's call sheet, she saw he was called for afternoon rehearsal. *Maybe we can talk then*, though she didn't like the idea of chasing him down. He needed peace to work. *He doesn't need drama; not outside the rehearsal room, anyway.*

The more she argued with herself, the less calm she felt. Where was he, and more importantly, what was he doing? Kate feared he might be packing his bags as she sat staring at her computer monitor. *There's nothing I can do if he is*, she realized. *If he doesn't want to talk with me, I get it. He sees me with Richard. He knows where my loyalties are. Where they have to be. And that will be that.*

Well. This day couldn't get much worse, so she might as well act on a decision she'd made after seeing Peter and Beth together. Checking to make sure her office door was shut, Kate punched a number into her phone.

Smile, she told herself. *This is for Beth.*

ACT 2

SCENE 9

PETER

Peter was off his game during afternoon rehearsal. Normally precise in text and blocking, he called for lines he'd known cold a week earlier and had to be reminded several times where to stand. Bryce widened his eyes at Tahoma, who shrugged. In addition to rehearsing *Hamlet*, Peter was now working through his role in *Midsummer* as well. And it was Friday, after all.

They were rehearsing the part of act 3, scene 2 in which a group of players perform a play before the Danish court, causing the usurping King Claudius to leave the room in anger. There was much for Peter to do: Hamlet flirts with Ophelia, goads the King and Queen, and says wild things to their advisor, Polonius. Peter gave his lines with half a heart and refused to meet Richard's eye.

He'd almost talked himself into packing his bags. *Fie on Richard, anyway, for setting the whole weight of the Rose's salvation on my shoulders. What's the Rose to me, or I to it, that I should weep to see it fail?*

As rehearsal went on, sharing the afternoon's work with his friends in the company dampened his impulse to run. Bryce might make a fine Hamlet, but he deserved the full six weeks of rehearsal to prepare for the role, not the three that remained. LaShia, Isabelle, Ted; how could he strand them? Fawn was finding beautiful details to play in Ophelia. Rosencrantz and Guildenstern, the inseparable Aaron Jensen and Carissa Karvelas, longtime fan favorites at the Rose, had become his friends.

They brought energy and enthusiasm to the rehearsal hall every day. If he left, the show would go on. But Peter wanted to be at the center of it, creating a world with this troupe. They would keep his secret, he felt sure of it. And he would somehow persuade Richard to do the same.

As rehearsal ended, Peter resolved to distract himself from his roiling thoughts. The best way he could think of had a damn-it-all quality he found attractive, and instantly he decided to act on it. While he still had his anonymity, he might as well make use of it. He'd been out in public a dozen times without being noticed. Turning on his phone as everyone packed up for the night, he called Kate: "Rehearsal is done. Can I take you and Beth to dinner at the 1899 Bar and Grill?"

"Beth is sleeping over at Lauren's house tonight," came the quick answer.

He grinned.

She dressed up for him in a flowing, midnight-blue dress of her own design, with seams that showed off her curves. Its turquoise silk lining, revealed by a slit in the hem, accented her calves. She'd paired it with a turquoise bolero jacket, also her design, tailored with flourishes that paid homage to her Spanish and Mexican ancestors.

For his part, Peter had cut his hair, or to be more accurate, he'd had Bryce cut it. "Just make it shorter, that's all I'm asking," he'd said to his friend. "I have a date."

"Who's the chosen lady, or can I guess?" Bryce teased. "Freja?"

Stung, Peter said, "No, Kate Morales."

Bryce gave an admiring whistle. "Lucky man."

Yes, he was.

Now he took her hands at her front door, kissed her on both cheeks, and said, "You're stunning." He'd briefly considered wearing a ball cap but was glad he hadn't. Kate looked too pretty, and nothing screamed celebrity like making an effort to hide it. He'd have to trust that his red-gold hair and beard, so different from Onyxx's clean-shaven look and raven-colored locks, would continue to provide sufficient cover from fans of *Thirst*.

The restaurant was lit more brightly than he'd hoped, but Peter and Kate were soon seated in a booth, his back to the door. She told him she liked his haircut, and that was all he needed.

Peter considered ordering ribs but discarded the idea when he imagined combing barbecue sauce from his beard. Not an attractive look on a date, especially one as important as this. When Kate ordered the salmon, he said, "Make that two," and they smiled at each other as they both ordered Chardonnay. "We'll take the bottle," he told the waiter.

She seemed a little down; an aftereffect, he assumed, of their meeting with Richard and his abrupt departure. He wished he hadn't flared up at Richard, wished even more that Kate hadn't seen it, but he decided not to invite workplace drama to join them at dinner. Instead, he asked how she got started in theater. Her smile told him he'd guessed right. She wanted easy conversation, too. Kate told the story of trying out with a high school friend for bit parts in *Tartuffe*.

"She got a role, and I didn't." Kate rolled her eyes. "The drama teacher asked if I would be interested in stage managing instead, and I said, 'For three units of credit? How hard can it be? Sure, I'll do it.'"

Peter laughed at "How hard can it be?" and asked, "But you loved it?"

"Not stage managing so much, though I've done a lot of it now," Kate admitted. "What I loved was diving into a script, doing research with the director and cast, figuring out what things mean. The words were like a puzzle, and I love puzzles. It was fun to watch our drama teacher. He was really good at helping actors shape their roles without telling them what to do."

"Sounds like a pro."

"He worked at the Utah Shakespeare Festival before taking up teaching. The summer before my senior year, we took a field trip there. He was a mentor to a lot of us—I ended up taking drama as my extra credit every semester until I graduated."

"A good teacher makes a difference."

"Definitely. He taught honors and AP English, too. Gerald Berglund was his name. The first time I heard 'To be or not to be' was in his classroom."

"A toast to Mr. Berglund, then." Peter raised his wine glass.

"Cheers, Mr. B." They clinked their glasses together.

"Who was it for you?" Kate asked.

"That's easy: my mum." Peter paused, remembering. "She was an actor, so I caught the bug early, following her to rehearsal and later, seeing her perform on tour. She was flawless, completely invested in every role, absolutely a master of the craft. Lady Macbeth, Beatrice, Portia, all of them. I didn't see her Cleopatra, but, erm, my dad told me she was the most beautiful woman ever to play the role, not excepting Elizabeth Taylor."

"Tell me about your dad," Kate asked. "He's in London?"

"He is. Bert is his name. He's rattling around our house in Chelsea. He was a set designer back in the day; retired now. He was very creative, especially with drawing room plays; he always nailed the details. A good egg." Peter hesitated on the edge of saying more but decided to leave it there. "What about your mum, then? Where's she?" He hoped he wasn't pushing Kate into difficult territory.

"She lives in Cambria. That's a fancy town on the coast of California. She's remarried, and they do a lot of cruises and golfing trips. He's quite well off. I don't see them much."

Both of them looked away and were glad for the distraction when the salmon came.

The restaurant was popular on Friday nights, and the room bubbled with talk. Peter and Kate amused themselves by looking at the other couples and guessing how long they'd been together by their body language. A couple holding hands were newlyweds, Kate suggested.

"Lovers, and for less than a month," Peter replied.

"Cynic."

Peter claimed that couples who talked least had been together longest. They discussed whether silence meant a relationship had played itself out or reached a state of contentment beyond words. Kate said body language was a more reliable test.

"Are they leaning toward each other? Are they looking at one another or looking away?" She looked at Peter. He held her gaze with such warm intention that she finally blushed and glanced down at her plate.

"What would people make of us, do you think?" Peter asked, raising his eyebrows. He set his hand on the table, palm up.

She set hers into it. "Does it matter?"

Just then, his ears caught a few words of the conversation at the table to his left. Someone had said "Hamlet," or had he misheard? He glanced at the family, parents and two kids, then at Kate, whose eyes had widened. He felt her squeeze his hand.

"She said they found someone famous to play it," the woman at the next table was explaining. "Somebody everyone knows. I wonder who."

The man pulled a steaming bread roll from the basket and slathered it with butter. "Remember when Patrick Stewart played Prospero in *The Tempest*?"

"Maybe he's coming back."

"He's too old for Hamlet," the man said. "Needs to be younger, someone in his thirties, maybe even twenties." He popped the bread into his mouth.

At their table, Peter narrowed his eyes at Kate, thinking of great actors who played Hamlet in their forties; John Gielgud, for starters. Peter was thirty-four and sometimes felt he'd taken on the title role too young.

"Dix, name some famous actors," the woman nudged her son.

"Double-oh seven, Daniel Craig."

"Too old," said the man, and Peter nodded.

"Iron Man, Robert Downey Jr.? Batman, Christian Bale?"

Peter leaned his head to the side, weighing these possibilities. *Bale, maybe.*

"Now you're talking," the woman said. "How old is Robert Downey Jr.?"

"Old. In his forties at least."

"Ouch," the man said. Peter snorted.

"Christian Bale isn't old," the boy said. "Maybe it's him."

"Wouldn't that be exciting," said the woman.

As the family discussed other possible Hamlets, Peter didn't know whether to feel relieved when his name didn't come up, or miffed. It stung his pride not to hear his name on the teenager's list. After all, *Thirst* had been one of the top-grossing American films of the previous year.

Kate squeezed his hand again to get his attention, and when he shifted his gaze to her, she widened her eyes and shook her head. "What, no *Thirst*?" she whispered.

Peter laughed along with her at his ridiculous ego that craved recognition even as he went to great lengths to avoid being recognized. Tuning out their neighbors' conversation, he dropped her hand to lift the glass of golden wine to his mouth.

"Tell me about Broadway," he urged Kate. They talked about shows she'd seen or worked on when she was studying at Columbia. Some had come over from London, including *Skylight*, with Michael Gambon and Lia Williams, which Peter had seen at the National Theatre. But he was finding it difficult to stay focused. The nearby family had moved on to other topics, leaving Peter wondering who was spreading a Hamlet rumor through town. Would all of Flagstaff be in on the guessing game soon?

"I think it's time to head out, don't you, Peter?" Kate said for a second time.

"What? Sorry," he sighed. "Bollocks."

"You're distracted! I get it. We can go." She signaled for the check, and soon they were walking out into the cool spring night.

He opened the car door and saw her settled in before going around to the driver's side. The night was theirs, and he'd hoped to see it through until sunrise with her, but this wasn't how he'd wanted things to begin.

"I wonder how people are hearing about *Hamlet*." Kate pulled out her smartphone as he drove north through town toward her house and the Arden. She'd read his mind again. He was consumed by curiosity and could think of nothing else. Well, there was one thing he could think of, but now he wasn't sure he could suggest it.

"I'm looking at the comments on our cast announcement blog post," she said. "It's from February. Nothing is popping out at me. Looking at our most recent posts now. Oh, wait. Here?"

"What?"

"You know a couple weeks back we did a post a day for each of the main actors in *Hamlet*. There's a new comment on yours from someone called 'Jack Russell,' saying he thinks you're going to be replaced. Jack Russell—that can't be a real name."

"I wouldn't think so. A pseudonym for someone in the company?"

"I can't tell. The comment was added yesterday, that's all I know."

"Oh, great." Peter thought it was anything but.

Kate read on. "He thinks our Hamlet will be Michael Sheen."

Peter laughed in relief. "That's quite a compliment."

"Who's he?"

"Welsh actor; he played Tony Blair in *The Queen*. I understudied him on *Frost/Nixon* at Donmar Warehouse. Sheen has a Hamlet in him, that's certain. Maybe Richard should call him."

"Oh, Peter, don't say that. You're our Hamlet."

"I'd like to be. But this is becoming difficult."

They had just about reached the intersection where a right turn would take them up to the Arden. Another mile straight on was the gravel road to Kate's house.

"I know," Kate said. "I'm sorry. If you want to call it a night, I understand. You can just drop me off."

"No!" Peter blurted without thinking. "I mean, not unless you want me to. Of course I will drop you off if that's what you want." He wished he could see her face.

"It's not what I want, but I thought maybe, if you're upset, then tonight's not the night for..."

“Would you come with me to the Arden if I asked?”

“Of course I would. I want…this. To see what this could be, because it could be so…”

“Yes, I think it could be.”

And so it was decided. Parking in his reserved spot behind the motor court, Peter shut off the engine, pondering his good fortune. He hadn’t looked for this when he came to Flagstaff, but it had found him, and he knew enough to be grateful.

He took her hand as they started up the trail toward his cabin. Bringing it to his lips, he kissed her fingers, and then the skin on the inside of her wrist. She gave a little sigh as he stopped and folded her into his arms. Still holding her hand in his, with his other hand he brushed her long hair back from her face, burying his fingers in those soft strands.

Around them in the darkness, conifers scented the air. He could see lights in a few cabins twinkling between distant trees. Their privacy was complete. Asking the world and its rumors to leave him be for a few stolen hours, he led her to the home he called his nutshell and brought her inside.

ACT 3 *April* 2009

ACT 3
SCENE 1

KATE

The next day, on a rehearsal break, Peter found Kate in her office. "'Good morrow, Kate, for that's your name, I hear,'" he said jauntily as he walked in.

"'Well have you heard, but something hard of hearing,'" Kate answered right on cue, arching one eyebrow. "'They call me Katherine that do talk of me.'"

Peter continued, "'You lie, in faith, for you are called plain Kate, and bonny Kate, and sometimes Kate the curst. But Kate, the prettiest Kate in Christendom,' erm, how does it go?"

"He says, 'Kate of Kate Hall, my super-dainty Kate (for dainties are all Kates)—'" the real Kate cued, smiling.

"Oh yes. 'And therefore, Kate, take this of me, Kate of my consolation: hearing thy mildness praised in every town, thy virtues spoke of, and thy beauty sounded.'" Peter paused, and Kate's grin widened.

With a sparkle in his eyes, an undaunted Peter completed the speech, "'(Yet not so deeply as to thee belongs), myself am moved to woo thee for my wife.'"

Kate laughed. "A bit soon, don't you think, Petruchio? We'll see. For now, a kiss will do."

Peter complied, stepping around her desk to offer a deep, sweet answer to her wish. Hearing footsteps in the hall, they broke apart, blushing.

"How about dinner tonight?" asked Kate once she'd calmed her breath.

"Bryce is setting up an outing to a club for country and western line dancing, whatever that is," Peter said. "How about that instead?"

How about going dancing with you? Having survived dinner at the 1899 Bar and Grill unidentified, Peter had apparently decided his disguise would remain impermeable. Nobody had added more rumors to their blog post about him, and Kate had asked their marketing manager to block "Jack Russell." With that situation contained, she wished she could go out with the cast and then bring him home to an empty house and indulge in another night like the one they'd shared at the Arden.

What a revelation, to find herself capable of such pleasure. His kisses were like matches, her body a flame where he caressed her.

There will be other opportunities, she told herself, hoping it was true. It had to be—she would make sure of it. In the meantime, there was work, and homework, and lessons; all the elements of her busy life with her daughter.

"I have Beth tonight," she told Peter. "Can I get a rain check?"

"Yours for the asking," he replied.

There was one conversation Kate couldn't put off, no matter how strongly she wished to. Beth continued to find annoying little ways to mention her father, and finally Kate had thought, *Enough*. When it happened once more on the way home that afternoon, she said, "Honey, I have something to tell you, and I need you to be patient and listen."

In the kitchen, she fixed them crackers and cheese and poured a glass of juice for Beth. After a longing look toward the wine rack, she filled a second glass with juice and brought everything into the family room where Beth sat, an expectant look on her face.

I hate to let her down.

"I'm going to tell you something, and you can ask me questions," she began. "You're old enough to know the truth, you've said. So that's how I will treat you."

"I am," Beth said. "I want to know."

"I see that. But you're also old enough to understand when I say some things are private. I'll tell you what those are and why they're private and what that means."

"What things?"

"Let's start here: I talked to the person who is your biological father. I'm not going to call him your dad."

"When?" Beth's voice glowed like a sunbeam.

"Yesterday."

"So you do know who he is."

"What? Of course I do." Kate gave a little laugh. "Let's go back a sec. You thought I didn't know who he was?"

"How would I know?" That Beth's voice held no judgment gave Kate something to reflect on.

"Fair enough. Here's what I can tell you about him."

Beth leaned forward, eyes wide.

"I went to school with him in New York. You love to sing and dance and act, and so does he. Every woman in my class fell in love with him. When I found out he liked me, I had—we had sex." Kate had practiced that, yet she still found it hard to say. She took a deep breath. *She needs to know what's what.* "We should have used protection, but we didn't. And I got pregnant." *Probably the third time we had sex,* Kate thought but chose not to say out loud. *Reckless.*

"He was your boyfriend?"

"I might've told people so at the time, but it would have been wishful thinking."

"He didn't want to be a dad?"

Kate shook her head. "But once I found out I was pregnant, I wanted to be a mom, even though I would have to leave New York to afford it. They let me do my final semester here, and my final internship for credit. It was at the Blue Mountain Rose. I lived with your grandma and granddad until I had you, and they took care of you when I was doing schoolwork. Richard gave me a job the day I graduated. Which is how you and I ended up back here where I grew up."

"What's his name?" Beth asked eagerly.

Kate shook her head again and saw her daughter's face darken. "I'm sorry, honey. I'm not going to tell you that. When I told you some things would stay private, this part is what I meant. Back in 1997, he had the choice to be a dad, but he said no. He's saying no again now. So I—we—need to respect his privacy."

"Why? I don't! Why do I need to?"

Kate gave her daughter a long look that was meant to be reassuring.

"He has a life that doesn't include us," she explained. She thought about what Wyatt had told her: the wife, the three kids, the need to maintain an image. She'd known the bare facts already. With his successful Hollywood career, as an actor and now with his own production company, he couldn't exactly hide, not that he'd ever seen a need to. He'd always trusted her to respect his decision, and she had. The pregnancy might not have been entirely her doing, but the choice to be a mother was.

"I'm not saying he's doing the right thing, but it's his choice, Beth."

"I want to talk to him."

"I'm sure you think you do, but that's not on the table right now."

"Why!" Beth was angry.

"This is tough to explain, but it's important, so I'll try. You're here because I wanted you to be here. That was my choice, to keep you and to be your mother." She waited, and finally Beth gave a little nod.

"If—this person we're talking about—had said, 'I don't want to be a father, so you can't keep this baby,' I would have told him, 'It's my body, and that's not your choice to make.' But I believe that along with my power to choose, as a woman, comes a huge responsibility of living with the consequences. I didn't force the other person to live with them as well. Other people would have done this differently, and that's up to them. But for me, when I chose to be a mother even though—he—didn't want to be a father, I accepted all the responsibility for you."

Kate looked at her daughter, who was staring at the floor. Had anything she said gotten through? She couldn't tell.

"I'm happy I accepted that responsibility," Kate added. "You can take time to think, and you can ask me questions. I expect you'll have some once this all sinks in. But here's the bottom line, Elizabeth." Beth slowly raised her eyes to Kate's, demonstrating all the reluctance an eleven-year-old could muster.

"I was just twenty-five when I made that choice, but I've been glad every day since. I knew what I wanted, and I was right. Honey, you have a parent who loves you with all her heart and always will. And that parent is me."

The first Kate heard of it was later that night by a text from Serena. "Website down temp, working on it, s/b back up soon."

She was sitting beside Beth in the family room, watching a rented copy of *Kung Fu Panda*, when the message came. It wasn't a surprise when her phone beeped a minute later and Richard's number came up.

"It's Richard," she told her daughter. "I have to talk with him." Beth nodded without taking her eyes from the television. The deep freeze, again. Kate sighed as she walked to her bedroom.

"Katherine!" came his booming voice. "The website has crashed."

Why does he sound excited? Kate wondered.

"The Serene One tells me it's a rush on ticket sales that's done it. Too many people coming on at once to buy seats for *Hamlet*. She says they're adding bandwidth or some such to handle the load."

"Does that mean Peter—"

"Aye! Our delectable Hamlet has been found out, it seems."

"Oh, no."

"Oh, yes! T'was not me, I swear it. But someone must've talked, and word has gone out. There's nothing for it now but to hang on for the ride. It's 1993 all over again, is what it is."

"He won't want to do it. You know he won't." She heard Richard clear his throat.

"He has to now, don't you see. Think of it: a new generation, filling the seats at a live performance. They'll hear the brilliance of Shakespeare perhaps for the first time in their lives. This is important, Katherine. Peter loves this work for a reason. Surely now he will stay to see the thing through."

ACT 3
SCENE 2

Peter

Nancy, their enthusiastic cheerleader of a line dance teacher, turned out to be a Shakespeare fan who took her family to the Rose every summer. As she taught the cast of *Hamlet* the "electric slide," the "cowboy hustle," and the charmingly named "tush push," she asked who was playing which role.

In the rustic setting of the Museum Club, Peter relaxed in a friendly crowd comprising mostly his castmates. The beer helped—the first pint of dark ale went down so easily he ordered a second.

All around him, actors stomped and scooted in time to the music. Freja positioned herself next to him and made flirtatious comments about his so-called skills. Margaret, a lively woman in her middle years, showed the younger cast members some flourishes she'd picked up when performing at the Texas Shakespeare Festival.

When Nancy finished her class to a round of applause, a band began warming up on the small stage. The actors crowded at the bar to order snacks and more beer.

"Two-step comes next," Bryce announced. "Who knows how?" Fawn, Margaret, and Carissa raised their hands. "The women, of course," Bryce laughed. "And me. That's it?" Seeing Aaron and Peter hang their heads, he said, "Guys, we're going to have to prove our manhood here—and that means following wherever the women lead. Pair up!"

Peter claimed Margaret for the first dance, disappointing Freja, but Bryce, the loyal wingman, gallantly stepped in. They eased onto the dance floor, trying not to get in the way of other couples who looked like they'd been making the Museum Club a weekly date for decades.

"Do you waltz?" asked Margaret.

"Yeah," Peter answered. "My mum had me in partner dance growing up, and I've taken some modern dance as well, though I doubt that will be called for here."

She took his hands lightly and set them into frame, with his left hand up. "This should feel familiar, from waltzing."

She set her left hand on his shoulder and told him to set his right palm on her shoulder blade. "Good!" she said. "Now let's go for a walk, quick-quick-slow, slow. Short steps, with you walking forward and me backward. You'll start with your left foot, yes?" He nodded, biting his lower lip. "We'll move counterclockwise around the dance floor and try not to run over anyone."

The band started up a tune, and Peter took a breath. Margaret gave him an encouraging smile. "Nothing fancy here. We're just going to walk around the floor, quick-quick-slow, slow, listening to the music."

All his concentration was required, but line dancing had warmed him up and now, as lively music played, he began to walk Margaret around the circle. Once he found the beat, he could even breathe again.

"Well done, you!" Margaret cheered. "I'm going to attempt a turn. Just keep walking, relax your left hand, and let me do it. Ready?"

Not ready! he thought, but before he could voice it, she lifted his hand and turned beneath it. They didn't run into each other and he didn't step on her foot, so he counted it as a win. Peter told her, "You're making me look good."

Then he glanced to his right and narrowed his eyes. Margaret followed his look. Their enthusiastic dance teacher was talking on her cell phone and looking straight at Peter. Or was she? Maybe Nancy was just looking at all her dancers absent-mindedly as she took a call. He raised his eyebrows at Margaret, who shrugged.

As he and Margaret danced closer to their teacher, Peter thought he heard the word "McKenzie." He avoided eye contact with Nancy as they moved away.

When the song ended, he and Margaret were close to Freja and Bryce in the circle. "Everybody trade partners," Bryce suggested. "Margaret? May I have this dance?"

Freja was turning toward him as he felt a tap on his shoulder. He turned and looked down at their dance teacher.

"You're Peter McKenzie, aren't you?" Nancy asked. "My son loves your movie *Thirst*. Can I get a picture with you? For my website. He's going to die when he sees it."

In his head, Peter heard a rushing sound. He took a reflexive step back. The shock on his face must have been apparent because Nancy continued, more hesitantly now, "Just one quick photo? I've never taught someone as famous as you the 'tush push' before."

Seeing the look in Peter's eyes, Bryce rushed to his aid. "I'm sorry, but Peter isn't doing photos tonight. I hope you'll understand."

"I'm not Peter," Peter blurted out, then hearing what he'd said, he added, "I'm not Peter McKenzie."

"He's not," Freja lied loyally.

"Didn't you play the leader of the vampires in *Thirst*?"

Aaron and Carissa had joined them. "Doesn't that guy have black hair?" Aaron suggested.

"I sent a picture to my son. He went online and saw what Peter McKenzie looked like when he was in *Macbeth*," Nancy told Aaron. To Peter, she added, "You had blond hair in *Macbeth* just like now, and your beard in a goatee."

Peter groaned inwardly. *I go back to fair to hide from black-haired Onyxx and run straight into the bloody sometime Scottish king. "So foul and fair a day I have not seen" indeed.*

"I know who you're talking about," Margaret said in a conciliatory tone. "He does look like that guy, sort of. But our Hamlet is Peter Dunmore, from New Zealand."

"That's right, eh." Peter pulled himself together. "I'm from down Wellington way." He'd never sounded more Kiwi than just then.

Their teacher looked from one face to another in confusion. "My son is sure about the actor from *Thirst*. He told me it's on some chat room thing for fans, that you're here. It says 'the elusive Onyxx is hiding out' at a 'weather-beaten outdoor stage in Arizona' of all things." Loyally, she added, "They must not know the Rose is the best Shakespeare festival in the country."

Overhearing the conversation, a couple from the line-dancing class walked over. Aaron imposed his lanky frame protectively between them and Peter. "My friend is just here to dance, so let's give him some privacy, OK?"

"It's a public place—I have the right to ask for an autograph," the man said gruffly.

"That's not in the cards tonight," Aaron answered with equal force.

"Hey, Aaron?" Bryce said. "Let's go back to Peter's so he can open a bottle of that New Zealand wine he brought over for us."

Peter dearly wanted to stay. It was almost in him to bluff it through. *How many fans of* Thirst *could be hanging out at a country bar in Flagstaff anyway?* Then he looked at Bryce, who was trying to pacify the couple and calm Aaron down, and at Carissa, Margaret, and Freja, who had closed ranks around him. This was becoming a scene he didn't want his actor friends to have to play.

"Leave it, mates," he said. "I've got some of my famous, erm, pavlova at home. That's a dessert we make in New Zealand. Let's go eat, eh?"

That quickly, the cast was spilling out through the big double doors and into the night. As soon as they reached the parking lot, Bryce had his arm around Peter's shoulder on one side, and Margaret on the other.

Peter's heart was thudding so forcefully in his chest he was sure they could hear the beats. He felt more hands on his back and his arms, his friends giving what comfort they could. He stopped on the gravel drive and closed his eyes for a moment, saying goodbye, though whether to his friends or his privacy he wasn't yet sure.

"We're sorry, bro," Bryce said in his ear.

"It's going to be OK," added other voices, and "We're sorry," echoed the rest.

"Those friends thou hast, and their adoption tried, grapple them unto thy soul with hoops of steel," Peter thought. *If Hamlet had known friends like this, he might not have lost his mind.*

ACT 3
SCENE 3

KATE, PETER

Kate took a call from Richard the next morning, inviting her to a rare Saturday-morning staff meeting.

"The Serene One has worked miracles for us," he reported. "Serena had the website back up and taking orders before the clock struck midnight, but there remains much to discuss between the Rose and its Hamlet."

Kate knew she should be glad but was not. She wished they'd let the website stay down until they knew what Peter wanted. She was worried about him and eager to talk with him before they met in the formal space of Richard's office.

He picked up after the second ring, sounding groggy.

"I'm sorry if I woke you," Kate said.

"You didn't," Peter lied. "It was just a short night. After the dancing, we came back to the Arden. There may have been a bit of drinking." He snorted. "It's a good job this place is tucked in the forest. If we'd had neighbors, they would certainly have set the bobbies on us."

"Has Richard called you?"

"Richard the Great has indeed blessed me with a royal invitation this morning. I am giving it all the attention it deserves."

Kate registered the sarcasm in his voice. "You've heard about the website."

"That I have. Fans of Onyxx are lining up to see him in the flesh. They all want a taste of him, it seems."

"I can tell you're not in the mood to be serious."

"'Speak. I am bound to hear,'" he said in a theatrical voice. She closed her eyes briefly.

"What are you going to do?"

"Do?"

"About playing Hamlet. Are you going to stay?"

"That, I have not decided. I was recognized last night at the Museum Club. The dance teacher's son is a fan of *Thirst.* There was a bit of a scene."

"I'm so sorry."

"It didn't amount to much. She wanted a picture for her website, not my blood. My comrades in arms came to my aid. For their sake more than for my own, I am weighing my options. Well, for them . . . and for you, good Kate, wild Kate, my pretty Kate."

They both paused, considering what he'd said. Finally, Kate sighed. "Don't do it for me, Peter. You have to do what's best for you."

"I appreciate that. I'm trying. But sometimes it's devilish hard to know what that is."

Along with Kate and Serena, Richard had called Gavriella Marconi, the company's house manager, to let her know they were now looking at sellout crowds for the length of the *Hamlet* run and *Midsummer*.

Kate scanned everyone's faces as she walked into Richard's office. Gavriella looked excited, while Serena's drooping eyelids showed the effect of her long night. Richard looked like a coyote with a rabbit in its jaws. On Peter's face, where she expected defiance, she found exhaustion instead. *All the morning's bravado is gone,* she thought. *Now what will he do?*

Richard broke the silence. "On this bright morning, we are faced with a challenge, one that is also an opportunity, if we choose to take it." Kate saw Peter's jaw working as he looked down.

"Here is the opportunity: We can fill the Rose with an eager audience. For many, it will be their first encounter with Shakespeare. This is a good and an important thing. If we are going to do it, and, yes, I said 'if,' then we must protect our Hamlet." Richard had Peter's full attention, that much was sure.

"By the way, Peter," he added, forcing Peter to look up, "I heard about the scrum at the Museum Club. A reporter from the *Arizona Daily Sun* called this morning for comment. What you do in the Forest of Arden is your own concern, but I cannot have the members of this company out brawling in public places."

Richard, the master debater, establishing the upper hand, Kate thought.

"It was hardly brawling." Peter sounded provoked.

"That's what I told the reporter," Richard said, his tone now as sweet as honey. "Be that as it may. The question I would put to you all is this. Can we protect Peter so he may deliver the grand Hamlet of which he is capable, and, if so, how?" He looked around the table expectantly.

Gavriella, mistress of all things related to the Rose as a theatrical house, asked, "Could we explain 'how to behave here' in the program?"

"That's an idea," Serena agreed. "Make it light, even make it funny, but set the expectations."

"I can have my ushers gently remind people as they enter, no talking during the performance, and no photos."

"And we could build it into the recorded announcement before the prologue."

"Whatever rules we set, we'll have to enforce," Gavriella concluded. "I may need to bring on extra security. We'll seat ushers in the crowd to encourage good behavior."

Peter was biting his cheek as he listened courteously. *So much he wants to say and can't,* Kate mused. *Or won't let himself.*

"Speaking of security," Richard interjected, "I offered to hire you a bodyguard, Peter, and I meant it. Are you interested?"

Peter leaned forward to rest his forearms on the table and looked at his fingers. "Since this all began, I haven't lived that way. I've preferred to run, rather than turn and face things straight on." His eyes flicked to Kate's face, then Richard's. "I'm having second thoughts about that strategy now."

A nugget of hope began gleaming in Kate's mind at his words.

Richard nodded, apparently seeing it, too. "What think you, Katherine? Can we devote some budget to these measures?"

Kate swallowed. "Yes, we can, especially if..."

"Yes?" prompted Richard.

"We would have to get buy-in from Peter and the other actors," she said, keeping her eyes on her boss, "and rewrite the contracts, but what if we added a Wednesday matinee to every full week of the *Hamlet* and *Midsummer* runs? The increase in ticket sales revenue would more than cover the higher personnel costs."

She heard Peter lean back in his chair. *I'm sorry*, she thought, *but Richard and I have to consider anything that might help the Rose.*

"If it works, and I think it will, Peter will be able to deliver his Hamlet as planned," Richard said. "How does this sound so far, lad?"

Kate turned to meet Peter's eyes. He searched her face for a moment. She kept her expression neutral, trying not to side with either him or Richard.

Peter sighed. "If I am going to be here, I'd be a fool to turn down more chances to perform on the Rose stage. But I can't speak for the other actors."

He's decided to stay? Kate's heart lifted at the thought.

Seeing the encouraging smile on Kate's face, Peter widened his eyes at her. *Did I just agree to stay*?

"Are we allowed to say who you are?" Serena asked. As marketing manager, she needed clear guidance on this point. "The word's definitely out, thanks to some superfan of yours named Jack Russell who's dominating the *Thirst* fan chat boards, but so far, our website still says 'Peter Dunmore.'"

"Do we have to change it?" Peter said.

"If the houses are already full, maybe we just leave it the way it is," replied Gavriella. "What's the harm?"

"Lots of actors use a different name for stage work," mused Serena. "As long as we don't deny who you really are, we aren't lying. But here's the other thing: I'm already getting interview requests. Everyone from our local paper to the *Daily Mirror* in London wants to talk to you. I can't tell them they have the wrong person when we all know they don't."

"No interviews, especially not the *Daily Mirror*," Peter said sharply.

"I can coach you," Serena offered. "You wouldn't be on your own."

Peter's smile didn't reach his eyes. "I don't need coaching; I'm not going to talk to them. You wouldn't believe the things they wrote about me last spring, when I quit doing media for *Thirst*. They twisted my words and made up the most outrageous—"

He paused, unwilling to bring his mother into the conversation, though she was right there, a ghost at the edge of his vision. He looked from Gavriella to Serena to Richard and, finally, to Kate.

"Never mind," he said, as if speaking only to her. "I've been telling myself I could hide out here for one season—one vampire-free run on the Rose stage. I see that's impossible now. It's not that I mind the attention, truly. I'm an actor, and a full house is an actor's dream. But the media?" He shook his head. "I don't want to talk with strangers about my workouts or which protein bar I prefer or who I'm dating this week. I just want to act."

The emotion swelled in his voice as he added, "I don't want to say once more how it feels to go overnight from being a player at what they loved to characterize as 'obscure British regional theatre' to an actor everyone knows. Maybe nobody knew me before *Thirst*, but the Chichester Festival Theatre was the seedbed for the National Theatre of Britain. Still, they love to pretend I rose 'from obscurity to the height of fame,' when all I really did was sell my soul to Hollywood for the proverbial thirty pieces of silver."

Richard knit his brows. "Laurence Olivier trod those boards."

Peter finally met Richard's eyes. "I don't expect people to feel sorry for me." His voice was quiet. "Thirty pieces of silver these days will be worth about twelve million American dollars, when all is said and done. I'm not asking for pity."

"We can help you," Serena urged. "I can keep the media at bay, and Gavi and her team can make sure you're safe when you're here."

"The offer of a bodyguard still stands," added Richard.

"If it comes to that, I can pay for my own security," Peter answered slowly. "That's the best I can say right now."

"You're staying on?" asked Richard, his voice warm.

Peter remembered Bryce and his other friends, standing up for him at the Museum Club, then keeping him company until the wee hours. They'd asked him about working on the London stage. They'd let him know he wasn't alone. And then there was Kate.

With three weeks to go in rehearsal, am I really going to abandon them all now? Abandon her now?

"I'm staying."

ACT 3
SCENE 4

KATE

After the meeting, Kate invited Peter to the house for dinner and was pleased when he accepted.

"I have to warn you about Beth, though," she said, wanting to give him some advance notice. "She's not happy with me, and her punishment of choice is the silent treatment."

"What's going on? If you feel like sharing it, I mean."

"I don't mind, really; I just need to get back because Beth's home without a sitter. It's about her biological father. She wants to meet him. She's never asked to before."

"Oh. That's a big question."

"Yes, and she doesn't like my answer. So if I'm still in the doghouse with her, you and I may be doing all the talking at the dinner table."

"I'm sure we have enough to talk about."

"I'm sure we do."

Late light was slanting through the dining room windows when Peter's car pulled into the driveway. Kate's table would have made her mother proud, with yellow floral dishes and a centerpiece of yellow daisies and violets in a Delft pitcher.

Beth had broken her silence as they decorated the table together, suggesting they add her favorite duck-shaped porcelain salt-and-pepper shakers to the central scene. Encouraged, Kate invited her daughter to help bake the yeast rolls, which she did with a willingness that gave Kate some hope.

Greeting Peter at the door, Kate noted they had an hour before dinner and suggested music to fill the time.

"May I?" Peter asked, indicating the upright piano in the family room.

"You play?" asked Beth. Looking at Kate, Peter cocked his head as if to say, "She's talking!"

"My Aunt Dianne taught me," he told Beth. "Let's see what you have." He began riffling through the music on the stand.

"How about this one?" Beth asked, pulling out a book of Rodgers and Hammerstein songs and opening it to "Oh, What A Beautiful Mornin'."

"Brilliant." Kate watched with pleasure as Peter played the introduction and Beth began to sing. On the chorus, Beth waved Peter in, and he added his warm tenor in a sweet harmony.

They went on together for several more songs, with Kate popping in from the kitchen to listen and applaud when she could.

Their duets gave them something happy to talk about over dinner. It turned out that Peter's Aunt Dianne liked American musicals, so Peter knew some of Beth's favorite songs. When he found out she'd been in a production of *Mary Poppins*, he said admiringly, "Singer, dancer, actor: You're a triple threat."

"Quadruple threat," said her proud mother. "She plays the piano, too."

"Mom, quit it!" Beth protested, blushing.

"Make that a quintuple threat: You also bake. You're a singer-dancer-actor-pianist-baker."

Beth rolled her eyes. "Now you're being silly."

"Can I get your autograph?" Peter asked.

Everything went swimmingly until Beth invited Peter back to the piano after dinner.

"You've done your math homework, right?" Kate knew Beth often left it until Sunday night.

"I can do it later."

"How about if you work on it at the table before dessert? It won't take long, and it will feel good to have it done."

"Feel good for you," Beth pouted. "I wish there was no such thing as homework on Sundays."

"Me, too," Kate agreed feelingly.

"You're just so—" Beth began, then stopped.

Kate raised her eyebrows.

"You never let me do what I want to do."

"Never? I don't think that's fair," Kate replied.

"There's such a thing as freedom, you know."

"All right, that's a conversation we can have another time," Kate said in a reasonable tone.

"Like the one about my dad. Another time. Sure, Mom."

Now it was Kate's turn to feel a flush of anger. "Yep, that one, too. We can have both conversations another time. Right now, we have a guest. Maybe Peter can help you with math." She thought that might deflect Beth's attention, but her daughter just glared at her.

"I bet I can. I like maths," Peter said.

Beth sighed and turned for the stairs, her feet dragging.

"No thank you."

"That was fun," Kate said as Beth's bedroom door slammed. "As if we didn't have enough drama today."

"No worries. You all good?"

"I will be. In about seven years." She shrugged as she delivered the joke.

"What's the situation, if you don't mind my asking? About her dad."

Kate invited him into the kitchen, where they could sit and eat the cookies she and Beth had baked together just two hours earlier.

When a wise mother would have been helping her with homework, Kate thought sadly.

"Tea?" she asked. When Peter said, "I don't mind," she set the kettle on. Peter's face grew somber as she explained the decisions she and Wyatt had made in their twenties that were playing out today.

"You told him, and he walked away?" As she set the steaming cup of chamomile tea by his hand, he took her fingers in his and gripped them, hard. "Bastard."

"I was upset at the time, but I understood his reasons," Kate mused, leaving her hand nestled in his. "He didn't love me. I told myself he did, but for him it was just a hookup. When he said he didn't want to be a father, I took it personally, but it also made sense."

"A real man accepts responsibility for his children," Peter said forcefully.

"For me, responsibility has something to do with the ability to choose. I was the one with all the options. If he couldn't choose to end the pregnancy—which he couldn't—then it didn't seem right to make him live with the consequences."

"I see what you're saying, but I still think he's a prick."

Kate shook her head. "I understood him back then, or I tried. And letting him go meant I was free to be the mom I wanted to be, without interference from anyone; except my mom, I guess. But I'm less on board with his reasoning now. I reached out on Friday and told him Beth asked about meeting him. He said no."

Dropping her hand, Peter stood up. "He still doesn't want to know his daughter?"

"Um, not that I'm defending him, but he has a wife and children now. He doesn't see the point in—revisiting?—a decision he felt like we settled a dozen years ago."

"It's not a decision like whether to go out or order take-in. It's not just two parties involved. It's a child we're talking about. Quite a wonderful child."

"I agree—"

"And she has the right to know her father." He was breathing rapidly, and his expression was fierce. *What are we really talking about?* Kate suddenly wondered. Before she had time to voice the question, she heard Beth at the doorway.

"Don't fight," she said in a small voice. "I'm sorry. Please don't fight."

They both did what they could to help Beth feel safe again. Kate realized that as the only child of a single parent, Beth hadn't experienced many arguments between significant adults in her life. *Just my mom and me*, she thought ruefully. The sound of raised voices in the kitchen had disturbed Beth's peace of mind, and comforting her took some time.

Afterward, when Kate walked Peter out to his car, there was just a long, silent hug and a kiss on the cheek before he folded his tall frame into the driver's seat. Determined not to show her disappointment, Kate gave him a smile as she swung his door shut. Then she started the long walk back up to her front door, where a sad Beth waited.

ACT 3

SCENE 5

Peter, Kate

An email to the *Hamlet* and *Midsummer* casts on Monday resulted in a round of yes answers to the question, "Would you approve adding a Wednesday matinee to each full week of the run if we increase your compensation by an appropriate amount?"

Truth be told, Peter felt relieved now that everyone he cared about knew who he was. No more Kiwi accent (even if he was proud of his efforts). No more glossing over the facts of his stage career. He might even talk again with the costume designer about shaving his beard. He'd grown fond of it, but his facial fur no longer provided the anonymity he'd craved.

About Richard's repeated offer of a bodyguard, he still hesitated. His agent thought it was a good idea, but Martin didn't understand how rural Flagstaff was or how isolated the Rose and the Arden were. Peter felt that if he stopped going out in public until the show opened, he might be safe enough.

Rehearsals were a refuge. They'd finished blocking and were starting to run full scenes. Peter and his colleagues continued to find insights into their characters as they responded to each other in word and gesture. The large rehearsal hall filled with the energy of concentrated effort, punctuated by an occasional comment or query from Richard. For everyone involved, the days were long but rewarding.

On Wednesday evening after rehearsal, Margaret suggested they run lines the next day for the scenes Hamlet and Polonius shared and finish developing their characters' backstories. Thursday morning, Peter was clearing dishes after breakfast when he heard a knock at his cabin door. He swung it wide, expecting to see Margaret's kindly face. Instead, two young strangers stood on his porch. They were clean-shaven, with short hair. Both wore ruffled black shirts and black jeans, trademarks of his modern-day vampire clan.

"Onyxx!" said one. The other cleared his throat and nervously quoted, "'If they're going to treat us like monsters, then monsters we shall become.' Man! We're stoked we found you."

Sod that. "You're on private property, and you need to leave," Peter said.

"We came all the way from San Francisco," announced the braver of the two.

"Just an autograph. Please! And then we'll go," his friend explained.

Hot rage flooded Peter's body. "I don't care if you came from bloody Mars, you're not allowed to be here," he shouted, slamming the door.

Through the front window, he could see their shadows. They had anticipated a friendlier reception, that much was clear. It sounded like they were talking, trying to decide what to do.

Eventually, they took seats on his porch chairs where he could see them through the curtains.

How old are they? Eighteen? Twenty? Unemployed and free to roam the country, evidently. Free to hang out on my deck for who knows how long?

Peter felt his heart thudding in his chest. All they wanted was an autograph, and here he was, becoming the monster.

Why? The break-in at my flat was nearly a year back. This time, I've locked the door.

Trying to calm himself down, he stalked through the cabin, dropping and closing the blinds until it was as dark as a vampire's lair inside. He thought about calling Kate, then Bryce, then Margaret. Then he thought about the person he really wanted to talk to, the voice that had always calmed and encouraged him; silent now. Instead of reaching for the phone, he sat down on the couch and let the tears come.

It was Margaret who saved him, of course. Coming up the porch stairs, she spotted the young vampires taking their ease on Peter's deck. When they told her they were friends of his, waiting for him, she wasn't fooled.

"Get on home with you. You've no right to invade his privacy." She stood with her arms folded across her chest, and like chastened little boys, they eventually did as they were told, grumbling and dragging their feet but leaving at last.

She watched them go, then knocked on Peter's door.

"Peter? You there, luv?" She heard a stirring inside, and then the door swung open.

He did his best to hide his anxiety, drying his eyes before he invited her in. He began circling the cabin, opening the blinds to let the light back in, but he could tell she wasn't fooled.

"Here, let me do that," she finally said. "You have a sit." He sat at the dining table, chin in his hands, watching her make tea. Finding a tin of Scottish shortbread, she exclaimed, "From home! Brilliant," and set a full plate at his elbow.

While she worked, he told her what had happened. Seeing his low mood, she suggested they run lines while the tea steeped.

"Let's not," he said. Instead, he asked about her; her home in Yorkshire, her husband and kids, how she'd become an actor. Listening to her story relaxed him, and when she reminded him they had a costume fitting at eleven o'clock, he stirred himself far enough to collect his things and go with her.

Once they reached the Rose, Margaret went to Richard's office. Finding it dark, she sought Kate instead.

"I'm worried about our young friend," she said after describing the morning's event. "It wasn't much of a kerfuffle, but he seems to be at sea."

Kate thanked her and said not to worry; she would talk with Peter and follow up with Richard when he returned. But when she checked in the costume design office, Hamlet hadn't shown up for his fitting. Nobody knew where he was.

I have an idea, though, Kate thought.

Sure enough, he was sitting at their table in Calliope's Grove, staring dejectedly at the Rose's half-timbered frame.

"I'm feeling a bit down," he began. Kate listened to his version of events, watching his face. *He's going to leave this time*, she thought. *I don't know why it hits him so hard, but it does. It's just too much.*

Finally, she asked whether they could bring Richard into the discussion. *May as well let him say it.*

Peter did indeed tell Richard he needed to go. His quiet voice, drained of emotion, set a weight on Kate's heart.

"I told you this thing would catch me. I have to go now, while there's still time for Bryce to get Hamlet on his feet."

She didn't think Richard would argue: Peter's anguish was too evident. It surprised her when he said, "It's too late for that."

Peter closed his eyes, drawing a long breath.

"I'm sorry, truly I am, but there's no going back now," Richard went on. "I've already told the other directors we have a movie actor among us who will raise ticket sales to gratifying levels. We've added shows, changed contracts, sold tickets, even scheduled work on the plumbing—if you don't perform, we're done."

"Then I guess you're done, because I'm not going to perform!" Peter's voice was hot.

"I offered you security, but you haven't taken me up on it. Let's at least try that," Richard said in a placating tone.

"You can't secure the Arden," Peter fumed. "It's in a forest. There are paths everywhere. If people haven't driven right up to my front door yet, that's only because they haven't tried it."

"Then we move you."

"Where?"

"Let's think about it." Richard paused. "One of the hotels in town?"

"Too public."

"Or we rent you a house? Somewhere outside of town. Williams, maybe, though that's a bit of a drive."

"Or you could come stay with Beth and me," Kate suggested. Both men turned to look at her. She lifted her chin.

"We live on a gravel forest road, at the end of a long driveway in the woods," she reminded Peter. "It's posted private property. There's a driveway gate; I can close it." Warming to the idea, she continued, "Beth likes you. She'll enjoy having another adult around, as long as you don't tell her to do her homework."

Peter formed a small smile. *At least he's not arguing with me,* Kate thought.

"I go back and forth from here all the time anyway," she added. "And so do you, for *Hamlet* and *Midsummer*. I can bring you on rehearsal days. We'll make sure we aren't followed. We'll have a private parking spot here where the public can't see how you get in and out."

When Peter still didn't answer, Richard said, "That's a kind offer, Katherine. I can see how it might be just the thing for our lad here."

Peter looked from Kate to Richard, and back to Kate. His shoulders slumped as if all the fight had gone out of him. Finally, he shrugged. "Thank you, Kate," he said, his voice rough.

He couldn't go back to the Arden, Peter told Kate after Richard went inside. He doubted his young fans had gone away for good, and even if they had, surely they'd shared his address on the Internet for others to find.

"Will you get my things for me?" he asked her. "You're the only one I trust to do it." Moved by his faith, she said she would.

"I'll find some boxes here and go while Beth is at dance," she promised. She gave him her house key so he could let himself in after rehearsal.

Suddenly feeling shy, she tried to stay businesslike. "Make yourself at home, OK? Feel free to eat anything you find."

"The cupboards will be bare by the time you arrive," he joked, but his heart wasn't in it.

It felt so intimate, entering Peter's cabin without him there. *I'm not a trespasser*, Kate told herself as she collected his food into a cooler and a box. *He asked me to be here.* In the hallway closet, his clothes were neatly folded. She packed his suitcase. Upstairs was his laptop and yoga mat, a World War II novel, and a set of weights. She groaned when she saw the weights. *Bryce can get those.*

The hardest thing was walking into his bedroom. Memories of the night they'd spent together here beneath the colorful quilt danced across her mind. They'd both been ravenous at first, like starved creatures, but later, they held each other close, talking softly, laughing now and then.

There was much to appreciate in the simple pleasure of skin-to-skin contact with another human being. He'd stroked her as if petting a cat, making her purr. She remembered the tenderness in his eyes as he brushed his fingers over her face and tangled them in her hair. Their second round had been sweet, its pleasures subtle and lingering. They'd fallen asleep together afterward, exhausted but not sated.

It was the start of something, or so she'd thought. Now, she paused. He would be living in her house, under the roof she shared with her daughter. This was a big step.

And she hadn't thought to ask Beth.

ACT 3

SCENE 6

PETER, KATE

Kate needn't have worried; Beth was delighted. Having Peter around gave her someone to talk to other than her mother.

That first night, Beth made Peter tell the story of the boy vampires who chased him away from his cabin. He did it over dinner, another of Kate's delicious soups, ornamenting the tale with flourishes that made Beth laugh. When he explained why the cabin was called "the nutshell," Kate laughed, too. In their company, he even poked fun at himself for shouting and slamming the door.

"I was rude. I shouldn't have done it," he told Beth. Kate appreciated his attempt to set an example for polite behavior, though she understood why he hadn't succeeded in the moment.

"They shouldn't have gone to your nutshell without being invited," Beth defended him.

The three of them joked about what an invitation to a nutshell might look like: perhaps a "welcome" sign made from pine cones? A bag of walnuts with words carved into their shells, like candy Sweethearts sent for Valentine's Day? That led Beth to ask if the British had Sweethearts candies (hearing them described, Peter called theirs "Love Hearts"). The conversation wandered on through different holiday traditions in America and Britain. Kate saw Peter relax in the warmth of Beth's attention and was glad.

After dinner, Beth sat at the kitchen table to do her homework without complaint. Inviting Peter to join her, she asked why he called the subject "maths." From her seat on the couch, Kate watched them. Beth twirled a lock of her dark brown hair around her finger as she puzzled out a problem, while Peter leaned across to read the workbook. They both seemed content.

She sat with her sketchbook, polishing up a costume idea for the fundraiser cabaret, now just eight days away. Richard and Serena had gone ahead with plans for the event. Many of the actors from *Hamlet* and *Midsummer* would take part, along with invited groups of local talent.

Kate was creating a costume for an aerialist, the Rose's own Fawn Tucker. It was supposed to evoke a bird in flight. The assignment challenged her design skills. Aerial athletes like Fawn worked with equipment such as silks and ropes and even a hoop that hung from the ceiling—their costumes needed to allow free movement without risking entanglement. Dangling feathers were forbidden. So, how to make this bird fly?

It was hard to concentrate. Having Peter in the house gave her much to think about. He could conceivably be with them until August when *Midsummer* closed. That was a long time. She hadn't exactly thought it through before she blurted out the offer. Now, she began examining the consequences of that hasty suggestion. For one thing: Where would he sleep?

Sharing her bed with him tantalized her. But since their night together, they'd disagreed about Beth's desire to know her father, and their working relationship was feeling the strain of Peter's difficult situation and its effect on the Blue Mountain Rose. She wanted him—very much so—but it wasn't that simple. She couldn't just move him straight into her bed, and her heart, without consequences to her work.

And what about Beth? There was a reason Kate didn't bring men home. Now that she'd broken her own rule, her daughter's life would change. In good ways, Kate hoped, but who knew?

"Penny for your thoughts," Peter called out from the table. Kate blushed. Seeming to read her mind, Peter narrowed his eyes, then smiled the wide, guileless smile that always melted her. Quickly, he turned back to Beth and asked, "What does a fellow have to do to get some dessert around here? Any Love Hearts in the house?"

"We need to talk about something," Kate announced as they sat down at the kitchen table with bowls of vanilla yogurt and strawberries.

She'd debated trying to get Peter alone for a talk without alerting Beth, but it didn't seem like an effort with a high probability of success. Besides, the conversation's outcome would affect all three of them.

"Peter, we're really glad you decided to stay here with us." Her smile smoothed the edge from her formal words.

"You'll be here awhile, and we want you to be comfortable. You're used to living alone—"

"Like a squirrel in a nutshell," Peter supplied.

"Squirrels don't live in nutshells!" Beth laughed at him.

"Yes." Kate fought to stay on topic. "There's a guest room upstairs with its own bathroom, but upstairs is Beth's domain, and I think it would be smart if we kept it that way—"

"I don't mind," Beth interrupted, but Peter assured her he didn't want to intrude.

"Peter, I was thinking you might want to stay in the studio instead."

Beth's eyes grew round. "Granddad's starship, Mom?"

Peter looked from Beth to Kate and back. "What's this about a starship?"

"It was my dad's studio. He had it built so he could paint and store his canvases and supplies—and get away from the family sometimes, I'm sure. I use it for sewing now. It has a sleeping loft with great big skylights that show off the stars on dark nights, so my sister and I always called it 'the starship.' It's nice and private."

She searched his expression, wondering whether he'd thought he would be sleeping in her room, but nothing showed on his face but curiosity.

"The starship is so cool," Beth said.

"I won't be in the way there?" he asked. "What about your sewing?"

"You won't be in the way anywhere!" Beth declared.

"I don't mind about that," Kate said, trying to think whether she did mind. She would need to sew Fawn's aerialist costume. She could set up her machine and fabrics in the upstairs guest room for the time being.

"Let's go show him!" Beth was so excited, she forgot about dessert. The adults cooled her down by finishing their own, but Kate noticed Peter wasn't meeting her eyes. She wondered again what he might have expected when she offered him a place to stay.

Following Kate and Beth, Peter carried his suitcases along the pathway from the back porch, through the garden to the dark building at the forest's edge. Kate unlocked the studio and stepped aside, letting Beth enter first.

"Hi, Granddad," Beth said cheerfully.

"Hi, Dad," Kate echoed as she entered, flushing a little at sharing their personal ritual with Peter and wondering what he would think.

Beth explained to Peter, "This was my granddad's favorite place, so we always say 'hi' when we come in, in case he's hanging around."

"Remind me of his name?" Peter asked, unphased by this idea of talking with ghosts.

"Jaime," Kate said, pronouncing the *J* with a Spanish *H* sound.

"Jaime Enrique Ramos Morales," pronounced Beth, rolling every *R* proudly.

"Hello, Jaime," Peter said as he walked through the door.

When Kate switched on the lights, the night bloomed with a thousand hues. Along the far wall, fabric swatches filled floor-to-ceiling cubbyholes with rainbow colors. To the right, her colorful costume sketches festooned a giant corkboard; to the left, Kate had set her sewing table and machine beside the big, south-facing window where her dad had always painted.

Peter's jaw dropped. He set his suitcases down with a thump and stood in the center of the room, turning in a circle to take it all in as Kate and Beth watched with delight.

"It's going to be like living in a flower garden," he said finally. "Are you absolutely sure?"

"Of course I'm sure." Kate smiled at him. "Beth, can you show Peter the loft, please?"

As Peter followed Beth up the staircase, Kate busied herself tidying the cups she'd left behind yesterday. Her dad had set up a basic camp kitchen for washing brushes and palettes and later added cabinets, a larger countertop, and a small refrigerator. Kate had left his brushes on the narrow drying shelf he'd built over the sink, a little altar to his art. When she started using the studio herself, Kate had brought over a hot plate and kettle, completing the setup. Peter could make tea or coffee and his breakfast here if he liked.

As Kate set her things on the sink drainer to dry, Peter and Beth clomped back downstairs. Peter was praising the sleeping loft, which made up for its low ceiling with a set of "sky windows." The city ordinances that preserved Flagstaff's starry nights for the benefit of nearby observatories had earned the town a designation as the nation's first "dark sky city." The sky windows gave a view both outward into the forest and up at the bountiful stars.

Kate told Peter about the sleepovers she and her sister had hosted as girls. "There was room for four sleeping bags, so we could each have one friend over." To lie on a pad in the loft, cozied up in a sleeping bag with a flannel-cased pillow beneath your head, and look up at the Milky Way had always been a magical treat. After her dad died, Kate slept in the loft bed every night for a month, comforted by Jaime's lingering presence in the space where he'd spent many happy hours.

"I amend my earlier statement," Peter declared. "It's like living in a flower garden inside a spaceship that's exploring the galaxy. I'll be quite happy here."

The hour was growing late, and, as always when tired, Beth was chatty. She pointed out Jaime's small Impressionist-style oil painting of the San Francisco Peaks above the door. Then she flitted around explaining to Peter what everything was: the cubbyhole drawers that held sewing notions, the bookshelves with Kate's costume history and design books, the closet under the staircase "like Harry Potter's." She showed off the kitchen setup, and when it threatened to become a cup-by-cup introduction, Kate intervened, asking whether Peter needed anything else. He didn't.

"Well then, we'll leave you to settle in."

She could tell by his look that Peter wanted to talk, but she didn't want to make things awkward for Beth. As they stepped outside, her sleepy daughter throwing silly "goodbyes" and "adioses" over her shoulder like a multilingual princess, Kate looked back. Peter was standing in the center of the room, hands at his sides, head tilted sideways. The look he gave her held such intense need that it sent a flare of heat through her body to the soles of her feet.

Kate pulled the door shut with a click, listening to the voice in her heart shouting its simple, impossible desires.

ACT 3
SCENE 7

Peter, Richard

That first night, Peter slept deeply beneath the blanket of stars, words from *Hamlet* rolling through his dreams.

Kate had invited him to the main house for breakfast before she drove him to the Rose Friday morning for fight rehearsal, but it was too early yet. After a yoga session, he sat at her drafting table next to the big window, looking into the forest. Not feeling silly at all, he said, "Hi, Mum, it's me. I'm staying someplace new. It belongs to a chap named Jaime."

Peter looked over at Jaime's quietly beautiful painting of the Peaks all dressed in greens and grays beneath a cloud-dappled, cerulean sky.

"Jaime is Kate's da. He's an artist, a painter. I have a feeling you two would get on well together. If you're there, if you're listening, maybe go say hullo to him?"

Having introduced his ghost to Kate's, he felt a wave of peace wash through him. That feeling was still in his smile when he knocked on Kate's back door. Two seconds later, Beth let him in.

"Peter! It's Finnish pancake and peaches for breakfast. She never makes that anymore, but only for you! Thank you for being here!"

Peter laughed as Kate shut the oven door. She turned and rolled her eyes, laughing with him. "Tea?"

They sat together in the sunny breakfast nook. Peter persuaded Beth to try a dollop of milk in the English Breakfast tea he'd brought, while Kate enjoyed her coffee. The talk turned to the approaching end of school, and then summertime, and then junior high for Beth, who said she was nervous.

"You have loads of time before then, and all your friends will be out of school, too," Peter encouraged her. "Don't give it another thought. What do you and your chums like to do in the summer?"

As Kate cleared the dishes, Peter was listening to Beth explain the Aquaplex, evidently a Shangri-la of water slides and water games, when his phone beeped. He gave Beth a sheepish look as he pulled it out.

"No phones at the table!" she squealed.

He looked at the caller's number. "You're right, no phones at the table," he agreed, clicking "Decline."

"Who was it?" Beth asked.

"Beth," warned Kate.

"All good. It was my, erm, my da."

"Bert, right?" Kate said.

"Right; Bert."

"He lives in London, Beth," Kate supplied. "He used to design stage sets."

Peter met her eyes, trying to relax his mouth from the unhappy curve Bert's call provoked before she could see it.

"Family calls are OK," Beth said. "Mom takes those, too."

"Well. I didn't want to interrupt our pleasant conversation," Peter answered gallantly. "This Aquaplex has two different pools? Say more."

Peter soon learned that Kate's house came with its own trail, which connected to nearby Observatory Mesa. Kate pointed out the access point after breakfast. "It's just uphill from our fence line, along that wash; see it?" When he nodded, she added, "Our trail eventually crosses the main trail. A right turn there takes you out onto the mesa. There are miles of dirt roads, lots of great running. Take a map so you don't get lost."

Peter said he would, privately thinking what every man does, which was that he didn't need a map. Then he conveniently forgot to bring one. Saturday afternoon, he spent a disorienting hour lost in the zig-zagging trail system. A four-mile run had turned into five miles by the time he found his way back. The lengthening days of early May were forgiving, though, and the weather was so pleasant he wished he had the whole day to explore.

Yes, Peter thought, *I can live quite well at Kate's, even though she exiled me to Jaime's starship.* He wasn't sure where things stood in that regard. She had to safeguard the company's interests, and their personal relationship could make things difficult at her job. And, of course, there was Beth. He understood why Kate, living under the same roof with an eleven-year-old, hadn't felt comfortable inviting him to move into her bedroom.

He didn't press, choosing instead to be the good houseguest who made himself useful and otherwise kept out of the way.

As he sat beside Tahoma in the rehearsal hall, watching the actors warm up, Richard was a happy man.

His Hamlet, evidently settling in well at Kate's, was aimed like an arrow at the target of his role, and Richard had every hope of hitting a bull's-eye. Peter had shown up at the first table reading already knowing his lines, and now that they were running full acts, he knew the blocking cold. The lad had a prodigious memory, capacity, and affection for the work; those facts were clear. By offering him a secure home, Richard felt confident they'd given him what he needed to deliver a Hamlet well worthy of the Rose.

Thank goodness for Katherine and her kind hospitality, Richard thought.

He still planned to retire at the end of the following season. His plan was to get through *Hamlet*, then give notice to the board and start helping them write the job description.

To find the next executive director would mean months of head-hunting of an international, and very public, kind. Though he admired

Kate's ambition, he still felt reluctant to support her bid to succeed him. *I simply like her too much,* he thought. *Far better to hand it over to a "hated new captain," as Art so memorably framed it.* Once the board named a successor, he could work with them throughout the 2010 season. Then he could step back gracefully, perhaps even finding a spring 2011 directing contract in London to give himself something to look forward to.

After all these years, he would feel like a stranger on what had once been familiar ground, but he relished the idea of proving himself once again. *I will turn 70 that year. To begin anew at such an age is an intriguing prospect.*

Everyone on the administrative staff knew he was set on leaving, but he didn't need to think about the details much yet; directing *Hamlet* and running the company absorbed his mind.

I'll stay on long enough to welcome the Hated New Captain and introduce them to my throne and kingdom with suitable pomp and honest assistance. And then ...

A tap on the shoulder startled Richard from his reverie. Serena bent down to whisper in his ear, "So sorry, Richard, but have you seen it?"

"Seen what?" Richard asked. Serena pressed a paper into his hand. He scanned it.

"Tahoma, something has come up that needs my attention. Please start without me. I'll be back in ten minutes."

"Thank you Ten," Tahoma said.

Settled in his office chair, Richard rubbed his temples.

"We can work with this," Serena began, but Richard was not that easily mollified.

"What does the man mean, what can he possibly mean, by calling our company 'a thousand-pound gorilla in a twenty-pound town'?" he asked rhetorically.

"Well—" Serena began.

"From the very beginning, when the Rose was nothing more than a few sheets of plywood set up on blocks, a herd of folding chairs in a meadow, and a painted backdrop, we have worked hand in glove with our fellow artists and artisans in our beloved town of Flagstaff. Have we not?"

"Of course we have—"

"And in this time of shared travail, the economic whirlwinds are battering all of us, from the lowest to the mightiest, are they not?"

Seeing which way the wind was blowing, Serena simply nodded.

"We've been given something like safe harbor in the person of our celebrated Prince of Denmark, which is nothing of our doing, but simply a spin of blind Fortune's wheel. How then have we earned the ire of the press?" He brandished the paper on which Serena had printed an email from the editor of the local newspaper.

"At least they gave us a chance to review it; they wouldn't have done that for just anyone," Serena said, relieved to get in a few words. "They recognize our place in this town."

"Indeed. We're afforded the favor of an advance look at tomorrow's opinion piece, which paints our actors as hooligans."

"I don't think it goes quite that far," Serena protested.

"Quote: 'Celebrity has apparently gone to the head of this year's Hamlet, movie actor Peter McKenzie of *Thirst* fame,'" Richard read aloud. "'At the Museum Club recently, he stormed out when asked for a photo. There was a time when the likes of Lynn Redgrave and Alan Rickman signed autographs between bites of breakfast at the Grand Canyon Café. These days, when locals encounter the Rose's actors, it seems no such requests will be honored by the glitterati who deign to perform here.'"

"We can ask Bryce what happened. He'll give us something we can use in our reply," Serena suggested.

"We'll ask, but that's not the part that sticks in my craw."

"It's the part about the money."

"Precisely. 'The Blue Mountain Rose attracts the lion's share of every arts dollar that flows into our fair city.' Leaving other artists to beg on the street corner, I suppose. If only they knew. Productions scaled back, pinching pennies to keep our stage high and dry. Every spare dime is going down the plumbing right now, quite literally."

Serena chuckled and was instantly serious again. "Maybe he makes a point when he says the NEA seems to favor us. Other than the museum and maybe the arts council, do you know anyone else here that reliably receives federal grants?"

"If the National Endowment for the Arts sees fit to bestow its largesse on the Rose, that's because we've been here since the 1940s. We're an institution, with a Tony Award to our credit; too big to fail, is what we are."

"Don't say that," Serena interrupted. "That's what they said about Lehman Brothers."

Richard sighed. "Eric Oliver is a grant-writer extraordinaire. The Rose spends its money on local plumbers and painters and crew; we buy local advertising, including in this very newspaper; we support local restaurants and hotels from May to the first of October. Why this attack?"

"That's what I'm wondering. What's in it for them, to take us down a notch? I think what happened at the Museum Club startled someone who has the ear of someone important; maybe the mayor, maybe the publisher, who knows. The important thing is, they've given us a chance to respond."

"Respond we shall."

"Leave it to me, Richard, please! Don't give them a juicy soundbite of outraged virtue. Invite the editor out to lunch at Josephine's and pick up the tab. Show up with an olive branch gripped between your teeth. Then let me write a gracious response they'll leap to publish."

Richard laughed. "My dear Serena," he said, adopting a tone of wounded innocence. "I never planned to do anything else."

ACT 3

SCENE 8

PETER

Monday night, Peter cooked up his famous "breakfast for dinner," hearty veggie scrambled eggs with cheese mixed in, and toast.

Over the meal, they talked about the cabaret fundraiser, coming up on Friday. In an email to the company that morning, Richard had shared the letter Serena drafted for his reply to Sunday's editorial.

> **The Blue Mountain Rose Theatre Company is partnering with other artists throughout this community to produce a cabaret evening that's sure to please. In addition to our mainstage performances, school matinees, and educational offerings, this is the kind of magic the Rose creates in Flagstaff. Come see for yourselves, and I'm sure you'll agree that we're right where we belong and doing what we've always done: supporting a vibrant local arts scene that benefits the whole community.**

"What are you doing for the cabaret?" Beth asked Peter.

He smiled at Kate as he answered. "I won't participate, unfortunately."

"Why not?"

"Richard asked me to, but I didn't want to create a distraction when the others have worked so hard. They deserve to be seen."

"Aw, Peter, but you're great. You could play the piano and sing. You would be marvelous."

"I'm flattered you think so, but—I'm flattered."

"But what? No *buts*." Beth was insistent.

"What are the others doing?" Kate interrupted.

"Bryce and Freja are singing a duet from *Rent*. Ted and Isabelle are tap-dancing to 'La Vie en Rose.' Fawn has her aerial routine with Circus Bacchus, as you know. Tahoma is doing Mark Antony's speech to the mob, in Navajo. I'll be sorry to miss that; he's going to wear some of his tribal regalia."

"You can't even sit in the audience?" Beth asked sadly.

"I think after my recent drubbing in the press, I should stay out of view," Peter said. "Until *Hamlet* opens, that is."

Peter sat at the piano after dinner, patiently accompanying Beth as she practiced "Tomorrow" for an upcoming recital. Kate had escaped upstairs to finish Fawn's costume. It was turning out beautifully, but Kate had high standards, and the costume had to be not only beautiful, but strong.

Peter tried to focus on the keys, but some part of him was watching the stairway for Kate to come down and make their little circle complete again. Finally, Beth gave up on her practice piece and said, "Peter, could you help me with something on the computer?"

"I dunno. What is it?"

She pointed to her school laptop on the dining table. "I want help looking something up."

"What's it for?"

Beth put on her most innocent face. "Mom was saying she was sorry she missed her ten-year reunion last year. Can we find her class at Columbia? Maybe they've got photos from the party."

"Maybe," Peter mused. "Let's just try a search on the school's website. Graduates of theatre management, what year?"

"I think she graduated in 1998?"

Peter's fingers clicked over the keyboard. "Reunions? Only upcoming. Alumni registry? No, only through 1931. Student directories! No, that ends in 1944."

"What are you guys working on?" At the sound of Kate's voice, Peter and Beth both jumped.

"Nothing," Beth said. "It's a surprise." But Kate had already circled behind Peter to scan the screen. She gave Beth a searching look. Beth widened her eyes, the picture of innocence.

"You can come back to this tomorrow, maybe. It's time to start getting ready for bed. Quick shower tonight, OK?"

"Sure, Mom," Beth said with forced cheer as she headed for the stairs.

"I'll be up at nine to say good night," Kate called after her. Then she turned to Peter.

"I'm not big on surprises, I'm warning you now."

Peter could hear the tension in her voice, though he couldn't guess the source. "Beth said you missed your college reunion last year, and she wondered if we could find photos from the party online."

"Why?"

"So you could see their faces, ten years on? I dunno. I didn't think much of it. She asked me to help her."

Kate's brows knotted. "And you did, without checking with me."

"I didn't think a search on the website at Columbia University could do an impressionable kid any harm. I mean, I know the Internet can be a dangerous place—"

"It's not the Internet I'm worried about," Kate interrupted. "It's Beth. You know why she wanted to find my classmates. I told you about—her dad."

Shite. Peter closed the browser and then the laptop lid and sat back. "I didn't think."

"You have to, with kids." Kate stayed firm. "And be honest with me. Didn't you want to see him, too?"

"I had no such thought in my head. You have to believe me. Why would I care who this prick is?"

"That's my question. Why would you?"

"I wouldn't." Peter stood up, and they faced each other across the table. "What does it matter to me?"

"It doesn't. It shouldn't."

"I see that."

Having run out of words, they stood looking at each other for a moment. Peter looked away first. "I'd better head out to the starship."

Kate nodded.

After taking a few steps toward the door, Peter stopped and turned. "I'm sorry I didn't ask Beth more about why. If she'd told me, I wouldn't have done it without involving you."

"Thank you for that."

"But if I'm honest, I would have asked your permission to help her." He saw the sadness in Kate's face, but he couldn't help himself. "Every child deserves to know who their father is."

Kate raised her eyebrows. "Even though he's said no?"

"I don't care what he said," Peter said, his voice a wall. Then, more softly: "That's not what I mean. Beth's wishes matter, too, don't they?"

"It's not that her wishes don't matter. Wishes don't always come true the way we imagine they will. She's not old enough to handle the consequences yet; at least, I don't think she is."

"But she thinks she is."

"I'm aware," Kate said with a wry smile. "But as her parent, that's a call for me to make."

Peter met her eyes, then looked away. "I'm sorry," he repeated. "Please don't be too rough on her—it was my mistake."

"I won't. I know what she can be like when she wants her way."

Peter shrugged, then turned for the door. "Good night, then."

"Good night."

ACT 3
SCENE 9

PETER

Cabaret week was also the final week of regular rehearsals for the *Hamlet* cast. The first run-through of the entire play would be this Thursday night. Everyone would have Friday off to get ready for the cabaret except Peter and Bryce, who were called for morning fight rehearsal with Devon to practice their rapier and dagger work. "You have to stay sharp," Devon had said, a joke so well-worn nobody thought to laugh anymore.

The cast tried to focus on *Hamlet*, reminding one another "This one's for Richard" as rumors that he planned to retire began to circulate. But the cabaret proved a powerful distraction. On breaks, people practiced indoors or outside, wherever they could find space. For Peter, especially, all the activity was a challenge. He did want to join his friends in presenting the cabaret and felt guilty for sitting it out.

"It's not too late," Bryce told him. He and Freja had just finished practicing their duet "Another Day" in Calliope's Grove as Peter listened. "We could put together a line dance group, show off what we learned at the Museum Club. You remember how to push your tush, right?"

Peter demonstrated that he did indeed remember the steps, and Freja whistled. Bryce laughed.

"We could turn it into a skit where someone interrupts us to ask for your autograph, and you punch them. Put on green body paint and tear off your shirt to become the Hulk. Play with your image and show them we know what they think."

Peter shook his head. "I see where you're going with this, but my being there wouldn't help the cabaret."

"It's all about raising money. You'd send ticket sales through the roof. Or maybe—" Bryce's smile turned to a laugh.

"What's so funny?" Freja asked.

"Let's lean all the way into it. Let's give them a Chippendales act." Bryce looked from Freja to Peter. "Come in wearing a tearaway cowboy outfit. A guy starts in on a snare drum to give people the idea. I'll get on the microphone and tell people it's a minimum hundred-dollar bill to play. We'd raise a grand in two minutes."

Freja fanned herself theatrically as Peter laughed. "You have an outsized idea of my dancing talents," he told them. "They're not worth a dollar, much less a hundred."

Tahoma had taken to bringing a bell to rehearsal so he could ring it when break was nearly over, instead of having to track everyone down. The bell sounded now, briefly setting Peter free from the pressure to perform anything other than his Prince of Denmark.

Early Friday morning, Peter dressed for a solitary run up onto Observatory Mesa before fight rehearsal. Shorts and a T-shirt would do on this late-spring morning that threatened to turn breezy. Kate had loaned him a running belt with two water containers. He slipped his phone into its pocket out of habit, despite the mesa's unreliable reception. He added an energy bar in case he needed a boost.

"Bye, Mum; bye, Jaime," he said as he locked the door. "You kids be good." He was convinced that in some realm, his ghost and Kate's were friends.

With Kate at the office and Beth at school, Peter started out alone up the path that connected to the mesa's expansive trail system. The previous night's run-through gave him much to mull over as he trotted uphill. On their first try at such a major piece of teamwork, they'd created a messy success. Despite the occasional dropped lines and needed adjustments to blocking, though, they'd been happy with the result.

Afterward, Richard gave the cast an encouraging note. "You have it in you to deliver a splendid *Hamlet*," he'd said. "Next time we'll push the pace a bit; try to take five minutes off the run time for every act and see how that feels. In the meantime, enjoy your day off. Tomorrow night, you're going to give this town a cabaret night it won't soon forget."

Heading up the hill at a mellow pace, Peter let his thoughts turn to his situation vis-à-vis Kate. After they'd gone crosswise Monday night, he'd stopped by her office the next day to apologize.

"I was thinking of Beth as someone I want to be friends with, and that's true," he explained, "as far as it goes. But it's not far enough. I have a responsibility to you, and to her, to be an adult. I wasn't thinking that way. But you have a right to expect it of me, and I promise to do better."

Kate's face had softened. "I appreciate your saying that, and to the extent any forgiveness is needed, I forgive you." She gave him a half-smile. "That feels like such a strange thing to say. But you're right: I was expecting something."

"You had a right to." His voice was fierce.

"I need you to be on my side if it comes to choosing between her and me, I guess—which I hope won't happen too often."

Peter nodded. "She's your only, and you're hers. And never the two shall part, nor should they on account of any action of mine."

Kate drew a deep breath. "There's something else I think I should say."

"What is it?" Peter steeled himself.

"While you're staying with us, while we're working together, I think we should try to be friends."

"I hope we are friends."

"We are." Kate smiled as if to reassure both of them that she believed it. "What I mean is—"

"I know." There was a pause. "For now, I agree."

"You have *Hamlet* to concentrate on, anyway. That's big work."

"You're not wrong about that. But Kate?"

"Yes?"

He swallowed. "It's not the only work I want to be doing. You and I had started something, or I thought we had. Was I wrong?" He looked at her sitting in her office chair, spine straight, face composed.

"No, you weren't wrong." Kate blinked quickly and looked away, then back at Peter. "I just think maybe, with everything here, and with Beth being so—challenging—maybe we should concentrate on being good friends awhile and see how that goes."

As he ran up onto the mesa and started a clockwise circuit of the main trail, he turned her words over in his mind, searching for a path toward a different outcome. Oh, in the moment he had agreed. What choice did he have? He saw both her reasoning and her determination to act on what was wise rather than what he sensed they both still desired.

Taking a right turn where several dirt roads met, Peter continued on around the vast meadow at the mesa's heart. As he looked north, his spirits rose at the sight of the Peaks. They wore shades of green, but patches of snow still shone in the alpine rocks of the upper ridges. He'd lived in Flagstaff for four months now and seen these mountains awaken from white winter slumber to this bright promise of summer. Their ever-changing beauty was a reliable surprise.

Distract himself though he might, his thoughts turned again to Kate. Being her friend was easy. They shared the dinner hour with Beth, and when their paths crossed at the Rose, they connected warmly. It was the rest of it he found difficult, fighting memories of sharing his bed with her; her passionate responses to his touch, the gentle look on her face afterward as she caressed him to sleep.

When he'd told Bryce about Kate's decision, his friend told him,

"She doesn't mean forever. Just be patient." Easier said than done.

On he ran, finding his way along the forest roads. The day was warming, so he paused for a moment to strip off his singlet and tuck it into his running belt. Then he returned to a mellow pace, balancing his breathing with the cadence of his footfalls.

What was he meant to do with all that? Channel it into his performance, he supposed. Consider Hamlet and Ophelia, former lovers now separated by the forces of revenge and madness at war in Hamlet's soul. Thwarted desire could fuel Hamlet's cruelty in the "get thee to a nunnery" scene. *And was it a nunnery or really a brothel Shakespeare was thinking of?*

Even his work couldn't distract him for long. Truth be told, Peter would gladly trade any great night on the stage for one chance to lead Kate up the stairs into the studio loft. He wanted to lie down beneath its magical sky windows and travel with her again along routes of passion up to the stars.

Used to being alone on the mesa or at most, occasionally encountering a hiker, mountain biker, or another runner, Peter was startled from his thoughts by the noise of an engine. Not a car, he didn't think; the motor sounded too rough and too loud. *People sometimes tow caravans up here to camp out. Maybe that?*

No sooner had the comforting thought crossed his mind than the dirt bike was zooming past him, driver navigating the rutted road so the passenger could steady his camera, swinging its long lens up like the barrel of a rifle.

Peter didn't have time to dodge out of the way as the bike swerved to block his route and stopped, idling. The photographer picked up another camera that dangled from his neck, the long lens being unnecessary at such close range.

Not again.

ACT 3
SCENE 10

Kate, Peter

Kate was in her office Friday morning when a sweaty Bryce walked in with Devon on his heels.

"I've been working the choreo on my own because Peter missed call," Bryce said. "We don't know where he is."

"Fight rehearsal isn't extra credit that actors can skip once they have the moves down," Devon growled.

"We thought you might know what's up," Bryce said.

Kate shook her head, a concerned look on her face. "At dinner, he told us he was going for a run this morning before your rehearsal. I assume he was out early. He would have to be, to get a decent run in and then shower and breakfast before call. He hasn't missed it before, right?"

"No, never," Bryce said.

"Let me call him." But Kate's phone rang through to voicemail. Despite the situation, she smiled when she heard his voice, still cloaked in his New Zealand accent. She was used to his natural British tones now.

Kate and Bryce shared a worried look. "Maybe I should drive home and see if he's there without his phone somehow?" Bryce agreed to her plan. "And we need to let Tahoma and Richard know," Kate added.

Devon nodded. "We'll call Tahoma, if you'll do Richard?"

Half an hour later, the group gathered in Richard's office for an update.

"He wasn't in the studio, and his running shoes and belt were gone," Kate told them. "I couldn't see any sign he ever came back from the mesa. I'm worried he's gotten seriously lost." She hesitated. "Maybe even hurt?"

"It's hard to get that lost up there," Tahoma said. "You can usually orient yourself by the Peaks, and even if you don't know which direction to walk, all the trails take you to town, eventually."

Richard drew a heavy breath. "I hate to do it, but he's two hours overdue. Perhaps I should at least call search and rescue to see how long we should wait before they look for him."

Kate nodded assent as Bryce said, "It's not like him. He's a trouper. He wouldn't miss call without telling Devon and Tahoma."

"He's always on time, never skips," Tahoma said.

Bryce added, "Beating me up at rapiers and daggers is a highlight of his week."

"What if he forgot, and we're doing all this for nothing?" Devon asked. "He could just be out on a long run on his day off. We'll waste police resources for nothing."

"Why isn't he answering his phone then?" Kate replied. "He's seen half a dozen of our voicemails by now. He wouldn't ignore all of us."

"Maybe he doesn't have it with him or isn't looking," Bryce said reasonably. "Hamlet is a big role, tough to prep for. A little time off duty isn't out of line."

"It is when you haven't checked out with the stage manager," Tahoma countered. "Wasting other people's time is not cool, and I don't see him doing that."

"I agree. I doubt our Hamlet is AWOL on purpose," Richard finally weighed in.

He was just lifting the receiver on his desk phone when Kate's phone beeped in her hand. A text. "Richard! It's Peter. He says, 'I'm fine, please tell everyone.'"

Kate waited a few seconds, but her phone remained still. Her fingers flew as she texted a reply. “Worried here. You OK?”

Then it was Tahoma’s turn. “Sorry I missed rehearsal,” he read aloud to the group. “Apologies to D. and B. ”

They all looked at Kate, who looked at her phone, waiting. But nothing more came through.

Out on the mesa, Peter turned off his cell phone and resumed walking, slowly. *To save the battery*, he lied to himself. *No, I’m not OK, but how can I admit that to Kate?*

He was well off-trail and determined to remain so. Surely they couldn’t find him here.

After that first encounter, he’d knitted his wits together and darted off the road into the pine forest. He’d heard the dirt bike engine revving and the fat tires scravening on the dirt. *They wouldn’t follow me into the trees*, he told himself, but no sooner had he thought it than the engine grew louder. These open forests didn’t offer many barriers to such a vehicle.

They’d roared ahead of him again, and the photographer lifted his lens. Peter raised a hand to shield his face.

“Looking good, Peter,” the paparazzo taunted him. “Nice abs. Give me something I can use, and I’ll leave you alone.”

Instead, Peter had darted behind the nearest big ponderosa, wider in girth than two men, a long-lived, red-barked giant. The engine revved again. *They’re going to come around the tree*. A surge of anger sent energy coursing through his legs. He took off running, racing despite the rough ground, jumping over a small log, looking for denser forest. He’d done some running events in the fells of the Lake District several years back, before everything in his life skidded sideways via illness and celebrity into chaos. Practice staying on his feet over uneven terrain paid off now.

That looks promising. Down he’d sped into a shallow ravine that gathered into a deeper one. He heard the dirt bike behind him, its engine flaring loudly when it found flat ground, then quieting when it met some barrier to the machine's progress.

Breathing hard, Peter had thrown himself down the ravine as quickly as he dared. Small pines and oaks grew thickly there, where water collected after every storm. In his haste, he brushed against them, heedless of his own skin, feeling only the animal determination to run from his pursuers.

The light dimmed as trees blocked out the sky. He'd slowed to a jog, still headed downhill, listening for the engine. When he hadn't heard it for more than a minute, he stopped, gasping for breath. He hunkered down next to a lichen-covered rock to collect himself. Arms: scratched from encounters with rough bark. Legs: the same, and tired from sprinting. Heart: pounding.

A few of the scratches were deep, running with blood. He'd tried to calm his pulse, but fear and anger pounded his heart like a war drum. *These wankers are never going to leave me alone*, he thought.

From a distance came an engine's growl. It sounded like they'd returned to the road system and were idling along, waiting for him to come out.

Let them wait, he'd thought.

Now, walking through the sheltering forest, his anger at being chased ebbed, leaving behind a weary sadness the likes of which he hadn't experienced since the days following his mother's death. Always before, he had seized on plans to be made, paths of escape to pursue. Deep in his soul, he'd believed there was a way out, one he could find or build for himself. He had financial resources and networks of colleagues and friends; his faith in them was strong. With their help, surely he could outrun the celebrity that hounded him and return to the life he loved.

No more. No more fighting, no more running, no more pretending: It was time to face facts. Sitting next to a horse-sized rock, legs stretched out in front of him, Peter turned his face toward the sun. Expecting tears, he found he was too deeply tired even to cry.

He no longer believed he held any power to change his own fate. The vampires would come for Onyxx, and the stage would not protect Hamlet from their hungry gaze. He couldn't run again, not with dignity; he couldn't abandon his fellow actors, his friends, and he no longer had the luxury of imagining the show would go on without him. Not this close to dress rehearsal; no way.

He had to stay, but the prospects looked bleak in every direction.

I give up, he thought. *Paparazzi want to chase me across the forest for a stupid photo? Fine.*

Kids dressed in black ruffled shirts want to show up at my door, follow me on the street, watch my every move? Fine.

Richard wants me to give a performance people will talk about for years to come? I don't see how, but I'll try. Maybe I can win a Tony for Best Hamlet Ever Performed by a Movie Star Vampire.

Looking down at his scratched arms, where the bleeding had finally stopped, he thought, *I just don't care anymore.*

He was at the mercy of great forces; that was abundantly clear. Hamlet's words rolled through his mind: *"There is a special providence in the fall of a sparrow. If it be now, 'tis not to come; if it be not to come, it will be now; if it be not now, yet it will come. The readiness is all."*

He pondered that fallen sparrow. Was it knocked from its nest, where it felt safest? Perhaps it had been caught mid-flight by a hawk wrapping golden talons around its defenseless, feathered throat.

Am I ready? I guess I have to be, he thought. *Ready or not, the time is now.*

That "now" felt as bleak as the dark side of the lifeless moon. *Ready to perform Will Shakespeare's greatest role in front of tossers like the ones who invaded my flat? I'll be vulnerable as a rabbit.*

Loneliness clouded his soul. Once, he'd imagined his feelings for Kate like a glowing ember. He'd held that ember safe in his heart, convinced that, at any moment, he could set it into the tinder of her affection for him, where it would spark a bonfire that could set their nights alight. *Who knows? Maybe for the rest of our lives*, he thought, swallowing hard.

Now she held him at arm's length, and, despite Bryce's assurances to the contrary, Peter trusted the firmness of her resolve. Oh, he believed her concern for his well-being was genuine. She'd been kind to him since they met. But try as he might to accept her friendship as a gift, as a foundation to build on, he couldn't stir himself to the effort just now.

Sitting on the dusty ground, examining his own heart, he found nothing but passive acceptance. *She doesn't want to see what we could be together? Fine. I'll get through this alone. I have to leave Jaime's starship now anyway. Paparazzi are as relentless as a vampire army. I can't bring this invasion down on her and Beth.*

But I don't have to do anything about any of it right now, he decided. The energy it would take to get up, find a trail, avoid his pursuers on the dirt bike, and get back to the studio without being seen; he didn't have it. All that could wait.

"'Come death and welcome,'" he whispered, feeling none of Romeo's bravado. Sore, scratched, and heart-weary, he let his thoughts fade into sleep.

ACT 3
SCENE 11

KATE

Standing backstage at the Orpheum Theater in downtown Flagstaff, Kate had to force herself to focus on the night's work. She felt so distracted, it was like being torn into pieces. She hadn't heard from Peter since the one, cryptic text; nobody had. Still, as she and Bryce had reminded each other at least three times since meeting at the backstage entrance at six o'clock, "The show must go on."

Peering through the curtains, she saw the stage and beyond that, the audience that was gathering around the banquet tables. The first patrons had paid handsomely to sit in the best seats, enjoy heavy hors d'oeuvres, and spend two drink tickets at the otherwise cash bar. Behind them were rows of chairs where the less well-heeled would sit. Hopefully, they would also drink; in addition to 55 percent of the ticket income, the Blue Mountain Rose would take home 70 percent of the bar.

She'd looked forward to the cabaret for weeks, but now Kate wanted it to be over so she could go home. She willed the lights to be on in her dad's studio and Peter to be waiting there, ready to tell her what had happened. Her imagination was vivid; a dose of reality would be welcome. She hoped so, anyway.

Checking her watch, Kate called into her headset, "Ten minutes."

She heard "Thank you Ten" from the tech running lights and sound, then from her two stagehands. Time to check in with the actors. Turning for the backstage dressing rooms where everyone was getting ready, she almost bumped into him.

Peter.

How long has he been standing there? She gasped, then bit back the words "Where have you been?" as she took in the sight of him, dimly visible in the red backstage light. He wore a white button-down shirt, its tails out over a pair of dark pants. He appeared to be carrying a dark coat over one arm. His face was still and serious, without any of the energetic positivity he usually projected in her presence. His face: She could see his face. He'd shaved his mustache and beard, leaving a shadow of stubble behind.

"Can you add me to the call sheet?" he asked in a low voice. "Maybe after Circus Bacchus."

Kate was finding it hard to breathe. "What are you—" she began. The top three buttons of his shirt were unbuttoned. Was that a bow tie resting on the warm skin of his neck?

"Could you have one of the stagehands give this to the board operator?" he asked, reaching out his hand. A thumb drive dangled at the end of a cord.

"What is it?"

"Orchestration," he answered without answering. "And this is the cue sheet for lights and sound. It's a bit complex. Tell them to look for my signals."

Kate looked at the paper, where a few lines were written in his neat handwriting.

"Peter, I can't just add you without—"

"Yes, you can," he interrupted. "It's only about four minutes of run time."

That's not the point. She wondered whether he could see her expression. Trying to hide her shock, she reached out for the thumb drive and cue sheet. As she called into the headset for a stagehand, he turned away.

"Don't tell them I'm here," he said.

But Kate told them, of course; first Ted, who would be emceeing the night's festivities, then Richard, who came backstage to open the show with a short speech. He'd been working the crowd since the doors opened, with an ebullience that only Kate could see was dimmed by Peter's disappearance. All he said when she told him Peter had turned up was, "Ah. And planning to perform? A fascinating turn of events."

When it was time for his entrance in the first set, Bryce set his hand on Kate's shoulder just before his cue and whispered, "Ready." Kate set her lips to his ear and shared the news. "I know," Bryce answered. "It's going to be a showstopper."

"Wait. What?" Kate exclaimed, but Bryce and Freja were already making their entrance.

Somehow, the night moved along, through the first set and a break for drinks, through the second set and another break, and into the third set. Now performers from Circus Bacchus were dancing in the aisles with any audience member brave enough to stand up from their seat. Onstage, jugglers threw flashing knives in time to carnival music pulsing through the hall's giant speakers. Above them all soared Fawn's birdlike form, flying on a hoop suspended from the ceiling.

Standing next to Ted, Kate fairly vibrated with tension. Half of her thought he wouldn't show up. The other half feared he would. When he set his hand on her shoulder and whispered, "Ready," it was almost anticlimactic. She turned, imagining herself prepared for whatever she might see, but he surprised her again.

With a glance, she took him in, from his slicked-back hair, down his bare chest, to the tailored black tuxedo pants, to his bare feet. He was still wearing the bow tie, a detail that set off alarm bells in her mind even as she felt her skin flush. *He looks like…*

She didn't have time to stop their emcee before Ted pushed out through the curtains and announced, "That was Circus Bacchus, one of the treasures of our town. Let's give them another hand!"

"Peter, wait," she whispered, setting her fingers on his bare arm.

Where she'd expected smooth skin, it was rough as sandpaper. Seeing him flinch, she drew back her hand.

"'Not a whit,' my Horatio,'" he said in a low voice. "'We defy augury.'"

From the stage, she heard Ted proclaim, "Now we have a special bonus performance not listed in your program, from none other than this year's Hamlet." The crowd erupted in a babble of talk mixed with clapping and cheering.

"He's here all the way from London, where he's been hailed as the next great interpreter of Shakespeare on the stage."

Loyal Ted. Kate heard Peter snort.

"Please give a warm Flagstaff welcome to—Peter McKenzie!"

Peter moved to the center break in the black curtains and parted them just when his soundtrack began. As the instantly recognizable first mandolin notes of R.E.M.'s "Losing My Religion" crashed through the air, he took one decisive step forward with the beat, then another, claiming ownership of all eyes. He was teasing his way toward a single spotlight at downstage center and now, he began to sway his hips from side to side.

The crowd soon saw what Kate had realized just moments before: Peter was dancing like the star of a striptease.

Kate froze into place, clipboard forgotten as she watched Peter. He held nothing back as he moved to the music, pulling the chords through his body, using every muscle.

What will the crowd do? Kate wondered. This was a fundraiser with an audience mostly in their forties and older, people with reputations in town. For many, being seen supporting the arts mattered as much as actually supporting them. Kate thought of it as a toe-tapping crowd not given to emotional display. But at least a few of the women had, at some point in their past, been to a Chippendales show, and they remembered the proper way to behave. As Peter danced in the spotlight, whistles and cheers flew toward the stage. With each one, Peter sent a nod or a small smile to its source, driving the noise level higher. Someone started clicking their high heels on the concrete floor, and soon the sound of stomping feet rolled through the hall, coming as close to drowning out the music as anything could, given that the speakers were the size of Volkswagens.

He isn't really going to strip, is he? Kate thought. *He doesn't have much to take off.*

"Ready," Bryce said in her ear, nearly causing her to jump out of her skin. "What do you think of our boy?" he whispered. "I guess he's been using that weight set I loaned him."

"What is he doing, Bryce? Are you part of this?" Kate's whisper had a sharp edge.

"He gave us parts in his act." Smiling, Bryce tilted his head toward a tall figure at his side. Like Bryce, the woman was dressed head to toe in black. Vaguely, Kate recognized her as Bryce's dance partner, the actor playing Hippolyta and Titania in their *Midsummer*.

"That's my cue," Freja whispered. The music had segued from the driving beat of a striptease to a spooky soundtrack Kate vaguely recognized. The theme song from *Thirst*.

"'Onyxx, change me, Onyxx, take me,'" Freja chanted to the beat as she stalked downstage. The crowd quieted a moment to hear her. Entering the spotlight, she raised her voice as she continued to chant. Peter turned toward her and smiled, flashing white teeth.

Now he was dancing for her, inviting her into his world. Taking in Freja's slicked-back hair and pale face, Kate wondered how many in the audience had seen *Thirst*. Did they understand the vampire references? When Peter set his mouth on the skin of Freja's inner wrist, Kate had to look away for a moment, cheeks flushed.

Whether they understood vampire iconography or not, the crowd had no trouble interpreting the action onstage. The whistles flew once more as Peter and Freja swirled and slid around each other, dancing like people who would soon share a bed.

Kate forced her eyes back to the spotlight. Peter had one arm around Freja's waist and the other tangled in her blond hair, exposing her pale neck. He leaned in to take the fatal bite. In that instant, the music crashed to a halt, and the spotlight cut out. From the loudspeakers roared a voice Kate recognized as Peter's American accent. "'If they're going to treat us like monsters, then monsters we shall become.'"

The spotlight surged back to life, instantly finding Peter. Freja had disappeared in the momentary blackout. Facing the audience, Peter stood still, his spine straight. He wasn't even breathing hard. Kate saw Bryce beside him, at the edge of the light. Wearing a long-sleeved black T-shirt and sweatpants over black tennis shoes, he looked like a stagehand to Kate, and, indeed, he was setting a mic stand in front of Peter with one hand and holding a jacket on a hanger in the other.

What is this? Kate thought. The crowd had quieted, apparently wondering the same thing. Bryce swung the black jacket off the hanger, revealing a white tuxedo shirt. With the jacket over his arm, he pulled the shirt from the hanger and handed it to Peter, who set his arms into the starched sleeves and began to button.

"'To be or not to be,'" Peter said calmly into the microphone. "Is that the question?" He shook his head.

"'I have of late, but wherefore I know not, lost all my mirth, forgone all custom of exercises,'" he continued, his tone conversational. The shirt now buttoned, he undid the hook on his tuxedo pants. That nobody whistled showed Kate how much the room's mood had changed. Peter tucked his shirt in carefully as he continued Hamlet's speech.

"'And, indeed, it goes so heavily with my disposition that this goodly frame, the Earth, seems to me a sterile promontory.'"

Bryce handed him a white cardboard box, its lid open. Peter lifted a golden cufflink and pinned it on his cuff, then the other, each one catching the light.

"'This most excellent canopy, the air, look you, this brave o'erhanging firmament, this majestical roof, fretted with golden fire—why, it appeareth nothing to me but a foul and pestilent congregation of vapors.'"

Shaking his head as if to dismiss those vapors, Peter returned the box to Bryce. Still speaking, he unhooked the bow tie from his neck, lifted his collar, and set the tie and collar in place.

"'What a piece of work is a man, how noble in reason, how infinite in faculties, in form and moving how express and admirable; in action how like an angel, in apprehension how like a god: the beauty of the world, the paragon of animals.'"

Bryce handed Peter the tuxedo coat, and as he slid it up one arm and across his shoulders, he did indeed look like the paragon of animals. Kate wasn't the only person in the room who felt herself leaning toward him as he pulled his shirt cuffs down with a flourish. His movie-star charisma was on full display.

Bryce offered a white pocket square, which Peter tucked into place with precise fingers. Freja had quietly returned to the stage. Kneeling, she set a pair of shining black dress shoes next to Peter's bare feet and held them as he slid his toes into them. He reached out his hand to help her to her feet, and she joined him in the spotlight.

"'And yet, to me, what is this quintessence of dust?'" he asked, turning his head and looking briefly into her eyes.

"'To be or not to be' is just a question, after all," he said, taking Freja's hand in his. "But how to be? Our answer to that question matters far more."

Bryce had moved around to stand at Peter's other shoulder. Kate saw Peter take Bryce's hand too.

"My answer is this," he declared in a ringing voice. "'Those friends thou hast, and their adoption tried, grapple them unto thy soul with hoops of steel.'" He looked first at Freja, then Bryce, and each returned his glance before all three turned their eyes back toward the silent audience.

"'This above all: to thine own self be true, and it must follow, as the night the day, thou canst not then be false to any man.'"

The three actors stood for a moment, shoulder to shoulder, centered in the crowd's gaze. Then they bowed, and a bright wave of applause crashed over them.

ACT 4 *May* 2009

ACT 4
SCENE 1

KATE, RICHARD

When Kate retrieved Beth from Lauren's house the next morning, the interrogation began even before their seatbelts clicked.

"What happened at the cabaret? Did you make a lot of money? Were the actors amazing? Did Fawn Tucker fly?"

In spite of herself, Kate laughed. "Yes, yes, and yes, Inquisitive One," she said, as lightly as she could. "The income will help the Rose get through this season, the actors wowed the crowd, and Fawn flew like a magical bird."

As they drove home, she added details, her mind always circling back to the act she didn't want to discuss, the one she couldn't pull her mind away from: Peter's striptease. *Reverse striptease?* She didn't know what to call it. Certainly, the sight of her scruffy friend from New Zealand commanding the spotlight, dressed in a tuxedo and looking every inch the British movie star, was burned into her mind—along with every other image of him dancing, shirtless, as the crowd whistled. And then with Freja.

Enough, she thought finally. *Just tell her something*.

"Guess what?" she asked brightly as they turned off the highway and onto their gravel road. "Peter showed up."

"No way!" Beth squealed. "To watch, you mean?"

"He performed! Something he made up at the last minute with his actor friends Bryce Benedict and Freja Lund. It began as—well—a dance. Then he spoke lines from *Hamlet*. And he did something else that's even bigger news."

"What!" Beth demanded as they rolled up the long driveway.

Kate couldn't help looking toward her dad's studio, hoping for a sight of Peter. She wished she didn't care so much. But ever since his disappearance yesterday, she'd been worried. She couldn't shake the feeling, despite his reappearance at the Orpheum. After the cabaret, she'd looked for him in the dressing rooms, but LaShia told her he'd already gone.

Kate had hurried home, expecting to find him in Jaime's starship, but his car wasn't in its parking spot. She'd kept herself awake with a video about movie costume design until nearly two o'clock. Every time she went into the kitchen, she looked out at the studio. Its windows remained stubbornly dark.

"Mom! What did Peter do?"

Beth's curiosity brought Kate back to the present. As they opened the car doors, she reached for her purse and said, "Without asking the costume designer, he shaved off his beard."

Her daughter's scream of delight could be heard for a mile.

Richard had just fed his cat, Tybalt, when the phone rang. He padded into his study already knowing who would call at the ungodly hour of nine o'clock on a Saturday.

"Arthur!" he said into the receiver, confident of his guess.

"Is life a cabaret, old chum?" came his friend's cheerful rejoinder. "Are we in clover yet again?"

Richard had told Art and the other directors that half of the cabaret night income would go to their production budgets. Nobody thought the entire shortfall would be covered by a single fundraiser, but every dollar counted.

"'All's well that ends well,'" Richard said. "Katherine will punch up the numbers Monday afternoon, but we seated a full house and the liquor was flowing, so I have every reason to believe we'll get the result we were hoping for."

"Paul will be delighted. He wants fairy costumes that glow in the dark."

"It will be high summer on an outdoor stage," Richard reminded him. "Paul won't have full dark to play with."

"Dusk is dark enough. He's going to have fun with the lighting. We'll all have fun, will we not?"

Richard's thoughts had strayed back to the previous night, and he replied distractedly, "I think so, yes; there will be money in the coffers for fun of some type."

"What's on your mind?" Art asked. "Something, I can tell."

Richard sighed. Briefly, he sketched a description of their Hamlet's unanticipated appearance on the cabaret stage.

"We hadn't expected him to perform—he's wanted to remain in the background since he arrived. Hid his identity even from us at first, you know. Wouldn't let me tell a soul once I did find out. But now it seems his mind has changed. As a player, he is a singular generational talent. But as a person? He seems erratic in ways that might prove troublesome over the course of a long run."

"Who is this lad?"

"Surely I told you. I'm certain I did."

"Someone from New Zealand who's done a Hollywood movie, is all I know. When ticket sales went skyward, it was his fans who sparked the sales. Which movie? Is it one I know?"

"I have no idea if you know it; it hardly sounds the thing. Have you heard of *Thirst*?"

"*Thirst*; that vampire movie from last year? Your Hamlet is Rory MacNair?"

"No, not him, another lad—his costar, I'm told. Peter McKenzie. It sounds like the casting director was a Scot."

"Your Hamlet is Peter McKenzie. You're telling me the fellow playing your Hamlet is Peter McKenzie?"

"McKenzie, yes. Why must you repeat his name?"

"Just to be sure I'm hearing you."

"He did the Scottish play at the Young Vic a few years back; you must've seen it. Trained at RADA. Can't believe I didn't guess it the first day. Losing my edge, I'd say. But he had the accent and the beach bum beard to back up his tale of hailing from New Zealand. I didn't think to dig further. It was my ego—purely my ego. I thought I'd discovered the next Laurence Olivier. Turns out you lot found him first."

There was a pause on the line. It went on so long that Richard took the receiver away from his face and shook it.

"Did I lose you?"

"I'm here, Richard," Art said.

"Have you seen him? Do you know the lad I'm describing?"

"Know him? Yes. Peter McKenzie from *Thirst* is Helen McKenzie's son."

Richard didn't hear the doorbell at first, sitting on his back deck, lost in thought as he was. Morning light slanted across the Peaks, but the grand scene was wasted on him. His mind had traveled to another time. It was among the best of times at the Rose, in his estimation; those early years when his friends followed him from London to play Shakespeare on a classic outdoor stage hidden in a wild forest in the American West.

The bell's clamor finally roused him from his reverie. He rose slowly and went in through the sliding glass door.

"I'm coming!" he announced gruffly across the living room. "I'm coming," he said again more quietly in the hallway. He set his eye to the peephole. *Well, well. Hello, Peter McKenzie.*

A few minutes later, seated at the table where they had pored over the soliloquies so many times, Richard assessed his visitor. Even relatively clean-shaven, Peter still looked scruffy. Wearing yesterday's tuxedo pants with a gray sweatshirt that seemed too small for his broad shoulders, he appeared far less self-assured than the previous night's spotlit showman.

Warming his hands around a mug of tea, the lad seemed unwilling to return Richard's gaze, choosing to comment on the Peaks instead. Richard joined him in the comfort of small talk. *Where else to begin but here? Let him take the lead.*

But Peter soon fell silent, leaving it to Richard to chart their course.

"You astonished us last night at the cabaret. It was a memorable performance."

Peter snorted and looked down at his steaming mug without smiling. "Good word."

"And I see you shaved your beard. Without permission, or I miss my guess." Peter merely nodded. This was like pulling teeth. "No more hiding?"

"What's the point? They find me no matter what I do." Peter's voice held the heat of restrained rage. When Richard lifted his eyebrows, Peter continued, "Yesterday when I disappeared, that wasn't by choice."

"Something happened?"

In disgusted tones, Peter explained about the run that had turned into a chase, while Richard's exclamations of dismay egged him on.

"But you eluded them," Richard said as Peter described hiding in the forest. "Thank the stars for that."

"Finally, yes. After I escaped, I even fell asleep. When I woke up, I couldn't hear anything. No dirt bike. The day had moved on, and I had to move as well. Walking back to Kate's place, I knew I was at the end of my tether. That's when I came up with the plan."

"Your bravura performance."

Peter met his eyes in a brief acknowledgment of the praise. "I had to show them I wasn't scared anymore."

"So no more hiding?"

"Erm, about that."

Richard leaned back, waiting for whatever might come next from this surprising young man who was Helen McKenzie's son. He fancied he could see something of Helen now in the green eyes looking at him with such resolve from across the table.

"I can't stay at Kate's anymore."

Richard sighed. "Ah, that."

"Yes that. I can't bring this down on her and Beth. The paparazzi will find her house, back road or no, gate be damned. As soon as they do, the vampires will know where she lives. We can't risk it."

"I suppose not," Richard agreed. "But the time for a precipitous departure from the country has passed. What do you propose?"

"You're the one who needs me to play Hamlet. Let me stay here with you."

Richard regarded Peter for a moment. Behind the mask of his level gaze, his mind raced.

Peter urged, "This is a gated community, so you already have security in place. I'm not saying I don't want to play Hamlet; I do." He paused. "More than ever. I'm just saying, evidently this is what it takes to do it."

"No more hiding means more than that," Richard countered. "It means we're riding the tiger of your fame now, and so are you. You'll do media interviews, public appearances, all of that?"

"Is that your price?" Peter asked.

"It is." Richard's firm voice belied the softer feeling in his heart.

"Then what else can I say? Yes." Peter uttered the word like a curse.

"And so I agree," Richard affirmed, taking momentary delight in the effect of his quick answer on Peter. The lad sat back, eyes wide.

"You need to play Hamlet. We need you to do it. We must keep you safe, and Katherine and Elizabeth as well. We've tried everything else. Let's try this."

ACT 4

SCENE 2

Peter

With the first technical rehearsal just a few hours away, they needed to get Peter fed. Richard gave him free rein in the kitchen, where he made enough veggie scrambled eggs to feed an army and then promptly devoured all but Richard's chaste portion.

"I usually call this 'breakfast for dinner,' but I suppose it's a bit early for that," Peter said as he slid Richard's plate across the gray granite counter.

"You'll have to revise it to 'breakfast for lunch,'" Richard replied. "If only there were a name for that."

Seeing the joke, Peter laughed. "Perhaps if we put our heads together, we can come up with something. Short and to the point, that's what's called for."

"Think, man, think!"

After they cleared the brunch dishes, Richard suggested, "With tech this afternoon, you'll need to get to Kate's to box up some things, unless you've already done that?"

The light demeanor Peter had projected during the meal dropped away before he could rescue it.

"I hadn't thought about it, but you're right."

Truth be told, it was all he'd been able to think about. How to get his things from Jaime's starship without seeing Kate?

"I'd rather not draw attention to her house. I don't suppose you could go?" As soon as he said it aloud, he knew it wouldn't do. He didn't want Richard boxing up his things. The photos of his mother; her scarf and perfume on the windowsill. No.

"Would it pose such a risk for you to make the drive?" Richard asked. "Take my car, in case the paparazzi know yours."

"Never mind. It's kind of you to offer the car. I may take you up on that." *No way out of this, but perhaps a bit more delay.* "Right now, I'm knackered. Do you mind if I catch twenty winks before heading over?"

Taking the hint, Richard led Peter downstairs, past the laundry room and garage exit and into the guest bedroom. Tybalt followed them down and twined himself around Richard's legs before stalking into the room. Framed posters Art had brought from Stratford on his visits brightened every wall, competing with picture windows offering a view east across a flagstone patio into the pine forest. An elaborately carved headboard anchored the king-sized bed. In one corner, set on flagstones and surrounded by yellow brick, stood a wood-fired stove. The room offered a restful, masculine retreat that reflected the host's interests and good taste.

Peter felt a pang of longing for the skylights in Jaime's starship, the company of ghosts. "Beautiful," he said aloud. "I can't thank you enough for letting me stay."

Richard clapped him on the back quickly. Peter flinched without meaning to, hoping his host hadn't noticed. Stepping away, Richard said, "I trust you will be both safe and at ease here, at last."

Peter smiled. How many times had he moved since coming to Flagstaff? The home of Richard James Aloysius Keane was the last place he'd ever expected to land.

When Peter rolled up Kate's driveway in Richard's silver Volvo, he hoped not to see her sedan parked in its customary spot, but there it was. Pulling in beside it with a sigh, he shut off the purring engine and opened the door.

"You're not Richard!" shouted Beth. Taking the porch stairs two at a time, she came running toward him. "Peter! Mom said you shaved your beard!"

"No more hiding in the shrubbery!" He forced the joke into his voice.

"And she said you did *Hamlet* while dancing in a tuxedo!"

"Did she?"

"I wish I'd been there. Were you marvelous?"

"I don't know about marvelous. Committed to the part, maybe." *Still no Kate.* "Is your mum in?"

"She's in the kitchen." Beth grabbed his hand. "We're making cookies for tech. They're so good! You definitely want some."

Peter squeezed her hand, then let go. "I have to get to the starship. Tell her I'm here, would you?"

He could tell he'd confused Beth. *Just go in and face it,* he thought. But he couldn't bring himself to do it.

"Tell her I'll come over in a bit to say goodbye."

"But where are you going so soon? You don't have tech until three." Trust the daughter of Richard's right-hand woman to have intimate knowledge of theatrical rehearsal schedules.

"I'm going to Richard's," he said, angling for the half-truth.

"For line practice?"

Peter widened his eyes at her. "May purple squirrels nibble your toes for thinking I don't have my lines! I'm just—erm—Richard and I have a few things to talk about." *Not that I plan to talk with him about them.* Could two half-truths add up to a whole? Evidently.

"I'll tell her." But as Beth turned to run back up the stairs, she tossed over her shoulder, "If you're lucky, she'll bring the cookies to you."

"Hi, Mum. Hi, Jaime," Peter said as he unlocked the studio. *If you're even speaking to me,* he added morosely.

Inside was the mess he'd known he would find, having created it himself in the hurricane of rush the afternoon before.

Opening the studio door after escaping the chase on the mesa, he'd looked across at Kate's kitchen window; dark, as expected. She would be at the Orpheum early, clipboard at the ready, checking the call board for stragglers as soon as the clock struck six. He'd have to hurry if he wanted to reach the cabaret before curtain.

In the shower, a dozen reopened cuts stung less than his absolute dejection at having been found yet again. He'd worn out his razor with a rough cut of his beard and mustache in the steaming water. Out and dry with a towel that soon looked as if it had cleaned a crime scene after a grisly attack, although he couldn't convict the innocent Gambel oaks just for having scratchy bark.

Am I really doing this? he'd asked himself, and then, an actor to the core, *Will it work?* A quick finishing job with the electric razor had left him with a two-day stubble and the bathroom covered in fine blond hairs. His tuxedo hung in its dry-cleaning wrapper, ready for the opening night after-party. He'd ripped the plastic away and dressed, leaving the shirt off so his cuts could dry, wrapping the bow tie loosely around his neck.

What else? Cufflinks. Shoes. Socks. Unable to find his dress socks as the clock ticked, he'd thought, *Sod that; I'm off.*

Now, surveying the damage in the bright afternoon light, Peter sighed. *Where to begin?* His running gear and shoes were in one dirty pile. His computer sat open on the drafting table where he'd spent precious seconds copying the theme song and voiceover from his *Thirst* ad and the song Bryce had sent as a joke after he and Freja teased Peter about Chippendales.

Bryce.

Freja.

Frozen in place, fighting off memories he wished he didn't have, Peter barely heard the tap at the door.

"Come in," he called out absently, still lost in the night, thinking it was Beth.

"Peter?" said a soft voice. "Are you all right?"

It was too much to hear, the note of hope and, beneath it, the harmonic line of sadness. He didn't want to turn around, didn't want to see her face, so quickly dear to him, so quickly lost. But he made himself do it; made himself turn and face her and explain.

He packed as he talked, picking up the piled gear as he described fleeing the dirt bike on the mesa, pulling his suitcases from the closet and shoving dirty clothes into them as he told her about coming up with the idea for his act, taking shirts from their hangers as he said he was moving to Richard's. He packed so he wouldn't have to see her face, though he did see it, the expression of sympathy so honest he wanted to cry, mixed increasingly with confusion when she realized he wouldn't meet her eyes. Finally, she said, "Peter, stop. Just stop."

He drew an impatient breath. "I have to return Richard's car before tech."

"I know. But I see this has hit you hard." She set a plate of cookies on the counter and took a step toward him, as if to push through the barrier he'd built with his flurry of activity. "It must have been terrible, being chased like that. What can I do to help?"

"Don't try to fix it," he said, his voice rough. "You're not responsible for this."

"What do you mean? I just want—"

It hurt, seeing the sympathy in her eyes. *I don't deserve it*, he thought, disgusted with himself. Out loud he said, "I appreciate what you're trying to do. But you're always taking responsibility, Kate. You're responsible for managing Richard and keeping the company afloat, you're responsible for Beth. You don't have to be responsible for me, too. You can't fix this. Nobody can."

"I'm not trying to fix it. I just want to help!"

"Those are the same things, don't you see?"

She shook her head. "I just see someone who needs a friend."

"I may need a friend, but I don't deserve one."

"Everyone deserves a friend, I think." Her voice was gentle.

Peter started folding T-shirts to give his hands something to do. Keeping his eyes on this task, he said, "Please don't be so nice. Not to me. You'll regret it when you know."

"Know what?"

"Please don't make me say it." He closed his eyes briefly, as if trying to shut out the world.

"Peter, I'm not trying to make you say anything."

Opening his eyes, he tried to read her expression. *She knows I didn't come home, right?*

"It's about last night."

Now it was her turn to be silent, and, in the silence, he knew she had waited up for him, because of course she had.

"I didn't come back here after the cabaret. I'm so sorry I didn't. I went with Bryce and Freja back to the Arden. I spent the night there."

"With Bryce."

His look was fierce, his voice a dagger aimed at his own heart. "No. With Freja."

ACT 4
SCENE 3

KATE

Kate looked at Peter, tumult in her heart.

Don't be nice to him. He doesn't want it. Because he's ashamed.

But it wasn't that easy for Kate to turn off her empathetic spirit, even if Peter had described it as trying to take responsibility where none was offered, trying to fix something she herself hadn't broken.

"Tell me what happened," she said, her voice soft. "Please, just sit for a moment and tell me."

His shoulders dropped. "You don't want to hear this."

"Not all the details, no." She gave him a sad smile. "But I want to know what really happened yesterday, not just the facts but what happened inside you. You think it isn't necessary, but maybe just saying it to someone will help. Because I doubt you told Richard."

"Ha. No, I certainly did not tell Richard."

"Take me back to your morning run." She gestured to the table by the window. "Please?"

He closed his eyes for a moment, and when he opened them, Kate was sitting, looking out at the forest, waiting for him.

Perched on a chair, he began to describe the fear and despair of running like a deer before the hunter's bow. He wondered aloud at how he'd fallen asleep sad and awakened angry, fired with a rage that made him feel he could take on the world.

"I came up with the idea for my cabaret show on the long walk back. Once the idea took hold, it was all I could think about: how to make it happen in the scarce time I'd have. It was a rush, in every sense. I was high on it, higher than I've been since opening night at the National. That carried me through the whole event—seeing you, telling Bryce and Freja, walking out onstage as the crowd lost their bloody minds. All of it."

He took a cookie and bit into it.

"And then what?" Kate took a cookie as well and began nibbling the edge in a circle.

"You mean, how did I end up at the Arden?"

"I guess so, yes."

"I crashed." She met his eyes for a moment, before he looked away. "Usually after a performance, I go someplace quiet, grab a snack, listen to music, unwind a bit. This time I lost track of myself. They could see it—Bryce could. I was still pumped, but I'd lost my edge, and everything else was rushing back in. The chase, being photographed again, knowing for sure they'll be following my every move from now on."

"I wish you'd come and found me."

"You're not the only one. But I was beyond exhausted. I couldn't see how to take care of myself; not last night, not in my life going forward. I have nothing left to fight it with. Bryce said, 'Let's get drunk at Uptown Pubhouse,' and all I could think to say was, 'Not a bar. Too many people.'"

"So you went to the Arden."

"We signed ourselves out on the call sheet before the closing act and went to Freja's cabin. She had the good stuff: the beer Bryce drinks, some top-shelf gin. It went down easy. You don't want to hear the rest of this."

And you don't want to say it, but this is what we're doing. "It must have been such a letdown, after the wave you'd been riding."

He drew a breath. "We talked how fame wrecks lives. A fine talent like Heath Ledger, dead by its hand. I said it fills your pockets with diamonds and steals the air from your lungs. Then we had another drink, and they listed all the things they would do if the diamonds were theirs. Freja wants to create a new Atlantis in the Caribbean and swim with dolphins every day. Beth would have loved that." He paused.

"They tried to understand, but truly, they think I'm mad for running away. Bryce said I should do the next vampire movie. Buy myself an island with my share and then tell the world where to get off, and the paparazzi, too."

"I suppose you could."

Looking down, Peter took another cookie. "These are really good."

Kate didn't answer, and when he looked up, there was a challenge in her eyes.

"Well. The night grew old and then young again, and every time Freja got up to pour us more drinks, she sat down closer to me. Bryce finally said he was leaving. 'Come sleep on my couch,' he said. I'm an absolute arse. I know he likes her, and—there's you, as well—but I said no, I was grand where I was." Peter swallowed. "Not that it makes a difference, but when I did *Macbeth*, she was Lady Macbeth. We have a history. It was easy to contemplate a return to the past, though this morning I can't imagine why."

Enough. "Maybe you can't, but I can," Kate said. "It's because of everything that's happened, not just yesterday but since you came to Flagstaff; maybe since losing your mom, even?"

Peter's eyes flicked to her face, then away. What Kate offered was the mercy of compassion. But when Peter shook his head, she realized he wouldn't allow himself to take it.

"This is the part where I say it didn't mean anything, but I hate it when blokes say that. As if it's admirable when we sleep around without letting it touch our heart." His tone was bitter. "As if being a psychopath is just built into the masculine DNA, and we simply can't help ourselves."

Their eyes locked while Kate held her breath, dreading what came next.

"It did mean something. It meant for a little while yesterday, after everything, I wasn't alone."

Kate and Peter sat looking at each other, the silence of Jaime's starship wrapped around their shoulders.

Then, keeping her eyes on Peter's, Kate stood. *I refuse to say thank you for telling me. You owed me the story.* Aloud, she said, "I need to tell Beth you're moving to Richard's. She'll be sad to see you go."

Not until she was on the other side of the door did she let the tears fall.

Peter had changed clothes and was gathering his things from the bathroom when they returned twenty minutes later. Beth bounded into the studio, but her voice was heavy as she said, "Hi, Granddad. Hi, Peter."

Kate gave Peter a sharp look as she explained over Beth's head, "She wants to help."

"I wish you didn't have to move out!" Beth exclaimed, making a pouty face.

"Me, too, but we can't let the vampires find Jaime's starship," he told her.

Kate turned to the sink, where she busied herself with washing dishes. She brushed him away when he said, "Let me do that."

"You need to get to tech," she replied, unable to keep a curt tone from her voice.

Oblivious to the tension, Beth helped Peter box up his books, notebook, and script, taping it shut and writing "Script! Important!" on the side. Peter handed her a smaller box and asked her to write "Helen! Important!" on it. Taking the labeled box, he sent her up to the loft with instructions to throw everything down to him but the weights and the things on the windowsill. Clothing came fluttering down, then sheets and a pillow, and his game of catching it all midair made Beth laugh.

Too soon, he was packed and ferrying things out to Richard's car. Kate and Beth walked him out with the final items in their arms.

"Are you coming to opening night?" he asked Beth.

"Of course! Right, Mom?"

"Right. You'll see Peter Friday. What do you say?"

"Break a leg! Break two legs if you can!"

"I'll do my very worst." Peter bent to hug Beth. Then he stood and met Kate's eyes. She'd been thinking about this moment for the past hour. *No point hesitating now.* When he opened his arms, she stepped into the hug, choosing to recall the months of their friendship rather than his night of—*Don't think about it*, she reminded herself.

As she set her head against his chest, the image that came to her heart instead was of the night he helped Beth with math. He'd caught her watching them and returned her look with such soft warmth that the memory still made her melt. She felt his chest lift with a slow breath and wondered what he was thinking of. Then she loosened the pressure of her hands on the firm muscles of his back, feeling her body's reluctance even as she resolutely stepped away. When she looked up, she was able to muster a genuine smile.

"We'll miss you," she said, then swallowed. She was surprised, but not entirely, to see tears sparkling in his eyes as he answered gruffly, "I'll miss you, too." She took Beth's hand, and they waved as he backed the car into the driveway and drove away.

"I wish they hadn't chased him on the mesa," Beth said plaintively as the dust settled in his wake.

"So do I," Kate said. "Let's finish in Dad's starship, so we feel better."

"The only thing that will make us feel better is Peter coming back or if we get to eat the rest of those cookies!"

"Food isn't feelings," Kate answered automatically, not needing to look to see her daughter roll her eyes.

While Beth pushed the battery-powered vacuum across the lower floor, Kate went upstairs with an armful of sheets. She liked to keep the bed ready in case of unexpected guests. The low mattress, set up off the floor on a custom-built frame, was bare and rumpled. It was hard not to remember Peter as she made it up with fresh sheets and a light quilt; the weight of his body on hers in another bed, a lifetime ago. *Freja*, she told herself sternly.

We've hardly spoken two dozen words, and already I hate her, Kate thought. *Now Peter and I…*

She hardly knew where to go with that thought, so she willed herself to stop moving for a moment and just sit down.

Looking out the sky windows from a perch on the edge of the bed, Kate searched her heart. *Freja isn't the enemy*, she told herself. *Freja didn't chase him from his cabin at the Arden to Dad's starship and now to Richard's. Fame did that, or maybe—celebrity is a better word?*

"All done," Beth called.

"Be right down."

You can be famous for something and still go for a run without having photographers chase you down. But when you're a celebrity, they watch every step. That's been his reality since his mom got sick.

Kate stood and walked slowly downstairs, thinking about what else they could do to reclaim the space.

"Are you sad, Mom? I can tell you're sad."

Joining Beth at the drafting table, Kate picked up a cookie. "Yes, I'm sad. Peter is a good friend, and he's going through a rough time." She began nibbling the edges in a circle.

Picking the biggest cookie on the plate, Beth broke it in half and bit into its center. "You like him." It wasn't a question.

"You're right, I do," Kate admitted, unable to use the past tense. "So do you, I can tell."

"I think he's awesome, and not just for being a movie star."

"I'm proud of you for that. He's a special person. I wish . . . ." *So much.* "I wish he could just have a normal life, like he wants."

"And not be chased by motorcycles and vampires."

"And ghosts," mused Kate. *How much of this is about losing his mom just as this wave of celebrity came crashing over him?*

"Ghosts?" Beth was confused. "What ghosts?"

Kate gave her a meaningful look. "You know that box you labeled 'Helen! Important!'?"

"Yeah?"

"Helen was his mom. He packed that box with things he keeps around to remind himself of her. He misses her, a lot."

"Oh, no!" Beth's eyes were instantly moist with unshed tears. "He doesn't have a mom?"

Kate reached for her daughter's hand. "Well, his mom died, about a year ago, or a little more than that. But you know how it is. The people we love never leave us. They stay in our heart, in our good memories of them. Their memory stays in places where they were happy, like with Dad and his starship." Looking over at Jaime's brushes on the drying rack, she remembered him sitting at his easel, whistling tunelessly as he painted. *I miss you, Dad.*

Beth nodded, comforted a little.

"Helen's ghost has gone with Peter from England to New Zealand to Arizona. Can you imagine? She's traveled halfway around the globe to stay beside him."

The corners of Beth's mouth turned up slightly.

"So he still has a mom, just not the kind who can give him a hug when he's scared like he was on the mesa, or cheer for him when he fights off the boy vampires like he did at his nutshell cabin, or give him a standing ovation when he takes a bow as Hamlet Friday night."

"I'm sad for Peter," mourned Beth, looking down at the blue and green beaded bracelet on her wrist, the kea bird dangling onto her hand.

"But he has his friends in the cast, and Richard," Kate added. She paused, imagining what things might be like at Richard's house once his leading actor moved into his guest room. Richard, who was accustomed to living alone, who liked things a certain way. *I'll have to ask how that's going when I see him.* She smiled a little at the thought.

"And he has us," Beth said.

Kate found it surprisingly easy to echo, "Yes. He has us."

ACT 4
SCENE 4

Richard

Watching Kate unlock the theatre gate before tech that afternoon, Richard noted the coin on her key ring, its embossed masks of Tragedy and Comedy glinting in the sun.

Adam Condell gave me that, he recalled. *I passed it to Katherine, thinking she might succeed me someday. Someday seemed so far away, then.*

While Kate walked backstage, Richard entered the echoing yard. *In these past few months, it's become clear she's ready. With the most urgent repairs to the Rose now underway, perhaps it's not cruel to revisit the idea?*

He looked around at the empty galleries, then over to the stage, his mind turning to the day's work. As he always did upon entering the Rose, Richard quietly recited an invocation from *Henry V*: "'Can this cockpit hold the vasty fields of France? Or may we cram within this wooden O, the very casques that did affright the air at Agincourt?'"

Yes, we may, Richard thought, *though it's the emotional battlefield of Elsinore and a villa in Messina where we'll lay our scene this summer, William.*

Climbing the stairs into the middle audience gallery, he turned to look at the Rose. A week ago, Kate had overseen the work of preparing her for the season. The stage was bare, the doorways clear. *All is in readiness for your thirty-ninth debut,* he thought. *I pledge it shall not be your last.*

At tech rehearsal, every piece of the *Hamlet* production came together for the first time. In addition to fine-tuning lights and sound, tech gave the design team a chance to make sure their creative work looked the way they wanted it to. And it gave the *Hamlet* cast time to get comfortable with the stage where they would perform for the next three months. But before the year's first tech could begin, they had a stage tradition to uphold.

As Richard settled himself in the gallery, Tahoma led the actors onstage. Behind him came Aaron, holding a stemmed blue rose in his hand. Aaron had worked more seasons here than anyone else in the cast, so he had the honor of introducing the Rose to its newest players.

The rest of the cast gathered around as Aaron set the rose downstage center. "'Of all flowers, methinks a rose is best,'" he said, looking toward Richard, who nodded.

Aaron turned to his friends. "She's a grand stage and, at the same time, the most intimate space you'll ever play," he announced. "You can hear a person crying in the back row of the upper gallery. The groundlings can rock this house with laughter so you can't hear yourself think. If they hold their breath with tension or shuffle their feet in boredom, you'll know. Right, Fawn?"

"Keep a grip on yourself or they'll blow you away," Fawn answered.

"You learn to not just withstand the crowd's energy but work with it, and then you'll come to love it," Aaron continued. "No other space will ever give you the rush of the Rose." He grinned wickedly. "But there's something I have to warn you about. She's partly open to the sky. Or how does Hamlet describe it?"

Peter heard his cue. "You mean, 'This majestical roof, fretted with golden fire'?"

"That's it. At 7,000 feet elevation, you can throw a stone and hit that golden fire. Forget your sunscreen one summer matinee, and you won't do it twice. And that majestical roof?" He pointed skyward, and they all gazed into the unruffled blue of May. "Our monsoon storms can soak the yard in two minutes. Right, Tahoma?"

"The groundlings all run to the protection of the gallery and stage roofs to wait it out. You're dry here onstage unless it's raining sideways—which it sometimes does. But we don't hold unless the audience can't hear you or if there's lightning."

"Prepare to shout yourself hoarse until your hair stands on end, my friends," Aaron concluded. "Those dry and lucky souls seated in the covered galleries paid handsomely, and they expect the show to go on. The groundlings usually know to bring rain ponchos. It's a tough crowd. I mean that as a compliment. Welcome to the Rose."

Seated at the production table, Richard and Tahoma watched as Margaret and a few other actors started dancing the "hokey pokey" for warm-up. Richard smiled, remembering other casts and their traditions: sun salutations, Tongan power stances, the memorable group whose primal screams always startled the watching ravens into flight.

Try as he might, Richard couldn't remember anything special they'd done to warm up for *As You Like It* in 1974—the year he'd lost his heart to Helen McKenzie. Rosalind of the golden hair and startling green eyes, the feminine, husky voice. *I saw her beauty, but I saw her player's heart as well.* She'd heard her calling at a young age. It mirrored his own development, from a brawling Galway lad to a "young lion" of the Dublin stage, where he discovered Shakespeare like he was the first person in history to hear its music. He'd been delighted to meet others who heard it, too. She was one; his fiery Helen of Troy.

Onstage, the actors were now stretching into yoga poses or doing vocal exercises, trilling and croaking and running scales in their throats, a chorus of mad bullfrogs. Peter was stretching his legs as he ran through a tongue twister.

What is her son like when the leaden cloak of celebrity isn't laid about his shoulders? Richard wondered if the lad would ever be lighthearted again. Would he do more American movies once he concluded this detour at the Rose? Would he become richer than Croesus, selling his soul as he claimed to have already done?

Richard hoped not. Helen had stayed with stage work throughout her career. She'd earned awards and accolades and even been made a Dame by order of Queen Elizabeth II. Helen McKenzie, still lovely and strong; with her patrician air and trained voice, she'd played queens and matriarchs.

When she stepped back, Richard had read the rumor she was ill. He'd imagined a temporary setback, something minor and easily gotten over.

How could she be so suddenly, so early gone? Richard shook his head as if to banish the thought. But here they were, a year on and a bit more, and the tall, broad-shouldered blond man standing on the very stage where his mother once commanded all eyes was now looking to him.

They were all looking to him. *What did I miss?* Richard thought in confusion.

"Richard," Tahoma said at his elbow, causing him to jump. "I'm ready to call Places for act 1. But did you want to say something to the cast?"

"It all began right here in 1947, with a group of players, a plywood stage and handsewn curtains, an audience seated on picnic blankets," Richard said, rising from the bench. "Imagine a crowd hungry for entertainment, actors who love the work enough to play for dimes, props and costumes repurposed from whatever was at hand."

"Downstage center, we see Adam Condell, our founder and later, my mentor. There he stands, young and alight, fired by the pure joy of sharing Shakespeare with a company of players." Richard smiled as he remembered his friend. *I must have told this story at tech more than a hundred times, Adam. I hope you're listening in.*

"In 1970, the jerry-rigged first theatre, constructed in pieces over decades, was torn down and this magnificent wooden O stood up. She has the lines of the original Globe Theatre, where played the Lord

Chamberlain's Men, Shakespeare's own company. She's graceful and tall and well-built, for her time."

Time was carving its initials into her skin, he admitted to himself. Even Richard could see that despite her new coat of paint, his beloved Rose was showing her age. *She has so much more to give to audiences yet unborn and actors who've yet to speak their first lines onstage. Damned if I'll be the person who locks the gates for the last time.*

"Within the embrace of this gracious frame, bright lights of the theatrical world have made their entrances and their exits." Their names winked like fireflies in Richard's mind. Since 1971, when Adam hired him, Richard had been the Rose's servant and her most passionate admirer. "And soon, your names will be voiced alongside theirs."

He looked at Peter, his Hamlet. Like all the actors, Peter was in costume; his mourning suit was a study in grays, above which his golden hair shone as if spotlit. *I want him to play as I know he can, and then I want him to stay and keep playing here, if he chooses. Helen McKenzie's son deserves anything I have in my power to give. Surely his fanged fans will forget him eventually. In the meantime, with his name attached to this place, is it too much to hope we'll earn the funds to save the Rose?*

"I know you've heard the rumor of my retirement," Richard said. "And it's true that I've been here since before some of you were born. But I'm still here. I'm here for you and for the *Hamlet* you'll soon give our audiences. And a grand gift it will be indeed." He looked down at Tahoma, who nodded.

"But why do I speak of tomorrow?" Richard turned back toward the cast. "When you play, play for today. Play for yourselves and one another. Play for the Rose. The stage is yours."

As their applause rang in his ears, he thought of Kate. As he had followed Adam, she was eager to make her mark here. *She's earned my support when I step down, but I'll not walk away yet, not with this great stone still poised to roll downhill and crush her.*

Settling regally back onto the bench, Richard admitted to himself, *I do not wish to hand Katherine or anyone else the keys to a failing kingdom. First, we must save the Rose.*

ACT 4

SCENE 5

PETER

Peter normally delighted in the drudgery of tech, and *Hamlet* was no exception.

During tech rehearsal, they ran the show "cue to cue," working through the production from first line to last. The actors used tech to adjust the actions they'd created in the rehearsal hall to the real stage. Occasionally, they might speed through a scene, speaking their lines in double time until Tahoma called, "Hold." But long speeches stayed as rehearsed, giving actors accurate timing for costume changes and other offstage business.

It reminded Peter of the hurry-up-and-wait of the movie set, but better than that; it took him back to other stages and shows, other directors and casts. And better still: Saying the lines and moving through the blocking and listening to Tahoma and his castmates claimed all his attention. He didn't have to think about anything else but Hamlet. There was no pressure to do anything fresh or new, anything difficult or unpleasant. He could just be.

On break that Sunday, the second full day of tech, he picked up his phone, hoping for a voicemail from Kate, knowing he had no right to wish for it. There was nothing from her, but his father had called.

Again. He briefly considered listening, if just to hear a familiar voice, then decided not to. *I can't deal with him right now.* There was also a message from Freja. That one he would answer. *But first, I may as well set the wheels in motion. There'll be nothing to keep me here.*

His agent picked up on the second ring.

"You've gone woodsman on us!" Martin greeted him.

"What now?" Peter asked.

"A captivating photo of you racing shirtless across the Arizona mountains. Those are fantastic shoulders, my friend. What happened to the slender willow of an ashen-faced lad who played Onyxx, eh?"

"That's the question, isn't it," Peter said. "As you can see, I've been found again."

"You're about to deliver the performance of the decade; of course you've been found."

"I wouldn't say that."

"No, but your agent would. 'He's at the famous Blue Mountain Rose, preparing to play Hamlet under the direction of Richard Keane, and when he's done, the world will be his oyster.' That's what I tell everyone who will listen. The offers are pouring in."

"Really? Like what?" Peter was intrigued despite himself.

"Like the West End; name your part. Broadway; they've heard of you now, and they want you. They want you BAD. And movies, of course. Pirates, superheroes, sensitive sagas of the human spirit triumphant. And then there's the next installment of *Thirst.* Their wallets open wide. They've as good as said my favorite three words."

"Name your price."

"Name your price!"

Peter sighed. *Be grateful.* "What will it cost me to keep playing Shakespeare?"

"Running shirtless through the Arizona forest."

"No, not here. I can't stay here."

"Ah. Might I ask why?"

"No, you might not. After my contract is up, the day *Midsummer* closes, I'm ready to go. But I won't give up the stage for good."

"How about this," Martin said in a more serious tone. "Play Shakespeare every other year, alternating with movies. Variety will keep your skills sharp, and you can rake in the profits while keeping your artistic soul intact."

"Maybe."

"Others have done it."

"I'm not saying I can't do it."

"Choose a new festival every year if you want. There isn't a Shakespearean stage here or in the States that would turn you away. You'll drive ticket sales to unheard-of heights, delivering your trademark Hamlet or Macbeth or what have you."

"A gypsy life."

"Why settle down? A lass in every port."

"Because I want—"

"Fame, money, adoring fans, the chance to play Shakespeare and Onyxx, too. What else could a man want?"

"The love of wife and family?" *Not that I deserve them now.*

"Overrated!" Martin shouted cheerfully. "Between festivals, you can do another *Thirst* movie and make ten million on the front end, and that's just for the next one. They're casting two more. They would sign you today if they could."

"There's going to be a series for sure?"

"The fans are thirsty for vampires." Martin laughed at his own joke.

"You don't know what you're asking me to do."

"Sure I do. Act and get rich. How many actors ever hear those words in a single sentence? One in ten thousand. You're a vampire now; it's bite or get bit on the silver screen, then take your shirt off onstage and watch them go insane. You'll be the shirtless Shakespeare guy."

"The shirtless Shakespeare guy." Peter sighed again.

"Can I enter negotiations with the *Thirst* team?"

There was a pause. "Let's go ahead and see what they put on the table. But Martin?"

"Yep?"

"See if you can find me one of those 'sensitive sagas of the human spirit triumphant,' too, with a good director attached."

"It'll cut your payday nine parts in ten."

"Let's just look at the offers."

Martin knew when to take his winnings and leave the table. "Will do! Good luck out there. You open this week, right?"

"Right, and don't say good luck; it's bad luck."

"Actors," Martin laughed as he rang off.

ACT 4
SCENE 6

PETER

By Monday, the final day of tech, even Peter could feel the freshness and excitement of their first experience onstage at the Blue Mountain Rose wearing off.

Tech work required patience from the actors, who might have to stop abruptly and stand in place for as long as ten minutes while crew refocused lights or musicians set their notes into the action or Richard fiddled with blocking to achieve just the right picture.

All the actors had to find ways to keep themselves moving through the work with good energy. They made a game of finding the board that creaked the loudest, adding note after note to Tahoma's list of things to be fixed before opening. Everyone looked forward to the big Tuesday run-through, when they would perform the entire work with only one break, for intermission. But they had to finish tech first.

Bryce was still upset over Freja, which meant Peter was upset, but he didn't see there was much he could do but endure his friend's mute anger and hope it eased. He'd tried to apologize backstage on Sunday, but Bryce shrugged him off with a muttered "Not here." Onstage, he met Peter's eyes when the blocking called for it.

Fortunately, they just had the three scenes together, and they'd already survived the first. Peter could only hope he would survive the second, where Hamlet and Laertes wrestle over the corpse of Ophelia, and the third—in which Laertes would seek to kill him. *I'd better check the rapiers myself,* Peter thought.

He'd made his peace with Freja in a quick call Sunday afternoon. She cut him off mid-apology with the question, "What are you apologizing for? We both knew what that was." Evidently, it was triumphant closure for Freja, who hadn't liked being the one who got left when *Macbeth* closed. Now she could say, "It was fun! But that's all I'm looking for." Peter didn't even have to say what he was looking for, which was fine; he didn't relish the idea of putting Kate's image into Freja's head.

Not that he had reason to. He knew that door was closed.

Tahoma had set a fight call for just after lunch, giving the other actors a longer break so Devon could work with Peter and Bryce. "I'll time it, to see how long you'll need on performance days," he'd told the choreographer. Fight call was required before every performance, giving the actors time to get their minds and bodies ready. The athletic choreography was both a battle and a dance, intricate in its patterns. Bryce and Peter were seasoned pros, and their weapons stage props with dulled points and edges, but they were still metal tools. Fight call was just part of the bargain.

Peter felt butterflies in his stomach as he checked in. He looked at Bryce, who looked away with a set jaw.

"Get your heart rates up, and then it's rapiers and daggers for you," Devon said.

"Warm up together, Bryce?" Peter offered and was glad to receive a "Sure" in return, though Bryce didn't smile as he began following Peter through jumping jacks, then dynamic stretches.

When they told Devon they were ready, the choreographer said, "Go on, then. Peter, you're the rabbit." Peter walked carefully down the steps into the yard, then began jogging with Bryce on his heels. He darted to the right; behind him, Bryce adjusted. Now left, then a reverse of directions, and Bryce was close behind him still, mirroring his movements. Peter began feeling like a rabbit indeed, one pursued by a hungry wolf.

Finally, Devon called, "Halt!" and the actors stopped, breathing hard. "Good run," Peter told Bryce, who didn't answer.

Tahoma had wheeled out the wooden cart that held four stage rapiers and two daggers. Onstage, Peter walked over to select his weapons. Bryce hung back until he was finished.

The stage now set, Devon cued them with, "'Come, begin. And you, the judges, bear a wary eye.'"

Looking at Bryce, Peter said, "Or how about if we go from Hamlet's earlier lines: 'Give me your pardon, sir. I have done you wrong; But pardon 't as you are a gentleman.'" *Worth a try.*

Bryce narrowed his eyes. "Too early. We don't need to start there. 'Come, begin' is fine."

Devon called "Places," and Peter crossed to his mark. On Devon's cue, Peter and Bryce raised the swept hilts of their rapiers to their foreheads, then settled into fighting stance.

"'Come on, sir,'" Peter said.

"'Come, my lord,'" Bryce replied, with a note of sarcasm not called for in the script.

The choreography of the first "phrase," as Devon called it, was gentlemanly, "by the book." In Shakespeare's day, a rapier was a courtier's dress sword, and the goal of a demonstration fight for points, such as King Claudius had set for Hamlet and Laertes, would have been to maintain honor and demonstrate skill, not injure the opponent.

"'One,'" Peter said at the proper moment.

"'No,'" Bryce called out dismissively.

"'Judgment!'" Peter said, looking to Devon, who read Osric's line: "'A hit, a very palpable hit.'"

"'Well, again.'" Bryce gave Peter a glare that was in keeping with the scene but a bit strong for fight call.

"Bryce, come on," Peter said. "'Let my disclaiming from a purposed evil free me so far in your most generous thoughts: that I have shot my arrow o'er the house and hurt my brother.'"

"Wrong lines. It's 'I'll play this bout first.'"

"I know my lines. I'm trying to apologize."

"'You mock me, sir,'" Bryce told him, using earlier lines spoken by Laertes.

"Second phrase now, guys," interrupted Devon.

"All good," Peter answered. Then to Bryce, on cue, "'I'll play this bout first. Set it by awhile. Come.'"

He and Bryce moved through the second phrase, which took longer and was slightly less courtly than the first. They used the daggers in this one to block each other's points: "Starting to mess with each other's heads and show a higher skill level at the same time," according to Devon. But Peter was distracted and missed a defensive step backward, which put Bryce right up in his face. Bryce swept his weapons out to his sides. "Start over."

"Sorry, mate." Peter hung his head.

"You keep saying that, but I don't know what you're sorry for."

"Second phrase again, guys." Devon's voice was firm. "Let's get it right."

Peter concentrated, and his steps were in place this time. As he passed Bryce and turned, he said quietly, "For Freja." Then, touching Bryce lightly on the back with the point of his rapier, he said more loudly for Devon's benefit, "'Another hit. What say you?'"

Turning, Bryce lifted the hilt to his forehead. "'A touch, a touch. I do confess 't.'"

"And I'm really sorry for it. I was a jerk to both of you," Peter said.

Devon growled, "Can we stick to the script, please? Let's skip ahead to 'Come, for the third.'"

"No, let's hold a second, fight master, if we can. I need to talk to Bryce." Peter ignored Bryce's groan.

"Two minutes," Devon said.

"Thank you Two," Bryce and Peter replied in unison.

As Devon busied himself upstage to give them some privacy, Bryce said, "You don't have to apologize. You didn't do anything to me. It's between you and Freja. And Kate, I guess."

"And you. I wish I'd made a better decision. But I didn't, and it hurt you to see us together, and I'm sorry."

Bryce tried to shake it off, but Peter, who knew he had another apology ahead, wanted to get this one right. "Bryce. I was a jerk, and I admit it freely. You've been a staunch mate ever since I came here. You stood up for me half a dozen times. In a bar fight, you're the person I'd pick for my side."

When Bryce snorted, Peter continued: "'Since my dear soul was mistress of her choice and could of men distinguish, her election hath sealed thee for herself.' What I mean is, of all the people I could hurt, you're the last one I'd want to. Except for Kate," he admitted.

"What about Freja?" Bryce asked.

"We talked. She says it was just the one time, for old time's sake. I wish it hadn't even come to that."

Bryce considered his words. "If they're OK, then I guess I am."

"You've always been on my side, but I failed you when it mattered. Forgive me, yes?"

"I can write it up to the big day you had. It's not like I've ever been chased by paparazzi. But I know what it's like to be strung out on adrenalin." Bryce paused, shaking his head. "How else could you pull off the cabaret show you did?"

"With your help, and Freja's."

"Thanks."

Peter put out his hand. "'Give me that man that is not passion's slave, and I will wear him in my heart's core, ay, in my heart of heart, as I do thee.'"

Bryce took it. "'Something too much of this,'" he quoted wryly. "Shall we get back to stabbing each other with daggers?"

ACT 4

SCENE 7

PETER, RICHARD

Tuesday morning, Peter woke up from a dream of being chased by hissing beetles through a forest of leafless trees. *Those trees were grabbing at me, too,* he thought, recalling their tugs even as daylight seeped in through his closed eyelids and lured him into wakefulness. Then, grimly: *No need to guess where that dream came from.*

He finally gave up on sleep and sat upright, looking around the cozy guest room Richard had lent him. *What am I doing in Richard Keane's house?* he wondered, and not for the first time.

He looked toward his suitcases and boxes sitting by the door. Tech had given him a convenient excuse to delay unpacking, but he couldn't put it off any longer.

Stirring from bed, he pulled on sweatpants and a T-shirt. He dreaded setting up house again, but it wasn't the repetition alone that bothered him. It was his mother's scarf, her perfume, the photos. Always before, he'd set them on a windowsill where they could catch the light. He'd talk to her as he placed things just right, telling her about his new place. It felt important to let her spirit know that no matter what, she was with him.

Not here. He couldn't imagine uttering the words, "Hi, Mum," in Richard Keane's house, or setting out her pictures where Richard could see them. But what then? If he didn't tell her, would she know where he was? If he didn't talk with his mother, how could he get through the next few months alone?

After yoga, he heard Richard moving around upstairs, so he threw on a fresh T-shirt and walked upstairs to the kitchen. *I'm a guest in the home of Richard James Aloysius Keane, lion of the theater, and who am I to be fed breakfast by such an august personage?* His stomach knotted with the same nervous tension he'd felt when he and Richard first met.

But when he walked into the kitchen, it was just Richard, wearing a dressing gown and slippers. Not a theatrical god, just Richard, the person he'd been meeting with since March, silver hair pointing in several directions, looking smaller and more ordinary in his morning attire than he normally did in the tailored suits he wore at work.

Richard was unloading the dishwasher, a decidedly mundane act. Peter felt a wave of affection and was surprised at himself. He'd held back for months, watching Richard, looking for a sign, but his heart had made its own assessment, it seemed.

"Good morning, lad," Richard said, turning. "You're a tea man, I assume?" When Peter nodded, caught speechless, Richard busied himself with a copper teapot at the six-burner stove.

"Shall I whip up veggie eggs for breakfast?" Peter finally asked. "I'll order in groceries today so I don't eat you out of house and home."

"I'm not worried by it, but if you want to scramble some eggs, I wouldn't say no. Toast?"

It was comfortable sharing the kitchen with Richard; Peter decided to stop marveling at it or questioning himself and simply relax. He had enough to worry about with the first full run-through tonight.

Richard, too, had decided to relax about something and stop worrying about how to bring it up. *All in good time.*

Once they were seated at the breakfast table, steaming plates of eggs in front of them, Peter said, "I don't know that I ever properly thanked you for taking me in, but I want to. Thank you for letting me stay here. It's, erm, an unexpected treat and certainly beyond the call of duty."

A gracious lad, Richard thought. *His mother raised him well. Of course she did.*

"The pleasure is mine. I'm glad of your company." Then, seeing his opening: "I knew your mother, you know. Helen."

Peter had taken a sip of tea at just the wrong moment and commenced coughing, finally worrying Richard so much that the older man rose and patted the younger man on the back until Peter gathered the strength to wave him off.

"I'm all right; just took some tea down the wrong pipe."

So casual, Peter thought. *"I knew your mother, you know."*

"She came here with a company in the early 1970s. Perhaps you weren't aware?"

Peter fought through the roaring in his ears to force out, "Yeah, I knew she'd played here. It was her only time in the States, I think. I just didn't know you knew. That she was my mum, I mean."

"Arthur Ryerson told me a few days back. Thought I'd given him the name of my Hamlet a month ago, but it turned out not. Your mother played Rosalind for the Rose. Incomparable. Among the finest actors I've ever directed."

And that's all? Did you give her another thought once she left? Aloud, Peter said, "Yes, she was a terrific actor, and she loved the work. Shakespeare, especially, I think."

Richard hesitated. "I'm sorry for your loss. I was shocked when I heard."

MY loss. The roaring in Peter's ears was getting louder, but he'd had to respond to expressions of sympathy so often in the past year that it came easily now simply by the fact of much practice. "Thank you, yes. Erm, it was a shock to all of us."

Peter forced himself to glance at Richard and was surprised to see the older man fighting with a series of emotions. *Hold on,* Peter thought. *Is Richard Keane nearly in tears?*

They sat in silence a moment, each at the edge of his own precipice, wrestling their emotions for reasons that couldn't have been more similar, both choosing to do so in private. *Was it* MY *loss,* Peter wondered, *or ours?*

Finally, he cleared his throat and picked up his teacup. "Delicious tea," he said.

ACT 4
SCENE 8

KATE, RICHARD, PETER

The actors were called for one o'clock, giving them time to dress, warm up, and do their makeup before the final run-through began at two. Then they would present the entire show from first line to last, without the pauses they'd had during tech.

The run-through was private, but Kate and others on staff had been called, as had Gavriella and her key assistants. Tahoma's seating chart gave them all the worst seats in the house—not that there were any truly bad seats at the Rose. They would sit in the back row and corners of the upstairs galleries, monitoring sight lines and sound levels to make sure every paying patron could see and hear the action.

Kate chose third tier balcony corner stage left, hoping to avoid sitting in Peter's view. She had the idea that seeing her might throw him off; she wasn't sure why. He was a pro. But he had avoided her at the cast dinners during tech, or really, they had avoided each other. Once, she'd sent a smile his way. He'd returned it, then ducked his head and turned away. *Feeling guilty,* she'd thought. *As he should.*

Today he won't see me at all. That was Kate's intention. This was a big week for Peter and all the actors, and Kate had lived in their world for a long time. She knew this was no moment to rock the boat.

The actors from *Midsummer* came in as a raucous group just before curtain. They were there to "lean forward," encouraging their comrades onstage with timely responses, giving the *Hamlet* cast their first sense of how a real audience might behave. In a clump, they laughed and chatted as they claimed seats in the center gallery. Freja was among them, of course. Kate felt a bit sick as she watched Peter's lover—*former lover*, she told herself sternly—cross the yard in the middle of the gang. *Evidently, she has no qualms about sitting in Peter's view.*

Yellow legal pad at the ready, Richard sat next to Tahoma at the production table and took notes as he watched it all unfold. He might also provide comments after the public dress rehearsal the next day, but by and large, this was his last chance to catch anything he might want to change.

It has a pleasing shape, he thought. Peter made a brilliant Hamlet, focused and intense. Though the rest of the cast were all excellent in their own right, a central performer of his caliber raised their game. Their director was gratified, but one bit didn't yet satisfy him: the final part of act 5, scene 2, in which all the surviving major characters but Horatio meet their ends.

After the run-through, as the actors went backstage to change out of costume, Richard received reports from staff seated throughout the house. Both Kate at upper left corner, and Gavriella at lowest right corner, had found it difficult to see the faces of key characters at crucial moments in that final scene.

This won't do. "I'd like to call the actors for just the last part of five-two back here after dinner," Richard told Tahoma. "No costumes. We'll walk it a couple of times and try different things. We'll need people sitting in the corners again. Who wants to come back for us? Katherine?"

"I have Beth," Kate reminded Richard.

"Bring Elizabeth with you," he suggested.

"To watch her friend Peter die a few times, so we can gauge sight lines?" Kate asked. "I'd rather not."

"Of course! I stand corrected." Richard found the volunteers he needed among the rest of the staff.

After a quiet dinner on his own in Calliope's Grove, Peter rejoined his scene partners onstage, where they were loosening up in an unstructured way. He began stretching his neck and shoulders.

"Ready to die by the sword?" called Bryce.

"Hamlet will acquit himself well enough!" LaShia jumped to Hamlet's defense, the loyal Horatio even when not in character. "And against someone who's supposed to have a fearsome reputation," she taunted Bryce.

Peter quoted, "'I'll be your foil, Laertes; in mine ignorance your skill shall, like a star i' th' darkest night, stick fiery off indeed.'"

"Live by the sword, die by the sword," said Ted, "though I don't think it applies here since Hamlet lives more by his books than by swordplay."

"His books or his looks?" LaShia teased.

"What is all this talk of swordplay?" asked Isabelle. "I thought we would pass by the swordplay tonight."

"I think the third phrase is essential," Richard said from the yard. "Bryce, Peter, do you want to use the props?"

"We can mime it, and I think it will be faster that way," Peter answered. Bryce agreed.

"Then it shall be so," Richard said. "Let's start from the King's line, 'Our son shall win.'"

"Places," Tahoma called.

They played it once as they had when the scene was blocked, with Richard standing in the yard at stage left, watching the sight lines along with his helpers in the galleries. Peter's final mark was on a creaky board. "That won't do at all," Richard said. As Tahoma made a note to have the board nailed down more tightly, Richard asked Peter to adjust downstage.

On the second round, Peter adjusted perfectly. After a quick conference, Richard gave notes to Isabelle and Ted, shifting their final positions. Then he went to stand at stage right, to make sure he hadn't cost one side too much in benefiting the other.

How many times must we play this? Peter thought. *The scene in which Hamlet watches his mother die? I'm prepared to do it four times a week in performance, but four times in one night?*

They played it again; again a conference; a fourth run. By this time, the actors were tiring, Peter especially. The day had been a long one, and he was drained. Once more:

> Hamlet: How does the Queen?
>
> King: She swoons to see them bleed.
>
> Queen: No, no, the drink, the drink! O, my dear Hamlet!
>
> The drink, the drink! I am poisoned. *She dies.*

Holding as Richard and his helpers conferenced, Peter thought again about the moment when Hamlet sees Queen Gertrude die by treachery. *That's when my peaceful, thoughtful prince finally finds the rage to commit murder. I understand it: Chemo was a poison, and I would have walked a thousand miles through hell to kill Mum's cancer.*

An image he always fought to keep from consciousness now rose before his mind's eye: his mother's wan face as she lay in her hospital bed on that last, longest day. *It's only when I'm really tired that I see you this way, Mum,* he apologized. *God-a-mercy, what does it matter? There is no good death here; no good death anywhere.*

Peter took a breath, trying to calm himself, but he was shivering.

When it mattered, I was helpless. Maybe that's why I've been so angry this whole time, fighting Onyxx's fans as if they were out to kill me. Hamlet at least has an enemy he can see.

Richard's voice broke through his distraction. "One more time and that's done. We're nearly to it."

When Tahoma called "Places," Peter drew a deep breath, sure he wouldn't be able to move a step. Then a new face appeared in his mind: Kate's. *I miss her laughter,* he thought, *and the contentment in her face when I caught her watching Beth and me doing maths.*

Love can stir a man to action, too. Try to be worthy of it. Taking another breath, he crossed to his mark opposite Laertes once more.

ACT 4

SCENE 9

PETER

Peter woke up late and groggy on Wednesday, the day of dress rehearsal. *I'd rather stay asleep awhile longer*, he thought. But though he tried, he couldn't return to the dreaming world. Nor could he force himself out of bed. He lay in its cushioned luxury, looking out through the French doors at the nearby forest, thinking about nothing.

Distant sounds filtered in, of Richard puttering around upstairs, a cupboard door slamming; then Richard's voice, chiding Tybalt for some feline transgression. Still, Peter didn't stir.

The list of things to do began fluttering through his mind. He had two major media interviews at the theatre today, one for the American television show *CBS News Sunday Morning*, the other for *American Theatre* magazine, plus three phone interviews. And, of course, preparing for and performing *Hamlet* for a full house on the Rose stage for the first time. *Let's not forget that,* he thought wryly.

As was tradition at the Rose, high school students and their families would make up the dress rehearsal audience. Most upper-level English classes at the town's high schools had focused on *Hamlet* during the spring semester, and their teachers offered credit for attending this show. *I hope it's Hamlet they come to see, and not Onyxx. Not much I can do about it either way.*

His thoughts had the weight and substance of butterfly wings, appearing swiftly and as swiftly gone. Still, he lay in bed, stirring only to glance over at the windowsill where, last night after the run-through, he'd set his mother's photos, her scarf, and her perfume. The crystal bottle glittered in the sunlight now, flinging shards of pale gold into the room.

Shite, Mum, do you hate that I'm here, looking for the answer you couldn't give? He asked his ghost. He listened for her voice, wishing for the thousandth time he held the key that would open the door to a real conversation with her. As always, the door stayed locked. His mother had packed her bags and moved to "the undiscovered country from whose bourn no traveler returns" without sending a forwarding address. If any answer came to his question, he knew it would reflect his own hopes or fears alone.

"O, my prophetic soul!" Hamlet cries out when the Ghost tells him that his uncle is a murderer. *It's the explanation he's been looking for, to make sense of his overwhelming grief. He's right to wonder whether it's an honest ghost or just a reflection of his own tormented mind. If the soldiers and Horatio didn't also see that haunting spirit, this would be a different play; more like real life. More like my life.*

On the nightstand, his phone buzzed. A text from Martin. "Can you dance?"

"I'm flattered, but I prefer partners of the female persuasion," Peter texted back, setting the phone down in irritation. Quickly, it buzzed again.

"Broadway: a Sinatra jukebox musical, choreo Twyla Tharp, previews March."

"A bit grand for me," Peter typed.

"Broadway: Merchant of Venice? Al Pacino rumored attached."

Peter drew a breath and released it slowly. *Be grateful*, he reminded himself, but it was hard to muster the energy. "Maybe," he typed, then turned off the phone.

A tentative knock at the door told Peter the morning was passing. "Peter, lad, you up? Would you like breakfast?"

"I'm up," Peter lied. "Just doing yoga. I'm not hungry yet. Nerves, I guess."

"I'll leave you to it." As Richard's steps faded, Peter returned to his haunting thoughts.

Do you hate me for being here, Mum, or were you behind it all along? Did you chase me from my Denmark to the nutshell to Jaime's starship to this—I don't even know what to call it—"rat hole" seems accurate if I'm the namesake rat. Did you want me here in Richard's house all along?

Peter's mind wandered awhile across the terrain of yesterday morning's conversation with Richard. *Has he mourned my mum, too, this past year?* Try as he might, Peter couldn't force any other interpretation on Richard's anguished face when they ventured out beyond where words could go. He'd been on the verge of tears, Peter felt sure.

Why would Richard grieve my mum? What's Helen to him, or he to Helen, that he should weep for her? Peter paraphrased. *Truly, Mum, what were you to Richard Keane?*

Peter closed his eyes, listening. Silence.

Is it possible you two were more than you said?

Still no answer.

Then his eyes flew open at the thought, *There is one person in this house who might answer the questions that plague my dreams, and he isn't the dullard in this bed. I'm here, whether I should be or no. And it's time this rat left his hole.*

When Peter entered the kitchen, Richard stood up from the table with a welcoming smile. "Sit! I'll start water for tea. Big day for you today! Let me know what you'd like to eat, and I'll make it."

"Big day for everyone," Peter managed to say. "One of many for you."

"Always exciting, dress," Richard agreed. "I can guarantee a full and enthusiastic house. The students have been focusing on *Hamlet*; they may be our best-prepared audience all season."

Moving to the breakfast table, Peter pulled out a chair. "I expect to have company when I launch into 'To be or not to be.'"

"I expect you're right," Richard laughed. "Good, you're prepared for it. Stay in your own lane and pay them no mind. I doubt they'll have the other speeches down by heart." Peter laughed half-heartedly along with him, but the sound soon died away. Richard gave his actor a long, appraising look.

"Darjeeling or English Breakfast?" he asked. When Peter expressed an interest in the latter, Richard added three bags to a teapot and poured in boiling water, carrying the pot to the table to steep. Tybalt leaped onto Peter's lap. He twined his fingers in the cat's thick black fur.

"How are your nerves?" Richard asked as he pulled out a chair. "Did you have a good yoga session?"

Peter met his eyes. "To be honest, I haven't done my yoga yet. I was having trouble getting out of bed this morning."

"Ah. Don't let it get the better of you, lad."

Hiding a sigh, Peter answered, "It's not nerves, or at least I think not. Last night's rehearsal took it out of me a bit."

Richard leaned back in his chair.

"I started thinking about my mum and couldn't shake it. I've thought about her before, of course, doing that scene, but somehow the repetition made it tougher than it's ever been."

"*Hamlet* is a difficult play for someone who's recently lost a parent." Richard's voice held a warm note of empathy. "Grief isn't an undercurrent here, it's an ocean; those tides drive much of the action. But we've run it through, and now that the choreography is set, you'll do fine."

"I don't know, Richard. When it comes to it, I just don't know."

"You have a great Hamlet in you, and it's due at least in part to her. You'll be honoring her legacy when you go out on that stage, final scene and all."

"Oh, yes, the show must go on and all that." Peter's voice had acquired some heat. "No matter what happens, you're five minutes early for call and grateful for the work."

"The work matters, lad. The work is what will get you through. You can trust me on that."

Lad, Peter thought. *He's called me that since our first days together.*

"Can I?" he wondered aloud. Tybalt jumped to the floor and stalked away, tail held high.

"You're grieving her; of course you are. But your mother of all people would want you to show up and give it your best. She was a trouper."

"Yes, and more than that." Peter could no longer hold his tongue. "To you."

"Ah." Richard shifted uncomfortably in his chair. "So she was."

Peter had been holding his breath. Now he let it out slowly. "What was she? Please, tell me."

"This is; well. This is more than I thought to discuss over toast and tea."

Peter searched Richard's face. "I can't . . . I have to know. Were the two of you—"

"Lovers?" Richard returned Peter's gaze for a moment before dropping his eyes. "Aye," he confessed. "For a short while, until she left for London, never to return. How did you know? Surely she never spoke of it? Of me?"

"She did, just once," Peter said, adding reluctantly, "toward the end." Now it was his turn to look down. "She didn't say for how long."

"Not long enough," Richard said after a moment. "Not nearly long enough."

"But Richard, if you were lovers—if you loved her?—did you know? I mean, did she ever—did she tell you?"

"You've lost me," Richard said patiently.

Peter forced himself to say the words. "Did she ever tell you about me?"

The two men sat looking at each other for a moment that seemed eternal to Peter.

"About you?" Richard broke the silence with a whisper. His shock answered the question that had gripped Peter's heart since their breakfast-table conversation the day before.

"What about…you?"

"Richard, I'm sorry. I didn't mean to tell you this way. Mum would never have—"

"You're not saying you're my…you're mine?"

"I—I guess I'm saying I don't know. I wondered if you did."

Richard shook his head as if to clear it. "Wait one moment. What do you mean?"

"She didn't know, and that's the truth. She told me she wasn't sure."

Peter watched as Richard stood and walked to the cupboard where plates were stacked. His back to Peter, he opened it, but then didn't move. *I've lost him*, Peter thought.

"She said after she came home, she and my—Bert, I mean—when she figured out she was pregnant, it wasn't clear who the father was," he explained to Richard's motionless back. "And I gather it wasn't simple to get a paternity test. She would've had to tell Bert why. She hated to admit that to me, but she felt she needed to, before—"

Still facing the cupboard, Richard cleared his throat.

Unable to stop the flow of words he'd held back for so many months, Peter continued, "When you and I talked yesterday, and I saw how sad you were, I started to wonder if maybe she'd told you something. Back then? Or since?"

"No." The word seemed to be pulled up from the bottom of a deep well. "Once she left here, she never spoke to me again."

"I'm sorry, Richard. As you said, this is a lot to talk about over tea."

Richard's shoulders rose, then fell as he released a breath. "Please; please. I can't quite seem to take it in. Could you just…" He shook his head. "I'll need some time."

Fighting back the urge to stand and put an arm around those taut shoulders, Peter answered formally, "Of course. I'm sorry."

Richard turned away from the cupboard, only to busy himself at the sink. "I know you have press rounds to make," he said, his voice gathering strength. "We both need to be on our game today."

"Richard—"

Again, Richard shook his head. "Your news has given me much to think on, but I need to get to the office." He wouldn't meet Peter's eyes. "Have Kate come and give you a ride when you're ready."

Peter admitted, "Kate won't want to."

Richard's eyes flicked to Peter's hangdog face, then away. "Ring Tahoma. He'll arrange something. I shall see you tonight at call."

It wasn't a question.

ACT 4

SCENE 10

PETER

That went well, Peter thought as he descended the stairs to his rat hole, a plate of cheese toast in one hand, a teacup in the other.

His phone was on the bedside table. He picked it up to see another missed call from Bert.

Maybe after yoga, he told himself, taking his breakfast outside and setting it on the patio table. Birds flittered about near Richard's feeders: hungry juncos and finches, a swarm of territorial hummingbirds. Peter watched them as he ate, trying to ignore the heaviness in his heart that told him he'd done the wrong thing in telling Richard anything at all.

She wouldn't have wanted me to do it, especially not that way, he eventually admitted. *And what did I gain from it? He obviously didn't know. Nobody does.*

Peter's thoughts wandered back to the morning when his mother finally broke her silence about Richard. It was sunny then, too, but the view from the hospital window, across the rooftops of London, hadn't been nearly this nice.

They were all coming to terms with her leaving, in their various ways. Bert kept a stiff upper lip, acknowledging the situation only when forced to and falling back on platitudes rather than expressing any emotion. Peter's older brother, Luke, on the other hand, went to pieces on the day of the diagnosis and spent the long months fabricating ways to be elsewhere. When Peter confronted him, he said, "I just can't do it; I can't stand by and watch her die."

Peter had found little to say to his brother ever since. *My way of dealing with it was to get angry at everybody, I guess, and I've stayed angry this whole time.* Only Helen had pierced through her younger son's fierce exterior to the sorrowing heart within.

They'd broken the rules that morning when Helen asked Peter to crawl in beside her. He'd curled his tall frame into the hospital bed alongside his frail mother, careful of the lines connecting her to the machines.

It was hard to remember exactly what she'd said, though Peter had tried a hundred times. He tried again now, tea cooling on the table beside him.

"I need to tell you a secret." He knew she'd started with that. But how had she told him about Richard? Was it "We had an affair" or "I was in love with him"? And then she'd said, "So he was your father, or might have been, anyway."

At first, he'd laughed, unsure how to interpret her words. The pain medications were powerful. There were times she was clear, and times she wasn't. This seemed like one of the clear times, but when she said something so fantastical, it was hard to know. He told himself he didn't want her to say anything she would regret later. Then he realized how silly that was, given her diagnosis.

"What d'you mean, Mum?" he'd asked. When she blushed, he realized she was embarrassed. He hated to make her uncomfortable. But he had to know.

"Are you saying you and Richard Keane—were you pregnant?" he'd asked.

Then she'd shushed him, looking over his shoulder, and he'd looked, too, sure someone had come into her room. Seeing nobody, he'd turned back to search her eyes and asked again.

"Might have been," she'd repeated shyly.

He remembered asking, if she hadn't told Richard about the possibility, why not? And if she loved Richard, why hadn't she left Bert?

He remembered her voice, a faded echo of its former power. *"It wasn't so easy as you might imagine. I had Luke to think of, as well as you, and he was just seven, very tender and vulnerable, you know him. I couldn't think of uprooting him and going to America on a maybe."* That, Peter recalled clearly.

It had all been so much to take in, and when she had said she was tired and they could come back to it once Peter had time to get used to the idea, he had agreed.

Then she went downhill so fast, it seemed cruel to bring it up again. It was like unburdening herself of that secret gave her the peace to let go.

What would my life have been like if Mum had returned to Richard? The thought was beguiling, a familiar siren luring him into fantasy. *Growing up here, surrounded by people who loved theater, with a dad who*...and here, his thoughts broke away. *I did grow up surrounded by people who loved theater*, he reminded himself. *And I have no idea what Richard would have been like as a father. I only know one man that way, and it isn't him.*

Leaving his teacup and plate on the table, Peter went inside and picked up the phone.

Bert answered on the second ring with his usual gruff "Hullo." The two men exchanged small talk for as long as Peter could stand it, which wasn't long. Striving to be more thoughtful with Bert than he'd been with Richard, Peter finally said, "I'm sorry I've been ducking your calls, but there's a reason for it, and I'd like to come clean."

"Oh, yes?" Bert replied.

"I'm not in New Zealand anymore, to start."

He heard Bert's dry chuckle. "I know. Curtis and Esther Clark rang me up when they saw the photo of you running in the Arizona mountains. 'We thought he was in New Zealand,' they said. 'So did I,' says I."

"Oh." The air rushed out of Peter's lungs. "So you know I'm playing Hamlet at the Blue Mountain Rose?"

"You open this week."

"That's right."

"Break a leg, son."

"Thanks, erm—yeah."

"I may be wrong, but I don't imagine you're there by accident. Tell me, then. What's he like, this Richard?"

Thoroughly shocked, Peter paused. *Bert knows?* He briefly considered saying, "Richard who?" or otherwise pretending not to understand the import of Bert's question, but if he hadn't called to make amends, why call at all?

"Charismatic, I guess? Brilliant when it comes to Shakespeare in performance. Accustomed to being in charge." Peter realized he didn't want to say anything Bert might take as a comparison that cast him in an unflattering light. *I've caused enough sorrow for one day. Please don't make me say more.*

"A pale, handsome Irish devil with fearsome good looks and the voice to match, I've always imagined," Bert said.

"I don't—I can't judge that, but I suppose yes, he is good-looking."

"As are you, and always have been."

"Me?" The word came out as a squeak.

"Aye, of course you. Who d'ya think?"

Peter cleared his throat. "What about me? What did Mum tell you?"

"I figured it out on my own. Didn't want to believe it; didn't want to know. But one day, I took a long look at this fresh-minted coin of a miracle son who had his mother's green eyes, her light hair, good looks that haven't been seen in my family for generations, if ever they were. I looked at my other son, short like me, dark as a rainy day on Loch Canaird. The truth was too plain to ignore."

There it is, then. And Bert's known all along.

"When was it? How old was I?"

"Oh, you must have been seven or eight then, and Luke fifteen, I would say."

"Did you think about telling me?"

"No, no. That wasn't mine to tell."

Peter thought back to his childhood. He'd never been particularly close to Bert, but until his mother's revelation, he always imagined that was just how fathers were with their sons. If he thought about it at all, he chalked it up to the well-known lid the British keep on their emotional lives. It wasn't until after his mother told him of her affair with Richard that Peter wondered about the true source of his father's emotional distance.

"Are you angry?"

"Angry? No. Angry at what?"

"I dunno. At Richard? Mum?" He paused. "Me?"

"It was a very long time ago, you know. I've had time to get past it."

"Did you—did it change how you felt about me?"

"Well now. I don't know as I can answer that. I tried to treat you both the same as always."

Fair enough. I never felt like Luke got the inside track with him. There was no inside track.

"Can I ask—what did Mum say when you told her you'd guessed?"

"May as well ask it. I said to her, 'I can forgive it if only you'll tell me the truth.'"

"And she did?"

"She told me some, aye. She'd been sad when we didn't set a young brother or sister on Luke's heels when he was wee. I was working all the time, not giving her the attention she deserved. She'd been lonely when she went to America, and someone there made her feel special again. Said she wasn't sure which of us was your da. I suppose it would have been too much for her, admitting the truth of it after the years that had passed. Even to herself. But I could see it plain."

The two men paused, considering. Peter felt an odd desire to comfort Bert; after all, the man had lived with the consequences of Helen's choices for far longer than Peter himself had. And evidently with more grace.

"I think she must have loved you very much," Peter finally said. "She probably could have come back here, at least early on, but she didn't. She chose to stay with you."

"Well. I loved her too, innit. I tried everything I could to never let her feel lonely again, or unappreciated."

"I know that." Peter thought back on family outings to the seaside and date nights when their parents left him and Luke with sitters. "You did right by her, Dad."

Bert cleared his throat. "When your mum told me what she'd told you," he began, pausing to clear his throat again. "That's when I knew she was leaving us for sure. She'd stopped fooling herself. As she had done out of pride, I think, and a sort of protectiveness toward you and Luke, and because she wanted you to remember her a certain way."

Tears sprang to Peter's eyes. "I do remember her that way! But we're all human, aren't we?"

"I suppose we are."

"It doesn't change how I feel about her, knowing about what happened. I see the choices she made, and I just wish I could tell her—" Peter stopped, unable to speak past the emotion choking his throat.

"Well then," Bert said to cover the silence.

"Yeah," Peter echoed. *Richard may be my father in terms of biology, but Bert is my dad,* he thought wryly. *Just listen to the two of us.*

"I'm happy you rang me up," Bert said. "I've been hoping to hear from you."

"I think she would be glad." Peter looked at her photos and the patterned scarf she'd worn when chemo claimed her hair. "That we finally talked, I mean. Say hullo to Luke for me, would you?"

"That I will."

"And Da?" Peter tried to stuff everything into two words, hoping the man who'd stood by his mother and tried to be a decent father to both his sons could hear everything he meant. "Thank you."

ACT 4
SCENE 11

Kate, Peter

"Richard's in a mood," Gavriella confided when she saw Kate unlocking her office door.

Kate lifted her eyebrows. "He doesn't usually get nervous about dress, but he's directing, and with retirement on the horizon—"

"I don't think it's that. He's grouchy at the world. When I checked in to tell him everything was ready for tonight, he said, 'I expected nothing less,' and that was it. Brevity isn't Richard."

"He may have something on his mind," Kate said as she and her friend parted. Musing on the possibilities, given his new roommate, Kate was preoccupied as she walked into her tidy office to find none other than Richard himself sitting in her guest chair. She shut the door and moved around her desk with a cheerful, "Good morning, Richard! Happy dress."

"Mmmm? Oh, yes. Happy dress, and all that."

Kate looked him over quickly but carefully, taking in his slightly disarranged hair. It was the only detail out of place in an otherwise impeccable presentation comprising a lavender shirt, a lavender and peach tie, and an elegant dark suit with a subtle peach pinstripe.

"What can I do for you?" she asked. *This is going to be something about Peter, I'm guessing.*

"How's the house tonight? Are we full up?" he asked. As company house manager, Gavriella always shared that report a few hours before every performance, but any staff member could run it, including Richard if he'd been of a mind to. Apparently, he wasn't of a mind to. So Kate ran it, engaging Richard in talk about the sold-out houses they anticipated once the show opened Friday night. That should have perked him up, but he remained dour even when she set the report in his hand.

"The yard will be filled with teenagers, as usual, and their parents have claimed all the seats except the last rows in the middle and upper balconies," Kate said. "That's a big crowd, for dress. No doubt some are coming to see the movie star, but I'll bet they're also excited to see their studies play out in real life in the *Hamlet* performance."

"Another dress," Richard said, his voice heavy. "Would that this year were behind us. To be safely ensconced in Tucson, a book on my lap and a tumbler of Jameson's ready to hand."

"It's been stressful, but things get easier starting tonight."

"Do they?"

"Of course. We're dark tomorrow. After the show goes up Friday, Tahoma will hold the reins. Do you have media calls today?"

"Serena has done her usual masterful job of setting all that in play, aided no doubt by the added attraction of, as you call him, 'the movie star.' I have three calls before lunch, and something in person at two o'clock in the Rose, 'for the atmosphere.'"

Kate smiled. "Those will be fun. You have every reason to be proud of your *Hamlet*."

"*My* Hamlet," Richard mused, sounding quite far away.

"Is something on your mind, Richard?" Kate asked, trying to bring him back into the room.

Richard gave her a searching look before shaking his head. "It's not my mind that's burdened."

"Is it Peter's? Something about Peter, I mean?"

"That, I can't say. Not with the two of you on the outs as I gather you are."

Kate held his gaze, determined not to give herself away.

"The lad and I had words this morning, and it's left me a bit at sea," Richard admitted finally.

"You two had a fight? I'm sorry to hear it."

"Not a fight. Words were exchanged. But we mustn't let it shift us from our course today."

"Are you—is it—did you work it out?" Kate asked.

"That would have required mighty effort on both our parts, which we could not give; the tincture of time, which we do not have; and perhaps divine intervention, upon which we did not call."

"So, no, you didn't work it out?"

Richard jutted out his jaw. "That is what I said."

"Well, I hope you will, and soon. With dress tonight, there isn't much time today, I know. But maybe tomorrow?"

"'Tomorrow and tomorrow and tomorrow creeps in this petty pace from day to day to the last syllable of recorded time.'" Richard rose from the chair. He was still quoting Macbeth's speech as he shut the door behind him, and she heard his voice long after he disappeared down the hallway.

Kate gazed at the door a moment longer, fighting the urge to call Peter.

Peter wrote his name on the call sheet at twenty past five, then went upstairs and out through the center door onto the stage for fight call.

This long day isn't over yet, not nearly, Peter thought as he started stretching. After ringing off with Bert, he'd resisted the bed's insistent whisper and set out his yoga mat instead. The familiar poses helped him hold onto the calm he'd felt when he and Bert said goodbye. That calm had faded, though, as he handled the media calls Serena had set up for him.

Serena had sent a briefing message encouraging him to be open and engaging with "our friends in the media, whose good opinion we need." Knowing the stakes, Peter had tried to come through, failing in his estimation only once, when the public radio reporter asked how playing Onyxx informed his interpretation of *Hamlet.* He was afraid his reflexive laughter at the question might have wounded the reporter's feelings. He went out of his way to smooth it over, comparing the two characters and their leadership styles, responses to challenge, and eloquence when expressing their inner lives. It was anything but a sound bite, and he wondered what the reporter would do with it.

Tahoma had picked Peter up from Richard's house at half past three o'clock and taken him to the Rose stage for in-person interviews with news outlets that needed video and photos for their stories. Such interviews were both easier and more difficult than phone calls. Those reporters had big reputations and long experience in the game.

Peter slipped as easily into the role of "star being interviewed" as they did into the role of "arts reporter." Serena had warned everyone ahead of time to "respect the actor's privacy when it comes to the personal matter of the loss of his mother," and nobody dared bring it up. But Peter could feel his mother's ghost hovering just behind the curtain as he sat onstage, legs casually crossed to indicate an ease he didn't feel, leaning into the reporters' questions with all the attention they deserved and then some.

As he shook the tension from his arms and legs now, Peter could feel the weight they carried, of long hours and emotional conversations. He nearly jumped out of his skin when Bryce tapped him on the shoulder and said, "Ready to play?"

"You be the rabbit," Peter replied. Instantly, Bryce took off with Peter right on his heels. The two were soon breathing hard as they chased each other through the yard. After three laps, Bryce had a solid lead. Finally, Peter shouted, "'A touch, a touch. I do confess 't,'" their agreed-on signal for the end of the chase.

Tahoma came on from backstage, where he'd been monitoring their warm-up while checking the props. Every actor would also check their own, but Tahoma was both a meticulous and a superstitious man, and a props error during dress rehearsal would be a bad omen.

As they climbed the steps, panting, he shook his head at their antics.

"All you need to do is warm up and loosen your muscles. You don't need to wear each other out," he suggested. They grinned as they agreed.

"Places," Tahoma called, and Peter crossed to his spot.

After they'd practiced the ballet of rapiers and daggers, Bryce and Peter shook hands.

"The others are at Calliope's, eating their snacks," Bryce said. "Shall we join?"

"I didn't bring any food," Peter replied. After everything he'd said to Richard, he'd been reluctant to raid the man's refrigerator.

"I'll share mine. Let's go!"

In Calliope's Grove, the other actors welcomed Bryce and Peter with calls of "How was it?" and "Break any legs?"

Peter sat munching half of one of Bryce's turkey sandwiches and a few slices of apple. He knew Bryce could read him, so he tried to stay positive. He made sure they all could hear it when he said he was looking forward to going on before a crowd at last. But as they walked toward the stage door for six o'clock call, he dropped back, weary to the bone.

The show must go on, he prodded himself, looking for any sign of the preshow jitters that would signal he was ready to perform. Instead, he felt the day's weight on his shoulders. In the past twelve hours, he'd performed half a dozen times at least. *Only one performance left to go*, he chided himself. *Then you can go back to bed.*

He looked over his shoulder at a break in the pines, seeking solace. Through their branches, the Peaks glowed serenely in the day's final light. He let the vision settle into his heart for a moment before turning toward the stage door.

Margaret was waiting for him. "All right, luv?" she asked kindly.

"All right, thank you," Peter answered automatically, giving her a smile that didn't quite reach his eyes.

Margaret gathered a few cast members and started a quick receive-and-pass game that soon involved the whole group. After they separated for vocal warm-ups, Peter felt her eyes on him. Once again, he searched himself for the nervous energy he'd used for *Macbeth*. Hamlet's first line, "A little more than kin and less than kind," rolled through his mind. *And then eight hundred more lines, and we're done for the night*, he joked to himself, trying to jostle his brain into something more than a woolen apathy. *Nothing?*

He did a few jumping jacks, telling himself *Listen* as he swept his arms up and *Respond* as they dropped to his sides. *Listen and respond; that's all I have to do.* The mantra improved his spirits, and by the time they lined up for the "tush push," he was feeling slightly more ready.

Around him, the others were laughing at the silly dance and their nerves and the quiet house that would soon fill with high school students and their families. When the dance ended, everyone turned for the dressing rooms, but Margaret's powerful voice called them back.

"Before we go, I have one more thing," she said. "Circle up." Walking over to Peter, she took his hand. The others also linked hands to form a circle, looking to Margaret, unsure what she had in mind.

"*Hamlet* is a big play, and it rests on the shoulders of one actor," she said. "We all have our parts, and they're important, of course. None quite as important as Polonius"—she paused for the laugh—"but you're all essential to what we create tonight. Still, I think we can agree that this play asks a lot of its Hamlet."

There were nods as everyone rested their eyes on Peter. Moved, he let his gaze circle the group, stopping briefly to connect with each actor, each friend in the cast.

"Let's give him some love, people," Margaret urged. She dropped Peter's hand but kept hold of Isabelle on her other side and walked behind Peter, continuing around the outside of the circle. "Group hug with Peter at the center!" she shouted. "Peter, stay where you are."

Everyone but Peter started walking, still holding hands, following Margaret, until one circle had taken on three additional loops. Margaret was back where she'd started, but now there were two people between her and Peter. He stood still, spine straight, swallowing down the lump in his throat.

"Five seconds of love," Margaret shouted cheerfully, and everyone pressed in. "We love you, Peter!" she called out, and the others chimed in, "Love you!" and "You've got this!"

"Now I've seen it all," Tahoma said as he entered from the wings. "Thirty minutes."

"Thank you Thirty!" They were all laughing—all but Peter. Holding Margaret's hand, he bent to kiss her cheek.

Sitting unnoticed in the uppermost gallery, Kate released the breath she'd been holding. *Beth was right,* she thought. *He has all of us—including me.*

ACT 5 *May* 2009

ACT 5
SCENE 1

Richard, Peter

Richard watched dress rehearsal from the sound booth, legal pad at his right hand. He had covered the first page with notes in his elegant handwriting, but midway down the second page, the writing ended. *What's the point?* he'd thought, setting down his pen. *It's all one note: Where is Peter?*

"Dead behind the eyes" was the stage phrase for an actor who doesn't show up for the work. They're speaking the lines and performing the movements as blocked, but the character's essence is lost. The audience senses it, their fellow actors see it, and their director knows it right away.

Halfway through the third act, Richard began pondering ways to guide Peter back to the path. *Choose whichever soliloquy he most enjoys speaking and work it through again.* Recalling their Tuesdays together, Richard smiled fondly. *That might do it.*

Or call a small group of actors for tomorrow. Perhaps Polonius and Ophelia—Margaret and Fawn. Take them through a scene rehearsal to remind him he has Hamlet in his bones. I hate to call them on their day off, but they would do it for me, and for him.

Reviewing his options, Richard came to the most difficult one: doing nothing. *He doesn't need more work. It's rest he needs. But knowing he's struggling, can I truly leave him to find his own way back?*

When the audience rose for a standing ovation, Richard gathered his notepad, capped his pen, and set it securely into his chest pocket. Then he said to Tahoma, "Time to rally the troops. I'll be down in fifteen minutes."

"Thank you Fifteen. I'll let them know."

Peter gamely spent the Fifteen at the stage door. There were no programs for dress rehearsal, but some students had printed out the cast list, and others brought copies of *Hamlet.* He gave each person a smile as he signed and returned the keepsake. Peter remembered being a kid at the stage door; this was easy work. He even managed to be polite to the teenagers dressed in black ruffled shirts who greeted him as Onyxx, though he stepped back out of arm's reach if they came close.

Teachers and parents also clustered around, congratulating him. In return, he thanked them for "nurturing the next generation of theater lovers."

Seeing their smiles lightened his heart, but the weight he'd felt all evening returned as he went back into the Rose for notes. He dreaded what Richard would say.

What a joke, he thought, *to come all this way and do all this work and be shite. Joke's on me, I guess, for thinking I still had it.*

In his own estimation, he'd fallen far short, leaving his scene partners to carry him through. He felt sure they'd spent the show fearing the moment when Hamlet would go off the rails for real. The uncertainty takes a toll on an actor's wits and energy. He hated that he'd created such stress for them.

Playing a vampire can make you a zombie, evidently, he chided himself. *But I can't let my failure bring the show down. I simply must be better.*

Sure, it had been a challenge, carrying the show on shoulders burdened by the day's revelations. *I never should have told Richard, and especially not today. It was too much for him; for us. He had every right to push me away as he did.*

As he trudged up the back stairs, Aaron, Carissa, and LaShia all said, "Good show," which only made him feel worse. Even as he praised their performances warmly in return, he thought, *I'll make sure I never let you down again.*

During the Fifteen, Richard stood near the main exit gate, accepting the occasional congratulation from those who knew who he was, but mostly listening as people flowed past. The show buzz was positive. His players hadn't disappointed this crowd; the young people would go home convinced they'd seen a world-class show.

Now he sat in the lowest gallery, the actors ranged on the benches around him, awaiting his notes. Everyone but Peter had changed into street clothes and removed their makeup. Peter was sitting two rows back on the aisle, still dressed in the white linen shirt and loose gray slacks he wore for the final scene, looking calm but drained. Richard wondered where he'd spent the Fifteen, if not in the dressing room with his castmates.

That's my son. The thought appeared in Richard's mind. Ambushed by upwelling emotion, he swallowed a sudden lump in his throat. *Whether you believed it or not, Helen, I do. We had a son.*

Reluctantly taking his eyes from Peter's face, Richard admonished himself, *This must wait. Sentiment will only distract me from the task at hand.*

"Enthusiastic crowd tonight, wasn't it?" he asked, sending his gaze from one person to the next. The actors nodded.

"And well-studied," Bryce commented.

Richard risked a second glance at Peter and was proud of himself for keeping his face bland. "You did a grand job sticking in your lane when 'To be or not to be' became the predicted Greek chorus."

"You prepared me well," Peter replied. "And I always think that no matter what else they learn in life, it's never a bad thing to have Shakespeare in one's head."

"And heart," Richard amended, sending an encouraging smile

Peter's way. Peter tilted his head questioningly, as if unsure of his ground. Letting his gaze continue circling the cast, Richard said, "It was gratifying to see them rise to their feet at the end."

There were nods and smiles, but from the corner of his eye, Richard saw Peter hang his head. *He's taken it too much to heart. Knows he fell short and feels he let them down. I can't leave him mired in dismay.*

Richard considered his next words.

"We have a splendid show in us, and we're nearly there." Turning back to Peter, he added, "And it's a well-known fact that a bad dress earns a great opening night." His gaze moved on to Margaret. "They'll be eating out of your hands on Friday. And from then through the end of this sold-out run."

"Hear, hear," she cheered.

"We're dark tomorrow, so you have the day off, and here's what I suggest," Richard said. "We've been working flat out for months now, and we started this week early, with tech on Saturday. With nearly sixty performances ahead, let's not take resilience for granted. You have the lines. You have the blocking. Isabelle, I'll call on you and ask, beyond those things, what does an actor need to get through such a long run?"

His Gertrude pursed her lips. "*Il est essentiel d'avoir le vin rouge et le bain moussant.*"

"Red wine and bubble bath sound just the things," Richard agreed. "For you, Margaret?"

"Weekly calls home when my family's not with me, and morning walks before the town is stirring."

That's doing it, Richard thought. *Teach them to fish. Remind them they already know how.*

"For you, Tahoma?"

"Walking off-trail across the shoulders of *Doko'oosłíid.*" With a subtle move of the chin, Tahoma indicated the San Francisco Peaks, a presence in the darkness beyond the trees.

Richard raised an eyebrow. "For another person, it might be a hobby of watercolor painting, or making pizza every Monday. Whatever it may be, I urge you to spend some time tomorrow on the question, 'How shall I care for myself from now until the day we close?'"

Skipping past Peter, he looked at Ted. "What say you, Claudius?"

"No matter where I'm working, I always find the best Italian restaurant in town and treat myself to dinner once a week."

"Such small-seeming acts of compassion toward oneself can make a large difference," Richard said. "To perform any play, but especially this one, requires physical strength and a good mind, but also, I would say," here he paused and swallowed, "great courage. You each have that in spades. See you Friday."

ACT 5
SCENE 2

Richard, Kate

After the actors filed out, Richard lingered in his seat, gazing at the ghost light. Tahoma always brought it out before shutting off the backstage lights. The bare bulb in its wire cage, burning atop an ornate pole, would be the only source of light other than starlight when the theatre went dark. Around it, his beloved Rose was falling into slumber, a cat with a belly full of milk.

Can't stay long; Gavriella's crew will be waiting to lock up. Rising from his seat, Richard straightened his back. *To it, then*. He made his way backstage and down the stairs to the dressing rooms. Peter would still be there, removing makeup and changing out of costume, and he would need a ride home.

I'll pour us both two fingers of Jameson's, and we'll talk it through, Richard thought. *Man to man. Or dare I say, father to son?*

When he reached the narrow hallway that linked the dressing rooms, the light was indeed on in the dressing room Peter shared with Bryce and Ted. But as he approached, Richard heard voices. *Peter running lines?* No. It was the voices of two people he heard. The first was Peter's, but the second was Kate's.

She said something Richard couldn't make out. He heard Peter reply, "I need to say this to someone I trust. I know I messed up—"

Unwilling to eavesdrop, Richard rapped his knuckles against the half-open door before poking his head around. Peter had changed out of his costume and into a T-shirt and sweatpants already. *Caught him just in time.*

"Good e'en, good e'en, Katherine," he said to Kate, who was sitting at Ted's dressing table. Her arms were crossed.

"And the same to ye, Richard," Kate replied, politely but without her usual warmth. *I interrupted something. Not that it's my business*, he reminded himself for the tenth time.

"Sorry to intrude. I came to give you a lift home," he said to Peter.

Peter glanced at Kate, then blinked before turning to Richard. "I'm grateful, but I need to talk with Kate. If it's all right, I'll find another way to your place. So 'I thank you for your pains,' but no."

Seeing he was being boxed out, Richard looked to Kate. "Line?"

She smiled. "It's 'I took no more pains for those thanks than you take pains to thank me. If it had been painful, I would not have come.'"

"Well spoken. She has Beatrice by heart, you know," he told Peter. *Tomorrow is soon enough, I suppose.*

"She's a woman of many talents."

"Well. I'll leave you to it then." With a final glance that took in the firm set of Kate's jaw and the rounded slump of Peter's shoulders, he turned and shut the door behind him.

Kate returned her eyes to Peter's and saw his rueful look.

Softening slightly, she told him, "Richard the Great isn't used to being put off, but he'll get over it."

Peter sighed. "I've given him plenty of reasons to be disappointed. I suppose one more won't matter." When he added nothing further, she stepped into the gap his silence made.

"Gavriella needs to close the house. Did you want me to take you somewhere? The Arden?"

"The Arden? No. Why would I? Oh, no." He looked up at her with eyes that conveyed the exhaustion he felt. "Honestly?"

"Honestly."

"Jaime's starship, if we could reach it without being followed. But I have no right."

Kate shrugged. "You don't need to. I know it's been a refuge."

"I don't deserve refuge, especially not from you. What I was trying to say before is, I messed up. I knew we meant something to each other. I didn't live up to it, and I don't deserve your kindness now. But whether it's true for you or no, I wanted to say out loud—you still matter to me. Very much so."

Pausing to gauge her emotions, Kate answered, "I appreciate that."

"I've let people down. The cast, Richard, but mostly you. For *Hamlet*, I'll do my level best to deliver a worthy performance on Friday and every show that follows. If I do that, dress rehearsal will be just a footnote to the season. But if I don't make it up to you somehow, if I don't—say how sorry I am about Freja and ask your forgiveness, there's nothing I can do in future to make up for that."

Kate paused again as automatic answers rolled through her mind. "It's OK," or "No big deal," or "You'll be fine." *He deserves better from me; we both do.*

"You've had a big day, a tough day," she offered. He shook his head as if to shake off such consolations. "Don't worry. I'm not going to say 'all's well' in your Hamlet tonight, or with Richard, apparently, or between us." She met his eyes with candor.

"I see what you're going through; some of it, anyway. But I think too much of you to believe a lie would ease your mind."

"Thank you for that."

"We can talk about your Hamlet tomorrow, if you want, if you think it would be helpful. I hope you can also find a way to talk with Richard about it." She saw his chest rise and fall as he released a heavy breath. "He is your director, you know."

"Yes, he is that." Peter's voice was a stone.

"About the other thing; um, about behaving badly." She caught his gaze again. "I've thought a lot about it. I want you to know I don't take it lightly. But I also don't hold it against you."

Peter sat up straight in his chair. "How can you not? I do."

Kate nodded. "I know you do. But I also see—you, and—everything you were going through. You and I were just being friends. I'm not so sure that if an old lover hadn't turned up on a day when I'd been to hell and back, I wouldn't have slept with him under the same circumstances."

Listening to what she'd just said, she added, "That's a mess of a sentence. What I mean is, yes, I can forgive you, because you asked and because I understand. Is there anything else you need to say to me about it right now?"

He looked away, biting his lip.

"Then it's done," she said. "Let's get you to the starship."

Peter stood, scanning his dressing table to make sure everything was in place for Friday. Picking up his costume for the final scene, he said, "Let's go then." In the hallway, he hung the costume on the wash rack, then followed Kate upstairs. She turned out the lights at the end of the hallway, then at the top of the stairs.

As they emerged through the stage door into the darkness, Kate paused to text Gavi that the dressing rooms were dark, so she didn't waste a trip. Hearing Peter's footsteps stop behind her, she fought the temptation to turn and offer him a hug. He seemed in desperate need of one, after such a disappointing show.

She'd seen it from the back row of the upmost gallery, last seat stage right this time. Officially, she was there to listen and watch the sight lines, but Peter's performance claimed more of her attention as the show went on. He had the lines and movements, but his timing was off. He seemed like a swimmer fighting a riptide and gradually losing. *Richard saw it, too. Of course he did.*

She felt a touch of concern for their production, for Richard and the cast, but mostly for Peter. An actor could experience a slump, just like a baseball player or any other athlete. Maybe it would end after one performance; she hoped that would be the case.

Now, as she drove them along the short stretch of highway and down the dark, gravel road toward her house, she tried to think of something to say that would be honest but also encouraging. *Omens aren't omens until we attach a story to them*, she told herself. *And people say a bad dress rehearsal means a great opening night.*

Tucking her car in alongside the sitter's, she clicked off the headlights.

Peter hadn't said a word, just leaned his seat back and closed his eyes the moment his door shut. She wondered if he'd fallen asleep in the ten minutes they'd been on the road.

"Peter," she whispered. "We're here."

He reached his hand across the space between them and set it on her forearm. "Thank you," he said.

She looked down at his fingers, feeling the warmth of his touch all the way down to her toes. "I need to let my sitter go," she replied, keeping her voice calm. "Dad's starship is unlocked, and the bed is ready." Hearing how that might sound, she added, "I always leave it that way for when someone needs it." That still wasn't quite what she meant. *Never mind.* "You can go over and get settled."

He sighed but didn't move.

"Or spend the night in the car if you want?"

Still nothing.

"Peter," she said in a motherly tone of voice. He opened his eyes.

"You need to get to the studio now, OK?"

"Very well." He pulled the lever to raise his seatback. "I'm going. Will you come say good night?"

That's the question, isn't it, Kate thought. "You need your rest right now more than anything," she told him.

"I know it. Will you come say good night?"

She laughed. "If I say yes, will you go?"

"Say yes and find out."

"Yes."

Making a sound like a purr, he opened the car door and stepped out.

Kate tiptoed in to find the sitter reading a novel at the kitchen table. Hannah told her Beth had been "precious and well-behaved." Kate sighed, longing for the days when Beth was as sweet to her mother as to the world at large.

Kate wrote out the check and pressed it into Hannah's hands with a whispered, "Thank you." As the door clicked behind the sitter, the house quieted into familiar night sounds: a clock ticking in the living room, the refrigerator's hum.

I could just go to bed, Kate told herself. *It was a rough day. He's so tired, he's probably asleep already. He'd never know till morning.* She turned toward her bedroom but couldn't help glancing out through the kitchen window. A light was on in the studio. And she'd made a promise.

Not a player. Not ever again. No matter how sorry he is. As she brushed her teeth, the familiar refrain rolled through her mind. She'd broken her rule with Peter, and what had it brought her? *Freja.* "This is the part where I say it didn't mean anything," he'd told her, "but it did."

He and Freja were never close. Here is where he wanted to be tonight. He still feels safe here.

Spitting out the toothpaste, she thought, *And if I'm honest, here is where I want him. He matters to me, too.*

Kate stood at the sink arguing with herself, but she knew her choice had been made. *Beth was right; when he's in need, he has us. Right now, he's in need. After tonight, who knows? But that's for tomorrow.*

With a little laugh at herself, Kate shut out the light.

"Hi, Dad," Kate whispered as she opened the door.

Night lights glowed by the sink and up in the loft. In a louder whisper, she said, "Peter? You asleep?"

Before she had time to decide what she wanted the answer to be, he popped his head above the loft railing. "There you are. Come on up."

Yes, m'lord, she thought, still trying to spur herself to some rebellion. Climbing the stairs, she could hear him settling back into bed.

She wondered if he was naked and if she soon would be as well, and blushed. *I must have meant it when I said I'd forgiven him,* she thought. *And there is such a thing as makeup sex, or so I'm told.*

Peter was sitting up in bed with a pillow tucked between his back and the wall. He was still wearing clothes, or at least the T-shirt—a quilt rested over his legs. He patted the quilt and lifted the other pillow so she could sit beside him. *The more fool I,* she chided herself. *Good night is what he wants, after all.* She sat on the quilt and swung her legs up beside his.

Once she was settled, he took her hand. "Thank you for letting me return to the starship, and for coming to say good night. I appreciate both gifts more than you can know."

"I felt like you needed a quiet place to rest tonight."

"This is certainly that." He looked around, then up through the sky windows. "Despite the day it's been, I think I shall sleep very well."

"I'm glad. Is there anything you need? Anything I can get you before I say good night?"

"Yes, there is one thing."

She looked over at him, waiting, and he met her gaze.

Releasing her hand, he slid down into the sheets, then rolled over and set his head on her leg. One hand rested on her calf; the other he tucked under his cheek. Kate hesitated, then set a hand on his head and began lightly stroking his hair. She could see a tear carve a glistening path toward his jaw. She let him cry it out, running her fingers through the sweat-matted strands until his breathing slowed and the tears dried.

"All right, then; time for sleep," she whispered. He sighed like a little boy. Reluctantly, she disentangled herself, letting him stay curled where he was. She set a pillow under his head where her leg had been. Recalling nights when she'd tucked her daughter into bed, she leaned down to kiss Peter's cheek with a mother's care. As she stood to go, he only opened his eyes once, to give her a look of such soft affection that her breath caught in her throat. She returned the look, her heart in her gaze. Then he closed his eyes again and let Kate carry the memory out into the dark and singing night.

ACT 5
SCENE 3

KATE

The next morning, Kate woke up early. It had been a short night, and she was tired, but time and the list of things to do maintained their usual relentless pace. She rose and stretched, then put on a pair of yoga pants and a T-shirt. Grabbing an elastic hairband, Kate walked toward the living room, braiding as she went. By the time she reached the kitchen, she was as pulled together as morning required.

She didn't expect to see Peter, thinking he might sleep in and have breakfast just before noon. Once the run began, an actor would typically eat a second meal around five before call and a final meal after the evening performance. A schedule like that would function as effectively on two-show days like Wednesday and Saturday as on one-show days like tomorrow's opening. Although the theatre was dark today and Peter had the day off, Kate expected he would be getting himself into the rhythm of performance, if he hadn't already.

So it was a surprise to see the studio door swing open as she set water on the stove for oatmeal. He walked through the garden to the kitchen door, opened it halfway, and asked diffidently, "May I?"

"Of course," she said, giving him a reassuring smile.

"Beth?" he asked.

"She'll be up soon and very excited to see you. I should probably warn her you're here, so she doesn't . . . I'll be right back. Can you start my coffee?"

Kate knocked at Beth's door and heard a muffled "What?"

"I have a surprise."

"What surprise?"

"Somebody special is here, and you'll never guess who he is."

"My dad?"

Kate rolled her eyes while keeping her voice cheerful, a mother's skill. "Way better. It's Peter!"

A squeal, and the thud of two feet hitting the floor. Kate heard noises she equated with the throwing on of one set of pajamas, then another. Her daughter finally emerged, brown hair in a tangle, face aglow. To the river of questions, Kate replied, "After dress rehearsal, he told me he wanted to sleep in Dad's starship, for luck." *Not lying, just improvising.* "Visit the mirror first and then come to the kitchen to say hello."

"Can I skip school today?"

"No, why?" Kate was surprised by this request from her academics-oriented daughter.

"To spend the day with you and Peter!"

The idea tugged powerfully at Kate's heart. A day off, and a chance to play with a happy daughter.

No, I can't be away from the Rose the day before the season opens. Richard would be lost.

"I have work today, and Peter needs—" *What?* Kate wondered. "He's going back to Richard's to get ready for his big night tomorrow.""

A jutting lower lip indicated Beth's disapproval of this latest demonstration of her mother's lack of imagination, but she couldn't contain her excitement at Peter's reappearance. "What about this weekend? Can we do a picnic with him or something?"

"We'll see." Hearing her mother's stock synonym for "no" coming out of her own mouth, Kate added, "That would be fun. Let's ask him."

After hugging Beth and handing Kate her coffee, Peter was likewise pouty when Kate told him their day's schedule couldn't be changed. Apparently, he'd wanted ... *What?* Kate wondered again.

Over oatmeal, Beth asked about dress rehearsal. "I fell short," Peter admitted. "I let my castmates down, and Richard the Great as well." Repeating his nickname for Richard with delight, Beth consoled him with the wisdom of a theater kid. "Bad dress, great opening, that's what Ms. Fontes says." A font of theatrical wisdom, Ms. Fontes taught drama at the arts camp Beth attended each summer.

"Good to hear." Peter smiled briefly.

After Beth went upstairs to get ready for school, Peter and Kate lingered at the breakfast table as long as they could. Peter was still in low spirits, so Kate asked him for a story from London. He described an acting class in which everyone played a part traditionally given to the opposite sex.

"I did Kate in the wooing scene in *The Taming of the Shrew*," he told her. My friend Amy was Petruchio. It took me some time to calibrate my physicality without lapsing into caricature. You would have laughed at me, I'm sure." He brightened at the memory. "But eventually we made our way past the discomfort and found something that felt true."

Kate was glad to see him smile, but finally, with one eye on the clock, she rose to clear the table.

"Let me," Peter offered. Their shoulders touched as he stood to gather Beth's plate and cup. Kate was very aware of how close he was.

Swallowing, she collected her own items. As she walked to the sink, she replied, "I can drop you at Richard's if you like. Or you're welcome to stay here, but I know you need to get over there sometime."

"Do I?" He moved around her to open the dishwasher.

"All your things are there," Kate said practically.

"The only things that matter are right here," he said, turning toward her. "Kate? Do you—can you—truly forgive me?"

She hesitated, looking into his eyes, then stepped into his arms. He held her close, breathing slowly. For a moment, she rested her head against his chest, accepting the embrace for what it was: the last peaceful moment of her day.

"Thank you for letting me stay last night." His voice rumbled through his chest wall and straight into her head. "I know I need to face the morning and everything it brings. But like Beth, I have other wishes."

"Being an adult is so hard sometimes."

He held her one breath longer before opening his arms. "Truer words were never spoken."

They dropped Beth at school on the way. Just before Kate turned in at the gate to Richard's subdivision, Peter set a hand on her wrist. "Can we take one minute?"

Startled, Kate pulled off the road at a wide spot and turned to look at him. "What is it?"

"I know we don't have much time. But there's something wondrous strange I need to tell you."

ACT 5

SCENE 4

Richard

Solitary thought was leading him around in circles like the proverbial tail-chasing dog that morning, so Richard decided a call for help was in order.

"Katherine, when you get this, please ring me. I'll need the favor of your time."

He heard her rap at his office door a few minutes later. To cheer himself, he called out, "'Knock, knock, knock. Who's there?'"

As she entered, Kate chided him, "Not the whole porter scene, I beg you. It's tedious enough onstage."

"'Come in, tailor. Here you may roast your goose,'" he replied.

She stopped walking and stood, arms crossed, looking as if she could outwait time itself.

"Very well," he conceded, gesturing her to a chair. "Thank you for coming. I am in need of your wisdom."

She took her seat across the desk and waited, eyebrows arched.

"It's about Peter. The lad has been a continual surprise since the moment he arrived on our shore."

"Yes, he has," Kate said, giving Richard an encouraging smile.

"You must recall the day he washed up here like a shipwrecked Kiwi pirate. Only he wasn't that, was he?"

"As it turns out, no."

Richard thought back to the day Peter told him about *Thirst*. "He brought vampires trailing in his wake, haunting his dreams and bedeviling his waking hours, chasing him from hither to yon to your house to mine."

"I actually don't think it's vampires haunting him." Kate's tone was speculative.

Richard narrowed his eyes. "Whatever the source, his haunted soul is impeding his course of action. Somewhere within him there is a performance of Hamlet that 'Conjures the wand'ring stars and makes them stand like wonder-wounded hearers.' Sadly, last night was not that performance."

"He had an off night. He'll hit the mark Friday."

"I hope so. I'm counting on the adage 'Bad dress, great opening.'"

"That's what Beth told him."

Noting the implications of her statement, Richard decided to bite his tongue. *Still none of my business*, he reminded himself. Instead, he said, "The question I would pose to you is what should I, as his director, do to elicit the performance of which we know he is capable?"

"As director? Nothing, I don't think."

There was a knock at Richard's door. "Go away!" he called out.

"We've seen him in rehearsal," Kate reminded him. "You're right to say he has a great Hamlet to give. I don't think you need to do anything more to bring it out; not as director, anyway."

"And as executive director?" Richard asked. He saw Kate pause, gauging his meaning.

"If I were executive director, knowing the financial straits we're in and the importance of this show, I would still let the director make the call. He knows best how to get great performances from our actors. He always has."

Richard smiled. "When it's time for a successor to fill my chair, I hope you'll allow me to recommend your application to the board," he said.

One eyebrow curving upward, Kate answered, "Whenever that time comes, I'll feel honored to know you're in my corner."

"You've earned my enthusiastic support many times over, Katherine. I regret not saying that sooner."

"It's difficult for you to think about leaving the Rose, I'm sure," Kate said. "And it's hard for us to imagine it as well."

"I appreciate that." Richard sent Kate a look of gratitude before returning to the topic that had filled his thoughts since the previous night.

"Regarding Peter, I remain troubled by the consequences if he serves the audience such tepid porridge tomorrow night as he offered at dress. The groundlings will adore their vampire leader, but the media and our loyal fans will know. How can I do nothing to prevent that consequence to my—to our Hamlet?"

"I'm not saying you should do nothing at all, Richard. I just don't think it's a job for you as director or executive director."

She knows. Richard's face softened. "Peter confided in you?" A hopeful note had entered his voice.

"He told me this morning as I was dropping him off at your place. He feels he told you the wrong way, on impulse instead of with consideration for your feelings and the timing. He's afraid you're angry."

Another knock at the door brought Richard to his feet. "Go. Away." When the door remained closed, he settled back into his chair.

"What he told you yesterday is a lot to take in," Kate said. "I can understand if you're upset. He is, too. That's what we saw last night. What he needs from you isn't the advice of a director."

Richard looked at his shelves, stuffed with books and mementos of a life lived with Shakespeare. "But a director is what I am," he protested. "It's what I always have been. I hardly know what else to say, how to be anything else."

Kate took a moment. "How to be a father, you mean," she said gently.

Yes. "If that is what I am. Peter said his mother wasn't sure."

"What do you think?"

"Last night, watching him, it was as if a veil had been torn away. I saw myself in his movements, heard my voice in his. 'It is a wise father that knows his own child,' as the Bard would say. That it took me this long to recognize it says something about my powers of observation."

"We both thought he was a Kiwi pirate," Kate reminded him. "And you had a few other things on your mind. The company's finances, for one."

"Perhaps it isn't true anyway. Half of me thinks this is idle speculation built on a fond heart's misplaced hope. Helen was . . ." He closed his eyes.

"I see she meant something to you," Kate offered.

"For a moment all too brief, she was my moon and stars." Richard's mind was far away. "I can't tell you how—grieved—I am, to learn she held such a secret from me all these years."

"It changed your life, didn't it?"

He glanced at her kind face, then looked quickly away. "It hardly bears thinking on," he replied. "That I might have been a husband, a father; the chasm between what is and what might have been rivals the watery Atlantic that forever separated Helen and me." His gaze now firmly on the window, Richard pulled out his pocket square and dabbed his eyes.

Now it was Kate's turn to look away. "I'm sorry. I don't mean to pry."

He shook his head. "I've lived a good life, but not the life I might have led. Tears seem fit to the circumstance."

"All right," she said, adding after a moment, "you're not upset with him, just feeling a bit lost when you think about how to approach this new role he's offered you?" She waited for his nod. "Then let me say one more thing."

"Go on."

"When I look at Peter now, I see you in him, too."

Once Richard had regained his composure, she continued, "But here's what I think. It only changes things if you and Peter want it to. If you step up and choose each other. Let's say a paternity test proves you're related. If you don't want the role, or he doesn't, then it still won't mean anything. Do you see?"

"That it will mean nothing if he's my son?"

"That it's up to the two of you to decide what it means or whether it means anything at all."

"Well, like the Thane of Cawdor, 'I dare do all that may become a man.'"

"Mackers didn't have children," Kate chided him. "Richard, I'm going to ask nicely. Just this once, don't escape into quotation. If you want to be any kind of father to him, then he needs to hear you say it matters to you. Your own words would be best, I think."

"That it matters to me. Of course it matters to me. How could it—"

They heard a careful tap on the door, and then it swung open. If the trespasser had been anyone but Tahoma, Richard might have lobbed a paperweight from his desk. But the stage manager was not a person at whom things would be thrown.

"Sorry to interrupt, but we have a situation," Tahoma said, looking Richard in the eye, "with Peter McKenzie."

ACT 5
SCENE 5

Kate

Their feet crunching on the gravel, Richard, Kate, and Tahoma crossed the grounds toward the Rose. As they marched, Tahoma briefed them in terse sentences.

"He called me for a ride—said he'd left the dressing room in a hurry last night and needed to set things in order. When we got here, he went up onstage instead. I didn't think much of it. Every actor has their process. Actors." Tahoma shook his head.

"Actors," Kate echoed supportively.

"But then on the stage mic I heard him say, 'Angels and ministers of grace, defend us!' He was off on his scene with the Ghost. A speed-through, and he was walking his marks as if Ted and LaShia were standing there."

Gavriella met them at the backstage door, a worried look on her face. "He's still doing it," she said to Tahoma.

"He kept talking after the Ghost exits, now to Horatio and them, still at double-time," Tahoma went on. "I thought he'd stop when he reached act 2. Maybe he just needed to work his opening. But then he said, 'Well, God-a-mercy. Excellent well. You are a fishmonger.' And I saw he was going on through the whole play."

"My crew is in, sweeping and cleaning the house before opening,"

Gavriella added. "They can keep working, of course, but he's freaking them out."

"Why? There's nothing odd about a speed-through," Richard said as Gavriella opened the door.

"Alone? On your only day off before opening?" Tahoma asked pointedly.

"You said yourself, every actor has a process." Richard's tone was tolerant. "I don't see why this is an issue."

"Give it a listen, before you decide," Tahoma replied.

"We can hear him on the backstage speakers," Gavriella told them as they walked down the hallway. When they reached the waiting area called the greenroom, Hamlet's words raced from the speakers like a river in full flood. It took Kate a minute to catch where he was in the script. He was playing the scene with the "tragedians of the city," the acting troupe that comes to Elsinore Castle at the request of Rosencrantz and Guildenstern. Now and then, she heard Peter's shoes scrape against the boards as he moved across the stage.

"Again, I don't see why this is an issue." Richard's tone was firm. "If Hamlet needs the stage this morning, we can give it to him. Work around him, as Gavriella said."

"The *Midsummer* cast is called at ten for the first full run-through of act 1," Tahoma said. "Missy called Peter's understudy for Lysander because the *Hamlet* cast gets today off, but she still needs to get the props table ready and set furniture onstage."

Richard frowned. "Can Ms. Ivy change their call?"

"From ten o'clock? It's a quarter past nine now."

"Move them to the afternoon."

"Richard," Kate interrupted. "That show matters, too. And I don't think—" her voice trailed off. Something in Peter's tone was setting butterflies racing through her stomach.

"Speak your piece, Katherine," he prompted.

"Tahoma's right: This is the one day off for the *Hamlet* cast. I don't think Peter should be here. Especially after yesterday. He should be resting, taking care of himself. Talking with you, I think. Not doing this."

Richard blinked rapidly, measuring her advice. After a moment, he said, "Let's go up to him." To Gavriella, he added, "Tell the house crew they're on break. Send them out to Calliope's Grove, and raid our snack box for them."

"I will."

"Tahoma. Are you set for tomorrow?"

"I'm coming back after the *Midsummer* run-through to set us for opening. That's the plan, anyway."

"A good plan. Feel free to go now, or stay; I leave it to you."

"While I have an actor on the stage, my place is in the house," Tahoma said.

Richard nodded. "Gavriella, please tell Ms. Ivy the *Midsummer* cast is still called for ten, but don't let them into the Rose until Peter is done. At the rate he's going, it won't interfere much. Tell her they can warm up in the rehearsal room."

"Will do."

Richard caught Kate's eye. "All will be well," he promised her. "Shall we?"

They followed the soft glow of red floor lights up and around to the house left stage door. When they emerged into the yard, Peter took no notice.

Up onstage, he was moving with the precision of a martial artist. His voice flowed like a river in flood, pausing briefly at other people's unspoken lines, then racing onward.

Catching his muttered "'Hecuba . . . Hecuba,'" Kate realized he was delivering the "rogue and peasant slave" soliloquy. She looked at Richard, who glanced at her and then set a hand on her arm as if to say, "Wait."

They held still, watching Peter express Hamlet's agony of doubt at a sprinter's pace. Emotions raced across his face. He looked out across the yard as if unseeing.

Kate felt her own muscles tighten, mirroring the tension Peter must be feeling. Tahoma had been right to warn them. This wasn't the work he needed to do today.

Finally, she heard him say, "'The play's the thing wherein I'll catch the conscience of the King.'" Swallowing, she called out in a clear voice, "'Good Hamlet, cast thy nighted color off.'"

A shock wave rolled through Peter's body. Hearing Gertrude's line from earlier in the play, he scanned the yard and found Kate standing beside Richard. To Kate, he looked like a person struggling to wake from a dream.

"'Soft you now, the fair Ophelia,'" he quoted at a normal speed. "'Nymph, in thy orisons be all my sins remembered.'"

Richard prompted Kate in a whisper, "'Good my lord, how does your Honor for this many a day?'" Kate delivered the line to Peter with a hopeful smile. But no answering smile softened his troubled face.

"'I humbly thank you, well,'" he said soberly.

This could go on awhile, Kate thought.

Beside her, Richard shifted on his feet, apparently having the same thought. "We're sorry to interrupt, but we need the stage for *Midsummer*. They're called in half an hour."

"Thank you Thirty," Peter said, turning away from them. "'To be or not to be,'" he asked the back wall, then picked up his pace to double time again: "'thatisthequestion.'"

Kate looked at Richard, who shrugged. Kate drew a deep breath as she watched Peter struggle with Hamlet's thoughts of suicide. Images of his audition raced through her mind. *He was just some unknown actor from New Zealand with the audacity to perform this speech in front of the famous Richard Keane. Or that's what we thought.*

When a tear rolled down Peter's face, she couldn't stand it any longer. *Actors and their processes*, she thought. *He's going to drive himself crazy*. On impulse, she walked up the house right stairs onto the stage.

"Katherine!" She heard Richard's hissed warning. Second-guessing herself, Kate thought, *Am I right to break his concentration? Or should I leave him to it?* She hesitated, agonizing.

Finally, he returned to the lines, "'Soft you now, the fair Ophelia,'" the words so swift they might as well have been one word. Instead of responding with Ophelia's lines this time, though, Kate moved in front of Peter and said, "You don't need to do this. Peter, please. Stop."

He shook his head as if to shake her presence from the stage. "'I humbly thank you, well.'" He paused. When she didn't reply, he went on, "'No, not I. I never gave you aught.'"

"I'm not going to do this, and neither should you," Kate said. "This isn't how you rest."

"'Ha, ha, are you honest?'" he asked quickly. "'Are you fair?'" He raced through his lines, not looking at Kate until he blurted out, "'Get thee to a nunnery.'" Then, his green eyes met hers as he continued at regular speed, "'I am myself indifferent honest, but yet I could accuse me of such things that it were better my mother had not borne me.'" The words seemed to catch in his throat.

"That's not true." Kate's voice was soft. "I'm sure Helen is very glad she bore you. I know she must be proud of you. And so are Richard and Bert."

He shook his head again. Picking up speed from line to line, he said, "'I am very proud, revengeful, ambitious, with more offenses at my beck than I have thoughts to put them in, imagination to give them shape, or time to act them in. What should such fellows as I do, crawling between earth and heaven? We are arrant knaves all; believe none of us. Go thy ways to a nunnery. Where's your father?'"

At the sharp question, Kate stepped backward as if struck.

Peter's eyes widened. Reaching out, he took hold of her wrist just as she caught her bootheel at the edge of the stage. Kate gasped as she felt herself falling. From the yard, she heard Richard shout again, "Katherine!" as Peter pulled her back from the abyss and into his arms.

"I'm sorry, I'm sorry," he was repeating, his face buried in her hair. "I'm so sorry."

"No, no, I'm OK, I'm here." Kate's tone was gentle, even as she fought to calm her racing heart.

They stood like that for a minute, until the flood of emotion abated. Just before it grew awkward, Kate leaned back and loosened her arms.

"I didn't mean to say it," Peter whispered, looking her in the eye.

"I know you didn't. I know."

"I was just trying to get through the play one more time before tomorrow night. I need to find the heart of it."

"You have the heart of it. You don't need a speed-through to find it. It's in you."

"Not last night it wasn't. I need to do this right, for me and the cast and the audience, and for him." A tilt of Peter's head indicated Richard, who had climbed the stairs and was now standing still, watching them.

"He knows you have it. He told me you have a Hamlet to conjure the wandering stars."

"He said that?"

"Would I lie to you about *Hamlet*?"

Peter snorted as he pulled her close again. She felt him draw and release a deep breath. "Kate?"

"What is it?"

"'If by chance I talk a little wild, forgive me; I had it from my father.'"

"We're doing *Henry VIII* now?" Her tone held amusement as the adrenalin of her near-fall began to fade.

"You're right: I should stick to my script. 'I am but mad north-north-west. When the wind is southerly, I know a hawk from a handsaw.'" He relaxed his hold on her.

"It will come in handy when we need to sort them out," Kate said, a mother reassuring a small boy. Leaning back to look at her again, he offered her a half-smile.

Richard cleared his throat. Keeping one arm around her, Peter turned.

"'Angels and ministers of grace, defend us! Be thou a spirit of health or goblin damned, bring with thee airs from heaven or blasts from hell, be thy intents wicked or charitable . . . I will speak to thee.'"

"Will you? That's very kind," Richard said. Kate chose to focus on the hopeful fact that he hadn't answered in the words of the Ghost of Hamlet's Father. Then he intoned "'Mark me,'" and her shoulders fell.

"You just couldn't stand it, could you," she said, glaring at him. Stepping out of Peter's embrace, she turned to look at the two of them. Peter's hangdog expression was so much like Richard's that she had to pause. *Like father, like son.*

"Stop, both of you. I'm begging you. You need to quit borrowing the words of the Bard and use your own for once."

"'The lady doth protest too much, methinks,'" Richard said to Peter. Kate groaned.

"'Who is 't can read a woman?'" Peter answered.

"Wrong play again," she snapped.

"All right, all right." Peter held up a hand, smiling. "I'll stop."

"You need to talk to each other, in your own words." Kate's voice was resolute. "You need to talk about—" recalling that the stage mics were on, she continued, "—fathers and sons, and ghosts. Maybe ghosts most of all. Don't you?" She looked at Richard.

"Perhaps so, Katherine. Yes, I think we do. Ghosts most of all."

Kate turned to Peter, who was somber again. "No more soliloquies. Just talk to him," she urged him.

"About fathers and sons," he echoed.

"And ghosts most of all," Kate replied.

Turning to Richard, Peter was quiet a moment. Then he said in a voice meant to shake the timbers, "'I say, away!—Go on. I'll follow thee.'"

Kate looked to the heavens for strength and tried not to laugh.

ACT 5
SCENE 6

RICHARD, PETER

Even with Kate's prompting, it was surprisingly difficult to start. They'd gotten through "Where to?" from Richard and "I dunno" from Peter, but conversation stalled once they decided to go to Richard's house. The elegant car didn't seem quite the place for apologies or pronouncements. But then neither did Richard's kitchen, where they fixed a salad and a plate of cheese and crackers without exchanging more than a few words of suggestion and inquiry as to one another's tastes.

Once they were seated at the table where they'd spent so many sessions poring over the soliloquies, Peter unlatched the gate with a simple, "I'm sorry."

When Richard stayed quiet, he added, "Mum wouldn't have wanted me to tell you like that. She may not have wanted me to do it at all, if I'm honest. I'm truly sorry I made you angry."

Richard steepled his fingers in front of his chin. "I was taken aback, I will say, but angry I was not."

"No?"

"I thought I knew the strain you'd been under. *Hamlet* is a heavy weight; it burdens one to the breaking point. But you were bearing this other weight as well."

Peter closed his eyes briefly. "I hope you can forgive me for delivering the news like that."

"Of course I can forgive you. That was never in question."

They returned to their salads. Richard watched Peter take a cracker from the plate and layer it with a slice of cheese.

"I've been wondering: When you decided to come here, what was the plan?"

"There wasn't one," Peter admitted. "I wanted to meet you; I've wanted that since she told me. I thought I might know just by looking at you, whether you—whether we were related. As we spent time together, I found I wanted it to be true. I couldn't trust my eyes once that happened. It might be just wishful thinking then."

"Remarkable."

"What is?"

"I had that same thought. As I watched your dress rehearsal, there were moments, glimpses, when I thought, clearly, that's my son. But as you say, it could all be wishful thinking."

"We could get a test. That would tell us."

Richard narrowed his eyes, considering. "Is that what you want?"

"Yes, but only if you do."

"I do, I believe. But Katherine said something that has lingered in my mind."

"She has a way of doing that." Peter smiled fondly. "What did she say?"

"No matter the results, it's up to the two of us to decide what it means."

Peter picked up his glass and took a long drink. "She's right, as usual. I'm curious to know the answer. But does DNA make you my dad?"

"Does it erase the years I lost with Helen, with you?"

"See?" Peter said, his voice rough with emotion. "So many unanswerable questions we're left with when a person dies. I suppose it's the way of things, that when they go, they leave mysteries behind. The thing I can't grasp is why Mum didn't tell you, then or later. About the possibility, at least."

"Nor can I . . . or so I like to tell myself."

Peter waited.

"I was angry and hurt when she said we were through," Richard admitted. "Our parting scene is a memory I've long wished to erase. A young man's ego and hope, tangled together and delivered in tones of command rather than entreaty. Surely afterward, she felt she couldn't disclose her situation to me. I only blame myself, if that's the case."

As Peter gave him a sympathetic look, Richard fancied he could see something of his own features in that honest face. *I paid a high price for my pride; higher than I knew. How can I ever recover the time we lost?*

"My memories of her are softened by the years, but one thing has remained unchanged," he said. "Her fire. She had a flame inside that everyone could see."

Peter smiled softly. "That she did. Tell me what else you remember."

Once they'd begun talking about their ghost, it was easier. Richard traveled back in his mind to that summer of 1974, when he'd been a brash young director from London. In three years at the storied Rose, he'd become known among America's Shakespeare aficionados as a director to watch. Adam Condell himself had as good as said Richard would be likely to take his place if he ever stepped down.

Richard drew a deep breath. "I'll never forget the day Helen walked onstage and said, 'Dear Celia, I show more mirth than I am mistress of, and would you yet I were merrier?' She was charming, of course, and delightful to look at. But the clarity of her speech, the intention behind it; masterful."

"I think she was fantastic, but I'm biased. I do know she loved performing Shakespeare."

"I'm glad she stayed with it after she left America."

"So was she. Eventually, she played all his big roles for women, plus a few fools and clowns. And she played Lear in a gender-reversed production at the Old Vic; did you know?"

"Yes. Once the Internet came along, I followed her career from afar.

Eventually, I told my friend Arthur of my particular interest in her and revealed our affair. I'd hidden it for decades by then, even from him. She was a married woman and she'd left me; I suppose shame and pride tied my tongue until time loosened the knot. From then on, Arthur passed along such tidbits as he heard. Just not the important stuff."

"The important stuff?"

"You."

Peter looked down.

"I am mightily impressed with you," Richard said. "You are your mother's son in your attention to the text, the purity and power of your intention. You'll show it to everyone in the house tomorrow night." He waited, and Peter finally met his eyes.

"After that dress rehearsal, I certainly hope so," Peter said. "If I get there, I owe it to you. To be told I'm my mother's son is the highest praise I could receive."

"And the highest commendation I can give."

They smiled at each other, and then Richard looked down at his half-eaten salad, while Peter took a quiet moment to gaze at the Peaks.

After a pause, Peter prompted Richard, "Tell me more about her. I guess she would have been thirty-five then; a year older than I am now."

"Helen was well trained, but that only takes one so far. To her schooling, she'd added years of experience with different directors, on different stages. She knew more about the performance of Shakespeare than most actors twice her years. But there was something more; an ineffable grace and conviction. The stage was her calling, and she reminded us it was ours as well. We felt—ennobled is not too grand a word. She lifted us, by her demeanor and the quality of her work."

Peter nodded in encouragement.

"I was a player then," Richard continued, "offstage as well as on, as many of us were. The sixties had freed us of our, shall we say, 'moral inhibitions,' and the seventies seemed sure to end in nuclear hellfire anyway, so why not have our fun? You wouldn't think it, to look at me now." The corners of Peter's lips turned down to squelch a smile.

"But the moment I met Helen, I was captivated. 'Who ever loved that loved not at first sight?' No more playing around for me—this was the real thing. It took some time to convince her I meant it."

"Did you—do you have good memories of that time with her?" Peter asked.

Richard's gaze softened as he looked into the past. "After she left, I told myself to forget her, but I never succeeded for long. I recall—well, moments, really. In rehearsals, we knew we were making something true. It bonded us tightly together: picnics in Calliope's, music nights at the Arden, great long hikes up onto the Peaks. Striding along, running lines, startling the crows from the trees. It was a long time before she looked at me, but when she did—"

"You loved her?" Peter's voice was a sigh.

"To the very core of me," Richard affirmed. "I loved her 'more than words can wield the matter, dearer than eyesight, space, and liberty.'"

Peter teased, "You'll get in trouble with Kate for saying that."

"'Double, double, toil and trouble,'" Richard grumbled, then raised a hand to deflect a second warning. "Very well. Mustn't risk Katherine's ire. Something for you to keep in mind, or I miss my guess."

"No; like the arrow of blind Cupid, your words have hit the mark."

"Good. Very good. Or not good, I should say."

"Why not good?"

"Because you're leaving after *Midsummer*, aren't you? Broadway bound?"

"And so are you, I'm told. Into the glorious sunsets of Tucson next year, they say."

"Touché."

They sat quietly for a moment. "I don't know," Peter said. "I've been offered an audition for a Broadway *Merchant of Venice*. And they want me back for two more vampire movies. With a simple yes, I would possess a quadrupled fortune. But it's not a simple yes. I've been weighing my options, but I still don't know what to do."

"Nor I. Two months ago, it was clear in my mind, but now?"

Peter lifted his eyebrows.

"For one thing, I would like for us to learn more of one another."

"I would like that as well."

Richard cleared his throat. "Perhaps if I stay at the Rose, I can lure you back to our stage next year. There remains much to be done here, but I have stood at the cliff's edge and struggled with my conscience when it comes to the consequences of handing a broken-down stage to a successor, whomever that might be. A few years of energetic ticket sales might salvage us and allow me to retire with pride."

Peter measured his next words carefully before he spoke. "It would be worth our time to talk further about that. I have a thought."

"Oh?"

"What is the point of my ill-gotten vampire gains, if not to serve a cause I love?"

Richard leaned back, measuring Peter in a long glance.

"Are you ready to say more?"

"Soon. But right now, I need to go see Kate."

ACT 5

SCENE 7

PETER

It was Beth who suggested they take the bikes. When Kate picked her up from school that afternoon and said, "Can you skip dance today? I have an idea," Beth resisted at first. But when Kate explained her plan, Beth said, "It'll be more fun if we bike there."

"Right as usual, my brilliant daughter," Kate replied.

Thus, Peter found himself on a mountain bike for only the second time in his life, following Kate and Beth up the forest road and onto Observatory Mesa. Beth's backpack held sandwiches and chips, while Kate's protected their cups, napkins, and drinks. They'd left Peter free to fill his own pack with the rest of what they needed.

He'd been nervous about this plan at first. In his memory, Observatory Mesa was a place of danger, with paparazzi lurking behind every tree. "We'll go up the back way and get off-trail, out into the meadow," Kate told him. "Nobody can see us out there. But feel free to go in disguise."

Considering his options, he'd hidden his hair beneath a ball cap and donned mirrored aviator sunglasses. A loose T-shirt and shorts completed the ensemble. He felt reassured he was pulling off "outdoorsy local" if anyone cared to look. And if they did catch him out, a sturdy bike with fat tires would enable him to race away at top speed across any terrain.

Now, as he navigated up the rocky road in the bike's lowest gear, he realized this was not the escape vehicle he'd imagined. *Speed is for cycles under more competent management*, he thought. The idea of easily outracing pursuit had him laughing, even as he struggled to stay up with Kate and Beth.

It all served as a welcome distraction from memories of his long talk with Richard.

He wanted to tell Kate every detail—sometime. On their picnic, a short version would have to do. Kate had said it was OK to talk about it, but Peter didn't want to encourage Beth in the search for her own father against Kate's well-reasoned wishes.

As they spread the thick picnic blanket on the ground and unpacked their backpacks, he said casually, "So, Beth, I have a story for you and your mom."

"What is it?" she demanded.

"Have a seat, and I'll unfold the tale."

They sat, and Kate opened a can of lemonade for Beth. "Beer?" she asked Peter, indicating two bottles of dark ale in the soft-sided cooler.

"Not yet." He looked out across the meadow, seeking inspiration. Touching the neck of his T-shirt, his fingers found the outline of the medal Richard had given him, now hanging from a chain around his neck.

"This is a tale about a father and a son," he began. "I am the son in this tale. And as it turns out, Richard Keane is the father."

Seeing Beth's eyes grow wide as she looked from his face to her mom's and back, he went on. "When I was growing up, I knew my mum was Helen, and my dad was Bert, and I have a brother, Luke. They're still my family, even though my mum has—even though she's an angel now. I still feel her with me every day. You understand."

Beth nodded. "Like Mom and Granddad."

"Precisely. And my dad is still Bert, who raised me and who loves me." His eyes flicked to Kate's. She was watching his face intently. "In his way. Which is all any of us can do."

"You two spoke? Finally?" Kate asked.

"Yeah. Finally." He returned to the story. "But a long time ago, my mum came here, to the Rose. And, erm, even though she was married, she fell in love with Richard, and he with her. And they . . ." He looked again to Kate.

"They had sex with each other," Kate prompted.

"Yes. Erm, I think I'll take that ale now." As Kate popped the top off the bottle, he went on.

"When my mum went home to London, she discovered she was pregnant. Adults make hard decisions sometimes. My mum decided not to tell anyone that Richard could be my—father. So that's how I grew up with Bert. I am his son. But it looks as if I'm also Richard's." Peter took a long drink from the bottle.

"How did you find out?" Beth asked.

"My mum told me last year. It took me a long time to wrap my head around it. So I didn't tell Richard until a few days ago."

"Is he mad?"

"Do you mean angry? Why do you ask?"

"Did he kick you out of his house?"

"Oh! Because I spent the night in Jaime's starship?"

"Yeah."

"No, actually, he isn't angry. Now that he understands, he's pleased, I think." Peter's fingers found the medal again, and he rubbed it for encouragement.

"I'm so glad," Kate said.

Beth sighed, taking it all in. "You have two dads now."

"Let's eat," Kate suggested, pulling a bag of chips from her pack.

"Don't you wish your mom told you a long time ago?" Beth asked pointedly.

Peter considered the easy lie and decided to try another road, possibly one as rocky as the forest road he'd just traveled.

"Part of me does," he admitted, looking at Kate for support. "Part of me is telling stories about what my life might have been if my mum brought me here when I was a babe. Just like your brain is telling you stories about how fantastic it would be to know who your dad is."

He looked at Beth to see if she would follow him into these woods. She was gazing back at him intently, her fingers twirling the blue and green bracelet around her wrist.

"My tricky brain is pretending I would have been happier growing up as Richard's son," Peter offered. Seeing Beth's face darken, he made his voice more playful. "I would have been a famous child actor, with a crew of people to meet my every whim. I would've eaten ice cream and cookies every day for breakfast, just like famous people."

Beth allowed him a smile.

"My life would have been perfect. But I have a secret to tell you about those stories."

"What secret?"

"They aren't true, and I know it. Have you ever heard someone say, 'The grass is always greener on the other side of the fence'?"

"I guess so."

"That's because our tricky brains always tell us that what didn't happen would have been much better than what did."

"Why do our tricky brains do that?"

"I don't know," Peter said, looking to Kate.

"Our brains are really good at telling stories," Kate said. "That's how we get great works of art, great books and poems and plays. A mouse on a motorcycle and a school for wizards, talking bears and chocolate angels. But we can also make ourselves miserable if we believe what our brains tell us about how things would have been, 'if only' something else had happened."

"I had a grand childhood," Peter added. "I didn't grow up Richard's son, but Bert loved my brother and me. He was devoted to my mum. I wasn't famous as a child actor. I'm pretty famous now, but it isn't all ice cream and cookies for breakfast like I thought. Real life is never like that. So when my brain starts telling me stories, I just say, 'Hey, you tricky brain, I know that's not real, but good try, anyway.'"

"Good try anyway, you tricky brain," Beth echoed.

"That's it."

"I still want to know who my dad is, just like you do," Beth argued.

"Of course. But now you know it won't make life better or different if you find out."

"I guess." Beth's tone was skeptical.

"And if you don't find out until you're grown up, then you really will be just like me. We'll be in a club together. And in our club, guess what we always have for breakfast."

Beth smiled. "Ice cream and cookies?"

"All the ice cream we want and all the snickerdoodle cookies we can eat!"

"But first," said the practical Kate, "sandwiches for dinner."

The sun was settling toward the western horizon as they sat on the blanket, finishing their picnic. Before the stars came out, they would need to ride home down the rock-strewn road, something Peter dreaded. But that wasn't why he asked Kate to wait once they tucked away the containers and wrappers.

"There's something I want to do, and I need you both to help me do it." Reaching into his backpack, he pulled out a candle in a tin holder and a set of matches. "It's all right to light this?"

Kate nodded.

"Beth, could you go find us a flat rock?" he asked. She scrambled up and walked away into the meadow, eyes on the ground.

"Trust me?" he asked Kate.

"Absolutely."

"Found one!" Beth called, holding it up.

"Perfect," Peter called out. Once she'd brushed it off and set it where he pointed, in the center of the blanket, he placed the candle on its sturdy surface and lit the flame.

"This is something I need to do for my mum," he said seriously to Beth. "Let's all sit quietly so I can hear her voice. Can we do that?"

As Beth folded herself into a cross-legged position, Peter opened his pack again. He pulled out his mother's scarf and his favorite photo of the two of them, sitting together on a bench in St. James's Park.

Wrapping the scarf around the rock, he nestled the photo frame into it.

"I know this may seem a bit crazy," Peter said.

"It doesn't," Kate reassured him. "We talk to ghosts all the time."

Peter let the evening's quiet settle into him. "Hi, Mum," he said, tears filling his eyes. He blinked them away.

"Hello, Helen," Kate echoed, and Beth copied her a second later.

"I'm here with Kate and Beth," Peter continued. "You know them. They're my special friends; my family here in Flagstaff." His eyes went to Beth's, then Kate's, and the candlelight on their faces reflected the warmth in his heart.

"I'm so grateful. They've helped me more than they know. They helped me with my fans, and my grief, and Richard." He reached out to hold their hands.

"Richard and I talked today, Mum." He looked at her face in the photo. "Things are shaping well. We have more to say. And we have *Hamlet* to get through. But I'm not scared of that anymore. I'm not scared of any of it, now." Kate's hand squeezed his.

"Thank you for telling me your secret, Mum." His voice roughened. "Thank you for trusting me. I don't understand everything, but I know you were strong, and you did what you felt was right for our family. I can live with what I know and try to be a good son—to both my fathers."

Peter drew a deep breath, letting the sweet scent of spring grasses fill his lungs. "And thank you also for this," he said. Letting go of their hands, he reached up and took off the ball cap. Then he opened the clasp and pulled the chain from around his neck.

"Richard gave it to me today," he said, showing the medal on its chain to Beth, then Kate, before lifting it over the candle. He watched it dangle, glinting in the soft light of dusk.

"Do you know what it is?" he asked Kate.

"A Saint Christopher medal?" she replied.

"That's what I thought, too, but no. It's Saint Francis."

"Oh," Kate said. "Like our mountains?" Peter nodded.

"The San Francisco Peaks were named for Saint Francis," Kate told Beth. "For Catholic people, he's the patron saint of animals, I think."

"And ecology," Peter added. "He cared for the poor and the sick and for all the living things on Earth."

"Why did Richard give you that?" Beth asked.

"That's the best part of the story." Peter lifted his eyebrows, still amazed by what he was about to say. "My mum gave this to him the year they met. He said she was quite in love with this grand volcano." He gestured toward the mountains that filled the northern horizon, sending the medal swinging.

"She wore it the whole time she was here. When she left, she wanted him to have it. She said it would remind him of their time together at the Rose, protected by the sacred San Francisco Peaks."

"Romantic," Kate said.

"He's kept it on his dresser ever since. But you haven't heard all yet." Peter smiled mysteriously at her, then at Beth. "Guess what my middle name is."

"No!" Kate blurted when she guessed.

"What!" Beth shouted.

"My mum kept her secret all those years, but she couldn't resist one gesture in the direction of . . . what might've been, I suppose. So I am the son of Helen Marie Dunmore McKenzie," he said slowly, savoring the names on his tongue, "and Bertram Niall McKenzie, and also of Richard James Aloysius Keane. And my name is Peter—Francis—McKenzie."

Their laughter was still ringing out across the meadow as Peter set the medal in Kate's hand. "Would you mind?" he asked, leaning forward.

Swallowing, Kate separated the chain and latched it back around his neck. He tucked the medal into his shirt and took her hands in his. Looking into her eyes, he stood and pulled her up beside him. Then he kissed her with sweet longing, while the sun settled its last rosy rays around their shoulders and across the waving grasses of the vast meadow beneath the mountains for which he was named.

EPILOGUE

Richard

The cast and crew of *Hamlet* were not as raucous a company of players as some Richard could recall, but they'd hit his wine stash with vigor and now ranged around his house and porch, talking with one another and the season's corporate sponsors as they enjoyed the catered midnight supper traditionally served here following the opening-night performance.

Everyone looked their best, whatever that meant to each person. Some women wore formal gowns, others cocktail dresses. The men were in dark suits or tuxedos. And here and there, someone had put together a more flamboyant look or cross-dressed. *Shakespeare and his comrades in the Lord Chamberlain's Men would enjoy this good company,* Richard thought.

He looked around with pride from his post at the bar. He was waiting for two more people before tucking into his own repast. Soon enough, the door swung open and Peter and Kate walked in.

Richard felt a glow of contentment when he saw they were holding hands. Catching his eye, Peter gave Richard a happy smile, and Richard nodded in return, noting that this time, Peter was wearing every piece of his tuxedo. *Is it* Hamlet *or Katherine that's brought a swagger to his step? Either way, I'm glad.*

Kate was wearing one of her handmade dresses, in scarlet velvet with sequined trim. She'd braided her hair elaborately for the occasion and tied it off with a yellow silk ribbon.

Everyone set down plates and glasses and sent a spontaneous wave of applause washing over the couple. Peter blushed and ducked his head. Kate caught his eye and gave him a reassuring smile. Dropping his hand, she took a step to the side and joined in the applause.

When the room quieted, Bryce walked over to welcome them, his plus one at his side. *The Scandinavian woman playing Hippolyta and Titania,* Richard thought. He saw Peter wrap an arm around Kate's waist as he accepted their congratulations. *What a couple they make, my son and Katherine. I'm a proud man tonight. And not just because Peter gave us such a* Hamlet *as dreams are made on.*

The performance had gone as smoothly as anyone could hope. At Peter's first entrance, many in the crowd applauded. Richard had warned him about this tradition of American theater, so Peter ignored it.

More importantly, the feared vampire uprising had failed to materialize. When Peter started Hamlet's first soliloquy, alone at stage right, someone standing in the crowded yard whispered his vampire name in a vain attempt to draw his attention. Nearby audience members quickly hissed the boor quiet. Later, when it happened again, Gavriella's crew intervened. There had been no further outbursts.

Richard poured Kate a glass of Chardonnay, then hesitated, not knowing whether Peter would prefer a Pinot Noir, which he also had on hand. *So much to learn about my son, on so many levels. In time.*

Other cast members surrounded the couple now, and Richard saw they were in danger of missing out on the meal. He poured the Pinot Noir and, taking both glasses in hand, walked toward Peter and Kate. The crowd parted to let him through.

"As Balthasar says, 'Small cheer and great welcome makes a merry feast.'" Handing them the wine, he cleared his throat and asked Ted, "Quiet the room for me, would you?"

Ted tapped his glass lightly with his fork as Richard returned to the bar for his own wine glass. The room grew quiet when he stepped up onto the entry landing and turned. He smiled as he looked into the happy assemblage.

"Thank you all for coming to the opening night supper. This is a tradition that's been celebrated at the Rose since before my time, and that's a long time."

Drawing a deep breath, he said, "First, won't you join me in lifting our glasses to toast the goddesses of theater: Melpomene, goddess of Tragedy; and Thalia, goddess of Comedy." Richard raised his glass.

"They have blessed us mightily tonight." He took a sip of wine, and everyone followed suit.

"You have, each one of you, showed them a grand *Hamlet* in return. I congratulate you." Around the room, there were scattered cheers.

"You should cheer!" he encouraged them. "Some would say theater is nothing more than light entertainment for the well-heeled few. But I say otherwise. At its best, live theater engages the hearts and minds of players and audience alike. It joins everyone in a shared enterprise that enriches, inspires, and encourages empathy. Please give yourselves a round of well-deserved applause for what you have created together." The cheers and applause grew more robust.

"I have been working in theater since 1962," Richard continued, more soberly now. "I saw Peter O'Toole play Hamlet at the National Theatre in London under the direction of Laurence Olivier in the very first year of its existence. I've watched many actors take on the role since then. Never have I seen a Prince of Denmark superior to the one performed tonight by Peter McKenzie."

As everyone applauded again, Peter blushed, rooted to the spot by the force of Richard's praise and his friends' support. Finally, Richard gestured to Ted, who tapped his glass again to reclaim the room's attention.

"Just two things more, and then I'll let you return to your meals. As you're aware, I have been contemplating stepping down at the end of my contract next year." He saw Kate's eyes widen. "The year 1962 was a very long time ago. Perhaps the hour had come, I thought, to draw the curtain on my time at the Rose. But watching you all create this *Hamlet* has changed my mind." Around the room, people murmured their support.

"I no longer contemplate leaving. I have been talking with—certain people—about what the Rose needs if she is to continue serving our audiences and actors in decades to come. Those people—that person, really—has decided to fund a significant renovation to our beloved theatre." Richard saw Kate look at Peter, who returned her gaze with a smile.

"She will still be her regal self, only a more comfortable and sustainable version of herself. And we've decided to take up this work in honor of someone who means a great deal to us. Before her passing a year ago, this actor played many roles, including a Lear that rewrote the book on how that tragic king could be performed.

"When she played Rosalind here at the Rose, the fiery Helen McKenzie—that's Peter's mother—stole many hearts. I speak simple truth when I say mine was among them, and she never returned it to my keeping. She was—" he paused to collect himself. "I shall only say she was incomparable. Her son and I wish to honor her memory by making positive changes, necessary changes, to a place that means a great deal to all of us.

"Here's to the Blue Mountain Rose. Long may she live."

ACKNOWLEDGMENTS

"I can no other answer make, but, thanks, and thanks, and ever thanks."

~William Shakespeare

If you visit Flagstaff, Arizona, hoping to see a performance in a renowned theatrical space like the Blue Mountain Rose, I regret to disclose that you won't find an outdoor Elizabethan stage here.

What you will find is the Flagstaff Shakespeare Festival. Founded in 2015, FlagShakes is an ever-changing company of gifted performers who lack nothing but an outdoor theatre of their own.

I was the founding board president of this festival, assisting the visionary Dawn Tucker, the founding executive director. It could be argued that *Blue Mountain Rose* is my way of doing something as a writer that I couldn't do as a board member: build a stage worthy of FlagShakes and our beloved mountain town.

Several generous members of the FlagShakes family helped me envision the theatrical world of the Rose. Christine Schmidle, a well-regarded stage director and text coach, gave the first version a careful reading that shaped the final product in countless ways. Hannah Johnson of FlagShakes and Marco Antonio Vega of Southern Utah University and the Utah Shakespeare Festival shared their insights into the actor's experience. And Cadence Lamb, who played a memorable Hamlet at FlagShakes, poured her enthusiasm into helping me shape Peter's experience as he learned Shakespeare's greatest role.

To Dawn, Christine, Hannah, Cadence, and everyone at the Flagstaff Shakespeare Festival, I offer my humble thanks. You inspired me to dream this dream of a great theatre in a small town.

The first seeds for this book were planted long before 2015, though. I grew up in the Central Valley of California. In 11th grade, I took AP English from Mr. Gerald Berglund. He taught *Hamlet* in class, then gave up his spring break to lead us on a field trip all the way up to the Oregon Shakespeare Festival, where we saw Mark Murphey perform the title role.

The day he assigned the "To be, or not to be" speech for us to memorize, Mr. Berglund set this book in motion. But I continued to think of theater as something other people did, until the day Ted Hawkins invited me backstage at a production of *Anything Goes*. He was playing Moonface Martin in that show, and he taught me to run the light board. It was a delight to watch Ted and his friends perform. I was hooked on the collaborative art form that is theater, and my life is the better for it.

Thanks to Ted's influence, I volunteered as a stage manager at Perseverance Theatre in Juneau, Alaska. That's where I met the great director Peter DuBois, whose fabulous hugs carried me through a rough patch in my personal life. I also worked with the brilliant Art Rotch, who almost talked me into pursuing dramaturgy as a career, and who had a brilliant career himself at Perseverance.

The three-volume set of Rowse's annotated Shakespeare that still graces my shelf was a gift from Ted. He would be surprised to see his name in these acknowledgments, but they would be incomplete without it.

It's humbling to contemplate the many good and kind people who supported my writing dreams.

I think first of my family. In the unconditional generosity of their love, my parents, Jim Hammonds and Catherine Bell, gave me everything necessary to set out on this journey and see it through. My husband, Matt Anderson, endured my frequent disappearance into this imaginary world with patience and good humor. And my sister, Jodie Hammonds, and my sister/cousin, Kristin Bontrager, often asked how the writing was going. My heart fills with appreciation when I call each of these beloved people to mind.

Shakespeare wrote, "I count myself in nothing else so happy as in a soul rememb'ring my good friends." Naissa Foster and Karen McKeever read early versions and offered the constructive criticism this book needed. Lillian Ruedrich, Amy Crook, and Judy Jones cheered every milestone. Other authors at Soulstice Publishing whom I'm now honored to call friends, including George Breed, Kathy Eckles Hooker, and John L. Vankat, encouraged me to pursue this dream. I am happy to remember all of them here, with heartfelt thanks.

The idea of an author who disappears into a garret one day and wakes up the next with a finished product in hand is a myth. It takes the time and energy of a committed team to prepare a book for publication.

My good friend and business partner at Soulstice Publishing, Myles Schrag, has supported this endeavor in every imaginable way. We've published a dozen books together since 2019. When I said I wanted to add my own book to the catalog, he gave the improv actor's classic response: "Yes, and." For our enduring partnership, my gratitude is as boundless as the sea.

The *Blue Mountain Rose* editorial team included Merlina McGovern, who did 24-carat gold work. She set diamonds of encouragement into her notes, and I valued every one. Milli Ondras proofed the final version. Her timely praise warmed my heart. I accept responsibility for every error that remains.

This book owes its beautiful form to graphic designers Lindy Kasler and Erin Stanford. I loved watching them bring this world to life with their skills and creativity. A better team could not be imagined.

And finally: Fascination with Shakespeare's plays has taken me from California to Virginia and from the Stratford Festival in Canada to Stratford-upon-Avon on a mission to "complete the canon." (I have four plays to go.) Each of those experiences helped me create this book. But I'm especially grateful to the Utah Shakespeare Festival. At their seminars, I've met and learned from experienced actors and directors.

In their theatres, I've experienced unforgettable moments of transcendence. The consistent brilliance of their productions and the relationships they create between actors and audience keep me going back to Cedar City year after year.

Richard Keane says live theater "joins everyone in a shared enterprise that enriches, inspires, and encourages empathy." As someone who loves the shared enterprise that is theater, I offer this book in humble tribute to every actor who takes on the challenge of performing Shakespeare. When you present the gorgeous power of his words and the depth of his insights into the human experience, you offer each audience member a gift. For enriching my life and the lives of so many, thank you.

About the Author

Julie Hammonds fell in love with *Hamlet* during a high school trip to the Oregon Shakespeare Festival and has nurtured her passion for Shakespeare ever since. She studied the plays in school, stage-managed *The Winter's Tale* and *Much Ado About Nothing*, and helped create the Flagstaff Shakespeare Festival. Her quest to complete the canon as an audience member has taken her from a community hall in Juneau, Alaska, to the Royal Shakespeare Company in Stratford-upon-Avon. She has four plays to go. This is her first novel.